**The Way of Life
By
Sue Curran**

Copyright © 2013 Sue Curran

All rights are reserved to the author. No part of this ebook may be used or reproduced in any manner whatsoever without written permission except in the case of brief quotations embodied in critical articles or reviews.

Published April 2013

This is a work of fiction. Names, character, places and incidents are either the product of the author's imagination or are used fictitiously, and any resemblance to actual persons, living or dead, business establishments, events or locales is entirely coincidental.

Dedication

To Heather, my great friend and fellow writer, thank you for all your support. Without your encouragement this book would never have been more than words in my head.

PROLOGUE

The bedroom was in darkness. Joy held her breath listening, straining to hear a sound from downstairs. There was only silence. She switched on the bedside lamp.

'Damn it. Why did I drink that vodka?' she muttered struggling to make sense through the fuzz in her head. 'Where the hell is he?' Gingerly she got out of bed, her legs alien to her as she crossed the room.

Her head bounced painfully with each step, as she went downstairs. She found Daniel in the sitting room, lying on the sofa, her heavy winter coat thrown over him. His eyes wide open, staring at the ceiling.

'Daniel,' she whispered.

He was lying so still, he could have been dead.

Her heart pounded as painfully as her head. Kneeling on the floor beside the sofa, she touched his face. He was icy cold.

'Oh my God. Daniel! What's happened? What's wrong?' Joy was scared. She'd never seen him like this before.

His eyes slid to the right, the pain she saw shocked her to the core. She felt as if she could see into his soul.

Her throbbing head forgotten, briskly she pulled off the heavy coat covering him. His clothes were soaked through. He'd obviously been caught in the torrential downpour earlier.

'You're freezing. Come on, you need a hot bath.' Joy rubbed at his icy hands, helping him to his feet.

Like a child, Daniel followed her up the stairs and into the bathroom.

The steam from the hot bath water distorted their reflection in the mirror tiles, misting over their faces. Joy sat on the bathroom floor, watching Daniel's body turn from grey to pink, as he began to thaw beneath the steaming water.

'I can't do this anymore,' Daniel whispered, his eyes locking on to hers.

'Can't do what, Dan?' Joy asked, her heart hammering at what he might be about to say.

'Come here,' Daniel gestured towards the bath water. 'I really need to hold you.' He stroked her hair.

One last time. He wants to hold me one last time before he tells me it's over.

Joy undressed, her eyes never leaving his, and stepped into the water to sit between his legs, leaning back against his warm chest. He held her, his arms wrapped tight around her waist, his chin resting on her head.

I'll hold onto that moment forever, no matter what happens. We never said a word. We just sat there until the water turned cool, my hands resting on his.

We said we'd never have secrets. Now, at two in the morning, here we are, sitting across from each other at the kitchen table. Dan said he has something to tell me. I feel calm; I think I'm ready to hear it, whatever he has to say. Since we're sharing secrets, I've written him a letter, afraid I'll bottle it when my turn comes. I can feel it, digging into my leg through my dressing gown pocket, pushing me, goading me.

SATURDAY
I

'What are these for?' Daniel asked. He dangled the glossy red sandal by its five-inch stiletto heel. 'This is a walking holiday. You know. Muddy boots, thick socks, sensible stuff.'

'I know. I booked it - remember?' Joy snatched the shoe. 'Maybe these will nab me some rich handsome Scotsman and I'll be out of your hair,' she said, shaking it in front of his face before stuffing it into her suitcase.

Daniel threw his battered rucksack on the opposite side of the bed. The revelations of the night before sat like unexploded firecrackers between them, making eye contact a frightening prospect. Joy sensed Daniel's eyes on her trembling hands as she folded the luxurious red dress; sensed his anger and disgust burning into the silky fabric. Flustered, she stuffed the dress into her suitcase, heedless of creases. How on earth were they going to get through the next seven days?

I've been so wrapped up in my own guilty secrets, how did I not see what was going on with Daniel? How could I think his erratic moods were the stresses of work? What do we do now? Months of planning have gone into this holiday. It's too late to back out.

The slamming open of the wardrobe door made Joy jump. Coat hangers clattered and fell to the wooden floor as Daniel, his shoulders taut with anger and frustration, yanked off shirts, folded them roughly and pushed them into his rucksack. Joy crossed the room, careful not to brush against him as she passed, quietly gathering together hair straighteners, moisturiser and sunblock.

Hauling the rucksack onto his shoulder, he pointed to her open suitcase. 'Can you manage that?'

Not waiting for a reply, he stomped down the stairs.

Anger bubbled in her throat. 'Looks like I'll have to,' she muttered under her breath.

She walked over to the huge bay window to stare down at the sleeping tree-lined street, where they had lived for nearly ten years. Everything was so familiar. Joy couldn't imagine living anywhere else. She was tired, they both were, and angry too. They hadn't slept at all, but had talked, yelled and cried late into the night, trying to digest everything that was said. Taking a deep breath Joy returned to her packing. It was already five a.m. and Tony was picking them up at five thirty. She leaned heavily on the case, squashing it closed and tugging at the zip.

This is just great fucking timing. Months of planning have gone into this West Highland Way walk. Why didn't we just plump for a week in Lanzarote like we usually do where we could snipe and snarl at each other without an audience? No, that would be too easy. Here we are spending seven days with our best friends, a man I can't stand and one I don't know. Well there's no way I'm putting on the entertainment for them all!

'Daniel!' Joy shouted from the top of the landing, her voice bristling with tension. She lugged the heavy suitcase down the stairs, banging it off every step.

He appeared in the hall as she reached the bottom.

'I can't do this,' she said.

Daniel remained silent.

'We have to talk.'

'The bus will be here soon.' Daniel's voice was flat.

'But how are we going to handle this all week? What will I say to Kathy and Trish? Or Ruth? You know what she's like - she'll pick up on the fact that something's wrong in a millisecond. What will I tell her?'

'Nothing.'

'Great! Nothing!' snapped Joy.

'Nothing. Anything.' Daniel sighed. 'Just tell them we had a row or something. Couples have them all the time.'

'Anything? OK, fine. I'll shout it from the hilltops. Our life is a sham. One big fucking lie. How does that sound?' Her eyes glistened with unshed tears. She pushed her feet into her well-worn Brasher boots and pulled the laces tight with shaking hands.

Daniel put a hand on her shoulder, giving it a reassuring squeeze.

'Joy. It'll be OK,' he told her. 'Just tell them we had a row. They'll accept that. And being away from here will be good for us. We'll have time to talk properly, find a way to work things out.'

Joy pulled away from him, fleeing up the stairs, two at a time. She stumbled into the bathroom and bolted the door. The sound of her rasping short breaths filled the room, as she struggled to quell the rising panic. Sitting heavily on the edge of the bath, she wrapped her arms tight around herself and rocked back and forth, her whole body wracked by heaving sobs. Her chest felt tighter. With eyes squeezed shut she clung on to the edge of the bath. *Breathe, Joy, breathe. In, one-two-three. Out, one-two-three. Nice and slowly.* Gradually, she felt the tight steel band around her chest begin to loosen.

As her breathing returned to normal, and the sobs subsided, Joy uncurled her fingers from the edge of the bathtub. On shaky legs she crossed to the basin, recoiling in horror at her reflection in the brightly lit mirror. Her expertly groomed sleek stylish bob of dark brown hair framed her ashen face. Shocked, she ran her hands over it, rubbing the skin frantically, trying to induce some colour into her cheeks. She stared into the empty dull-grey eyes staring back at her.

'Who are you?' she asked the stranger in the mirror.

A gentle tapping on the door startled her.

'Joy, are you OK in there?' Daniel tried to open the door.

Joy continued to stare into the mirror. She frowned at her reflection, then forced a smile.

'That's better,' she muttered seeing the steely glint in her deep blue eyes. 'I'm still in there... somewhere.'

Daniel rattled the door handle with frustration.

'Joy, open the door.'

She remained silent, holding her breath. The door shuddered as he kicked it.

'Fine, have it your own way. The bus will be here in five minutes.'

Joy sighed deeply as she ran water into the basin. She washed her tired face, drying it gently on a thick white towel. Running her finger across far too many elegant bottles and jars, she methodically selected the ones she needed, before beginning the cover-up process. She applied liner to her eyes, and then with slow, sweeping strokes, coated her lashes with thick black mascara, willing some life into the deadness she saw there. Finally, she painted her full lips with a ruby lipstick.

She gave her reflection a strained smile.

'Can we pull this off?' she asked.

'We have to,' was the only answer.

The rumble of a diesel engine outside told her it was time to go.

*****

Joy pulled back the sliding door on the minibus, hitched her small backpack onto her shoulder, and stepped inside.

'Morning, Joy.' Tony twisted round in the driver's seat to throw her his most charming smile. 'What's with the fancy suitcase?' He grinned. 'I thought we were off to Scotland, not a swanky hotel in Paris.'

Instantly irritated by his comment, Joy was determined not to react.

'A girl likes to be prepared, Tony,' she replied, her voice a little too bright. 'After all, you never know who you might meet. Isn't that right, Kathy?' She looked over her shoulder at her best friend.

'Ermm... Absolutely,' Kathy replied without looking up.

He is such a prat. I don't know how Kathy is still married to him!

Joy moved to the back of the bus, anxious to put as much space as possible between herself and Daniel, relieved that he had sat up front beside Tony. Kathy followed and slid into the seat across the aisle from her.

'You should buckle up.' Kathy pointed to Joy's seatbelt, as she snapped her own into position. 'Tony wants everyone to wear their seatbelts. He said that way, if we have an accident, everyone's responsible for themselves.'

Joy rolled her eyes. 'Right little ray of sunshine he is. We're not even out of the estate and he's casting doom and gloom over the whole thing.'

'I know, but honestly, Joy -' Kathy lowered her voice to a whisper. 'It's easier to do as he asks.'

Joy pulled off her jacket and began rummaging in her backpack.

'Who are we picking up next?' she asked. 'Is it Trish?'

'No, it's Brad next, then Ruth. Tony said seeing as Trish and Rob aren't far from the motorway, it makes more sense to pick them up last. Then we'll be on our way.'

Joy listened to Kathy reeling off the information. She took her bottle of water and iPod out of her backpack, wondering if it would be rude to put in her earphones.

'Sorry. I'm prattling on,' Kathy said. 'I'll be quiet.'

Joy smiled at her excited friend, wishing she could muster up the same enthusiasm.

'You're fine, Kathy, really. I'm just getting organised.'

'No, you listen to your music.' Kathy nodded to Joy's iPod, and picked up her book.

Joy glanced across the aisle. Kathy looked like a teenager, her tiny frame swamped in a pale grey hoody, her shoulder-length dark brown hair scraped back into a ponytail, highlighting her large brown eyes and long black lashes, as she shuffled to get comfortable in her seat.

It was only a few minutes from Joy and Daniel's home near Redcar Racecourse to the row of elegant Victorian town houses on the seafront. Joy loved these houses, so prolific in this seaside town, with their grand bay windows and gleaming paintwork. They had tiny front gardens, with wrought iron railings painted black. The matching arched gates opened onto stone steps, leading to glossy front doors with polished brass knockers. The bus stopped outside the only run-down house in the terrace.

Brad waved from a top-floor window. Seconds later, the drab red front door opened and he appeared, wearing khaki shorts, a white T-shirt, and a red baseball cap. He slung his rucksack onto his shoulder and ran down the few steps to the footpath.

Joy didn't really know him. She watched him now, walking past her window, having just thrown his bag into the back. He grinned at her and gave a mock salute. She remembered the afternoon in Macy's Coffee House, when Kathy had asked if he could join them on the walk. Joy's major concern had been: if he's a friend of Tony's would he be like Tony?

'He's suffering from stress,' she told Joy and Trish, her soft brown eyes peering at them over the rim of her coffee cup. 'His doctor said he could have a heart attack if he didn't take a break, and when Tony mentioned the walk to him, he really liked the idea.'

Trish was also cautious. 'We'd have to meet him first, Kath,' she said.

As it turned out, Brad was a pleasant surprise. He turned up at The Ship Inn straight from the accountancy firm where he was a partner, still in his suit and tie. His blue eyes twinkled behind black-rimmed, Armani glasses, and he looked every inch the successful businessman that he was. He seemed relaxed and got on well with everyone.

Now however, Brad couldn't have looked more different as he climbed aboard the bus, in the early morning sun.

'Hey Kath,' Joy whispered. 'Who'd have thought such a handsome hunk was hiding beneath that business suit?'

'Mmm,' Kathy muttered, looking up quickly before rummaging in her bag.

'Morning, ladies,' Brad said with a boyish grin, running a hand over his short blond hair. He took off his sunglasses, revealing a flirty twinkle in his blue eyes. 'All ready for the big adventure?'

'Can't wait,' Kathy said quickly and buried her crimson face deep into her book.

'Sorry, I'm not much of a morning person.' Joy smiled apologetically. She pushed her earphones into place. 'Ask me again in a few hours' time,' she said and closed her eyes.

Brad shrugged and slid into the seat in front of her. He shook out a copy of the *Financial Times.*

Joy increased the volume on her iPod, letting the soothing tones of Nora Jones cover the drone of the diesel engine. She leaned her head against the cool glass of the window. Watching the seagulls dive into the crashing surf in search of breakfast, she allowed herself to be hypnotised by the sight of the cold North Sea pounding rhythmically against the sandy shoreline, as the bus travelled along the deserted coast road. Soon the grassy dunes blocked her view of the grey water and Joy closed her eyes once more.

II

Kathy looked up from her book, stealing a quick glance across at Joy. *What was going on between her and Daniel this morning? The atmosphere between them was fraught with tension. God knows, I know enough about household tension to recognise the signs. What a shock though. Joy and Daniel's life always seemed so perfect.*

She shuddered hearing Tony's gruff tones filtering down from the front of the bus. She'd been looking forward to the holiday for a long time, but ever since Tony's announcement that he was coming with them, happy anticipation had been replaced with nervous trepidation.

It was during a girls' night in at Joy's house that she had agreed to go along on the holiday; predictably, Tony had put the kybosh on the idea immediately. Then, two weeks later, he made his announcement.

She'd been ironing when he arrived home from work. Hearing the front door slam she drew a mental picture of him kicking off his boots, leaving them in the middle of the hall floor, before taking off his jacket and tossing it over the banister.

'Kathy, I'm home,' he bellowed loudly, as if they lived in a twelve-bedroom mansion, not a tiny three-bedroom terrace on a council estate.

'I'd never have guessed,' Kathy muttered under her breath, then raising her voice called out, 'I'm in the kitchen.' She kept her eyes on the kitchen door, waiting for it to open; bracing herself for what would come next.

Tony opened the door, his bulky frame filling the doorway, pausing for a moment to look her up and down, as he did every evening.

Kathy smiled. 'You're home early today, love,' she said, trying to gauge his mood, watching his gaze travel over her appearance, wondering what she'd gotten wrong this time.

He picked up a freshly ironed shirt from the back of the chair. He examined it, turning it this way and that, then threw it back into the linen basket. He performed this ritual with a further three shirts.

Kathy continued ironing, her hands shaking, as she waited for him to speak. He left the kitchen without uttering a word. Annoyed at the extra work he had created, still she gave a sigh of relief. She knew the shirts were fine. It was just his way of controlling her.

'Kathy! Tea.' Tony's clipped command and the blare of the TV invaded the silent house.

'I've decided you can go on that holiday to Scotland, with your Trish and Rob,' he told her as she handed him the mug of strong steaming tea.

Kathy was dumbstruck, excited butterflies danced in her stomach.

'And I'm coming with you,' he added with a grin.

Kathy felt her heart plummet. 'But you don't walk anywhere!' she said.

'Oh, I won't be walking,' Tony told her. 'I thought I could drive a minibus to carry all the suitcases and stuff.' He patted the sofa. 'Sit down, Kath.'

'I need to finish the ironing,' Kathy said backing away.

Tony's eyes locked with hers and patted the sofa a second time.

Kathy sat on the very edge, her back straight and tense; her hands fidgeting in her lap.

'It'll be perfect, Kath,' he said, clamping a large grubby hand over her left knee. 'We can spend the evenings together, and I'll be there to look after you.' He squeezed her knee and grinned.

Tony's laughter bellowed down the bus once more. Kathy glanced across at Joy, envious of her earphones. *I could do with those to block out the grating drone of Tony's voice. Thank God he isn't fit enough to do the walk.* She closed her eyes. *Don't think about him, girl. Just savour the days and the hours of freedom. Remember the plan - and stick to it!*

III

Joy's head jerked forward and her eyes flew open, as Tony brought the bus to an abrupt halt in a narrow street, tightly packed with cars parked either side. She couldn't help smiling as Ruth emerged through the gleaming white PVC door, flamboyantly dressed in cerise pink Capri pants and a canary yellow T-shirt with 'Are we there yet?' emblazoned across the front. The leopard skin suitcase she pulled along behind her rattled across the deserted street.

Joy watched her best friend of twenty-five years with admiration, amazed Ruth was still smiling despite the heartbreaking decision she had made - to give up her children. Once she'd had it all; a loving husband and two active young sons.

'Love the t-shirt, Ruth,' Joy called out, as Ruth threw her ample frame into the seat in front of Kathy. 'Very apt.'

Ruth gave Joy a mischievous wink. 'I aim to please.' She peered through the gap in the seats. 'How are you, Kathy?' I'm so glad your Tony's driving this bus. I don't think there's a chance in hell that I'll complete the walk. I'm sure to need a lift more than once.'

Joy frowned. 'Don't set out with a negative attitude. Thousands of people complete this walk every year, and there's no reason why we can't too. We have to stay positive.'

'Bravo. Well said,' Brad piped up from behind his newspaper.

'Fasten your seatbelt, Ruth.' Kathy repeated Tony's orders once again.

'Yes, boss.' Ruth grinned.

Joy turned to the window. They quickly left behind the narrow streets filled with tiny terraced houses, heading out of town, and were soon whizzing past endless green fields. She saw cows forming a surprisingly orderly queue at a gate, ready for milking, and a beautiful foal, its coat milky white with large toffee-coloured splashes, loping after its mother who chewed grass contentedly in the early morning sun. She closed her eyes, willing the rhythmic movement of the bus to calm her churning insides. Since meeting Kathy at her front door, every word she'd spoken felt strained and unnatural. She hardly recognised her own voice. *Surely it's just a matter of time before one of the girls notices and asks awkward questions, I'll only get away with pushing in earphones and feigning sleep for so long.*

They entered an exclusive cul-de-sac and pulled up outside a large sprawling bungalow. An army of colourful bedding plants surrounded the pristine manicured lawn. Joy watched through half-closed eyes as Trish and Rob made their way down the drive. She wasn't surprised that Trish had managed to look glamorous in beige combats and khaki T-shirt. *Trish would look glamorous dressed in a black bin liner.* She kept her eyes closed when they came on board, knowing that Trish's perceptiveness would pick up on her fragile condition immediately, if their eyes met.

'Are we all ready for the great adventure?' Trish asked, her voice bubbling with excitement as she walked towards the back of the bus.

Joy could feel Trish's gaze upon her and kept her eyes tightly closed.

'She's still catching up on lost sleep,' Kathy volunteered.

'Right, I'll leave her be then,' Trish replied.

'Trish McLeod, are you going to find a seat so that we can get this show on the road?' Tony bellowed, as he revved the engine.

'Yes sir!' Trish saluted. Leaning towards Kathy she lowered her voice to a whisper. 'I hope he hasn't got any grandiose ideas that he's running this trip.'

Out of habit, Kathy defended her husband. 'He just wants to get us to Milngavie as early as he can.'

IV

Kathy could just about see the top of Trish's head a few rows in front. Her sister's short blond hair nestled against Rob's bronzed balding crown. She turned away, annoyed at her rising jealousy of her own sister's happiness, and looked down at her book. Tony's belly laugh reverberated down the length of the bus, making her body tense.

D-T-day is getting closer.

Kathy hugged the knowledge to her and then quickly looked around terrified somebody might read her mind. She had only said the words aloud a few times, high up on a hilltop in the Yorkshire Moors, or on a deserted Redcar beach, with the wind blowing a hooley around her. Her plans had to be kept secret. They had to be foolproof.

It's taken two years to prepare and pull them together. The idea of Tony finding out – or getting so much as an inkling...

She shuddered at the thought.

The vibrating pulse of her mobile made her jump. She pulled it from her pocket to see Alison's name on the screen. Smiling, she pushed the connect button.

'Hi, love,' she said warmly.

'Hi, mum.' Alison's sweet, singsong voice responded.

'You OK?'

'Yes, I just wanted to say have a good time.'

'Thanks, I'm sure we will. You behave yourself for your Gran.'

'Mum.' Alison let out an exaggerated sigh. 'When do I ever not?'

'OK, OK.' Kathy laughed. 'Go back to sleep for a while, it's Saturday. I'll speak to you tonight.'

'Bye, Mum.'

'Bye, love.'

Kathy slid down in her seat. She made a cushion with her fleece and rested her head against the window, allowing the vibration of the bus to lull her to sleep.

V

Joy straightened up in her seat and rubbed the sleep from her eyes. Amazed that she had slept at all, she looked out at the urban sprawl of Glasgow in the distance before turning her head from side to side to ease her stiff neck. She stretched her long and tanned arms high above her head then ran her fingers through her dark hair. She took the compact mirror from her backpack, flicked open the silver clasp and studied her face. Her eyes still looked dull, but her cheeks now had a rosy glow from the heat of the sun shining through the window. She decided the ruby lipstick was a little full on and carefully removed it, applying a rose pink lip-gloss instead.

Everyone was very quiet. Joy craned her neck slightly, to see over the seat in front. Although she could see the top of Daniel's dark head, she couldn't tell if he was asleep. *What is he thinking? Is he regretting his decision to be here, to go along with the holiday? Does he hate me for the secret I've kept from him?* She felt the lump rising in her throat again and took a swift gulp of water. It was lukewarm, making her shudder and grimace. She leaned back in her seat.

'All you sleepyheads at the back, Milngavie in ten miles. And according to Radio Clyde, it's going to be one hot and sunny day.' Tony boomed out his wake-up call.

Everyone cheered and clapped.

'Brilliant,' Trish called out over the back of her seat. 'All those books on the walk had stressed the need for waterproofs. Let's hope they are wrong.'

Kathy leaned across the seat, to call up the aisle, 'It's pronounced Mull-guy, Tony.'

Joy watched the excited grin slide from Kathy's face as her eyes locked with Tony's through the rear-view mirror, before she shuffled quickly back into her seat.

It was just after 10.30 a.m. when Tony manoeuvred the minibus into the car park in Milngavie town centre.

'We'll leave all the gear on the bus, guys, and grab something to eat,' Rob called out, taking on the unofficial role of leader.

Joy remained seated watching the others from the window. Rob stretched his arms above his head and looked up at the flawless blue sky. Trish straightened her T-shirt and ran her hands through her hair, before pushing her sunglasses back onto her head. Her eyes met Joy's and she smiled and waved. Joy waved back, well aware of her friend's perceptiveness; she was thankful of the glass between them. She took a deep breath, using the last few moments on the bus to suppress the uncertainty she felt about the week ahead. Daniel was crouching down fastening his bootlace. His eyes found hers as he stood up, a thousand unanswered questions clearly visible on his face. He pulled his sunglasses from his shirt pocket and put them on, hiding the hurt in his eyes before turning away.

Kathy gave Joy a gentle nudge. 'Come on Mrs, get a wriggle on. I don't know about you, but I could eat a horse.'

Joy pulled on her sunglasses and followed Kathy off the bus, into the heat of the morning sun.

'Hi. Did you sleep well?' Trish asked the moment Joy's feet hit the tarmac. 'You were out for the count when I got on the bus. I came down the back to say hello and you were giving it zees.'

Joy smiled at Trish, grateful for the cover of the sunglasses.

'I was wrecked. What with getting organised, the excitement of the trip and everything, I didn't get any sleep last night,' she said lightly.

'Daniel seems very quiet. Rob says he can't get two words out of him.'

'He's probably tired too.' Joy quickly changed track. 'I need to find a chemist before we leave here. My head's pounding – I'm probably dehydrated after the journey. I could do with some more painkillers, just in case I run out.'

'I'll come with you.' Trish nudged Joy. 'Maybe we should stock up on the sun block. This could be a sunshine holiday after all.'

The group had stopped outside The Pantry, a small cafe with a distinctive deep fryer smell wafting through the open windows. The shabby swinging pavement sign read, 'Full Scottish Breakfast with free tea or coffee top up.'

Tony was peering in the window. 'It looks like there's enough seats for us all,' he said moving to the door. 'Let's get stuck in.'

Joy hung back, putting off the moment when she would have to take off her sunglasses and reveal the turmoil of emotions inside.

'After you, madam.' Brad held open the door.

'Thanks.' Joy smiled. Pushing her sunglasses through her hair, she made her way to the long table near the back of the restaurant. Brad indicated for her to take the seat next to Daniel, and he sat between Kathy and Ruth. Unwilling to protest and draw attention to herself she sat down and quickly picked up the menu. Food was the last thing on her mind; she scanned the pages for something light, finally opting for scrambled eggs with tomatoes, orange juice and coffee.

'Did you sleep much on the way up here?' Daniel asked her quietly.

'A little. How about you?'

'No, Tony likes to talk.' Daniel gave a wry smile.

Joy looked at Tony sitting opposite her, already munching his way through a bowl of cornflakes. Milk dribbled down his chin, and he wiped it away with the back of his hand.

Joy felt sure there must be a neon sign above her head, advertising the rift between her and Daniel. The awkward silence between them seemed so obvious. She picked at her food when it arrived, glad of the excuse to be quiet, though not really eating anything at all. After a few minutes she gave up and placed her knife and fork, neat and straight, across her plate. She nibbled at a triangle of wholemeal toast and drank three cups of strong coffee.

While the rest of the group were still mopping up egg yolk, Joy pushed back her chair.

'I'm just popping to a chemist,' she said brightly. 'I'll meet you back at the bus in fifteen minutes.'

Outside in the sunshine, she put on her sunglasses and headed off in the direction of the chemist she'd spotted on the main street. The temperature was rising, making the coolness inside the shop very welcoming. She went straight over to the pharmacy counter and asked for strong painkillers.

A hand tapped her on the shoulder. Trish had followed her.

'Why didn't you tell me you were leaving the cafe? I would have come with you,' she rebuked.

'Sorry, I thought you were still eating.' Joy turned back to the counter and paid for her purchase.

'Are you OK?' Trish's gaze was intense.

'I'm fine.'

'You don't look fine. Where's your sparkle?'

'I'm fine, really.' Joy hoped her smile was reassuring.

Trish wandered over to the display of sun creams. Her hand hovered over the different brands.

'Has something happened?' she asked Joy.

Joy ignored the question.

'What factor are you looking for?'

'Is it Daniel?' Trish pushed.

'Factor 30 should be good enough.'

Trish shook her head, took the factor 30 from the shelf, and pulled a ten-pound note from her pocket, before marching over to the till.

Joy walked outside into the sunlight, shading her eyes once more. She knew avoiding conversation would be impossible. Trish was like a dog with a bone once she thought she was on to something.

Trish came out of the chemist, waving a paper bag containing the sun cream.

'OK, I have the factor 30. Now, has something happened?' she demanded.

Joy remembered what Daniel had said earlier that morning.

'We had a row, that's all. Another fucking row.' She gave a weak smile. 'It'll be fine. We'll get over it. We always do.'

Trish gave her a hug.

'You can talk to me. You know that, don't you?'

'I know I can. I'll be fine really.' Joy hoped she sounded convincing enough. 'Now let's get this show on the road.'

'Absolutely,' Trish agreed. 'Let's head for those hills, girl.' She linked her arm through Joy's as they began threading their way through the Saturday morning shoppers.

Back at the car park, there was a flurry of activity around the bus. Ruth had kicked off her flip-flops and was busy lacing up her hiking boots; her lime green socks peeking out from above them. Brad and Rob were sharing a joke as they rubbed liberal amounts of sun cream onto their necks and faces. Daniel sat on the back step, his red baseball cap pulled low over his face, shielding his eyes from the glare of the sun and prying eyes.

'You'd better put some of this on,' he said throwing a bottle of sun cream to Joy. 'Wear a cap too.'

Her catch was clumsy, chipping a carefully manicured nail. She winced. 'Thanks, I will.'

Trish squeezed her arm. 'You see,' she whispered. 'He's coming round already. You'll be little love birds again before the day's out.'

Joy didn't answer. She let the cool river of sun cream snake down her already bronzed arms. Out of the corner of her eye, she spotted Kathy and Tony, standing at the front of the bus, slightly out of view of the rest of the group. Tony's hand gestures were aggressive, threatening even, as he pointed a finger at Kathy's chest; his face was just inches from hers as he spoke, while Kathy looked at the ground.

'What's going on?' Trish nodded towards Kathy and Tony. She took the sun cream and began rubbing it into the back of Joy's neck and across her shoulder blades.

'Not sure, but whatever it is, Kathy doesn't look too happy about it,' Joy replied. She felt the pressure of Trish's fingers on her neck. *Daniel should be doing this.*

'He's such an arrogant pig of a man,' Trish said. Her dislike for Tony was no secret. She'd often sound off to Joy when they met for a coffee, and she had no qualms about telling Kathy what she thought of him either. Trish meant well, but often didn't realise how hurtful her words could be.

VI

Kathy stared at the ground, totally humiliated by Tony's lecture. A small spider scurried across the open space between her sturdy brown walking boot, and Tony's brilliant white trainer. She watched as it climbed the snowy white mountain, over the hills and troughs of the lace, before disappearing inside the leg of his faded blue jeans.

It's a pity that's not a tarantula, going in for the kill.

'Now, remember what I told you,' Tony said pulling her towards him into a bear hug.

Kathy recoiled at the sticky heat of his hands on her back as they crept inside her T-shirt.

'I'll be waiting for you at the pub. And keep yourself covered up. I don't want any strange Scotsman in a skirt ogling you. These are for my eyes only.' He squeezed her breast.

'Please, not here, Tony.' Kathy's protest was barely a whisper.

He straightened her T-shirt and stroked her cheek. 'Now enjoy your walk and try not to get lost,' he said, his voice sugar sweet before placing his mouth on hers.

Kathy tried to pull away. His lips were wet, his breath hot, and his stubbly chin rough, as he pushed his tongue against her teeth.

'Cut it out you two. You'll have plenty of time for that later,' Brad called across to them.

Kathy said a silent thank you as Tony's lips left hers, feeling her cheeks burn with embarrassment. She resisted wiping her mouth with the back of her hand.

He nodded to Brad. 'Not jealous, are you?' he asked with a grin, keeping a hand possessively clamped on Kathy's shoulder. 'Later, darling,' he drawled, and gently pushed her towards the waiting walkers.

VII

'Tony, will you come with us to the official starting point?' Rob called from the open door at the back of the bus. 'We'll need a photo for the holiday album,' he said waving his camera.

A yellow sou'wester appeared over Rob's shoulder.

'Do you think we'll need the waterproofs this morning?' Ruth asked.

Joy couldn't help smiling at her friend, 'It suits you, Ruth, but I think you're more likely to need a sun hat today.'

Ruth disappeared inside the bus, emerging seconds later with a floral sunhat, a riot of orange and yellow, pulled down over her blond curls.

'How about this?' She put on her sunglasses and struck up a pose against the bus door.

'No chance of losing you anyway,' Joy said. 'We'll see you a mile off in that.'

Rob captured Ruth's catwalk pose with a click of the camera. 'Right, show's over. Let's get started,' he said, closing the back door with a resounding thud and throwing his rucksack over his shoulder.

Back on the main street, they wove their way through the sea of shoppers and walkers to the granite structure marking the start of the West Highland Way.

Tony immediately took control.

'OK, everybody, gather round, lads at the back, girls in front. Kathy, you're the smallest, you stand in the centre.'

They shuffled about until they were happy with the line-up, and Tony took a series of snaps as they smiled, pulled ridiculous faces and made rude gestures.

'Right, off you go then, I'll see you in a few hours,' Tony said handing the camera back to Rob.

VIII

It was just before noon and within minutes they'd left the noisy hustle and bustle of the town centre behind them. Now the real journey began. Mile one of their ninety-five mile trek. They headed north, along an old railway line. The sun broke through the tall leafy trees lining both sides of the track, creating dappled dancing shadows on the gravelled path.

Joy strode along at a steady pace. She pushed her troubles into the deepest recesses of her brain, choosing, just for a while, to relish the beginning of this much-planned holiday. Her sturdy boots hugged her ankles as she crunched across the gravel. Her walking pole swung in time with her stride, its steel tip rhythmically tapping the ground with a very slight echo. She threw her head back to gaze at the cloudless blue sky above, feeling exhilarated and free.

Alongside the Allander Water, a shallow stream that sauntered through pleasant wooded parkland, Joy listened to the chatter behind her. Hearing Daniel's voice brought all the anger and frustration rushing back to the surface, so she quickened her step to widen the gap and be out of earshot.

'Hey, at this rate you'll run out of steam before we even get to the half way point,' Trish called out from the pack behind.

Joy turned, walking backwards for a second or two, surprised by the distance she had put between them already. 'Just glad to stretch my legs,' she said, stopping to wait for Trish. She looked down at the flowing water of the stream, alive with activity; tiny fish scurrying under rocks and minute flies hovering just above the water's surface. A pair of dancing dragonflies, all whirling wings and vibrant azure bodies, cavorted just inches away from her.

'Wow, look at them!' Kathy stopped beside her. 'They're just beautiful!' She whipped out her camera and began clicking madly.

'This place is gorgeous already,' Trish said as she reached them by the edge of the stream.

Kathy smiled at her sister. 'And the further north we go, the better it'll get,' she said. 'I can't wait to be in amongst the mountains.'

The others were now thirty metres or so ahead, disappearing around the bend. 'Come on, girls, make sure you take the right path up here,' Rob called out.

'Best get moving again.' Trish took a mouthful of water, and then pushed the bottle back into the side pocket of her rucksack.

Joy thought how unalike the two sisters walking beside her were. Trish, quite tall at five foot six and very slim, wore her blond hair short, in an almost boyish style. Her make-up was always natural looking, allowing her warm brown eyes to attract the attention of everyone she talked to. Very outgoing and self-assured, Trish oozed sex appeal, and looked nearer thirty than her true age of forty. Her style was classy, with a hint of sexiness. She usually wore tight jeans, boots with heels, and a fitted shirt or jacket. Zipping around town in her red Mini Cooper, the top down whenever the sun shone, she was clearly happy and enjoying life.

You'd never guess Kathy was the younger by five years. Her small round face, always so serious, her large brown eyes, too often dull and sad, and framed by fine straight nearly black hair that rested on her shoulders when it wasn't pulled back into a ponytail. On the rare occasion that she relaxed, her appearance was transformed. Her eyes glowed with warmth and her smile showed white perfectly even teeth. *She has none of her sister's confidence*, mused Joy. She nearly always wore baggy T-shirts or sweatshirts to hide her figure. *Maybe having her first child at seventeen and being married to that loud and arrogant man just knocked the stuffing out of her.*

Trish, on the other hand, had what appeared to be the perfect life. A husband who positively idolised her, a lifestyle she loved, and no money worries. What more could any woman wish for? On top of which, their only son Seb was a high achiever at university in Edinburgh, studying to be a vet.

Joy saw an image of her own life with Daniel and how many of their friends thought that they had the perfect marriage. She gave an involuntary laugh that came out more of a cackle.

'What's so awful it's funny?' Trish asked with a quizzical look at Joy.

'Just thinking. Walking gives you plenty of time to think,' Joy said.

'Would you like to share these wicked thoughts?'

'Perfection.'

'Could you elaborate on that?' Trish asked.

Joy sighed. 'I was thinking that people are not always as they seem. That sometimes what looks like the perfect life to an outsider may not be perfect at all. In fact it could be an utter disaster.'

'And are you thinking of anyone in particular?' Trish asked.

'No,' Joy said. She wasn't ready to share her problems just yet.

'I think you have a perfect life, Trish.' Kathy spoke quietly, without changing pace or looking at her sister. 'You're beautiful, you have a perfect marriage, and a lifestyle you enjoy. You're so lucky.'

Trish spun round to glare at her sister.

'You are so wrong, Kathy,' she snapped. 'Yes, I do have a husband who loves me and I adore him too. We enjoy our time together and we make the most of it.' Trish paused a second or two before continuing. 'But it's far from perfect. We spend half the year apart. For the twenty years we've been married we've had only ten years together, and I've had ten years of being alone, and a single mother - making decisions other couples can share. Ten years of Rob not being there to keep me warm on cold winter nights, or hold me when I'm upset. My life is definitely not perfect.' She turned away stony-faced, and jogged off to catch up with the others.

'Sorry,' Joy apologised to Kathy, as they watched her. 'Seems my simple comment opened a can of worms.'

'I didn't ever think of Trish's life that way,' said Kathy, shocked at her sister's outburst. 'I guess we never really know what goes on behind closed doors.'

'Too right we don't. Come on, they're all waiting for us.' Joy upped her pace, urging Kathy along with her to the next stile they had to climb.

For a few minutes the two of them walked in amicable silence, enjoying the heat of the sun on their backs. Joy watched Trish and Rob up ahead. They appeared to be in their own little world, holding hands, chatting, sharing the occasional kiss. She looked at Daniel, his usual long stride shortened to match that of Brad walking beside him. He appeared more relaxed than he'd been earlier. She heard his deep laugh at something Brad had said. His laughter annoyed her, and not wanting to talk she pushed in her earphones. She searched the play list on her iPod, looking for something lively, something to stop her thinking for a while. With Queen's 'I want to break free' flooding her ears, she marched along in time to the beat, heading for a domed wooded hill ahead.

*****

Kathy slowed down a little to walk beside Ruth. She was still pondering over Joy's parting comment on a perfect life – *too right we don't*. She could see her now, some distance ahead, walking alone. Kathy recalled the icy atmosphere in the Crathorne house earlier that morning. She had felt uncomfortable standing in the hallway, watching Daniel grab his rucksack and drag the suitcase through the front door. And she'd noticed the tremble in Joy's voice as she came down the stairs. Her face was puffy, despite the expert makeup and the brave half smile, and it was obvious she'd been crying. Kathy of all people knew that prying questions would not be welcome.

'How long before the first pub stop?' Ruth asked, breaking the silence. 'I didn't think walking could be such thirsty work. And the sun! Wow, who would have thought we'd get weather like this?' She wiped her face with a cool wet wipe. 'Here, it's quite refreshing.' She offered one to Kathy.

'Mmm, you're right.' Kathy ran the cool wipe over her face and neck. 'I reckon we should reach the pub in about an hour. Can you last that long?'

'Just about.'

'How are the boys and Paul getting on at the farm?' Kathy asked.

'They're doing fine,' Ruth said with a nod.

Kathy gave a knowing smile.

'You know, four years ago when we moved into the rundown farmhouse that Paul's father left him, I thought it was going to be the most idyllic country life for us all. Boy, did I get that one wrong. I must have driven Joy demented with my frantic phone calls.' She chuckled. 'Oh, Kathy, the place was filthy, I didn't know where to start, and did anyone else care? Not a chance. It was like having three kids, not two, all permanently excited, playing with the tractor or messing around with the animals. Joy always calmed me down, told me what a great opportunity it was for the boys to grow up in the countryside. She used to say don't stress about the house, start at the top and work your way down, it doesn't matter how long it takes, you've years ahead of you.' Ruth pointed to Joy in the distance. 'Easy for her to say, living in her mini palace!'

Kathy laughed. 'But you did it. You got the place looking nice in the end.'

'I did, you're right. I tried to make it work for the boys but I wasn't happy, Kath. Then when Mum got ill and I was driving the sixty-mile round trip from Stokesley, I realised how much I missed Saltburn and the sea.'

'Saltburn is lovely,' Kathy agreed. 'Its Victorian charm, the Cliffside lifts, I could see how you missed the place.'

'It was at Mum's funeral, when I looked at the three of them, perched on the edge of the sofa in their matching black suits, like blackbirds ready for flight, knowing they would have given anything to be back in their overalls and green wellies, that I knew telling Paul I wanted to move back to Saltburn would break his heart.' Ruth brushed the back of her hand across her eyes as grief at the loss of her mother and the life changing decision she had contemplated that day overwhelmed her.

'But he loved you, Ruth, surely he would have understood,' Kathy said, patting Ruth's arm.

'I knew he couldn't give up the farm. It was always Paul's dream to leave his fitter's job in the dirty steel works and move to the country. To work with animals. Farming was in his blood.' She wrinkled her nose with a loud sniff. 'Anyway, things hadn't been going well between us for ages. Probably from the day we arrived at the farm, our marriage began a downhill slide, gathering momentum until we hit the bottom, where neither of us had the desire to climb back up again – at least not together.'

'Can't be much further to the pub stop now, 'Kathy said, hoping to distract Ruth before the tears started.

'It was wrong, you know, separating the boys from their dad,' Ruth continued, her mind still in the past. 'They were so subdued at school and then at home they were like caged animals, stripped of their freedom. Instead of acres of green fields to roam and play in, now they had only a handkerchief-sized garden for their games. It was obvious to anyone that they weren't happy. I had to put them first, no matter how much it hurt me and let them go home to their dad.' She wiped away the tear that squeezed out of the corner of her left eye. 'Can you believe they've been back with him ten months now? They've settled back into school perfectly and Paul's a great dad. He idolises them.' Ruth gave a wistful sigh.

'You must miss them though.'

'Every day. And every day, I have to tell myself, I did the right thing.'

'It doesn't make it any easier, I know,' Kathy sympathised. 'It was a really brave thing you did - I envy your bravery. I wish I had the courage to do the right thing.'

'What do you mean?' Ruth asked with instant concern.

'Oh, nothing. Take no notice.' Kathy instantly regretted her comment and tried to backtrack.

'Is something bothering you?' Ruth stopped walking, pulling Kathy to a halt too. 'Is it the kids? Tony?'

'You two look as thick as thieves. What are you up to?' Trish called.

'Please, don't say anything to Trish,' Kathy pleaded. 'We'll talk again later. OK?'

'OK,' Ruth reassured her. 'Last one to the pub buys the round,' she called back to Trish.

'That'll be the lads then, trailing behind,' Trish said with a laugh, as she caught up.

'It certainly won't be Joy. What's with her today?' Ruth asked.

'We'll catch her up, shall we? Anyone fancy a jog?' Trish began running on the spot.

'Count me out, it's enough of an effort just walking in this heat,' Ruth puffed, wiping her forehead with the back of her hand.

Kathy started running.

'Come on then,' she challenged.

The two of them took off, each trying to outrun the other.

'You're mad, the pair of you!' Ruth yelled after them. 'Stark staring mad!'

IX

Joy could feel a trickle of sweat running down between her shoulder blades. Her palms were hot and sticky, and her damp hair was plastered to her forehead. Still she kept up her relentless pace. The beat of the rock music pounding through her earphones blocked out any noise around her.

'Are you in a race or something?' Trish asked, breathless after the two-hundred-metre jog.

Joy pulled her earphones out, her heart hammering at her ribcage.

'You scared the life out of me, you silly sod,' she said.

They fell into step, slowing the pace a little, neither of them speaking as they allowed their breath to return to normal. Joy debated what answer she would give, to the question she knew was about to come her way.

Trish was first to break the silence.

'Phew, it's getting hotter, I'm sure,' she said, knotting her T-shirt at the bust, exposing her taut bronzed midriff. 'What are you up to anyway, marching ahead like that?'

'We can't be expected to be in each other's pockets for the next seven days,' Joy snapped.

'No, of course not, but storming off in the first few hours isn't very sociable, is it?'

Joy looked down at her feet.

'You're right, I know. I just can't be sociable today.'

'You're not going to let a row with Daniel spoil your holiday, are you?'

'No, I'm just angry and confused at the moment. It'll be easier tomorrow, I'm sure.'

'Do you want to talk about it?'

'No.'

'Is it something catastrophic or trivial? On a scale of one to ten, how bad is it?'

'Trish. Drop it.'

'It's not good to bottle it up, you know.'

'Trish!'

'I just want to help.'

Joy was about to swear at her friend, but thought better of it. Instead she pushed her earphones back into place and pursed her lips.

Trish walked alongside Joy, despite the lack of conversation. After half hour or so of trekking along deep, uneven ruts, caused by huge tractor tyres, they arrived at a small pub at the end of the track.

Tony was sitting outside at one of the long picnic tables.

'Have a seat, girls,' he mumbled, through a mouth full of burger. 'Want a chip?' He pushed the plate towards them.

'No, thanks, I need to get out of the heat for a while,' Trish said. She pulled the rucksack from her back and began searching for her purse. 'Are you coming inside?' she asked Joy.

'Yes,' Joy replied. 'I need to find the ladies,' she added hoping to hide out in there until the others arrived, thus avoiding being the object of Trish's scrutiny.

'Who's Kathy with?' Tony asked.

'She's walking with Ruth,' Trish told him.

Joy pushed her sunglasses onto her head and stepped inside. The dimly lit atmosphere of the bar quickly replaced the glaring sunlight, and the clammy coolness on her smouldering skin felt good. Although it was busy outside with the Saturday lunchtime trade, it was relatively quiet indoors. A couple of men in their fifties, whose beer bellies were so huge they looked as if they were about to give birth any moment, sat on high stools, watching the football on a small television above the bar. A group of six elderly ladies, each sporting a blue rinse and a floral dress of equally gaudy colour combinations, sat primly eating roast chicken and vegetables, napkins tucked under their chins. Joy saw them all pause with forks mid air, to turn and stare at Trish and her exposed midriff.

'I think you're the hot gossip topic of the day,' Joy told Trish as they waited to be served.

Trish frowned.

'The old biddies. Did you see the looks they were giving you as we walked in?'

Trish glanced over her shoulder at the ladies who were still watching her as they gabbled to each other.

'I think perhaps they disapprove of your outfit.' Joy couldn't help smiling.

Trish looked down at herself. As the day had gone on, her T-shirt had been pushed up and pulled down to take the shape of her bra. Her cotton combats were rolled up above the knees and pulled down on the hips.

'I'm still decent, aren't I?' She grinned. 'They're probably just jealous.'

'Will you have something to eat?' Trish asked Joy, as the barman poured orange juice over the boulders of ice that filled the glasses.

Joy was peckish, and knowing they still had a few hours walking ahead, she nodded.

'I'll have a tuna salad sandwich in brown bread, thanks.'

'Can you make that two, please?' Trish asked the barman. 'We'll sit over there.' She pointed to a long table on the left of the bar, directly opposite the old biddies.

'Hello,' Trish addressed the curious ladies with a wave. 'Beautiful day, don't you think?'

'Yes, dear.' The lady in the pink and green floral number nodded and smiled, while the others tucked into their food, sheepish at being caught staring.

Joy was thirstier than she realised. The ice-cold river of juice wound its way down her throat sending cold waves through her body.

'Mmm, I needed that,' she said, and settled back in her seat.

'Me too.' Trish sipped at hers and then bent over to take off her boot.

'What are you doing? You don't have a blister already, do you?'

'No, I read somewhere that if you keep your feet well moisturised it helps prevent blisters.' Trish examined her exposed foot; the skin glowed hotly, ridged like corrugated cardboard from the ribbing on her thick socks. 'Look, no blisters,' she said as she plonked her foot on the edge of the table.

'Get your foot off the table,' Joy whispered.

Trish grinned and took down her foot. She pulled a large tube from her backpack, squeezed a dollop of thick creamy white moisturiser into her palm, and proceeded to massage it into her foot. She offered the tube to Joy. 'Want some?'

Joy thought of her hot weary feet, stifled inside the firm boots and thick socks.

'Go on then, why not?' She bent to take off her boots, aware of the disapproving looks coming from the blue rinse brigade. Welcoming the cool air that brushed her bare feet, she put them up on the bench. She spread the moisturiser gently, first one foot then the other, rubbing it into the sole, squeezing it between her toes, using long smooth strokes over the top of her foot and up around her ankle.

'Does that feel good or what?' Trish asked.

'Heavenly. Thanks.'

Braving yet more disapproving glances, the pair crossed the bar, relishing the cold tiled floor beneath their feet on their way to the Ladies room.

Joy threw cool water at her face and neck, feeling a cold trickle between her breasts.

'I never thought I'd hear myself say this, but I hope it's not this hot every day,' she said, pulling a paper towel from the dispenser and patting her skin dry.

'I'd rather heat than rain. We should count ourselves lucky.' Trish smiled at Joy's reflection. 'You look a little better now, more relaxed; less angry.'

'Mmm, I guess I was a tad overheated,' Joy replied. The pressure of the tightly coiled spring inside her had eased a little. 'That foot massage did the trick.'

At that moment, the door swung open and Ruth barged in.

'Make way, make way, weak bladder coming through. I need to spend a penny quick.'

'Sounds more like a pound than a penny,' Trish called out with a laugh.

The others were settling themselves at the long table when Trish and Joy went back into the bar.

Kathy looked down at their bare feet.

'Cooling off?' she asked.

'Come and join us. Take off your boots – it's great.' Trish patted the bench beside her.

Kathy sighed. 'Sounds inviting but Tony's outside, I should go and sit with him.'

As if on cue, Tony's voice boomed through the open doorway.

'Kathy! Kath, bring me another pint out.'

'It's so hot out there, Kath. Go and tell him you need a break from the sun,' Trish told her sister.

'I'll be fine; it's easier to do as he asks.' Kathy spoke quietly.

Joy hadn't realised how hungry she was until she tucked into her tuna sandwich. She smiled at Rob as he put his arm around Trish and kissed her. Trish gave him a bite of her sandwich. *It's all just a bit too much bliss.* She was glad of the distraction of her name being called.

'Joy, do you want another?' Brad was holding up a glass and pointing.

'Yes, please,' she replied.

Daniel was standing beside Brad. She wondered if he would come and sit with her. A part of her hoped he would, even though she knew she couldn't trust herself to put on a show of normality.

X

Kathy waited her turn at the bar. Her face was burning, not from the heat of the sun but from embarrassment. *How dare he? What right does he think he has, speaking to me that way in front of everyone?*

'Yes, love?' the barman asked.

Kathy paid for her drinks then took them outside, avoiding eye contact with anyone as she passed. She squinted, blinded for a moment by the brightness of the sun after the gloom inside.

'What's the matter with you? Your face is all screwed up,' Tony asked as she approached the table. 'You're not sulking, are you?'

'No, the sun's blinding me, that's all.' She banged the pint of lager down in front of him, spilling some on the table.

'Be careful with that.'

She mopped it up quickly with the used napkin from his empty plate.

'You're driving, you shouldn't be drinking.' Kathy threw the napkin back on his plate. 'You're responsible for the other people here, you know.'

'Calm down, woman, I have hours to kill before you finish for the day. I'll have a kip in the back of the bus before I drive on to Drymen.'

'Still, it doesn't look good. What will they all think?'

'This is my holiday too. Don't try telling me what to do, Kath.'

'I'm not.' She backed away, recognising the signs. She had almost gone too far.

He reached for her hand. 'Where are you off to now? Is it too much to ask that you keep your husband company for half an hour before you trek into the wilderness again?'

Kathy took another step back. 'Come inside, it's too hot out here.' She kept moving towards the door. She was determined not to sit beside him. She could see the pulsing vein in his temple, his bulbous eyes staring at her intensely, delving into her very soul.

Back inside the gloomy bar, Kathy gave her eyes a moment to adjust, before joining the others. She hoped desperately that Tony wouldn't follow.

Seconds later the door swung open, the sunlight blocked by Tony's bulky figure as he threw his gaze over the group searching out Kathy.

'Have you all cooled off enough yet?' he asked walking towards the table. He perched on the edge of the bench. 'Budge up, Brad. I want to sit beside my beautiful wife.'

Kathy cringed. Her heart was thumping as Tony pushed himself up close to her, his thigh pressed against hers. She shuffled further along the bench, and her cheeks flamed as he pushed her closer to Brad. She was like a sardine between the two of them. Tony draped an arm possessively across her shoulders and placed his other hand on her thigh, squeezing it with his podgy white fingers. She bit down hard on her lip, willing herself not to shout out. He leaned his body into her as he chatted to Brad, all the while kneading and squeezing at her flesh, the heat of his hands searing through her thin cotton trousers.

Rob clinked his glass with a spoon to get everyone's attention.

'OK, time please, ladies and gentlemen. We need to start making tracks. Boots on, girls...'

Trish placed her bare toes on the edge of the table and wriggled them.

'... and for anyone who feels the need, it's the last civilised stop for a call of nature for the next few hours.'

'That would be me.' Ruth waved a hand, like a schoolchild asking to be excused.

Kathy said a silent thank you to Rob for the distraction. Feeling the pressure of Tony's grip lessen she seized the moment.

'Can you let me out please, Tony?' She spoke clearly as she stood up, praying he'd just let her pass. 'I need to go to the Ladies before we leave.' She answered his unspoken question.

In the solitude of the cubicle Kathy took a couple of deep breaths before she pulled down her trousers. She examined the angry red marks left by Tony's probing fingers, knowing she would have bruises tomorrow.

'Are you ready, Kath?' Ruth called out to her.

'Two minutes.' Kathy flushed the toilet. She waited for Ruth to leave before stepping out of the cubicle, and then took a moment to check her appearance, frowning at her red face, her brown eyes glistening with unshed tears. She promptly ran the cold tap and began throwing water over her face, cooling her burning cheeks and washing away the tears.

Outside Kathy put on her sunglasses and joined the others.

'See you later,' she said to Tony as she passed him, keeping her tone light.

'Can't wait.' He winked.

Brad fell into step beside her. 'He idolises you,' he said with a grin. 'Every time we go out together he talks about you nonstop, saying he can't believe how lucky he is.'

Kathy gave him a brief smile.

'Don't be fooled. Things aren't always as they seem,' she said, before calling out to her sister. 'Trish, wait up!'

XI

Kathy felt the tension lessen and her shoulders relax once the pub and her husband were out of sight. The group spread out once again and Kathy fell into step beside Joy as the footpath cut its way through farmland, the fields a mass of long grass, standing ramrod straight, like vibrant green soldiers in the stillness of the afternoon sun.

'It's so peaceful out here,' Joy said.

'I know, that's why I love walking so much, it gives you time to think,' Kathy replied, hoping that Joy didn't want a heart-to-heart. She was relieved when her friend pointed to her earphones.

She nodded. 'Go ahead.'

The silence was comfortable and Kathy let her mind wander.

She'd been seventeen when she first met Tony. He worked as an apprentice mechanic in the garage opposite Redcar Tech, where she was doing a basic accountancy course. Kathy remembered how she would get off the bus at the stop before hers, hoping to see him. She'd steal quick glimpses from the corner of her eye, searching him out, spotting the black curly hair that rested on his broad shoulders, blushing and scurrying past, if his chocolate brown eyes met hers and he gave her a wink or one of his lopsided grins. Even when he began calling out things like 'Morning' or 'You'll need your brolly today', she was still too shy to speak to him.

On the last day of term, just before Christmas 1988, she'd gone into town with a few friends. They rushed through the doors of the arcades on the seafront, eager for warmth, after the cold north wind had whipped salty sea spray into their numbed faces. Smoothing down her tangled hair, Kathy collided into the solid chest of her handsome mechanic. Recognising her, he winked. Colour flooded her face. She mumbled hello and rushed off in the wake of her friends, towards the coffee bar.

Tony found her again by the Shove a Ha'penny machine. Kathy concentrated on rolling coins down the slot, hoping to tease the bundle of two pence coins teetering on the edge of the shelf to fall into the tray below. Tony talked nonstop, telling her stories of the customers who called into the garage, mimicking their voices and expressions. He made her laugh and she relaxed a little. She challenged him to a game of Ten Pin Bowling - even though she wasn't very good – and when her friends said they were off to the Dolphin Bar for a couple of drinks, she stayed with Tony.

After beating her three times at bowling, Tony walked her to the bus stop. They stopped to buy chips at the kiosk on the seafront, the aroma of hot fat and vinegar too tempting to resist. With a woolly hat pulled down over her ears and her shoulders hunched up against the cold, Kathy warmed her hands on the parcel of hot chips, as the two of them walked along the dark deserted promenade. At the bus stop, Tony kissed her goodnight. His lips were greasy and salty from the chips. Kathy grinned at her reflection in the bus window. She could still taste Tony's salty kiss and couldn't wait to see him again.

From that evening on, Kathy and Tony were an item. They met up almost every day after college. Trish, Joy and all her friends said she was spending too much time with him, and not to lose touch with her friends, Kathy didn't listen. She was totally besotted with Tony.

When Tony bought his first car, an old Ford Fiesta that he lovingly polished until it gleamed like new, they swapped walking the beach for zipping around the countryside. Kathy's favourite trip was across the moors to Whitby. They'd eat fish and chips on the pier before racing up the 199 steps to the Abbey, taking bets on who could do it without pausing for breath.

Some days she'd wait for Tony at the garage. Stretched out on the back seat with the radio tuned to Radio One, she'd work on her assignments until it was time for him to clock off. Then he'd climb into the car, bringing with him the fruity smell of citrus hand cleaner and spicy aftershave. His breath smelled of mint as he leaned across to kiss her, his lips soft and cool. He pushed his shoulders back into his seat and revved the accelerator as they set off in search of a country pub, planning their future.

They'd been together six months, when Tony moved out of his parents' house. There was a massive row. His father had caught him smoking in bed, and had been furious, almost raising the roof with his torrent of abuse, yelling at Tony that he could have 'burnt the fucking house down'.

Tony had retaliated smartly: 'Like you did last year, when you lit the gas under the chip-pan, then fell asleep in the chair, too hammered to remember what you'd done. You almost killed us all.'

His father's eyes narrowed with rage and he lunged at Tony with his fist, catching him full on the face. Blood had poured from Tony's nose and mouth, and instinctively he lashed out in defence, but his blows were no match for his burly father.

His mother dashed up the stairs, screaming at them both to stop. She was a small wiry woman and as she tried to get between them, his father tossed her aside like a rag doll. Tony could only try to protect himself as the blows rained down on him. He ended up in casualty, with two broken ribs and bruising to his face and body. Kathy cried when she saw him, he looked so dejected.

He only went back home once after that, to collect his belongings; a battered old holdall with a zip that wouldn't close, and a black bag filled with his clothes. He threw them into the boot of the car, along with a cardboard box with a picture of a deep fat fryer on it, containing everything else he owned. He slept in his car for a couple of nights, glad of the warmth of the duvet and pillow he'd dragged off the bed as he left.

Tony rented a bedsit on the top floor of an old Victorian terraced house on the seafront. The first time Kathy went there, she gagged at the stench as he pulled her through the front door. The peeling wallpaper in the dank hallway was completely torn off in places and the mould growing in one corner of the ceiling was spreading down the wall. The carpet, once red, was a murky shade of brown, pitted with dirt and Kathy shuddered to think what else, which had been carried in over the years, and was now ingrained in its fibres. The bedsit wasn't much of an improvement on the hallway. During the weeks that followed, they worked together to make it feel more like home, but the hallway never improved and Kathy always took a deep breath before she entered the front door, and then raced up the three flights of stairs, throwing herself into the flat before gasping another breath.

They didn't go out as much once Tony had the bedsit. They were happy to be on their own, snuggling up together under the single duvet, eating crisps and drinking cans of cider, listening to music or a late night talk show on the radio. Kathy was head over heels in love, never happier than when they were together, loving the kissing, the sex – and the tenderness Tony showed her.

'Ouch,' Kathy yelped as she stubbed her toe, jolting her thoughts back to the uneven footpath they were following.

Joy grabbed her arm to prevent her falling.

'Are you OK?' she asked anxiously.

'Yes, I was miles away, not watching where I was going.' Kathy smiled at her. 'Do you ever think back to when we were teenagers...?'

Joy nodded. 'Ah yes, you mean the still-at-school teenager - where the biggest problem in life was not doing your homework, or having a crush on the music teacher...'

Kathy laughed. 'I remember him. Mr Williams; long hair, tight jeans, nice bum.'

'He was just divine,' agreed Joy.

'We all had such high hopes and dreams back then.' Kathy sighed. 'We had no idea of the real world. Did your life turn out the way you imagined it would when you were seventeen, Joy?'

Joy paused a moment. 'No... not really,' she said vaguely. 'But look at you. Three lovely kids. You did OK, didn't you?'

'Is "OK" really enough?' Kathy drew inverted commas in mid air. 'I was studying accountancy when I was seventeen. I had dreams of being a highflying businesswoman with a top London financial organisation. Flitting around the world, to conferences and the like... and look how I ended up.' She glanced down at her well-worn navy cotton trousers and plain white T-shirt, both Primark end-of-season specials.

Joy stared at her. 'You're a fantastic mother, Kath, doing a great job of caring for your family and home. Most people would think your life turned out pretty perfect.'

Kathy sighed. 'I want more from life, Joy. Yes, I love my kids, and I think I've done well by them. But the boys are grown up now, and independent. Alison won't be far behind, and then what? It'll be just me and Tony.' She pushed a finger behind her sunglasses to wipe an escaped tear.

'Would that be so bad?'

Something inside Kathy snapped as she conjured up an image of Tony, seventy-something, obese, and still leering at her. 'It'd be a nightmare,' she spurted out. 'I can't do it. I won't. I'm planning my escape route - I hate him.'

Joy looked at her, speechless.

'Oh shit.' Kathy threw her hand up to her mouth. 'I shouldn't have said that. Please don't say anything, will you?'

'Is it really so awful?' Joy whispered.

'Worse than awful.' Kathy grabbed Joy's arm. 'Please don't say anything to Tony, or Trish, or anyone,' she pleaded.

'No, of course I won't. But what will you do. Where will you go?'

The sound of footfalls distracted them. Brad jogged to catch up then fell into step beside Kathy.

'What are you two plotting?' he asked.

'The trials and tribulations of husbands,' Joy said quickly, 'and how to get rid of them.'

'Oh, right.' Brad looked uncomfortable.

'Take no notice of her.' Kathy helped him out of his quandary. 'It's just girl talk.'

Still shocked at Kathy's confession, Joy said the first thing that came into her head.

'Somebody's ears should be burning big time,' she admonished, then trying to laugh it off, added, 'Be thankful they're not yours.'

Kathy tried to change the subject. Brad was Tony's friend; the last thing she needed was any hint of the conversation getting back to her husband.

'Do you have your map handy?' she asked Brad.

'Yes, sure, just in the front pocket.' He turned his back to present her with his rucksack, and she drew it out. They both pored over it for a short while, and then Kathy looked up.

'Do you see that knobbly ridge over there?' She pointed, hoping to distract Joy from her attack on the male species. 'Is it Conic Hill?'

Joy shielded her eyes as she looked into the distance.

'I read about that - it's one hell of a climb apparently.'

'Should be fun tomorrow then.' Brad looked up from the map. 'That's it all right.' He nodded. 'We're not far from Drymen now. I don't know about you two, but I'm looking forward to a long cold drink and a long hot soak ... just not sure in which order.' He grinned.

The girls nodded in agreement and the three of them walked on without speaking.

Kathy silently berated herself for letting her guard down with Joy. She had allowed her deepest inner torment to voice itself and was thankful for Brad's timely interruption. *Maybe it is time I spoke out and made a stand. I'm thirty-five; I still have a whole lifetime ahead of me. But is walking away failure? Will I leave a trail of irreparable devastation behind? Will the kids hate me? Will my friends turn their backs on me? After all, how could they support me when they don't really know anything about my life?* She continued her self-interrogation until the village of Drymen came into view.

XII

'Oh isn't this gorgeous?' Ruth was rapturous, throwing her arms wide, encompassing the panoramic view of the B&B, as they entered the driveway of Mountain View Guest House.

Joy nodded. 'It's exactly like the pictures on the website.'

The wide gravel driveway was lined either side with perfectly manicured lawns, vibrant and lush, despite the hot weather. The high hedges with their blocky shades of green broken by splashes of scarlet climbing rose weaving through them, gave privacy to the garden. The whitewashed house, with Georgian-style bay windows either side of the open front door looked welcoming.

The minibus was waiting for them on the driveway, its doors wide open, an array of rucksacks and suitcases heaped beside it.

Tony appeared from around the side of the house.

'Ah, the weary travellers. Your rooms await.' He gave a mock bow, gesturing to the front door.

'Our bags are inside already, Kath,' he said, putting an arm around her waist and guiding her. 'Come around to the back garden. It's great, there's a pond with fish and a stream and a bridge. The patio has a hammock and a swing, you'll love it!'

He was gabbling like an excited child, and Kathy's shoulders relaxed. His enthusiasm reminded her of the man she'd fallen in love with years ago.

'OK, but then I need to take off these boots and have a shower,' she said, following him around the side of the house. She gasped. It really was spectacular. A riot of colour spilt down from the hanging baskets secured on the walls and fencing, and from the overflowing tubs dotted around the patio. She peered into the depths of the pool, seeing shimmering lights of orange, silver and gold, as fish lazed in the late afternoon sun.

'There were sixty-three of them at the last count.'

Kathy turned to see a tall elegant woman, dressed in cool cream linen trousers and matching tunic top. She wore a wide-brimmed straw hat, pushed down on her head, with just a few silver tendrils of hair escaping.

'Helen McDougal,' she introduced herself, as she placed a tray holding a large jug of water filled with ice, surrounded by eight glasses, onto the chunky wooden table.

'This is my wife Kathy,' Tony said proudly.

'You have a beautiful garden, Helen,' Kathy said, taking the proffered glass. She smiled her thanks and sat down at the table.

'Thank you, dear.' Helen smiled. 'Are the others joining you for refreshments? I have homemade scones and Madeira cake.'

'If I mention the word cake, they'll be out in a flash. I'll give then a shout.' Tony said before disappearing inside to look for them.

'Excellent, I'll bring out a tray.' Helen said and followed Tony into the house.

Kathy unlaced her boots and pulled off her socks. The cold stone floor soothed her throbbing feet, and she closed her eyes. Tiredness from the day's walking, combined with the early start, was beginning to kick in. A long soak in a soothing Radox bath, before slipping between cool cotton sheets and drifting into a dreamless sleep, would be her perfect end to the day.

The kerfuffle behind her, as the others piled out onto the patio, interrupted her daydreaming. There was a scraping of chairs on the stone floor as everyone got themselves settled. Trish played mother, handing round plates of scones and cake and filling the tall glasses. Waves of praise rained down on Helen for her baking skills and already the men were contemplating what delights might lay in store for breakfast.

'What shall we do tonight?' Rob addressed the table, taking charge as usual. 'Is it posh nosh or takeaway after a few pints?'

'Definitely posh nosh,' said Trish. 'A celebration of our first day completed without injury, getting lost, or any other mishap.'

'I second that.' Brad raised a hand.

'You're more than welcome to a handful of forks and some wine glasses, if you want takeaway out here on the patio,' Helen McDougal offered, as she replaced the empty water jug with a fresh one.

'A few bottles of wine here in the garden gets my vote,' Joy said, hoping she could escape to her room unnoticed if they stayed put.

'Suits me, I'm with you, Joy,' Kathy said, catching a glimpse of Tony's warning glance. She knew he would want to go to the pub and expected her to vote for the pub too.

'All those in favour of posh nosh... one, two...' Rob counted the raised hands. 'OK, five hands beats three, posh nosh it is guys.'

'With a few pints thrown in?' Tony asked.

'That goes without saying, Tony.' Rob grinned. 'We'll meet out here in an hour. OK?'

'Hopefully it'll be out early and home early.' Joy sighed. 'I'm wrecked.'

'Know the feeling,' Kathy agreed. 'See you later.'

XIII

Joy closed her eyes, sliding further down the bathtub. She lowered her head back and pushed the soles of her aching feet against the end of the bath. Water ran into her ears, muffling all sound, distorting the voices coming from the TV that Daniel had switched on, and accentuating her throbbing head. She lay motionless, longing to feel the slowing heart rate of slumber, as her tension uncoiled beneath the warm water. Instead there was just the pounding in her head and the knowledge that Daniel was in the next room. The distorted voices grew louder and water lapped around her as she sat up.

Daniel pushed open the bathroom door.

'Are you asleep in there?' He didn't look at her, as he began filling the basin with warm water. 'We're meeting up in half an hour and I still need to have a shower.'

'I'll be five more minutes.' Joy soaped her arms with the luxury crème body wash; lathering it around her neck, under her arms and over her breasts. She sank down into the water again, allowing the foam to float from her body. *In another time, another place you'd have been in here with me, your firm hands massaging my shoulders before moving tantalisingly over every inch of my body.* She watched through half-closed lids. He'd stripped down to his boxers and was running a razor down his face, deep straight lines ploughing through the thick white beard of foam. She took in his broad shoulders, smooth back, and long muscular legs. Handsome Daniel, protective Daniel, loving Daniel... cheating Daniel. Angrily she pushed herself up. The bath water frothed and swirled around her calves, running down her body as she stood like a statue in a fountain. Their eyes locked through the mirror and clashed, filled with sadness, anger and betrayal. Grabbing a towel, Joy wrapped it protectively around herself and stormed into the bedroom.

She threw herself onto the bed, staring wide eyed up at the suede lightshade hanging from the ceiling. Her fists clenched and her fingernails cut into the flesh of her palms, as she fought to hold herself together. *Deep breaths, Joy, remember. In- one-two-three, out-one-two-three.* Gradually, her fingers uncurled, her heart rate slowed and she took control again.

She dressed quickly in a simple black wraparound dress that hugged her slim figure, falling just above the knee, revealing tanned shapely legs. She slipped her feet into a pair of flip-flops, deemed eveningwear by the shiny decorative toe loop. She whizzed through her hair with heated straighteners, perfecting the sleek black bob, before applying her regular makeup and completing the job with a ruby red lipstick. Satisfied with her appearance in the full-length mirror, Joy picked up her bag and knocked once on the bathroom door.

'See you outside,' she called.

XIV

'Come on, Kath, get a move on,' Tony called out as he hammered at the bathroom door. 'What's the door locked for anyway? There's only me here.'

Kathy sat, fully clothed, on the closed toilet lid, hypnotised by the steaming water filling up the bathtub.

'I told you: my stomach's a bit dodgy,' she said loudly. 'Anyway, it's not polite to barge in on a person using the toilet, even if you are their husband.'

'Well, don't be long.'

Kathy didn't miss the sulkiness in his tone. She heard the sound of the TV come to life and gave a small sigh of relief. He'd clearly been distracted, at least temporarily. But she knew he wanted quick sex before they went out. It was his usual routine. He'd grab her as she came out from the shower, whipping the towel from her, pressing his hot mouth on hers, pushing her down onto the bed and tasting of lager as his tongue nudged her lips apart. Afterwards he'd stretch out on the bed, naked, watching her dress.

'Wear the black bra and that black lace top. It shows off your tits,' he'd say, coming up behind her and squeezing her breasts.

She'd feel his breath hot against her ear.

'Strut your stuff, girl,' he'd say, squeezing a little harder. 'You'll look so hot. I'll be the envy of every bloke in the pub.'

Then he'd spin her around, hands on either side of her face, eyes boring into hers. 'You're mine, Kath... remember that,' he'd tell her.

Despite the warmth of the steamy bathroom, she shivered at the thought. Quickly she removed her clothes and stepped into the hot bath water, sinking down slowly, trying not to make a sound; hoping not to alert Tony that she had moved away from the toilet. With her eyes closed, Kathy allowed her body to relax, letting her aching limbs become weightless, soothed by the warm water. *Maybe, if I stay in here long enough, the lure of a pint will...*

'Kathy!' Tony hammered on the bathroom door again. 'Are you coming out any time soon, or what?'

She jumped at the noise, causing water to lap over the edge of the bath, onto the tiled floor.

He rattled at the handle. 'I can hear you're in the bath now – and why you need the door locked is beyond me. I'm your husband, for fuck's sake!'

'I'll try not to be too much longer.' She put on a pained tone. 'You go down and meet the others. I'll ring you. I can meet you later, if I feel up to it.'

'I could murder a pint all right,' he said. 'You will be down later though, won't you?'

'Yes, hopefully.'

'Right, I'm off then. Be sure to dress up nice for me.'

She heard him move away from the bathroom and waited, listening for the room door to slam shut before relaxing back into the comforting bathwater. She closed her eyes and floated on the edge of sleep.

A knocking on the bedroom door stirred her into action. The water was almost cold, and she had no idea what time it was. Quickly she sat up and pulled herself out of the bath.

'Who is it?' she called out as she wrapped a towel firmly around her petite frame.

'It's me. Are you OK? Are you ill?' Trish's concern was evident.

Kathy opened the door to her sister. 'I'm fine, really. I just needed a little time out before dinner, that's all.'

'Tony told us you were ill, diarrhoea, or something equally awful,' Trish said as she felt Kathy's forehead. 'You do look a little flushed.'

'I've been in the bath for the past hour. I'm bound to be a bit pink.'

'Are you coming down to the pub then? I told the others I'd wait for you.'

'I need to eat, so yes, I guess so,' Kathy said, pulling clothes from her suitcase.

She could feel Trish watching her, as she quickly dressed, brushed her hair, and slicked some tinted moisturiser onto her glowing skin, finishing off with a little coral pink lip-gloss to her lips.

'Ready,' she said, pulling a natural linen jacket over her black spaghetti strapped top. She'd discarded the short sundress Tony had picked out for her, in favour of black linen trousers. The strappy top was one of his favourites on her, and she hoped it would be enough to keep him happy.

Trish and Kathy caught up with the others at The Old Oak. There was much concern for how Kathy was feeling and she felt a complete fraud.

Ruth handed her a menu.

'You could have the watercress soup, with a little dry bread,' she said. 'It should be perfect for a dodgy stomach.'

Kathy wrinkled her nose.

'Thanks for the thought, Ruth, but the very idea of watercress soup is enough to make me throw up.'

She spotted the empty chair beside Tony and her heart plummeted. He was engrossed in a debate with Brad, so she squashed onto the end of the bench beside Ruth.

'Can your stomach take a glass of wine, Kath?' Ruth offered an open bottle of Shiraz. 'We should celebrate completing our first day unscathed.'

Kathy filled up her glass and clinked with Ruth.

'Cheers. Here's to more of the same tomorrow.'

'And the day after.'

'And the day after that,' Trish joined in.

Kathy laughed, glad now that she had come along. She pushed Tony and his annoyance with her earlier to the back of her mind. Her mobile phone pinged a message alert.

It was Alison. 'Hi mum, did u have a good day, have u got blisters? lol xx.'

With nimble fingers, Kathy replied: 'Perfect day, perfect feet. Love u xx.'

'Secret admirer, eh?' Ruth nudged her, giving an exaggerated wink.

'Alison.'

'Is she missing you already?'

'I very much doubt it. My mother'll spoil her rotten. She'll be lapping it up.'

Ruth took a long drink from her glass. 'The boys don't miss me,' she said.

'Of course they do.'

'Nope, they couldn't care less, now they're with their dad.' She topped up her glass, slopping wine over the side as her hand wavered, her forehead creased in concentration. 'You want some?'

Kathy took the bottle from her. 'They're only kids, Ruth, just getting on with their lives. They're always pleased to see you when they visit, aren't they?'

'Yes, but...'

'I know you miss them, it's only natural. You knew it wouldn't be easy when you made the decision to live apart...'

'But I couldn't have imagined how hard it was going to be.' Ruth blew her nose noisily into the red paper napkin. 'I don't know what to do with myself.' She was becoming loud and a bit maudlin.

'I think the wine's talking now. Here, have a glass of water.'

Ruth took the water and sat up straight, thrusting her shoulders back, her bosom out and fixed a grin on her face.

'Can't be a party pooper now, can I?' she said determinedly.

'Good girl. Now let's eat,' Kathy said, leaning back to allow the waitress to place a large bowl of warm chicken salad in front of her.

Later that evening, on the way back to the B&B, Tony caught Kathy by the arm; pulling her back into step beside him.

'You didn't sit with me. Why not?'

'Ruth nabbed me, then she got upset, I couldn't leave her,' Kathy defended herself.

'We're supposed to be a couple. You didn't sit with me all night.' His petulant whine irritated her.

'We'll have other nights.' She tried to keep her tone light, anxious not to cause a row.

'You made a right show of me. Brad kept asking if we'd had a fight.'

She wrenched her arm from his grip. 'Don't be ridiculous,' she hissed. 'I was at the same table, for God's sake. Just grow up.'

SUNDAY
I

Joy opened her eyes. Daniel was sleeping beside her. Disorientated for a few seconds, she took in the lilac floral curtains beyond the mound of his back. She reached out to him and then stopped, hand in mid air, like a freeze-frame in a movie, as reminders of the past two days assaulted her brain. Memories of the angry words, the betrayal, the hurt, jolted her out of her relaxed sleepy state. They'd barely spoken to each other the whole of the previous evening. And when they returned to the B&B, too tired to care that they'd be sharing the double bed, they lay tensely, back to back, trying not to touch, until exhaustion took over and they fell asleep.

Daniel turned over in his sleep, carelessly throwing his arm across her body, pinning her down.

Did he do this with HER? Protecting her as they slept? Did he stay with her all night? Joy tried to think. *Had there been any conferences lately, any reasons for him to stay away for a night? How do I know what's been going on? He often works late so I'm in bed before he gets home, and in the morning, he's always up and dressed before I wake.* She tortured herself further, every nerve ending in her body aware of the weight of his arm across her stomach. *Maybe he didn't come home at all some nights. No, that couldn't be. I'm his wife -I'd know if he hadn't been beside me all night. I'd sense it. Wouldn't I?*

His touch was suddenly unbearable. She flung back the duvet and jumped out of bed, leaving his fingers to fall, with a thud, onto the empty mattress. The heat in the room was oppressive and stifling, and Joy showered and dressed with lightning speed, eager to get out into the fresh air. She moved quietly through the sleeping house. Sliding open the patio door she slipped outside. The cool morning air wafted across her face. The rising sun cast its rays over the pond and caught the dewdrops on the lawn, like diamonds glistening on an emerald sea. The patio was still in shade, but Joy didn't mind that. She'd get plenty of sun during the day.

'You're up and about early, my dear.' Helen McDougal appeared, ghost like, beside her.

Joy jumped at the sound of the soft Scottish lilt. She'd heard nothing of her approach. Helen smiled at her.

'Would you like a cup of tea? I'm afraid breakfast will be another half hour or so.'

'Tea would be lovely, thanks,' Joy said.

A few minutes later Helen brought out a small tray laden with a 'tea for one' Wedgewood teapot and matching cup and saucer, along with a plate of buttered toast.

'Now, that should keep you going for a little while,' she said with a kind smile, and returned to the kitchen.

Joy sat in one of the patio chairs, and began nibbling the corner of a slice of toast. *How can we ever sort out this mess our marriage has become? Is it retrievable? No. How can it be? Can I forgive him?* She poured the tea, stirring in sugar, distracted by her thoughts. *Probably. But how can I ever trust him again? And can he forgive me? I very much doubt it. So that's it then. In a nutshell, it's over.*

Rob walked out onto the patio, disturbing her internal mutterings.

'Morning. Aren't you the early bird?' he said, scraping back the chair beside her.

Joy quickly brushed the telltale tears from her cheeks and gave a watery smile, embarrassed and annoyed with herself for being caught out like this.

He stroked his greying goatee beard. 'Are you ok?' His green-blue eyes, which twinkled blue when he smiled and became green when he was troubled, were now a definite green. 'Is it Daniel?' he asked. 'I know things aren't quite right between the two of you.'

Joy bristled.

'Has he said something?'

'No.'

'We had a row, that's all.' The words stuck in her throat. 'We'll sort it.'

'Hiya, you two. Isn't this just heavenly?' Trish materialised beside them and planted a kiss on her husband's receding hairline. Then her smile turned to alarm at Joy's tear-stained face.

Joy got to her feet, desperate to escape. 'I'd better wake Dan for breakfast,' she said, before fleeing back into the house.

She bumped into Daniel, quite literally, in the corridor. He reached out to steady her, as she fell against the wall.

'Take it easy. Where's the fire?' he said.

For a second he was the old Daniel, solid and safe. Then, scalded by his touch, she pulled away again, pushing past him.

'Breakfast is almost ready,' she called out over her shoulder. She saw the hurt confusion in Daniel's face as he continued watching her. 'I'll be down in a minute,' she added.

*****

Breakfast was a feast. The table was laden with fresh fruit, cereals and homemade breads. And then the full Scottish fry-up appeared, along with several rounds of toast and copious amounts of tea and coffee.

Joy kept her head down, looking busy with her food, yet eating very little. Her stomach was churning. She listened to the kind of conversations that take place at hotel breakfast tables the world over, and decided they were all way too jovial for this hour of the morning. And when Rob announced they would be setting off in half an hour, she was the first to move. She couldn't wait to get going again.

III

Kathy stood to one side as Tony threw the last of the bags into the bus. She knew he'd want a proper goodbye before she joined the others, and she couldn't face the humiliation of him calling her to heel, like a pet dog.

'Right, all ready for the off?' he asked, slamming the back door shut. 'Come here you.' He pulled her into a bear hug.

Kathy fought the urge to pull away. The closer she got to carrying out her plan, the harder it was getting to be even in the same room as him.

'Tony, I have to go,' she whispered.

He tightened his hold. 'See you later then.'

'Yes, see you later.' She pulled back as he relaxed, his hot kiss grazing the side of her mouth as she turned.

'Kathy!' He tried to pull her back.

'Bye,' she said, and waved, jogging down the drive to catch up with the others.

'Ahhh, he's missing you already,' Brad drawled, as he fell into step beside her. 'He talked about you all evening.'

'Then I'd sit somewhere else tonight if I were you.'

Brad smiled at her prickly response and wisely decided to ignore it. 'I'm looking forward to Conic Hill,' he ventured. 'It's our first real challenge.'

At the change of subject, Kathy relaxed. 'It's a steep climb all right,' she said. 'But the views over Loch Lomond are meant to be spectacular.'

'I wouldn't mind climbing Ben Nevis while we're up here.'

'Now that really would be a challenge... after seven days' walking.' Kathy raised an eyebrow. 'Are you mad or what?'

'Definitely mad, and probably a little "or what" too.' Brad grinned, laughter lines crinkling at the corners of his eyes. 'How about you? Are you up for a challenge?'

Kathy felt the gentle pressure of his hand in the small of her back, as they crossed the road to the path leading into the forest, and abruptly she moved away, whipping round to face him.

'What are you doing?'

Brad looked confused. 'Sorry?'

'Your hand.'

'It was just a gesture,' he said, obviously bewildered by her outburst.

Kathy glared at him saying nothing. After that, it was as if an invisible barbed wire fence separated them, as they walked along the meandering woodland footpath. Kathy was relieved the others were far enough ahead not to have witnessed her outburst. *What was I thinking of, overreacting like that? He'll probably tell Tony how touchy I was, and then Tony will say I was leading him on and all hell will break loose. Oh, I'm so stupid. Planning to leave him is just a dream, a stupid, pathetic dream. He'll never let me go.* She was acutely aware of Brad's presence beside her, his strides matching hers. *Should I say something? Tell him how Tony will react? Maybe I should just change the subject completely.*

Brad interrupted her thoughts. 'I'm sorry if I offended you just then. I didn't mean anything.'

'Don't be daft.' Kathy forced jolliness into her voice. 'You startled me. That's all. Forget it.'

'I'll try to remember you're an independent woman next time we cross a road,' he said, grinning mischievously.'

Kathy couldn't help warming to him. 'You do that, and we'll get along just fine.'

'So...'

Kathy looked up, waiting for him to continue.

'... what did you think of the B&B?'

'Really nice, did you like it?'

'Yes, great breakfast, powerful shower...'

'The homemade breads were gorgeous.'
'Mmm, and the room was nice.' Brad sighed.
'Well done to Joy. She chose well.'
'Lovely soft carpet, comfy bed, fluffy towels...'
Kathy burst out laughing. 'What are you going on about?'

He gave her a wounded look, making Kathy laugh even harder. Tears filled her eyes, her shoulders shook, and her sides ached. She hadn't laughed, truly laughed, in what felt like an eternity.

'It wasn't that funny,' Brad said.

She couldn't help herself - she couldn't stop. Brad handed her a tissue to wipe her streaming eyes. A smile spread across his face and he laughed with her.

They were still chuckling when they reached the others. Rob was talking to a guy who was obviously a seasoned walker, with his fully laden rucksack, wide brimmed hat and matching walking poles.

'Come on, you two. This kind gentleman has offered to take our picture, before we climb this baby.' Rob pointed to Conic Hill, looming beside them.

'What's tickled your fancy?' Trish asked Kathy, as they got in position for the photo.

'I don't know really. We were just talking about the B&B, and I got a fit of the giggles.'

'Well, whatever it was, keep up the smile for the photos.'

'OK, everyone, say cheese,' the man said. His weathered face creased into a smile.

'Take five or six, if you don't mind,' Rob called out from the back of the group. 'Just in case someone's got their eyes closed, or mouth open.'

Click, click, click. 'There you go, folks.' The stranger handed back the camera. 'Now, that's a fair hike you have ahead of you, just keep a steady pace and you'll do fine. Oh, and if you think you can manage it, go off the path before the descent, and climb that little bit further to the very top. You'll be well rewarded if you do.'

'Thanks for the tip.' Rob shook his hand.

IV

Joy stared into the distance, following the line of the path with her eye, from where they stood, to the top of Conic Hill. The yellow-coloured pathway snaked its way through the green grass and vegetation on the lower slopes, before slithering upwards between shades of copper and bronze, which she guessed were rocky outcrops.

Ruth came up behind her. 'So this is it.' She looked up, her eyes almost out on stalks. 'I'm really going to climb this mountain.' She pointed up with one hand, while stuffing the fist of the other into her mouth, stifling a mock scream.

'Hold that pose,' Trish shouted. 'It captures the moment perfectly.' She whipped out her camera.

'Thank God I've got my best friend to help prop me up,' Joy said.

'I know, I'm glad you're here too,' said Ruth.

Joy tapped her hiking stick on the ground.

'Sorry Ruth. This wins best friend of the day award today.'

Ruth pulled a face, pushing out her bottom lip.

'Come on, Ruth. We'll prop each other up.' Trish laughed, linking her arm with Ruth's.

They set off again, Trish and Ruth leading the way, marching off full of bravado and determination, with Rob and Daniel walking a few steps behind at a more leisurely pace. Joy followed slightly behind them, yet still close enough to hear the low murmurings of their conversation. Rob's deep baritone voice was most prominent, and Joy imagined that he was asking Daniel what was going on.

And what will you tell him, Daniel? Will you say it's just a silly row, or will you confess to your indiscretions? Will you tell him our secrets? She almost called out for them to wait for her, so that she could listen in and have some control over what Daniel might say. *Stop it. Do I really want to discuss our marriage out here, on this hill, with Rob, who'll tell Trish, who'll tell everyone? And then they'll all know what a bitch I've been.*

'Ouch, shit.' She stumbled on the uneven path and was only saved from falling by her new best friend, her walking stick.

'Are you OK, Joy?' Kathy called from behind.

'I'm fine, I just wasn't concentrating for a moment,' Joy replied.

Daniel looked back, waiting until she was level with him.

'I'm OK. Really,' she told him, seeing his frown. She focused on her steps and the tapping rhythm of her stick as it hit the stony path. Daniel walked along beside her, although neither of them spoke.

As the path got steeper, Joy's heart rate quickened. She was breathing hard, and realised too late that her fitness could have been better. She should have been more prepared.

'I need to stop for a breather,' she said. 'You go on ahead if you like. I'll just admire the view for a few minutes.'

'I could do with a rest myself.' Daniel stopped beside her.

'Admiring the view?' Brad asked as he passed with Kathy.

'Great idea.' Kathy smiled. 'You don't always appreciate what you leave behind.'

Joy noticed that she looked daisy fresh, with not a hint of breathlessness.

'We should walk from Fort William back down again next year,' Kathy added.

'Hey, slow down, you.' Brad nudged her playfully. 'Let's get this week over before we start planning the next trip.'

They were soon out of earshot; leaving Joy and Daniel surrounded by silence, save for the occasional cry of a warbler, or the buzz of a bee. Joy drank in the vista before her, the hazy sunshine creating a pleasantly fuzzy image.

'What a view.' Daniel shielded his eyes.

Joy followed his gaze along the footpath. 'Look how high we've climbed already,' she said. 'This is perfect. It's everything I imagined it would be.'

'Not perfect,' Daniel whispered.

His words were a silent sledgehammer, slamming her brain back to the present.

'We should make a move, or they'll get too far ahead,' she said, saddened and angry at the situation they had put themselves into. Spinning around she set her sights on the miniature figures in the distance.

Daniel kept pace beside her, as she stabbed her stick into the ground.

'We have to talk sometime, Joy.'

'Not here, not now,' she panted, keeping up her relentless pace, feeling every stab of the stick reverberating through her body, stabbing at her heart.

'She didn't mean anything.' Daniel increased his pace so that he was slightly ahead, and turned to look into her eyes. 'You have to believe me, Joy, please.'

Every inch of her body screamed out in protest as she pushed on, one foot in front of the other, up the ever-steepening hill. Her T-shirt clung to her damp skin, and rivulets of sweat ran down between her breasts and shoulder blades. Then, as he refused to look away, her eyes locked with his, and pain transmitted between them like a bolt of lightning. Joy tore her gaze away, wiping the back of her hand across her forehead. She studied the beads of sweat sitting on her oily sun- creamed skin, before drying her hand on her shorts.

'Not here.' She forced the words out between rasping breaths, pushing past him. 'Not now.'

*****

She caught up with the others at the top and collapsed onto a rock beside Kathy.

'Jeez, Joy, are you all right?' Ruth offered her bottle of water. 'You look like you've just run a marathon.'

Joy glugged the water thirstily, wiped the top and handed it back. 'Thanks, I needed that.'

'The lads are going to the top,' Trish announced. 'Are any of you up to it?'

'I think I can manage it.' Kathy stood up, joining Trish at the foot of the final climb.

'I'll just catch my breath,' Joy puffed, pulling a small towel from her backpack.

'This is as high as I fly this morning.' Ruth looked down at Joy. 'I'll stick around here, I think.'

Joy towelled her arms, then her chest and around the back of her neck, drying her damp skin, aware of Ruth's probing eyes.

'You shouldn't push yourself like that,' said Ruth. 'We've a long way to go yet.'

Joy nodded and pulled out a packet of wet wipes, offering it to Ruth.

'Thanks.' Ruth closed her eyes, placing it over her face as she lay back against the grassy hillside. 'Oh, that feels good.'

Joy's burning face welcomed the cool dampness as she gently cleansed her face and neck. Her breathing slowly returned to normal. She applied more factor30, pulled her cap down low, shielding her eyes, and lay down beside Ruth.

'I'm worried about you,' Ruth said.

'Don't be.'

'I'm here if you need to talk.'

'I don't, thanks.'

'You were a rock for me when I needed you. I owe you one.'

Joy felt Ruth sit up. She kept her eyes closed, staying silent for a moment. 'You owe me nothing, Ruth. That's what friends do,' she said quietly.

'Joy watched through half closed eyes as her friend's shoulders slumped.

'The boys would love it up here. I still miss them so much,' she said sadly.

She continued to talk, not needing a response. 'I guess I'll always miss them and that's OK. What I can't handle is how slowly time passes, and all the hours and days of silence in the house. There are no pots to wash, apart from my lonely mug, one knife and fork and one dinner plate. No muddy boots to clean, and never a full load for the washing machine.' A long sigh escaped her. 'I need a new purpose in life, Joy. I need a reason to get up in the morning.'

'You need a man in your life,' suggested Joy, pushing her own problems aside with an effort.

'That's one thing I don't need,' protested Ruth. 'Anyway, I said a reason to get up in the morning - not stay in bed all day.' She let out a raunchy laugh and flopped back down beside Joy.

There was a sound of approaching steps, and Trish's shadow fell across the two of them. 'You should have made the effort,' she exclaimed, brimming with enthusiasm. 'The views were amazing! We could see for miles; up Loch Lomond and back towards Glasgow! Apparently, on a clear day you can see the tower blocks in Glasgow city. Can you believe that?'

'Chilling out for twenty minutes after the latest endurance test has been pretty amazing too.' Ruth exaggerated her sleepy drawl. 'Wouldn't you agree, Joy?'

'Positively amazing.' Joy yawned and stretched out an arm to Trish. 'Give us a pull up.'

*****

The panoramic views soon disappeared when they began their decent. As usual, Rob took the lead, followed by Trish and Joy. Joy could hear Ruth and Brad laughing and joking behind them. She was glad that Ruth had perked up again.

'What do you think? Could they be a perfect couple?' Trish grinned at Joy as she pointed behind them with her thumb.

Joy turned, only to see beyond Ruth and Brad to where Daniel and Kathy appeared to be deep in conversation. She felt a stab of jealousy.

'Jeez, I thought going uphill was bad, but this is pure torture.' Ruth huffed and puffed as she negotiated the steep stone staircase, down the westward side of Conic Hill.

'Here, hang on to my arm,' Brad offered.

'Ooohh, the perfect gentleman,' Ruth gushed, her tone playful 'How come nobody's snapped you up?'

'I'm still searching for Miss Right.' Brad smiled.

'I could be onto a winner here, Joy.' Ruth winked at Brad and linked her arm through his.

Joy reeled in her gaze to focus on Ruth and Brad, just feet away from her. She forced a smile at Ruth before turning her attention back to her footing.

'So?' Trish asked.

'So what?' Joy gave her a puzzled look.

'Forget it.' Trish shook her head in exasperation. 'The joke's dead now.'

'Sorry.'

'Apology accepted.' Trish lowered her voice slightly. 'But will you please tell me what the hell is going on. Daniel is in bits, and you, well, you're on another planet. So this is not just a row over leaving the toilet seat up.'

Joy continued to focus determinedly on the steep steps.

'Rob has tried talking to Daniel...'

'What did Daniel tell him?' Joy interrupted her. 'What did he say about me?'

'Hey, calm down.'

'Is he blaming me? Because it's not my fault. There are two sides to this you know.'

'He's not blaming you.'

'So what did he say?'

'Nothing.' Trish touched her arm and they stopped, staring at each other. 'He just said it was a silly row and you'd get it sorted in a day or so. But Rob could sense it was more than that.'

Joy took a deep breath.

'We'll sort it in our own time, Trish.'

'You can talk to me. I won't judge, you know that.'

'I know.' Joy set off again, with Trish keeping stride beside her. 'But not here, not now.'

'You keep saying that. I just hate to see you this way.'

'I couldn't bear for everyone to know.'

Trish looked hurt. 'I don't gossip, Joy.'

'No, no, sorry, I didn't mean it like that, it's just that I know I'll cry – and once the floodgates open I don't think I'll be able to stop.'

'OK, but if it's so bad that you need to cry, then for fuck's sake just cry. Get it all out. And if you need to curse and swear at Daniel, then fucking do it. Either way, whatever it is, don't let it eat away at you like this.'

Their pace had increased as the conversation heated up until they had left the others far behind them out of sight. The steep decline had given way to a quiet path that curled through the mature woodland and finally emerged into a car park where the familiar minibus was pulling in - just as the two women arrived.

V

Kathy looked sideways at Daniel from behind the cover of her sunglasses. Her attempts at small talk had met with no response, so they walked in silence. Some of the steps were very high for her short legs, and he held her hand to help her down them.

Finally, Daniel broke the silence. 'Do you ever think that if you could change just one thing in your past, the events that followed it would be wiped out - and the future could be so different?'

'Wow, where did that come from?' said Kathy.

'Have you ever made a mistake, Kathy?' He looked at her, his eyes filled with anguish.

She took a deep breath. *What should I say? Is he talking about himself, Joy, or me? Can I trust him? Will he tell Tony?*

'A good few.' Kathy decided to try to keep it light, in the hope that she wouldn't give herself away.

'No, I mean a whopper of a one. Big enough to wreck your marriage, or turn your family away from you.'

'No, not so far. I guess there's still time, we're only young yet. Have you?'

'Too many.' Daniel's tone was deadly serious.

Kathy held her breath, knowing something big was coming.

'I cheated on her, Kathy.'

Kathy stopped dead in her tracks. 'You bastard,' she spat. 'When? Does she know?'

Daniel sat down on the steep step and put his head in his hands.

'She does, doesn't she?'

The briefest nod answered her question.

Kathy looked at Daniel. His confession explained a lot. Her heart was pounding with rage, and although she saw how distressed he was, she couldn't feel any sympathy for him. Her only thoughts were for her friend.

'Are you still seeing her... this other woman?'

'No, it was only once. Years ago.' Daniel pulled a tissue from his pocket and blew his nose.

'And you just told her about it? Now, this week? Why, for God's sake?'

'It was killing me. All the lies, the overcompensating, the guilt.'

Kathy gave a snort of disgust.

'My heart bleeds for you. You shatter her life because you can't handle the guilt. Well, you should have kept it in your pants in the first place.' Kathy was shaking as she marched off. *No wonder Joy's in the state she is. And there was me thinking she had the perfect life. What a mess. Her with a lying cheat, me with an abusive possessive control freak. Men. Who needs them? Bastards, the lot of them.*

'Kathy, wait, please.' Daniel was jogging up behind her.

She glared at him.

'You won't say anything, will you? To Joy, I mean. Or to anyone. We haven't really talked things through yet.' He was breathing hard and his eyes were wild with fear. 'Joy doesn't want anyone to know anything. She won't even talk to me properly.'

Kathy shook his pleading hand from her arm.

'Kathy, please.'

'I'd never do anything to hurt Joy,' she said.

'Thank you.'

'Don't bother thanking me. I'm not doing it for you.' She shrugged him away from her, and increased her pace, dismissing him.

*****

Her anger at Daniel made her even more determined than ever to create a new life for herself. Although she was almost certain Tony has never been unfaithful. Infidelity, or rather the suspicion of it, was a major factor in the decline of Kathy's marriage. Tony's reaction after Alison was born was a memory Kathy wished she could forget.

Alison came along six years after Joe. Kathy had been taking the pill for years, knowing they could not afford another child, but somehow it happened. Maybe she was ill or forgot to take it one day. She was four months pregnant when Tony noticed. She had been putting off telling him, knowing he'd blow a gasket. As she'd correctly predicted, he ranted on about how expensive kids were and that he was working every hour God sent to support his family. 'How could she have let this happen?' He demanded, conveniently forgetting that it takes two.

Despite all his ranting about expense, once Alison arrived he became besotted. She was his precious baby girl, with a mass of dark, downy hair and big blue eyes behind long thick lashes. By the time she was three months old, the baby down hair had been replaced with golden curls. Her eyes remained blue, unlike the boys', whose eyes were a warm, dark brown, like their parents'.

'She's not mine, is she?' Tony said one night, completely out of the blue.

He'd just rolled off her. The tenderness had gone from their lovemaking some time ago. He was always selfish, but this was the first time he'd been rough too. Horrified, Kathy tried to make light of his comment.

'What are you talking about? Of course she's yours. Look at her; she's the image of Anthony when he was that age.'

'She's blond. Who else is blond? Anthony, Joe, you, me?' His voice rose with each name. 'Not one of us. There's not a fucking blond hair in sight.'

Her whole body stiffened, and for the first time in her marriage, she was afraid of him. He flung back the bedclothes and stormed across the room, flicking the light switch and flooding everything in it with a harsh glare. Instinctively, Kathy curled up, to protect herself, shielding her eyes from the brightness and pulling the bedclothes back over herself.

'Who is he, Kath?' He loomed over the bed.

'Tony, you're just being stupid. I was blond when I was a baby. Of course she's yours. Why would I want anyone else? I love you.'

He dragged the bedcovers off her, exposing her naked shivering body.

'Look at you! If that's not a guilty look, then I don't know what is,' he sneered.

She was terrified of this man. He wasn't Tony at all. She lay waiting for the first blow, staring at him, wide eyed. Their eyes locked for a few seconds, and then he turned on his heel. At the bedroom door, he flicked the light switch again, plunging the room into darkness once more, before slamming the bedroom door closed behind him.

*****

'Kathy!' Tony called out, as he walked up the forest path towards her. 'What happened? Why are you so far behind the others?' He stood in front her, his chest heaving from the unaccustomed exercise. Beads of sweat, lined up like soldiers on parade, covered his forehead.

'No drama, Tony.' Daniel came up behind Kathy. 'Some of us just walk a little slower than others.'

Kathy saw Tony's eyes narrow with suspicion as he looked from Daniel to her. She sighed heavily. She was in no mood for one of Tony's lectures.

'Come on, let's go.' She pushed past, leaving Daniel to walk with Tony.

VI

The outside seating area of The Balmaha Inn was packed. Groups of tourists, mainly olive-skinned French and Italians, gabbled away in their singsong voices, gesturing animatedly with their hands. They sat among fair-skinned families out for Sunday lunch, who spoke in a thick Glaswegian accent - their conversations equally unfathomable to anyone not from the area. Then there were the walkers, looking hot and weary, sitting propped up against their rucksacks on the grass. The unusually hot weather meant that all the tables outside were full.

The group were more than happy to take a table inside, out of the glaring sun. There were just two free tables, on one of which lay the remains of the last occupants' meal. Unperturbed by this, Rob and Brad pushed the two tables together, and everyone settled down as the waitress cleared the table for them. Tony and Daniel were the last to sit down.

'Come on, you two, we're waiting to order,' Rob said, passing the menu across to Daniel.

Tony waved the menu away. 'The fish and chips'll do me, but I need a pint first. It's bloody roasting. You lot must be mad,' he panted, wiping the sweat from his beetroot face.

Kathy's eyes met Daniel's, as he followed Tony to the bar, and he silently pleaded with her not to say anything to Joy, who sat beside her.

'What are you having, Joy? You didn't eat much at breakfast.'

'Oh, I don't know.' Joy looked distracted.

'Earth to Joy.' Kathy watched a chain of expressions flicker across her friend's eyes. She understood completely what was going on in her mind.

'The baked potato with coleslaw.' Joy closed the menu and looked at Kathy. 'What was Daniel saying to you?' she hissed in a whisper.

Kathy hesitated, sensing Joy's hostility. 'Nothing specific.'

'Was he talking about me?' Joy raised her voice a little.

Kathy saw Trish and Brad look their way. 'The others can hear you,' she whispered, hoping Joy would lower her voice too.

'Was he talking about me?' Joy persisted.

'He just said how upset he was, I'll tell you more when we get out of here. It was nothing... honest.' Kathy hoped she sounded convincing. She'd never been so thankful to feel Tony's hand on her shoulder.

'Hello girls,' he said, putting his pint of lager on the table between them.

Joy gave him a withering glare before pushing back her chair. 'Sit here if you like, next to your wife.'

'Who rattled your bones?' Tony asked Joy as she pushed past him.

Kathy watched sadly, as Joy moved to the other end of the table. She felt Tony's hot hand rest on her thigh and her heart sank.

'So, what were you and Daniel up to?' he snarled, just loud enough for her to hear.

She edged away a little. 'Nothing,' she mumbled, through a mouthful of crusty bread.

Tony unwrapped his knife and fork, as a young waitress placed a plate of fish and chips on the table in front of him.

'Why were you walking with him and not with your sister?' He shovelled white flakes of fish covered with crispy batter into his mouth, never taking his eyes off her for a second. 'If I find out anything's going on you'll be sorry. You both will be. I mean it, Kath.'

He spat tiny particles of fish as he ranted, and Kathy kept her eyes lowered. She concentrated on her bowl of carrot and coriander soup; methodically lowering the spoon, watching the orange liquid flow into its silver hollow, as he continued his tirade. She hoped and prayed that no one was watching them. She spooned small amounts of soup into her mouth, forcing it down past the lump in her throat, willing herself not to cry. She could hear Ruth's raucous laughter at some tale she was spinning. Only when she felt Tony lean across the table and heard him join in the conversation, did she cautiously glance up. Her face flooded with colour when she saw Brad watching her.

'Are you OK?' he mouthed silently.

His kindness was more than she could take. She gave a brief nod as a silent tear squeezed from the corner of her eye. Quickly sliding out of her seat, past Tony, she escaped to the ladies.

*****

Kathy slammed the cubicle door and sat down heavily on the toilet lid. She was shaking with anger; fighting to hold back the hot, salty tears. *What was I thinking of? Coming on holiday knowing Tony and his preaching, self-righteous attitude would be in such close proximity to everyone for a whole week. I can't bear it. I'm going to blow it. I know I am. I'll blurt something out.* She stood up, brushing away the tears with the back of her hand. *I can't, I have a plan, and I need to stick to it. Get a grip, woman.*

Kathy was splashing water on her face and staring at herself in the cracked mirror above the sink, when Joy walked in.

'They're all ready to go,' she said, without even giving Kathy a glance, before entering a cubicle.

Kathy pulled a grey paper towel from the dispenser and patted her face dry. A final close-up look in the mirror showed her there was no telltale trace of redness around her eyes. 'I'm ready, see you in a minute,' she called to Joy.

Kathy stepped out of the gloomy darkness of the pub, shielding her eyes from the glare of the afternoon sun. She wove her way through the group of children racing around the beer garden, past mothers cradling babies or spoon-feeding toddlers in buggies. It seemed as though the entire population of Glasgow were spending their Sunday afternoon in Balmaha.

She joined the others at the start of the footpath.

'Think I'll join you for a while,' Tony announced. 'It's a nice afternoon and this stretch along the beach is fairly flat,' he added, looking across at Kathy.

They strode off again, heading northwards, leaving behind the bustling village and the marina filled with boats of all sizes, bobbing and bumping against each other on the gentle lapping waters of the loch. The footpath ran alongside the narrow road lined with cars bumper-to-bumper, parallel to the pebble beach beside the loch.

On the hot white sand, bodies in various states of undress stretched out, skin exposed to the burning sun.

'I propose we ditch the walking, rip off our clothes, and frolic in the water,' Ruth announced, fanning herself with her bright floppy hat. 'Any takers?'

'No time for such niceties, I'm afraid,' the ever-practical Rob called out. 'We still have over seven miles left to walk this afternoon.'

'Party-pooper.' Ruth pouted.

'I'm up for a bit of frolicking. How about you, Kath?' Tony winked suggestively as he squeezed her behind.

A wave of repulsion washed over Kathy, and she brushed away his hand. Sidestepping to the left, she walked off, moving a little quicker, threading her way through the kids playing football, stepping over abandoned trainers and sandals. All the while, she sensed Brad walking in line behind her, treading in her footprints. Kathy remained silent. She didn't want to talk to him; she just wanted to think. She dragged the D-T-Day plan from its hiding place deep in the recesses of her brain, and began mentally ticking off her reasons for going through with it. She could feel the butterflies in her stomach. The terrifying anticipation of what she was about to do.

She touched her hot cheeks, not from the sun... but thank God for the sun anyway. Sunburnt cheeks and sunglasses are the perfect camouflage for her humiliation.

Kathy jumped at Brad's tap on her shoulder, and then stumbled.

'Shit.'

'I've got you.' He grabbed her arm.

'I'm fine,' she said, shrugging off his hand, even though it had felt reassuring for those few seconds.

Brad stayed beside her. 'I didn't like what I saw back there. Tony shouldn't talk to you like that.'

'It's OK. I'm used to it,' she mumbled. 'He doesn't mean anything.'

She was defending him again. She hated herself for doing it; it was just easier that way.

'He deserves a thump.' Brad stabbed his walking pole into the sand.

'We don't need any hassle. It's fine. I told you.' Kathy was getting anxious. The last thing she needed was Brad having a pop at Tony.

'He's supposed to love you.'

Kathy felt uncomfortable under his intense gaze, and she was worried that Joy and Trish could hear, walking just behind them.

'Drop it, Brad, please,' she whispered.

'Do you love him?'

'No... Yes... for God's sake, Brad... just drop it.' The words came out in a whispered hiss. Kathy was mortified, convinced that everyone must have heard... but the world carried on around them. She quickened her pace, increasing the distance between herself and the others.

'I'm a good listener.' Brad kept his stride in line with hers.

'Well, I'm not a good speaker.' Kathy took a swig from her bottle of water, and then clamped her lips tightly shut. She couldn't believe his audacity; *who does he think he is? He hasn't known me five minutes and he's criticising my marriage, asking intimate questions. How dare he? If he's such an authority on love and marriage, then why is he on his own?*

'Kath, Kathy, wait up!' Tony's loud, coarse voice interrupted her ramblings. She turned, to see him crossing the sand towards her. His thin white legs covered in thick black hairs protruded from his knee-length shorts, and he carried his wobbling belly with a sort of pride.

'What are you doing, so far ahead?' he asked, wiping the back of his hand across his forehead.

Kathy shrugged and said nothing, acutely aware that Brad was still within earshot.

Tony's chest heaved as he waited for his breath to return to normal. 'I'm going back to the bus now; I'll see you at the hotel later. Right?' It was an order, not a question.

Kathy was tempted to say '*you might, then again you might not*'. She thought better of it and instead gave him the briefest graze of a kiss on his cheek, before stepping quickly out of reach.

'I need to get the sunblock from Trish,' she called out. 'Bye.'

She jogged across the sand towards Trish, relieved to have got away without too much fuss, but also conscious that Brad would be scrutinizing her from behind his glasses.

Kathy made a pretence of searching Trish's rucksack, knowing that Tony too would be watching her until she was out of sight.

'What are you looking for, Kath?' Trish tried to swivel round as Kathy delved into her backpack.

'Nothing, it's ok.' Kathy watched Tony's retreating figure, until he was just a speck amongst the day-trippers.

'What was that all about? Trish questioned.

Kathy pretended she hadn't heard, feeling Trish's troubled gaze from behind her sunglasses.

'You and Brad? It all looked a bit heated.'

Joy could see trouble brewing between the sisters and tried to defuse the situation. 'Trish, you have that bone between your teeth again,' she said.

'Kathy's my sister; it's my job to look after her.' Trish's voice prickled defensively.

'She's also a grown woman,' returned Joy. 'She's been living her own life for a good few years now, and managing fine.'

'Not very happily,' snapped Trish. 'Anyone with eyes can see that. You only have to...'

'Excuse me,' Kathy interrupted. 'It's my life – and anyway who are you to judge, Trish? Just because you live in that swanky house, all loved up and cosy, it doesn't give you the right to rubbish the way I live.'

'Kathy, that's not fair. You know I don't judge.' Trish looked hurt.

'She cares about you, Kathy,' Joy intervened.

'Yes, whatever.' Kathy knew she had over-reacted to Trish's comments.

The three of them walked in silence. Kathy felt the tension. *I knew this was a mistake. What on earth made me think I could keep up the pretence of a normal marriage, under the scrutiny of Trish and the girls?*

Giving herself an impatient shake, she marched ahead, needing to be on her own for a while.

They had left the Glasgow day-trippers and the beach behind now. Kathy walked a few yards ahead of Trish and Joy. She could hear their low muffled tones and knew they were talking about her. So what? What did she care? She pushed their voices out of her thoughts, concentrating instead on her D-T-Day plans.

VII

'Are you OK, Trish?' Joy asked her subdued friend.

'Yes.' Trish sighed. 'I should know better. Sticking my nose in where it's not wanted is asking for trouble, but I can't help caring. I'm sure there's more going on than she's saying.'

'And maybe you're imagining things that aren't there.'

'Oh, come off it, Joy. You know as well as I do something's not right in that house - and hasn't been for years.'

'Well that's as maybe, it's still none of our business.' Joy's own troubles loomed large in front of her. 'What goes on behind closed doors is a person's own affair,' she said.

'I only want to help. Is that so awful? We all need a bit of help sometimes.' Trish frowned in frustration.

'I know that. Kathy's a big girl now. I'm sure she'll talk to you when and if she feels the need.'

'And do you feel the need to talk to me, Joy?'

'I'm a big girl too,' Joy said, inwardly cursing. *This is such bad timing. I can't face telling Trish yet, but I know she'll get huffy with me if I don't.* 'Let's just change the subject for a while.'

'OK. Fine.' Trish tossed her head and stalked off.

'Trish!'

'I get the message. It's fine,' she called over her shoulder, and the gap between them grew wider.

'Shit, shit, shit,' Joy fumed. *As if my life wasn't complicated enough without alienating a best friend. It's time I got a grip, sorted myself out. I need to talk to Daniel.*

'You two fighting again?' Rob joked, as he and Daniel drew level.

'Nothing we can't fix.' Joy tried to keep it light. 'She was getting a bit clucky with Kathy earlier.'

'Clucky?'

'Yes, clucky. You know, like a mother hen.' Joy flapped her arms.

'Ah-ha, she's on one of her mercy missions.' Rob nodded solemnly. 'I'd best catch her up and douse the flames.' He took off in Trish's wake, leaving Daniel to walk beside Joy.

Their footsteps fell into line. The silence that echoed off the invisible barrier between them was crammed with unanswered questions. Joy immersed herself in the beauty of the scenery around them, the shimmering blue waters of Loch Lomond, the idyllic secluded island floating enticingly, just out of reach.

Daniel broke the silence, his deep voice almost a whisper. 'Joy...'

'I know. We need to talk,' she interrupted. 'But not now.'

He let out an exasperated sigh.

Joy ignored it, and called out to Ruth. 'Come on, slowcoach, we don't want you getting left behind!'

Daniel pursed his lips and shook his head, leaving her to wait for Ruth.

*****

'Damn it, I knew I shouldn't have eaten that steak pie and chips,' Ruth groaned clutching her side. Her forehead glistened with sweat, and damp tendrils of hair curled around her flushed face.

'I could say I told you so...' Joy's smile was sympathetic. 'But I won't. Do you feel ill?'

'No, I just have a stitch, trying to keep up with you lot,' Ruth huffed and puffed. 'I'm not super-fit like the rest of you.'

'You'll be fine. Come on.' Joy linked her arm. 'You can't be getting all defeatist on me already. We'll stroll along together until that stitch wears off. OK?'

'OK.'

The leafy canopy along the woodland path gave the women a smattering of shade from the relentless heat of the afternoon sun.

'I'd never have believed it could be so hot in Scotland,' Ruth gasped, as they climbed the steady incline. 'I've probably lost a stone since lunch.'

Joy laughed. 'We'll have to feed you up at dinner then,' she said.

'No.' Ruth shook her head vigorously. 'If I get nothing else out of this torturous trip, losing a couple of stone will make it all worthwhile.'

'That sounds a bit excessive,' Joy said, not sure if Ruth was joking.

'I could do with getting rid of these.' Ruth grabbed her generous love handles and gave them a shake. 'And these.' She slapped her thighs and watched them wobble. 'See? Legs like jelly... literally.'

Joy joined in the banter. 'Some guys like a couple of love handles to hold on to, you know,' she teased.

'Huh,' sniffed Ruth. 'I've had it with guys - and love handles too.' She stuck out her chest defiantly. 'This is my body, and I aim to have it just the way I want it.'

'No possibility of a reconciliation with Paul then?'

'Not a chance.' Ruth's shoulders slumped.

'Wouldn't you consider moving back to the farm for the boys?' Joy spoke tentatively. She never knew if the mention of Ruth's estranged family situation would instigate tears or rage.

'I think about them every day,' Ruth said. 'Every day, Joy. Every minute of every day. It won't work. Paul and I just can't live together. It's that simple.' She shrugged. 'I know I can't live on the farm and I know that he will never leave.'

They continued along the footpath for a few minutes, each lost in her own thoughts. Then Ruth pulled her phone from the side pocket of her backpack, scrolling through the photos to bring up the latest image.

'See how happy they are?' She handed the phone to Joy.

Luke and Adam grinned at the camera, each holding a tiny baby lamb.

'That's what keeps me going, you know. Looking at their happy faces, telling myself I did the right thing.'

Joy nodded. 'You know they're settled so perhaps it's time you thought of a career change. You could go back to college.'

'Oh, I don't know, I can't see me back at school somehow.'

'Well, what would you like to do? If you could do anything at all, what would you choose?'

'I guess I'd like to work with people. I like to feel needed and that I belong... an important cog in the wheel.' Ruth played with her earring.

'What about nursing?'

'I haven't got the brains for that.'

'A care assistant, looking after old people?'

'Haven't got the stomach for that.'

Joy gave her a puzzled look.

'You know.' She lowered her voice conspiratorially. 'Too many involuntary bodily functions.'

'Ugh, Ruth, only you could say that.'

'I believe in calling a spade a spade. No point in beating about the bush,' said Ruth firmly. Only her mischievous twinkle gave hint of the humour behind her solemn response.

'OK, OK, we'll keep working on it. We're bound to come up with something.' Joy smiled; glad to see Ruth looking more cheerful.

They could hear voices ahead and found the others waiting in a clearing at the end of the path.

'Finally! 'We were about to send out the search party for you two.'

'Well, excuse me, but some of us like to take in this magnificent scenery.' Ruth threw her arms wide, encompassing the views around her.

'Let's get a few photos while were all together.' Trish said. 'Everyone gather round on these rocks, where I can get the loch in behind.'

'Give us a minute to catch our breath,' Ruth puffed.

'Smile then.' Trish looked up over the camera. 'You all look like you're doing ten years' hard labour. We're supposed to be having fun!'

'Right, let's get cracking folks.' Rob hoisted up his rucksack.

VIII

Kathy continued to soak up the view for the final few moments, as Rob rounded up his flock. She closed her eyes, breathing in the sultry air, feeling the heat of the sun, with not a whisper of a breeze to cool her skin.

'I bet you could sit here all day. I know I could.' Brad stood beside her.

She took an involuntary sidestep, uncomfortable at the heat from his body so close to her.

'I wish! But we still have miles to go yet.' She grabbed her gear. 'We'd best get on with it.' She threw a quick smile to hide the brusqueness of her comment. *What is wrong with me? I feel like a jittery teenager. Why all this attention from him anyway?* He was half a step behind her, and Kathy stole a discreet sideways glance at him. *I should talk to him- he's probably only trying to be friendly, but he is just so infuriatingly nosy. No, nosy isn't really the right word...*

'I'm really glad I was invited along this week,' Brad interrupted her rambling thoughts. 'A month off work to de-stress was sounding very stressful to me.' He grinned.

Kathy watched him push his sunglasses into his short blond hair, observing how his blue eyes twinkled. Small laughter lines and dimples formed in his cheeks as he smiled. She thought he looked totally relaxed.

'You don't seem the type to let anything faze you,' she said tentatively, attempting a conversation that wasn't about her.

'My doctor would beg to differ.' Brad's tone was light. 'Said I needed to watch the ticker, change my lifestyle, or I might not have a life left to style.'

'But you look so fit.'

Brad raised an eyebrow.

'I mean...' Flustered, she tripped over her words. 'You play five-a-side and go to the gym and stuff.'

'Yes, work hard, play hard, work even harder. Not a healthy balance, apparently.'

She saw the light go from his eyes as his smile faded and his face suddenly looked old and tired. Her heart melted. 'So, how is the break going for you?'

'It's tough going actually.'

She waited, not sure whether to change the subject.

'When work has been your life for the past fifteen years, you can't just switch off,' he continued.

'It's your own business, isn't it?' Kathy knew he had his own accountancy firm in the centre of town.

'Exactly. It's taken so long to build and it could all fall apart if I'm not constantly at the helm.' He let out a frustrated sigh.

'Surely you have people you can trust?' Kathy stepped over the gnarled tree roots that crossed the narrow pathway, treading carefully, with her feet and her words.

'I guess so, but...' He took a swig from his water bottle. 'It's kind of like leaving the kids for the first time without a babysitter, while you go on a night out. You know they'll be perfectly OK, but it still doesn't stop you worrying yourself sick while you eat.' He gave a wry smile. 'I know they are all more than capable but it doesn't stop me worrying, or calling the office ten times a day.'

'OK, I get the picture. How long have you been out of the office?'

'This is the third week now.'

'And have there been any disasters?'

'No.'

'So?'

'So what?' He frowned.

'So... they are obviously doing just fine without you.' She was warming to the conversation now. 'What you need is a project, something to fill your day, totally unrelated to the business side of your brain. Something different...'

'This is different - a real challenge; I've never walked this kind of distance before.'

'This is a holiday. I mean an ongoing project that you can continue when you go back to work.' She looked at him. 'You're not getting what I mean, are you?'

'I am. I am, really. I just wouldn't know what else to do. If I'm not in the office, then I'm up half the night working on the laptop.'

'I'd say that doesn't go down too well with the girlfriend,' she ventured.

'Ha!' He let out a mirthless laugh. 'What girlfriend? I don't have time for one, and even if I had, I couldn't take her back there - the place is a disaster. I haven't even unpacked everything yet. Most of the walls are still bare plaster and I know that floorboards are the in thing, but not the paint-splattered unpolished variety.'

'That's it then,' Kathy announced with a flourish. 'The ideal project!'

Brad looked confused. 'Find a girlfriend? He shook his head. 'I don't think so.'

'No, you silly sod: renovating your apartment.'

They were walking along the shoreline again, and Brad picked up a pebble, caressing its smooth surface with his thumb.

Kathy noticed the gentle gesture, embarrassed at the picture she conjured up in her head, of his thumb on her cheek.

'I'll help you - I love doing stuff like that.' The words tumbled out.

Brad threw the stone. They watched it skim the surface of the gently lapping water four times before it disappeared. He took so long to answer that she wanted to retract her words. Kathy could see the others stopping just ahead, to sit beneath a large oak tree.

'Would you?' he asked. 'I'm hopeless at choosing stuff and organising people like plumbers and electricians. And I guess it really is about time I got the place sorted.'

Kathy's face lit up.

'I will, on one condition.'

'Oh no.' His eyes crinkled as he grinned. 'What's that... unlimited budget?'

'I took that as a given.' She smiled. 'No, my condition is that you don't ring the office for the rest of the week.'

He frowned.

'Oh, and you say nothing to Tony about this.'

'That's two conditions.'

'Just agree to them, Brad, and we'll get along fine.' Kathy laughed.

'I'll come back to you later. It looks like we're about to take a shade break,' he whispered, giving her the briefest glimpse of a wink, as they joined the others under the umbrella of the oak tree.

*****

'That looks like one angry big toe,' Kathy said, flopping down beside Ruth.

'You're telling me.' Ruth grimaced. 'And where's our knight in shining minibus when we need him? The other side of the water. Ouch!' She winced as she smothered the offending toe with Savlon.

'Turn your sock inside out,' Trish called over to them. 'The seam inside has probably been rubbing.'

'Such a smart arse, your sister,' Ruth muttered.

'Good advice all the same,' Kathy said sympathetically. 'We've a fair way to go still.'

'Shall we dress up for dinner tonight, girls?' Trish looked around the group. 'Let our hair down a bit; celebrate two days' walking done.'

'You'll be exhausted,' warned Rob. 'We still have Ross Wood to negotiate yet.'

'Oh, don't be a killjoy Rob.' Ruth massaged her sore feet. 'I need something to look forward to, to get me through these next few miles.'

'I like to party as much as the next man,' Rob defended himself. 'But, I have heard that Ross Wood is an absolute killer.'

'OK, so if we haven't been killed off you'll buy the first round?' Ruth stuck out a hand.

'Deal.' Rob shook it vigorously.

'Cocktails?' she raised an eyebrow.

'Cocktails it is.'

'Come on then, girls.' She grinned as she pulled on her boots. 'I don't know about you but the promise of Sex on the Beach is enough to get me through Ross Wood in half the time.'

'Mmm, and a White Russian,' mused Joy.

'And a Black Russian for me.' Trish joined in as they moved off, their spirits revived again.

IX

Kathy padded along the carpeted hallway in her socks, with the second key to room seven gripped tightly in her hand. Arriving at the hotel, she'd gone straight into the bar, assuming that as Tony hadn't been at the gate waiting for her, that's where he'd be. There had been no sign of him. Outside the room, she took a deep breath and turned the key. The lock released with a quiet click and Kathy pushed the door open.

'Oh my God.' Her hand flew to her mouth at the scene before her. The stench of alcohol filled every corner of the room. She quickly closed the door before the smell permeated the corridor. Tony lay spread-eagled across the bed, face down, wearing only his boxers. His discarded shorts and T-shirt were a puddle at her feet. This alone was no great surprise to her; at home, she would just climb into bed beside Alison. But here... she had nowhere else to go. And what disgusted her most was the sight of her empty, upturned suitcase, and its contents, which were strewn around the room.

Her first instinct was to pounce on him and pummel his doughy white back with her fists. *What the fuck are you playing at Tony? S*he struggled desperately to stem the flood of angry tears hovering behind her eyelids. Terrified of becoming the target of his drunken anger, she moved tentatively around the room, picking up items of clothing, smoothing the creases from her T-shirts, gathering her underwear. She spotted the black plunge bra that she loathed, lodged under Tony's inert hand. *What is all this about? What was he looking for? He knows what's in the suitcase. He told me what to pack, for fuck's sake. How do I explain this one away downstairs?*

Kathy almost jumped out of her skin when Tony groaned and turned onto his side. She stood frozen to the spot, praying his eyes wouldn't open. They didn't - it was only a matter of time, she was sure, until he woke. Grabbing the closest clean clothes she could lay her hands on she fled to the bathroom and locked the door. She leaned heavily against it, letting out a quivering sigh. Her hands were shaking. Her whole body trembled.

After a lightning quick shower, Kathy dressed at top speed and cautiously opened the bathroom door. Tony hadn't moved, and his breathing was deep and even. She seized the moment and quickly gathered up her clothes, pushing everything she could find back into her suitcase, before closing the zip slowly, cringing at the grinding sound it made, which seemed to echo around the room. Keeping one eye on her husband, she pulled the case upright and stood it beside the door. Nervously she moved towards the bed, took the pale green floral throw that had fallen to the floor, and placed it gently over the sleeping figure.

X

Joy walked out onto the hotel terrace. She spotted Trish straight away, leaning against the railings that looked out across the loch, and looking less than half her age in a low-cut olive green dress, which fell in soft folds just below the knee. Four-inch stiletto-heeled strappy sandals in a matching shade of green completed the outfit, and showed off her tanned, shapely calves.

Joy moved across the quiet patio, passing its only other occupants, a young couple. Newlyweds, she guessed, noticing their interlaced fingers, and sensing sparks of chemistry as she passed them...

'Well, if it isn't the green goddess herself.' She smiled as she reached Trish and kept her tone light, hoping to dispel any tension that might have been lingering after their heated words earlier.

'You don't look so bad yourself.' Trish pointed to Joy's equally high sandals. 'The dress is gorgeous.' She reached out to touch the silky red fabric that clung seductively in all the right places. 'You wouldn't be trying to impress anybody in particular tonight by any chance?'

'Ha ha... like who?' Joy raised her eyebrows and tossed her head. Her hair skimmed across her face like a curtain, before falling neatly into place again.

'Like a certain tall dark handsome guy coming our way.'

Joy spun around and then back again just as fast. 'No,' she retorted.

'Well, if seeing you tonight doesn't make him want to suck up and apologise immediately, I'll eat my hat,' Trish whispered, as Daniel reached them.

'He'd be wasting his breath,' Joy said bluntly.

'Rob's getting the drinks in.' Daniel smiled at Trish. 'Do you want to sit inside or out?'

'Oh, inside, I think, we'll be eaten alive out here soon.' She rubbed her arms as if to ward off imaginary mosquitoes. 'We'll follow you in a few minutes.'

Joy gave an involuntary shudder as she watched Daniel walk back towards the hotel.

'You cold?' Trish asked.

'No.' Joy pulled her gaze away from Daniel 'But I do need a drink. Come on.' She linked Trish's arm with hers, propelling them both towards the door. 'Let's find the girls and get this party started. Oh, and Trish...' she stopped and looked at her friend. 'I'm sorry I was a bitch earlier.'

'Forgotten already.'

'I'll tell you what's going on, I promise...' She crossed herself, an old habit she'd never got out of since school. 'I just have to talk to Daniel first – or at least hear him out.'

'OK, subject closed.'

'Thanks, Trish.'

'For now, that is!'

Inside, in the bar, the two women spotted Daniel and Rob sitting at a large round table in front of an equally large arched window. Seeing the empty chairs and the two glasses of white wine waiting for them on the table, Joy sighed, and wished she had stayed outside a little longer. The conversation might well get a little awkward with just the four of them there. She thought of texting Ruth and telling her to get a move on.

'Thanks, guys. Cheers.' Trish clinked her glass against Rob's before taking a sip.

There was still no sign of Ruth or Kathy. Joy was feeling panicky; she pulled out her phone and began quickly clicking with her thumb.

WHERE ARE YOU? Joy selected Ruth's name and pressed send.

'I was just saying to Daniel, the four of us haven't been out together in ages. In fact the last time we went for something to eat was that Sunday when we were planning this trip.' Rob patted the seat beside him for Trish as he spoke. 'Remember? We met up at The White Horse, up on the moors, and then we went for a walk.

Joy sat beside Daniel, knowing it would be churlish not to. She took a few long sips from her glass. She did remember that day, not in quite the same light as Rob. While the other three debated the last football match they'd seen at the Riverside stadium, and a technicality of the referee's decision, Joy recalled that day out in the Yorkshire Moors, and let her mind wander...

*****

'Do you think it'll be cold up on the moors?' she'd called out to Daniel, studying the row of neatly ironed clothes, hanging in colour co-ordinated order in the wardrobe. She turned to see Daniel busy stuffing walking boots and Gortex jackets into his battered old rucksack. 'Dan, what are you doing?'

'What does it look like? I thought we were going walking.'

'We are.' She turned back to the array of clothes, selecting a low-cut, short-sleeved, black and cream top.

'You'll be cold in that.' Dan was behind her, caressing her smooth arms, still bronzed from their week's holiday in Lanzarote a month earlier. 'Take a jumper.'

Ten minutes later, finally happy with her appearance, Joy was ready to go. She ran down the stairs and through to the kitchen, the heels of her black knee-length boots clicking across the hall floor. Daniel was sitting at the kitchen table, engrossed in the sports pages of the *Sunday Times*. She could hear the splutter of the percolator, and the pungent aroma of strong coffee hit her nostrils. She inhaled deeply, loving the smell.

'Do we have time for coffee?' she asked, 'I've booked The White Horse for one o'clock.'

'I know.' Daniel pushed back his chair and folded the paper.

She looked him up and down, taking in his comfortable brown cords and white T-shirt beneath his old cream jumper. 'I think you could have made more of an effort. You know how up market The White Horse is - you never know who we might bump into there.'

'We're going walking. I'm hardly going to wear a suit and tie.'

'I just wanted it to feel a little bit special, that's all.' She spun around on one shiny black heel and left the kitchen.

A minute later Joy was staring out of the large bay window in their bedroom, down onto the quiet Sunday morning activities in the street below. Her next-door neighbour was polishing his car, rubbing at it vigorously until it gleamed. The old lady from three doors down walked past in her Sunday best, clutching her bible. She gave their neighbour a prim smile.

Joy folded her arms protectively across her chest, her blue eyes glinting with tears of anger. She heard Daniel's heavy tread as he climbed the stairs.

His sigh was audible as he walked across the bedroom towards the window.

'Nothing I say or do is right anymore,' he muttered, placing two mugs brimming with coffee on the windowsill.

He stood behind her; Joy felt his hands lightly caressing her shoulders.

'I don't care who we might meet. I just want a day out with my beautiful wife and our friends.' He kissed the top of her head.

Joy jerked away, whipping around to face him. 'I care, Daniel. It's important to me. We need to be somebody. We need to be respected.' She took a deep breath, lowering her voice to a whisper. 'I need to be someone. Not just Daniel's wife.'

Daniel tried to rescue the day by changing into a casual, blue striped Ralph Lauren shirt and smart black jeans.

Joy didn't comment, except to say, 'I'll drive.' She took the keys from the hook by the door, and marched out to the car with Daniel trailing behind her. Sliding into the driver's seat, she started the engine with an unnecessarily loud roar.

They drove the forty-minute journey over the Yorkshire Moors in silence, passing Scaling Dam, where a few hardy sailors were out on their yachts, braving the choppy waters of the reservoir. They turned off, to drive deeper into the heart of the moors, to the White Horse pub.

Joy pulled up beside Trish's red Mini Cooper, and turned to look at her husband. She took a deep breath. 'Let's have a good time today', she said.

She kissed Daniel's cheek and took his hand in hers. They walked into the bustling country pub hand in hand, forced smiles on their faces.

Over a roast beef lunch, amid the hustle and bustle of the busy pub, they discussed the holiday idea, and every imaginable obstacle.

Trish tapped her glass with a spoon. 'OK, so we're all agreed?'

'Let's go for it. The worst we can do is kill ourselves trying.' Rob raised his glass. 'To The West Highland Way.'

'To The West Highland Way,' Trish, Joy and Daniel said in unison.

'Now, who's up for a walk on the moors?' Daniel asked.

'I'd rather have some of that sinful chocolate cake for dessert.' Joy and Trish said in unison.

Laughing, Trish said, 'Just listen to us, planning a ninety-six-mile walk when we're not even up to a Sunday stroll. We'll never make it to the end.'

'Well, we could always hole up in that luxury hotel planned for day three,' Joy said, laughing.

As a compromise, the girls ate chocolate cake while Rob and Daniel had another pint, and then they set off to brave the elements on the Yorkshire Moors.

Outside, by the cars, they put on their walking boots, jackets, hats and gloves. The sun shone high in the ice blue sky, casting its wintery light on the beauty of the moors. Their breath rose in swirls of white mist and the chilling breeze nipped at their ears. After two miles of clambering up and down rocky outcrops, and walking along the exposed ridge with its beautiful views of the valley below, they arrived back at the White Horse, exhilarated, cheeks glowing and noses reddened with cold.

After a round of coffees to warm themselves, they said their goodbyes and started the drive home.

As Joy negotiated the winding moor roads, Daniel chattered on about the excellent food and the walk.

'Today was a really great day,' he said, 'I think the holiday idea is brilliant. I'm not sure about staying in that luxury hotel though...'

'STOP RIGHT THERE!' Joy yelled. She shot him a furious glance, and swerved to the side of the road, screeching to a stop. She switched on the hazard lights and turned off the engine. 'What is it with you? Why does everything come down to money and how much things cost? We have enough, don't we? It's one night, Daniel. One night in a nice hotel half way through the week. Are things so bad that we can't even do that? I've had enough of it... all of it.'

Daniel sat in silence as she vented her pent-up anger and frustration.

'All the overtime you're doing, working late into the night.' She gripped the steering wheel, staring out at the dusky shadows. 'The lack of decent conversation - because you're too knackered to be bothered, the lack of sex these days...' She paused in her tirade, choking on the angry tears stinging the back of her eyes. 'I know you don't love me anymore,' she finished furiously.

At this, Daniel was shocked out of his silence.

'How can you say that?' he retorted. 'Of course I love you!'

Joy made an exasperated noise. She started the engine again and pulled away at speed. 'Well, you have a pretty shit way of showing it these days.'

'I know, I'm sorry, it's just work... and stuff.'

'What stuff? You need to buck your ideas up and talk to me. If we can't get things back on track, we may as well call it a day.' Although the words were killing her, she knew one of them had to do something. 'I love you, Daniel, but we can't live this way any longer.'

XI

Ruth arrived at the table and Joy focused her attention on the present once more. She realised she'd been gripping the stem of her glass so hard that her knuckles were white. She relaxed her grip, allowing the blood to flow into them.

'Hi, Ruth.' She gave a little wave to her friend. 'Wow! Look at you. Give us a twirl.'

Ruth spun around, before taking up a pouting, seductive pose, as she ran her hands down her body, skimming her ample breasts that threatened to escape the plunging neckline of her 'seventies print top. The flowing mass of fuchsia, purple and red skimmed the top of her thighs, which were clad in skinny jeans. She placed her lipstick-red, stiletto sandal on the chair beside Daniel.

A round of applause erupted, not just from her friends, from the group of walkers gathered around the bar too. Ruth sat down with a triumphant grin.

'You should be on the stage, Ruth.' Brad put a glass of white wine in front of her.

'Why thank you, sir.' she sipped at it. 'Believe me that was nothing compared to Joy's rendition of Sandy...'

'Don't even go there, Ruth,' Joy interrupted.

'OK, OK, your honour remains intact.' Ruth held up her hands. 'I'll tell you later,' she whispered to Brad.

'Where are Kathy and Tony anyway?' Trish asked. 'I don't know about the rest of you, but I'm famished.'

'I'll text her.' Joy pulled out her phone.

'No need,' Rob said, pointing to Kathy crossing the bar towards them.

*****

'We were just about to send out a search party for you,' Brad said, pulling out a chair for her. 'Where's Tony? Will he be long? We're all getting hungry.'

'He's not feeling well.' Kathy spoke quietly as she fiddled with her handbag. 'I'm not sure he'll be down at all. We'll just carry on and order. I'll check up on him later.'

'Right, come on then. Let's move into the dining room.' Trish picked up her glass as she stood up.

'I hope it's not catching. You look a bit peaky yourself,' Joy said to Kathy, curious as to why she was dressed so casually when they'd agreed to a glitzy night.

'No, I'm fine, really. You look gorgeous, by the way.' Kathy's smile was lukewarm as she looked down at her plain white T-shirt and blue jeans. 'I completely forgot we were getting dressed up.'

'Why don't you order, then run up and get changed while we wait for the food to arrive?'

Kathy pictured Tony, motionless on the bed, and shuddered inwardly. 'No, I'll be fine, really. Anyway I don't want to disturb Tony.'

'OK, whatever you want. Let's sit down and order some food.'

Their table was by the full-length windows, giving them stunning panoramic views over the darkening blue water of Loch Lomond, and across to the mountains beyond. All bathed in the orange, red and pink of the setting sun.

'Isn't it absolutely breathtaking?' Trish gazed out at the view, her arm draped casually around Rob's waist.

She nudged Kathy. Look at those two, isn't it sweet?'

Joy and Kathy saw the presumed newlyweds out on the terrace, feeding each other strawberries between kisses.

'Enjoy it while it lasts,' Kathy said.

'The calm before the storm,' Joy added.

'Oh, behave yourselves.' Ruth turned on them. 'Don't be so cynical.'

'What?' Joy looked at the couple and then back at Ruth. 'You of all people know it's not a bed of roses.'

'So I should write off romance altogether, just because it didn't work out the first time? Thanks a bunch.'

'I didn't mean to upset you.' Joy patted Ruth's arm. 'It's just a little too sickly sweet for my liking. Let's sit down.'

XII

After they had eaten a sumptuous four-course meal, they all wandered back into the bar.

Ruth flopped down, sinking into a black leather couch. 'God, I'm stuffed,' she announced undoing the button on her jeans.

'Have you given up on the idea of a Sex On The Beach then?' Trish plonked herself down beside her.

'Not a chance – bring it on.'

'Right so that's a Sex on the Beach with a Black Russian and a White Russian and...?' Trish turned to Kathy.

'Count me out this time. I'll just go and check on Tony. I won't be long.' She turned towards the reception area and the door marked Residents Only.

'And a podgy White Englishman,' Ruth finished with a wicked grin.

'Ruth! That's a terrible thing to say,' Trish admonished, with a hint of a smile.

'I can see this conversation is going to become very anti men,' Rob said, returning with Brad and a tray of cocktails. He kissed Trish briefly on the top of her head. 'Shall we leave them to it, guys?'

Brad and Daniel nodded in agreement before picking up their pints of lager and heading over to the bar, where the television was showing replay action of the day's football matches.

After a second round of drinks, the girls began to get giggly. 'Come on, keep up, Joy.' Ruth pushed the half-full glass across the table. 'I'm ready for another. Same again, is it?' She rose unsteadily.

'No, not for me.' Joy placed a hand over her glass.

'Oh, come on. Don't be a party pooper. Tell her, Trish,' Ruth pleaded.

'Come on, Joy. One more for the road,' Trish said. 'Anyway the lads are probably throwing the pints back without a care. They'll only be fit for sleep by the time they've finished.'

'OK.' Joy relented. 'I can't drink another long drink. I'll have a shot instead. A Baby Guinness I think.'

'Great idea! We'll all have one,' Ruth squealed, clapping her hands in excitement.

Joy watched Ruth, unaccustomed to wearing heels, totter across the room precariously. She wished she could muster as much enthusiasm for the evening as her friends had. She was tired and her face ached from forcing a smile, when all she really wanted to do was close her eyes and transport herself into another time, another place. A place where this thing with Daniel hadn't happened. Where they were still happy, still in love... She sank back into the soft leather of the sofa, closing her eyes.

*****

It was her eighteenth birthday party. Cindi Lauper was blasting out 'Girls Just Wanna Have Fun', accompanied by a horde of screeching teenage girls, when Joy answered the door to Graham, a friend from college. Daniel was with him. His thick black hair curled slightly where it touched the nape of his neck and his piercing blue eyes crinkled at the corners as he smiled, showing even white teeth. He mouthed the words 'happy birthday', and through the hazy fuzz produced by six bottles of cider, Joy fell in love with him even before he'd crossed the doorstep.

'Come dance with me.' She took his hand, pulling him towards her. She pouted her glossy red lips and fluttered her long mascara-coated eyelashes seductively.

They danced and drank the whole evening, ending the night locked in a tight embrace, smooching around the living room to a slow number that, years later, neither of them could remember. Joy's arms were stretched up around his neck, her head resting on his chest. Daniel's hands had strayed from her lower back to settle on the firmness of her neat behind, pulling her closer, letting her feel his excitement. She pressed her body into his.

From then on, Daniel and Joy were unquestionably a couple. They went out almost every night, to dances, or the cinema and quite often to house parties where the music boomed out and the alcohol flowed - usually beer or sometimes a punch, loaded with any spirits available – and all thrown in together, along with a couple of bottles of lemonade to sweeten it. Food was never important. An abundance of alcohol and cigarettes was all that mattered... and being together. Dancing, pressed close, hands locked in the other's, moulding their bodies into one, or finding a space in the narrow dark hallway, amongst others like them, wrapped up in their own worlds, bodies up against the walls, or in a tight embrace on the stairs. They would kiss, deep urgent kisses, and she would let him touch her breasts, or stroke her thighs, as she felt his longing for more.

'No, Daniel,' she'd say, pulling away and straightening her clothes. 'No further, not until we are married.'

*****

Trish gave Joy a gentle shake. 'Here, don't you be going to sleep on us, missus.'

'Sorry.' Joy sat up, straightening her dress and smoothing her hair. 'Cheers.' She took the Baby Guinness, and drank deeply. She crinkled her face at the bittersweet taste. 'Let's have another! The night is young.'

Three rounds of shots later, the girls began to sing, making their way through the sound track from *Grease,* quietly at first, then rising to a crescendo with Joy & Ruth's performance of 'You're the One That I Want'.

'I think it's time for bed, ladies.' Rob pulled Trish to her to her feet.

'Thought you'd never ask.' Trish fell, none too graciously, into his arms.

'Come on, Joy.' Daniel guided her towards the stairs.

Joy sank into the warmth and comfort of his solidness. Her brain was fuzzy and relaxed. *Just five minutes*, she told herself.

Daniel opened the door to their room, and Joy stumbled inside, falling unceremoniously onto the bed and kicking off her shoes. She closed her eyes and was immediately assailed by a nauseous spinning sensation. She sat up quickly.

'Here, drink this.' Daniel handed her a glass of water. He waited until the glass was empty then pulled her gently to her feet. 'Let's get you undressed and into bed. You'll be ok. You'll soon be asleep.'

Gently he unhooked the fasteners on her dress allowing it to fall at her feet.

Almost naked, she wound her arms around his neck, pulling his head down to meet hers. 'Kiss me, Dan.'

His lips grazed hers briefly. 'No, not like this,' he said.

'Yes, just like this.' She found his lips again, falling back onto the bed, pulling him down beside her.

XIII

Kathy unlocked the door, closing it silently behind her and tiptoed into the room. Her eyes took in Tony's inert bulk on the bed, and her suitcase beside the door. Everything was as she'd left it; he obviously hadn't woken up at all. She let herself breathe again. *Thank you, God - although why you'd do me any favours, I don't know. But thanks anyway.* She sat on the loo for a while, considering whether or not to go back downstairs to the bar. *The girls were all set for a lively night. I should join in, I guess. What if he wakes up? He's bound to; he's been asleep for hours. It'd be better if I were here, in bed, beside him. Maybe then, he won't remember...*

She almost leapt off the toilet seat as her mobile rang. She grabbed it quickly. 'Hello?' she whispered.

'Hi, Mum, it's me. Didn't you see my name come up on the screen?' Alison sounded hurt.

'Hi, love, sorry. How are you getting on with your gran?'

'Oh, you know Gran, fussing about everything; she's even polishing my shoes for school tomorrow. Honestly you'd swear she didn't think I could clean a pair of shoes.'

'And can you?' Kathy smiled, relaxing as she listened to her daughter's impression of her gran.

'Of course,' came the haughty response. 'Anyway, why are you whispering? It sounds very quiet there. Where are you?'

'I'm in our room. Dad's asleep. I don't want to wake him.'

'Already? But it's still early.'

'I know.' Kathy sighed. 'He's not well.'

'Oh, right...'

'I'll get him to ring you tomorrow.' Kathy tried to reassure her, even though she knew it was pointless. Alison had heard and seen more than a girl of her age should.

'No need. I have to go or I'll miss *The Simpsons*.'

'OK. You be good for your gran, and I'll speak to you soon. Bye, love.'

'Bye, Mum.'

Kathy flipped her phone closed. Brushing her hair in front of the mirror, she wondered once more if she should join in the fun downstairs or get into bed. It wasn't worth the risk, she decided – she'd pushed her luck already this evening. She proceeded to attack her face with a cleansing wipe, before vigorously brushing her teeth.

Ten minutes later, she emerged from the bathroom in candy pink teddy bear print short pyjamas. She padded lightly across the bedroom floor, lifted the duvet gingerly, and lay down beside her husband. Careful to avoid touching any part of his body and scarcely breathing, she perched on the edge of the bed, praying he wouldn't wake until morning.

XIV

Joy hugged the toilet bowl. She was still retching, the hollow sounds reverberating around the porcelain. She laid her burning face against the cool ceramic rim, not even caring that it was a toilet bowl. She hated throwing up. It made her cry. Her mascara, moistened by her tears, was running into her eyes, stinging, intensifying her sobs. Above all else, she was disgusted with herself. *What a weak, fickle cow I am. I can't believe I've just done that. What was I thinking of? Self-gratification, that's what. Stupid, stupid cow.* She retched again, her misery echoing around the bowl. Dragging the white towel from its rail, she rubbed her face, leaving mascara stains on it. *I've sent all the wrong fucking signals now, haven't I? What's he going to think... that I'm a pushover; ply me with a few drinks and all will be forgiven? Fuck.*

       'Joy.' Daniel tapped on the bathroom door.
       'Go away.'
       'Are you OK?'
       'Leave me alone.'
       'Drink some water, it'll help.'
       'Daniel, just go back to bed.'

*****

She didn't know what time it was, or how long she'd been sitting on the floor, but she was cold. She stood up shakily and wrapped the towel around her, rubbing at the goosebumps on her arms. Her legs felt alien as she crept towards the bed, holding onto furniture to steady herself. She almost retched again and stuffed her fist into her mouth, waiting for the feeling to subside. Daniel had left the bedside lamp on. He lay on the far side of the bed with his back towards her, his broad tanned shoulders visible above the cream duvet.

Taking no chances of any further bodily contact, Joy took the spare pillows and lined them up down the centre of the bed. She dropped the towel and lay down, pulling the duvet up, hugging it tight around her shivering body.

MONDAY

I

Joy pulled the peak of her cap down low until it was touching her sunglasses, hiding from the irritating glare of the morning sun. She shivered despite the heat, as she tentatively placed one foot in front of the other, trying to quell the vibration that raced up her trembling legs, around her already churning stomach, gathering in intensity, until finally exploding against her temples, like a thousand gunshots. *Oh God, I'll never make it to lunchtime, never mind do a full day's walking.*

'Hi... Ohhhhh dear.' Brad lowered his voice sympathetically. 'You girls had a great time last night.'

'Yes, really, great.' Joy said.

'Have you taken anything for the hangover?' he asked. Undeterred by Joy's sarcasm, he prattled on. 'I didn't see you at breakfast. You should have eaten something, even just a bit of dry toast; it would help settle your stomach.'

Joy stopped walking.

'Brad,' she said.

'Yes?'

'No offence, but will you shut up?' she whispered, adding as an afterthought, 'Please?'

'None taken,' he smiled, giving her a playful wink. He leaned in close. 'Drink plenty of water, it'll help,' he whispered.

Joy watched him walk ahead to catch up with Rob and Trish. She took out her water bottle and drank thirstily. As her feet navigated the uneven ground, she tried to focus her brain, pushing away the events of the night before, and concentrate on the task ahead. She could hear Ruth's raucous laughter coming from ten paces behind, joined seconds later by Daniel's familiar tones, and she seethed inside. *This is so unfair. He should be walking beside me. We should be the ones laughing together, sharing a private joke. How did we manage to screw it all up, Dan?* She walked faster, wanting to move out of earshot, wincing as the throbbing pain inside her head increased.

Once she was far enough ahead, Joy slowed down. Some of the boulders and tree roots were like mini mountains, she'd already stumbled twice, and she didn't want to end up with a broken ankle. She drank more water, relieved that the queasiness in her stomach was beginning to ease off, and, pushing her earphones into place, she searched her IPod for something soothing. Settling on an Eva Cassidy track, she tried to clear her mind. She knew there were issues that needed addressing, and that burying her head in the sand was no longer an option. Like the waves that lapped the shore she walked beside, the relentless ebb and flow of problems had washed away the façade of what now seemed a hollow life, exposing her to its harsh realities.

Joy was a list person: Christmas shopping list, holiday packing list, dinner party guest list, housework task list and now a how-to-sort-out-her-marriage list. And so she began...

Step1: Listen to Daniel's story.

Oh, God, I don't think I can. How many times has he done this? Will he do it again? Of course he will. A leopard can't change its spots... no matter what he promises me. And after the bombshell I dropped on him on Friday night, will he even want to?

Step 1a: *Don't, under any circumstances, let him kiss you, put his arm around you, or even touch your hand. There's too much anger and hurt, and it'll only mean your defences will cave in.*

Her face burned at the memory of their urgent, hungry lovemaking the night before. *You're such a hypocrite, Joy Crathorne. Sending out mixed messages like that, completely avoiding him - not even looking him in the eye one minute - and ripping his clothes off the next. I know he didn't want to, not at first, but he's a man, for the moment, he's still my man – and while his head might say no, I know my seductive charms can always break down his resolve.*

She tossed her head, shaking her brain into action. *Get a grip, girl. Ditch the emotional claptrap and get back to the list.*

Step 2: *What the fuck is step two?*

Do I leave? Why should I be the one to leave? But would I want to live there without him?

Does he leave? He probably would if I asked him to. Do I have the right to do that? After all, I did play a part in getting us into the mess we're in.

Do we kiss and make up? The way I'm feeling at the moment, that's definitely not an option.

*****

She stopped her mental list as she caught up with Trish & Rob. They were listening to a history lesson from Brad, on Rob Roy, the Scottish warrior.

'It's said that Rob Roy used the bigger crags of rock above the loch as prison cells,' Brad said, pointing them out. 'Although according to the guide books, and what I've read on the internet, there's no real evidence that he actually kept any prisoners.'

'Perfect spot for it though,' Rob agreed, surveying their surroundings. 'Miles from civilisation and expertly hidden amongst the huge boulders. You'd never know it was here if it wasn't for the word "cave" painted on the side.'

While Rob and Brad continued their discussion about Rob Roy and his antics, Joy and Trish followed the well-worn, and at times, rocky, footpath along the Loch Lomond shoreline.

Trish broke the silence. 'Glad to see a bit of colour in your cheeks,' she said. 'You looked pretty rough earlier.'

Joy smiled weakly.

'Mmm. I'm still a little fragile.' She knew where this was leading.

'Yes, I'm feeling rather delicate myself. I think we overdid it a bit, it was good fun though,' Trish said. 'And you, you little minx.' She nudged Joy. 'You were out to get your man. Does this mean everything in the garden's rosy again?'

'No.'

'Oh.' Trish frowned, as Joy offered no further comment.

The footpath began to climb, away from the water's edge, and Joy weighed up in her mind how much to say. *Will she understand me at all? How could she, safe in that strong relationship of hers? I'm sure neither she nor Rob would ever contemplate the idea of a fling; an affair; a one-night stand – because whatever you call it, it still represents a crack in a relationship the size of the San Andreas, fault.*

Trish's curiosity finally got the better of her. 'So, are you going to expand on the "no"?' Her perfectly groomed eyebrows rose above the rim of her sunglasses.

'I was totally out of it last night.'

'I'll second that.'

'I'm exhausted this morning. I hardly got any sleep at all...'

'Whoa. Too much information.' Trish put up her hands to ward off any details.

'No, not that. Clean up your dirty mind.' Joy couldn't help laughing. 'Well, there was that, and it was great... in a way. Still, I'm disgusted in myself and my total lack of restraint. After everything that's happened, all the betrayal and the hurt, what do I do? Pounce on him like a desperate housewife. God, I'm so angry, Trish.' She could feel hot tears starting behind her sunglasses.

Trish laid a sympathetic hand on her arm.

'I told you the other day, if you want to talk, I'll listen.'

'You'll be judgemental. I know you will.'

'How can you say that, Joy? We've been friends for years. When have I ever judged you, or Daniel?'

'Yes, but you're always on about Kathy's relationship.'

'That's different and you know it. We all want what's best for Kathy... and it's not that bigoted bully she's married to.'

'You'll take Daniel's side.'

'How do you know that?' Trish grabbed Joy's arm, pulling her to a halt. 'Can you please just have some faith in me?' she asked, pushing her sunglasses up onto her head.

Joy saw the hurt in Trish's eyes and gave her a quick hug, before pulling away, embarrassed. Hugging wasn't a big part of their friendship.

As they stood facing each other, a sentinel of conifers lining the footpath sheltered them from the blistering heat.

'He's having an affair.' Joy said the words aloud for the first time.

'Bastard,' Trish spat. 'Don't say another word if you don't want to. I'm sorry, I shouldn't have pushed you.'

The two women set off up the hill once more, this time in silence.

Seconds later, Joy felt nauseous again and pulled out her almost empty water bottle, draining it.

'It's OK,' she said shakily.

'Do you know how long?' Trish lowered her voice to a whisper.

'No.'

'Is it still going on?'

'I don't know... I don't think so.'

Trish said nothing.

'He said it was just the once.'

'And you don't believe him?'

'Would you?' Joy threw the question back.

'Rob would never do that to me.' The words were out of Trish's mouth before she could stop them.

'I'd have said the same about Daniel last week,' Joy said, totally deflated. *I knew that's what she'd say. Now I know she could never understand.*

'Fuck it. That was a stupid thing to say. I didn't mean it to come out like that. I'm sorry. I wouldn't have thought it of Daniel either. I thought you two were rock solid.'

'Well you know that old adage... behind closed doors.' Joy sighed. 'The signs were there, I just wasn't reading them.'

'Do you think it's fixable?'

'I don't know. I don't think so.'

'Do you still love him?'

'At this moment I hate him with a passion, but you can't just turn love off, can you?'

Trish gave Joy's arm a gentle squeeze.

'I don't know what to say to him, Trish. I can't face listening to the sordid details, how it's all my fault.'

'Fuck that. It's sure as hell not your fault. Did you introduce him to this woman?' Did you throw them into bed together?'

'She's called Stephanie,' Joy muttered distractedly. 'I don't know any Stephanies.'

'Do you want me to shut up?' Trish asked. 'I know I go on a bit sometimes.'

Joy shook her head as she listened to Trish trying desperately to find the right words, thinking that this was almost more difficult for her friend than for her. It was a relief to have actually said the word 'affair' aloud. Perhaps now she would be able to deal with talking to Daniel.

'When did you find out?' Trish persisted.

'Last Friday. He just came straight out with it.'

'What? The day before the holiday? Great timing.'

'It was awful,' Joy told her. 'He wanted to talk, and I just kept screaming at him that I didn't want to hear it, that we were going on holiday the next day with our friends, and I couldn't deal with it. I just wanted to shut it off, lock it away in a secret part of my brain, until we got home. So finally we agreed not to say anything, that we would try to act normally – whatever that is – until we got home.'

'I hate to say this, but the pair of you are doing a crap job of normality.' Trish voiced what Joy already knew. 'I think you should try opening up the lines of communication. At least listen to what he has to say. Throw it all back at him again if you have to; just give him a fair hearing. He deserves that much from you. And maybe it was just once. Maybe it's not insurmountable. I don't know. Only you two know the answers.'

'Unfaithful is unfaithful, whether it's once or one hundred times, Trish,' Joy said sadly. 'Look, the others are just behind us; can we change the subject please?'

'OK, if you promise you'll talk to him.'

Joy nodded.

'I will, I promise.'

*****

At the top of the hill, the path opened out into a clearing, giving fantastic views across the loch, to the Arrochar Alps mountain range on the far side. A village nestled on the shore in the distance and the brilliance of the blue sky reflected in the still water below.

Joy found herself a flattish boulder to perch on. The sun's heat on the stones radiated through her trousers, to her already clammy skin. She took a few deep breaths to regain her composure, just as the rest of the group approached.

'I don't know how you do it, girl,' Ruth said, placing her ample behind on the stone beside Joy. 'Ouch!' She jumped up again. 'Those stones are roasting,' she said as she danced around rubbing her bum.

'Do what?' Joy asked.

'Party all night, look like shit this morning, and yet still manage to be first up this bleeding hill,' Ruth said, sitting down again, carefully this time.

'Dogged determination and sheer madness, I guess.'

'Hey, girls,' Brad called out from behind them. 'Check out the lovely cold water. You should fill up your water bottles; it'll keep you going until lunchtime.'

Joy went over to the spring bubbling out from the rocks. She cupped her hands under the flow, catching the ice-cold water and taking it to her lips. It tasted pure and refreshing and she quickly topped up her bottle. It was too hot to be sitting around, and wanting to get moving, Joy set off again, while the others gathered up their belongings behind her.

'Joy, wait,' Ruth called out, jogging up to her. 'I need some of this dogged determination you seem to have so much of,' she said.

'Drink loads of water. That's what Brad told me this morning,' Joy said. 'It seems to be working.'

'If I do that I'll need to pee,' Ruth whispered.

'So?'

'There are no toilets until we reach The Inversnaid Hotel.'

'Then you go behind a bush, of course.'

Ruth's eyes widened. 'Would you... go behind a bush?'

'I don't have a weak bladder. But I would if I had to.'

'Lucky you.' Ruth sighed. 'See what happens when you have kids? They mess you up big time. You can't go through the night without getting up to use the loo, you leak when you sneeze, and your boobs go all floppy and sag practically to your knees.' She cupped hers and shook them vigorously to prove her point. 'Everyone will think I'm old and past it if I have to go for a pee in the woods. And I wouldn't put it past Brad to sneak up behind me with a camera. No, thank you. I'm very fussy about who I'd drop my knickers for, I'll have you know.'

Joy was laughing and it felt good. 'I'll be the one peeing in the bushes if you keep making me laugh,' she said, still chuckling.

'OK, let's change the subject,' Ruth said. Theatrically, she ran her hand down her face, removing the twinkle from her eyes and the smile from her mouth, before asking conspiratorially, 'What's the story with Kathy? I wouldn't have thought she'd have been the one to miss a day's walking.'

'I really don't know.' Joy's response was genuine.

Earlier in the day, when Trish said she'd had a text from Kathy saying she'd meet up with them at lunchtime, she'd been feeling too hung-over to take much notice.

'Don't you think it's odd though?' Ruth persisted. 'She wasn't drinking last night, and she went up to bed early. Surely she should be in a better state than any of us.'

'I don't know. Maybe she wanted some quality time with Tony.' Joy seriously doubted this, but in view of her own problems, she didn't think it was fair to be discussing Kathy's.

'Rubbish. More likely he's had a go at her about missing dinner last night, or being out without him, or something equally ridiculous - and she's trying to keep the peace.'

'Ruth, stop it,' Joy snapped. 'It's none of our business.'

'OK, OK.' Never one to be silenced, Ruth continued under her breath, 'He's such a pig of a man.'

Joy took a deep breath, knowing she had overreacted a little. 'Anyway, enough of Kathy. What did you and Brad get up to after the rest of us retired last night?'

'Oooh he's such a hunk. He walked me back to my room and...' Ruth winked suggestively and then sighed. 'He was the perfect gentleman. He wouldn't even come in for a nightcap.' Her mouth turned down at the corners, petulantly.

Joy laughed. 'He's a hunk all right. Do you fancy him? He'd be quite a catch. I could use my matchmaking skills to help you along, if you like?'

'No, thank you. I've been on the receiving end of your matchmaking skills before. Remember Barry Jenkins?'

Joy frowned, as she tried to remember. 'Was he in college with us?'

'Yes. You told him I fancied him and set him up to meet me in the art room. He was only after a quick snog...'

'And his girlfriend walked in ...'

'Yes, and I ended up with a black eye. So thanks for your concern for my love life, but I'll handle it myself,' Ruth said, tartly. 'Anyway, he's got too much baggage,' she added as an afterthought, picking up a stone from the gravelly beach and tossing it into the loch.

'What baggage? He's single, loaded and a workaholic. That's hardly baggage.'

'Trust me. When he lets his guard down, you can see it in his eyes. And, I can feel it in my water... Speaking of which, I really do need to pee. Looks like I'm going to have to brave the bushes after all. I'm going to run behind those over there – keep a look out, will you?' Ruth asked before scurrying away through the long grass.

Standing guard, Joy wondered about Brad. So far she hadn't spoken to him that much. *Too wrapped up in my own troubles...* She saw him now, walking towards her, chatting away to Daniel, both of them looking very relaxed. *How do men do that? Act so normal, when their world could be crashing down around them? But then haven't I just spent the past half hour laughing and joking with Ruth?*

They stopped beside Joy, followed closely by Trish and Rob.

'Where's Ruth?' Trish asked.

'She's gone to the ladies,' Joy whispered, hoping not to catch the attention of the men, knowing full well they'd exploit the situation. 'Behind a bush,' she added, seeing Trish's confusion.

Joy saw Rob's mischievous grin as he pulled the guidebook out of a pocket at the front of his rucksack.

'Apparently this is a very popular spot for birdwatchers,' he said. 'If we keep an eye open, we could see a jay or a woodpecker. Mind you, I wouldn't go dropping your pants around here. You never know who might be lurking behind a bush with a set of binoculars,' he added with a grin.

Ruth came scuttling out from the bushes, hastily adjusting her clothes.

'OK, thanks, guys,' she said, her face crimson.

The others roared with laughter.

Rob showed a red-faced Ruth the guidebook. 'I'm not kidding,' he told her, still laughing. 'That's what it says, right here – see?'

Ruth grabbed the book. 'Just you wait, Rob McLeod. I'll get my own back, when you least expect it,' she said, trying hard to keep a straight face.

Everyone was laughing as they left the birdwatchers' paradise behind them, heading north towards Inversnaid.

II

Kathy stared at the ceiling. She counted the flowers on the elaborate rose centre, for the tenth time that morning, wondering why she was still in bed, and not walking to Inversnaid with the others. She glanced at Tony, sleeping beside her, and checked the time on her phone. It was 10.30 already and they had to check out before midday. She slid silently from the bed and grabbed a T-shirt, pulling it over her head. She hated to walk around naked when Tony was in the room – even if he was asleep. It made her feel so exposed. So vulnerable. She tiptoed around the bed and into the bathroom.

Kathy locked the bathroom door with a gentle click and pulled off the T-shirt again. She wanted to have her shower in peace, and gather her thoughts. She still felt mystified by the events earlier that morning.

She turned on the shower and looked at herself in the mirror. Her face was flushed from sleep and lovemaking. *Lovemaking, not sex.* She mouthed the words silently to her reflection. She lifted her hair and turned her head from left to right. He'd been so gentle, she didn't think he'd marked her neck – no, for once there were no telltale signs. Her eyes travelled over her chest, down to her breasts. Nothing.

The swirling steam began to cover the glass, obscuring her vision. She turned away and stepped into the shower.

Hot tears of confusion mingled with the hot water running down her face. *Why does he do this to me? Every time I've made up my mind to fight back, he does something like this. I feel like a fucking puppet - and he's pulling all the strings.*

She'd lain awake for hours during the night, hoping he wouldn't wake, planning what to say if he did. She must have drifted off eventually, and when she woke, it was light outside. Tony's side of the bed was empty, and the clink of china made her turn over, to see him making tea. She said nothing, trying to gauge his mood.

He walked round to her side of the bed and put a cup on the bedside table.

'Thought you might like a cup of tea,' he said. He sat down heavily on the edge of the bed and instinctively she shuffled away from his touch.

'Thanks,' she said.

'Do I repulse you so much?' he asked dejectedly.

His eyes were bloodshot and his complexion mottled from his drinking binge the night before, and he looked so sad that Kathy suddenly found herself wanting to hug him.

'Of course you don't,' she lied, wondering where this was leading.

Tony groaned and leaned forward, resting his arms on his thighs, and dropping his head.

'Fuck it, I feel like crap,' he said.

'Take two of these.' Kathy handed him the packet of aspirin from the bedside table.

He held onto her hand as he took them, his rough calloused fingers linking with hers. Kathy's whole body stiffened. She wanted to pull away but was afraid to.

'Did I make a complete ass of myself?' he asked, before throwing the two tablets into his mouth. Grimacing, he swallowed them down without water. 'I can't remember a fucking thing.'

Kathy quickly debated with herself how much she should tell him. Could she lie? What if he remembered, then...? She shivered.

'You were in bed when we got here yesterday evening,' she said.

'What did you do?'

'I had a shower, I had dinner, and then I came to bed' *Can he really not remember or is this a test? He's waiting for me to have a go about the mess he made of my stuff.* You were still sound asleep when I came back up.' Kathy hoped desperately that she sounded convincing.

'I had a few drinks in the bar.' He was talking to the floor again. 'I remember seeing this young couple... I was drinking and they were laughing and joking. I had another pint, and then I had a whisky... I could see them, this young couple, through the mirror behind the bar. They were snogging - all over each other they were. I had another whisky and another...'

'No wonder you're suffering.' Kathy tried to keep it light. 'You never could drink whisky.'

'I got to thinking about you Kath, about us.' He sat up and there were tears in his eyes as he looked at her.

She tensed, hoping he wasn't about to lean over to kiss her, breathing rancid whisky fumes into her face.

'Sit up and drink your tea,' he said, taking the cup from her so she could shuffle up the bed. She dragged the duvet with her, wrapping it tightly around her.

He kept his eyes on hers as she took a sip of tea.

'I don't mean to get angry with you,' he said. 'I love you to bits, Kath. I worship the ground you walk on. But you're different since we came away.'

What's happening to him? It's like he's peeling off layers; going back in time.

'It's like you've stopped caring about us, our marriage.'

He looked so dismal that Kathy thought he might burst into tears.

'Of course I care. I'll always care,' she said, trying to reassure him, yet still cautious of how much to say. She had to admit, he did seem different, more approachable somehow.

'Don't ever leave me, Kath.' It was a pitiful plea. 'I couldn't bear to live without you.'

'Go and have a shower, time's getting on,' she said briskly, not sure how to handle him in this mood.

'Will you stay with me today?' Tony asked her. 'We could go off and do something on our own and meet up with the others later.'

Kathy cringed at the thought, but he'd asked so sweetly that she didn't have the heart to refuse.

'OK,' she said. 'We'll meet them at lunchtime. I'll let Trish know.'

'Thanks, Kath,' Tony said, before disappearing into the bathroom.

Once Kathy heard the shower running, she let out a long sigh. *God, he seems so vulnerable. Whisky must turn him soft in the head. Maybe, just maybe, he'll understand if I tell him how I feel. If I dare. Perhaps we can fix it. But do I want to fix it?* Confused, she pulled out her phone and began to text.

STAYING WITH TONY THIS MORNING C U 4 LUNCH X KATH

She brought up Trish's name and pressed send.

Within seconds, the phone pinged back a reply.

WHAT'S UP?

NOTHING C U LATER X

Kathy switched off her phone and took a sip of her tea. It was cold and she wrinkled her nose in distaste.

Tony emerged from the bathroom, a large white towel wrapped around his waist. He was rubbing vigorously at his hair and droplets of water clung to his broad shoulders. He crossed to the bed and stacked up the pillows, before stretching out beside her, on top of the duvet. His skin had that shiny scrubbed look, smooth where he'd shaved. He smelt of lemon burst shower gel and minty toothpaste.

'What's going wrong, Kath?' he asked, without looking at her. 'Once upon a time we used to be like those youngsters I saw last night. And now it's like you're not really here. Like you're just going through the motions.' There was no malice, no fight in his voice.

'You scare me, Tony,' Kathy said, in little more than a whisper. She instantly regretted her words.

'I don't mean to scare you.' Tony looked shocked. 'I love you. I'd never do anything to hurt you.' His eyes were bright with tears.

'You do, Tony, all the time.' Kathy was feeling a little braver. 'You say things that hurt. You embarrass me in front of our friends. You put me down in front of the kids.' Tears of sadness shone out from her brown eyes.

'What do I have to do to put things right?' he asked. 'I can't lose you. I'll do anything. Just name it,' he begged.

'I think it's too late, Tony. I don't know if I can forgive and forget, just like that.' Kathy tried to brush her tears away, but the floodgates had opened, and her body was taken over by huge, breathless sobs. Tony picked her up, cradling her like a child, kissing her hair, her face, her lips. She could taste a mixture of salt and toothpaste. And then she was kissing him back and it was as if they were nineteen again...

When Kathy emerged from the bathroom, Tony was up and dressed. He wore khaki shorts and a sage green T-shirt with 'I've walked the West Highland Way' printed across the front.

'How's my gorgeous wife feeling now?' he asked with a wide grin.

'Famished, I think we should go find somewhere to eat.' She smiled confidently, secretly crossing her fingers and hoping that his mood hadn't changed.

'Come here.' He held his arms wide.

She let him hug her tight and it was nice. There was no squeezing or pinching, no vile possessive whisperings in her ears. She relaxed.

'I mean it, Kath, I'll change. I'll do anything you want me to. I'll join AA.' His words were muffled in her hair.

'You're not an alcoholic.'

'I'll see a psychiatrist then. An anger management therapist. Anything.' He wrapped his arms even tighter around her. 'I love you. I won't lose you; I won't let you go without a fight.'

III

'Oh! We're here,' Rob announced, as the path unexpectedly arrived at Inversnaid.

It led down to the Inversnaid Hotel via a wooden slatted bridge crossing the Snaid Burn, just above the rushing water of its celebrated waterfall.

Ruth fished in her rucksack for her camera. 'We must take pictures near the waterfall - it's famous, you know,' she gabbled excitedly. 'Is anyone else coming down?' Not waiting for an answer, she set off down the steep steps.

'I'll come with you, Ruth. Just let me grab my camera,' Trish called after her.

Joy sat on the wooden slatted bridge, legs dangling over the crevice below, absorbing the atmosphere. She was feeling much better than she had four hours earlier and her head no longer throbbed with every footstep. She could hear Ruth and Trish laughing in the distance, and she smiled, glad that this holiday was a success for them. She'd worried about Ruth - that she might not be fit enough or that she'd drink too much and get maudlin. *I'm the maudlin one. She's having a great time, lucky cow.*

'How's the hangover coming along?' Brad asked, sitting down next to her and swinging his legs over the edge, too. 'Did you drink plenty of water?'

'I did indeed. Gallons of it. I'm amazed I didn't need the loo,' Joy said with a smile.

'Just as well. What with all those birdwatchers hiding in the bushes!'

'I know.' She laughed. 'Ruth's face was an absolute picture. I should have had the camera ready.'

'Glad to see you're feeling better anyway. Are you ready for the hair of the dog?'

'No way. Not another drop of alcohol will pass my lips until we reach Fort William.' She shook her head, relieved that the inside of it no longer felt like mush. 'I'll eat some lunch though. I couldn't face breakfast, and now I'm starving.'

Brad stood up and held his hand out to her. 'May I have the honour of escorting your ladyship to the dining room?'

'Why, thank you, kind sir.' Joy took his hand and he helped her to her feet.

At the bottom of the hill, they found the others, gathered near the small jetty. They were watching a group of teenagers jumping off into the cold loch – and then, shivering and teeth chattering, climb out of the water and do it all over again.

Joy didn't miss Daniel's enquiring look as she and Brad approached them, arms linked.

'Has anyone had an update from Kathy?' Rob asked. 'Are she and Tony joining us for lunch, or what's the story?'

'They'll have to come across on the ferry,' Brad said.

He left Joy talking to Trish and went over to read the ferry timetable.

'The next one's not due over until two p.m.,' he announced.

I say we go ahead and eat,' Trish said. 'They'll probably have something over the other side.'

Joy nodded in agreement and set off towards the hotel.

Daniel caught up with her as they walked through the manicured gardens, passing late-flowering Rhododendrons with their vibrant pink and red blooms. She tensed as he caught her arm.

'We have to talk, Joy,' he said, annoyed. 'You can't keep blowing hot and cold.'

'We will. Just not here,' she hissed. *I know we have to talk, but not in front of everyone. Fuck it, Daniel. Your timing is crap.* 'And for your information, I'm not blowing hot and cold. I was pissed last night,' she said, raising her voice.

'You can say that again,' Trish said, from just behind them.

Joy glared at her. Daniel was bound to pick up on her sarcasm and realise that Trish knew something.

Daniel shook his head in exasperation and stormed ahead, into the bar.

'For God's sake, Trish, did you have to?' Joy turned on her friend. 'Things are bad enough already, without putting him on the defensive.'

'Well, if he'd kept it in his pants in the first place, he wouldn't be in this mess,' Trish said tautly. Her voice softened. 'Seriously though, you're going to have to do something, before you destroy anything you ever had.'

Joy frowned and bit her lip.

'I know I am,' she snapped. 'And I will.'

IV

Joy knew she'd eaten too much at lunch, that chocolate cheesecake had been too tempting to ignore. Her stomach groaned under the assault of alcohol and now chocolate abuse, as she made her way to the ladies.

As she opened the door, she heard voices.

'You're a two timing bastard, Daniel Crathorne.' Trish's sharp tone bounced through an open window.

Joy stopped dead in her tracks, the colour draining from her face. Relieved that the room was empty, she quickly entered the cubicle beside the open window. *You just couldn't keep your nose out, Trish, could you?*

'She told you then?' Daniel's response was blunt, edged with annoyance.

'How could you?' Trish asked. 'Who is she anyway? Some young thing, to stroke your aging ego?' Trish had the bit between her teeth now.

'Did she tell you everything?'

'Enough for you to have gone way down in my estimation. I used to think you were one of the good guys.'

'Not everything, then. She's played her part in this too, you know. She's not the only injured party.'

Daniel Crathorne, don't you dare. Don't you dare tell her. Joy stuffed her fist in her mouth.

'What the hell is that supposed to mean?' Trish spat.

'Nothing. It's none of your business anyway, Trish. Just keep out of it.'

Joy heard Daniel's receding footsteps scrunching through the gravel, and she let out the breath she had been holding. Needing a few moments to calm down, she pulled the sun cream from her rucksack. Squeezing a dollop into her hand, she began covering every exposed part of her already tanned skin. With no letup in the weather, the relentless heat was wearing her down in a way she could never have imagined.

She left the cubicle, just as the door opened and Trish came through.

'We were about to send out a search party for you,' she said, her face all smiles.

Joy glared at her. 'I heard you both out there.' She nodded to the open window, 'Everything.'

Trish had the grace to look shamefaced. 'He just made me so angry.'

'And now you've made me angry. You said I could trust you,' Joy said with disgust.

Trish pushed back her shoulders and stood tall, jutting out her chin in defiance.

'You can!' she protested.

Joy sighed. 'How can I, Trish? Daniel and I haven't even talked properly yet and you just barge in there, confronting him like that!'

Joy swung around to the hand basin and turned on the tap, splashing water everywhere, rubbing at her hands with fury.

'I'm sorry. All right? I won't say anything else, OK?'

Joy yanked a paper towel from the dispenser, and marched out without another word.

*****

Outside, Joy walked down towards the rest of the group who were on the jetty. In no mood for small talk, she stood back from them a little. The ferry appeared to be full of tourists waiting to disembark, and Joy scanned the sea of faces in search of Kathy or Tony.

'There's Kathy.' Ruth pointed to the waving figure. 'She must have left Tony on the other side. Looks like she's on foot.'

'Great, she should be ready for the off straight away, then. ' Rob was checking the map, obviously anxious to get moving again. 'There's still over six miles to go, and according to the guide it could be rough going in places,' he said.

Joy glared at the back of Daniel's head. She was furious with him. *It was their business, and nobody else's. OK, if he wants to talk, we'll talk. If he wants to get it all off his chest, well, that's fine too. I can hold it together. I'm strong. I can live a lie; pretend I don't care, that I don't hurt. After all, what's new? My whole fucking life feels like a lie.*

'Joy.' Trish came up behind her.

Joy was in no mood to talk to her. She bent down to fiddle with her bootlace.

'Oh, have it your own way,' Trish turned on her heel, going to join Rob and Ruth, who were waiting on the pier to welcome Kathy back into the fold.

As soon as she left, Joy straightened up and swung the rucksack onto her back. She stomped over to Daniel.

'You want to talk, right?' she barked at him. 'Well, I'm ready to listen. Let's get ahead of the others first. I'm pissed off enough that Trish knows, without anyone else throwing in their two penn'orth.'

Daniel whistled to Rob and pointed to the footpath leading away from the hotel, indicating they were going on ahead.

V

They walked in silence until they were out of sight of the hotel and the walkers.

Joy was seething after the conversation that she'd overheard between Daniel and Trish, but equally she was scared of how she might react to what he was about to tell her.

'So,' she began. 'Her name is Stephanie.'

'Was... it only happened once.' Daniel spoke slowly, as though he too was dreading the conversation he had been pushing to have with her.

'Was?' Joy raised an eyebrow. 'So she's dead?'

'No. I don't know. For fuck's sake, Joy, stop being facetious; this is hard enough as it is.'

'Well S-O-R-R-Y.' It wouldn't be hard at all, if you hadn't slept with her in the first place. Would it?'

'You drove me to it, Joy,' Daniel said. 'You pushed and you pushed and then... she was just there and it happened.' Pain and disappointment was etched on his face. 'And I've never regretted anything more in my whole life.'

'I drove you to it?' Joy felt a heavy weight settle on her shoulders as she repeated Daniel's words. 'I've only ever loved you, Daniel. I wanted everything to be perfect for you.'

She was walking just a step ahead of him, as the footpath narrowed and the ground became uneven. She was relieved she could no longer see the icy numbness in his eyes.

'Things always had to be exactly right,' with you, Joy. Like in the magazines you read, or the stupid American films on TV. It was all a million miles away from the real world, and that was fine. You liked to keep up appearances and I could live with that, because I knew the real Joy. Passionate, funny and caring, behind the prim and proper exterior. I remember on our third wedding anniversary, you booked us into that luxury country house hotel – can't remember the name of it now.'

'Hayfield Manor,' Joy interrupted. She remembered the place too. It was all thick cream carpets and antique furniture. Their room had a four-poster bed and a bath made for two. It was a luxury they couldn't really afford, but she wanted the weekend to be special.

'We spent practically the whole weekend in bed and in your usual organised way, you announced it was time we had kids. You thought we should have two, you said. Two years apart. A boy first, and then a little girl. I laughed, telling you that you can't plan the sex of the baby. I told you we had to take what we were given, and that it didn't matter because whatever order they came in and whether they were boys or girls, we'd love them. You jumped off the bed then, rushing back seconds later with a magazine article all about how it's possible to determine the sex of a baby by making love in different ways. I thought it was a load of old rubbish. Still, we had fun trying anyway... for a while.' Daniel paused.

Joy was still walking a step ahead on the narrow footpath; she heard the crackle of plastic as he squeezed his water bottle. She remembered everything as clearly as he did.

'Suddenly, having a baby became an obsession with you, Joy,' Daniel continued. 'More so, as the months went on. We were only young. If it happened, it happened. We should have just got on with our lives. But oh no. In Joy Crathorne's world, things not going to plan was never an option.'

Joy winced at the venom in his voice.

'There was no love in our lovemaking. No passion or warmth, no affection, just pumping in those sperm. Although you never actually said the words, I could read your mind, and it was saying, "Don't bother kissing me, just get as many of the little buggers in as you can while the time's right." I was a twenty-eight-year-old man in love with his wife. Not a sperm bank servicing a robot.'

Daniel put a hand on Joy's shoulder, forcing her to stop and turn around to face him.

'Do you know how hard it was for me? Watching you continuously poring over temperature charts and any alternative medicine theory you could get your hands on. Then every month, when you weren't pregnant, you'd lock yourself in the bathroom for hours. It killed me to hear you crying, but you'd never let me in.' Daniel's eyes bore into hers. 'You hardly ever let me touch you unless it was part of the baby making process. It was hard, Joy, really hard.'

Joy felt the sting of tears as she stared back at him. She willed herself not to blink, in an effort to hold them at bay.

'I needed physical contact. I needed you, Joy. My beautiful, funny, loving wife. I needed to feel alive. I never felt I needed kids to be complete, as long as I had you.'

Daniel released his grip on her shoulder.

Joy turned and began walking again. This time she didn't bother to wipe away the tears that ran silently down her cheeks, before dripping off the end of her chin. *It is my fault. Single-handedly I've destroyed everything. You didn't know how I felt, Daniel. I was a failure. I was letting you down.*

She listened to Daniel blow his nose, and then begin talking again.

'Stephanie worked in the office; in payroll. It was Christmas 1998. There was an office party before we finished up for the holiday, and you wouldn't come. You'd had a bad day and you locked yourself in the bathroom for hours. I was annoyed with you; all the other guys would be with their wives or girlfriends. I said I'd look a right prick going on my own, but there was no budging you. So I went alone, just to show my face...'

'I don't need you to go on,' Joy interrupted. 'You win. It was my fault. I drove you to it.' She said it shakily.

'I'm not the winner, Joy,' he said sadly. 'I needed to tell you. I've carried this secret, this guilt for over ten years. I can't do it anymore. If I lose you...'

Joy was trembling inside, and feeling that attack was her only means of defence, she spun around to face him, her eyes glinting like cold steel.

'DANIEL. I GET IT.' She fired the words at him like bullets. 'It was an office fling. A one-night stand. She flattered you. Seduced you. Stuck her tongue down your throat. You fucked her. End of.'

Joy left the footpath, marching across the gravel beach to the water's edge. She began firing stones into the loch, with all the energy she could muster. Daniel didn't follow her, which was a relief. She was shaking with anger. She could feel his eyes boring into her from behind, with such intensity it scared her.

'Just go, Daniel, please. Give me some space,' Joy shouted out, without taking her eyes off the water.

After a moment she heard Daniel's heavy footsteps as he moved on, leaving her with only her demons for company.

VI

Kathy grinned at the reception committee waiting for her on the pier.

'Welcome back to the fold, you lazy cow,' Ruth said brightly. 'I never thought you'd be the first to dodge a few miles. Or did you get a better offer?' She winked.

'I just thought I should spend a few hours with Tony. After all, it's his holiday too,' Kathy said casually, hoping Ruth wouldn't comment on the flush creeping up her neck.

'Well, I too could have been tempted by other methods of getting hot and sweaty this fine Monday morning, if the offer was thrown my way.' Ruth rolled her eyes.

'Ruth!' Kathy tried to hide her embarrassment. 'What did I miss this morning anyway?' she asked hoping to change the subject. 'Where are Joy and Daniel?'

Trish walked over to join them.

'Well, you missed Ruth going for a pee amongst a field full of birdwatchers.' She giggled.

'That's right, take a pop at me, what do I care?' Ruth pouted good-naturedly. 'I'd better go to the loo before we set off again.'

Once Ruth had gone in search of the hotel loo, Trish turned to Kathy.

'Are you OK?' She asked. 'You didn't come back down last night. You missed all the fun.'

'I was tired, that's all,' Kathy said. 'Tony was comatose until six this morning, and then he was really embarrassed, and full of apologies. He wanted to make it up to me. Everything's fine now.' She smiled, hoping to reassure her sister. 'Where are Joy and Daniel by the way?'

Trish raised her eyes to heaven, and linked arms with Kathy, steering her towards the path.

'Rob, be a love and wait for Ruth, she's gone to the loo,' she called out over her shoulder, before turning to Kathy. 'Well, you know how touchy she's been since we came away…'

'Trish, if this is gossip I don't want to know,' Kathy said.

Trish looked wounded at her sister's remark.

'It's not gossip,' she said. 'She told me while we were walking. She wasn't upset. But then this is Joy we're talking about. Always in control, nothing bothers her, or so she'd like us to think.' She paused.

Kathy waited, knowing what Trish was about to tell her. *Had Daniel spoken to Joy? Did he tell her everything?*

'Daniel's having an affair,' Trish said. 'She told me eventually, when I'd convinced her she could trust me.'

Trish took off her cap and ruffled at her short-cropped hair.

She gave a long sigh. 'And then what did I go and do?'

'What?' Kathy knew her sister's meddling ways. They'd always got her into trouble when she was a kid and things hadn't improved much as she'd grown older. *Anyway, what does she mean, 'he's having an affair'? He told me it was just once, years ago.*

'I didn't mean to interfere. I found him outside, on his own…' Trish's eyes pleaded with Kathy to understand. 'And I just had to tell him what I thought of him. What a bastard he was.'

'Actually, I would have backed you up on that one.' Kathy nodded, for once in agreement with her sisters impulsive actions.

'No, wait. It gets worse. I didn't realise we were outside the ladies toilets. Joy was inside, she heard it all.'

'Trish.' Kathy sighed, her agreement quickly diminished. 'Why can't you just keep out of other peoples' affairs?'

'Don't you fall out with me as well, Kath,' Trish pleaded.

'I'm not,' Kathy said. 'But in future will you stop and think before you open your big mouth?'

Trish nodded obediently.

'He did say something odd though,' she said.

'I don't want to hear it.'

Trish ignored her reluctant listener.

'He said, "Did she tell you everything? She played her part in this too." What do you suppose that means?'

'It's none of our business. Drop it.'

'Mmm,' Trish pondered. 'Maybe she's been playing away as well. You never know with Joy, she's such a closed book. Don't you think?'

'I'm not listening to your pondering, Trish.' Kathy gave an exasperated snort and walked ahead, leaving her sister behind, relieved that the path dictated they walk in single file.

*****

Talking of closed books, she'd have a field day if she knew what was going on in my head. I actually enjoyed this morning with Tony; it was lovely more's the pity, that just makes things harder. How will I know if I'm making the right decision? He's just so difficult to handle sometimes. He's been really attentive today, but I know he'll blow a gasket if I tell him I'm helping Brad to do up his apartment, or that I want to go out and get a job. She checked her phone for the hundredth time, in case she had a missed call. She'd kept it on silent, not wanting Tony to hear the conversation if it had rung. There had been no calls. That was probably a bad sign.

She'd been for an interview for an office job two days before the holiday. She thought the interview had gone really well. *They were probably just humouring me. Why would they do that? I need to stay positive. It was the first job I applied for and I got an interview. That has to count for something. I've come a long way since that morning, over twelve months ago when... oh, what's that saying again. The straw that broke the camel's back...*

'Kathy, don't parade yourself in front of the kids like that.' Tony berated her as he entered the kitchen.

He took a slice of toast from the plate she placed in front of him.

Kathy popped more bread into the toaster for Alison's breakfast. She looked down at the vest top and shorts pyjamas she was wearing.

'What if their friends called to the door? Or the postman?' He pulled her heavy fleece dressing gown from the laundry basket beside the washing machine and threw it at her.

'You're not decent. Cover yourself up, woman,' Tony ordered. Still munching on toast, he went into the hall for his coat.

She sighed and wrapped the gown around her pulling the belt tight, feeling suffocated by its bulk in the warm kitchen.

Anthony, their eldest son, was cramming in a final few minutes' study before his history exam. He looked up from his notes; his eyes were bright with suppressed anger.

'He shouldn't treat you like that,' he muttered.

'Leave it, Anthony,' Kathy snapped, instantly regretted her reaction. 'Finish your breakfast, love.' She patted him on the shoulder and left the kitchen.

Tony was waiting for her in the hallway, by the front door. She leaned towards him to kiss him goodbye, following their usual morning ritual.

He pulled her close and pushed his hand inside her dressing gown, squeezing her breast.

'For my eyes only, and don't you forget it,' he whispered in her ear. He straightened her gown, kissed her on the cheek, and was gone.

Kathy stood in the open doorway and smiled - purely for the neighbours' benefit, should they be watching – although it didn't quite reach her eyes.

'See you tonight, love,' he called from the gate, with a wide-eyed smile.

Kathy closed the front door, leaning heavily against it for a moment, fighting the angry tears, annoyed with her lack of confidence to stand up to him.

'Mum, Muuuummm,' Alison yelled down the stairs. 'I can't get my hair to go right.'

Kathy looked up to see Alison standing on the top stair, hairbrush in her hand, and a pleading grin on her face.

By a quarter to nine, peace had finally descended on the house, and Kathy felt hot and sticky in the heavy dressing gown. She took it off, tossing it back into the laundry basket with an air of defiance aimed at Tony and his rules. She opened the back door, letting the morning sun flood the kitchen and began clearing away the breakfast things. When order was restored once more, Kathy made herself a fresh cup of tea, and, still wearing her pyjamas, she took it and the morning paper out into the garden.

'What he doesn't know, he can't complain about,' she told to herself. 'And who'd be interested in me anyway?' She addressed the blue tit that had perched on the back of the chair beside her. 'I'm just a dumb, scared rabbit, only fit to be Tony's puppet on a string.'

Sitting back in her chair, enjoying the feel of the warm sun on her bare skin, she tried to relax. But her mind was fraught with anger and frustration at how her life was going. If it wasn't for the kids, she told herself, as she had countless times before.

'What would I do? How would I support us?' She spoke to the bird again. 'I'd need a job, and who'd employ me? I've got nothing to offer.' She sighed and closed her eyes, deciding bitterly that she should resign herself to her lot.

Minutes later, she sat bolt upright in her chair. The blue tit took flight as Kathy jumped up and rushed into the kitchen. Grabbing a pen and paper, she dashed outside again and began scribbling. She had a plan.

In big bold letters, she wrote D-T-DAY. Next, she set a date.

'One year from now,' she told the bird, who watched from a safe distance, perched on the edge of an upturned plant pot.

She began to write, biting on her bottom lip as she concentrated on the task in hand...

Computer courses: *They're the things to have these days for any job.* Check out the colleges and the library for information. She wrote in bold capitals, hoping it would help instil confidence.

Job: *What can I do? It will take ages to get enough computer courses under my belt and then I'll need experience. Maybe I could clean. I'm good at that. Or stack shelves in the local supermarket. Or pull pints... no, Tony would never go for that one.*

House: *Will I need a deposit? I'll need a job first for that. Maybe housing associations, I could get my name on some lists.*

Kids: *Will it break their hearts? Alison will have to come with me. She loves her dad, I know she does, but she's already noticing things; picking up on the way he speaks to me. I don't want her thinking this is normal family life. He'll fly into a towering rage one day, I just know it. He'll look at her and yell out his obsession that she's not his - when of course she is. I never wanted anybody else except Tony, and now... well, forget it. I won't be sharing my bed with any man once I get out of here... never again. What about the boys? They see what he's like, how he treats me. Will they come with me too?*

She twiddled with her pen. 'How do I do all this without Tony becoming suspicious?' She said aloud. 'Can I really make it happen by myself?'

With a sigh, she dragged one of the white plastic patio chairs across the grass, and put her feet up. She picked up the paper and quickly flicked through it. She skipped the national news pages, thumbed past the story about a drugs haul off the coast near Whitby, until she found the classifieds. There was nothing much in the jobs section. *It's probably the wrong day of the week for jobs,* she mused. Under Training Courses, she found an ad offering a basic computer skills course for beginners. It was a six-week course, starting after the Easter holidays, on Wednesday mornings 10-12. Kathy stared at the ad. It was perfect! She had butterflies in her stomach – and she was excited in a way she hadn't been in years. She could still manage to get all the housework done and the dinner on the table at the right time. Tony need never know. Quickly, she wrote down all the details, careful not to mark the newspaper in any way that might alert Tony.

*****

Kathy stumbled on the bumpy footpath, bringing her back to the reality of her present situation, and the dilemma Tony had given her by being nice that morning.

She loved the rugged isolated terrain that surrounded her. This stretch of the walk wasn't accessible by road, only via the ferry to Inversnaid. People visited especially to see Rob Roy's cave, high amongst the boulders above the loch, although it was rare that they would venture this far along the track. She stopped and looked behind her. The others were nowhere to be seen, and she relaxed, loving the solitude. To be able to laugh or cry. To voice the deepest thoughts and fears – which often stay locked inside you, eating away.

'What is the right thing to do?' She called out, directing her voice towards the woodland behind her. But of course only Kathy had the answer.

Rather than wait for the others, she set off again. It was a well-marked path and she knew Joy and Daniel weren't far ahead.

She just wasn't in the mood for idle chatter. She needed time to think and find the answers to her questions. *Will he really change? Does he love me that much? I don't think so. I think this is just another way of controlling me. And do I still love him? I said I did last night. Did I lie? No, I don't think so. There's still something, buried deep inside- something I fell in love with. And when, occasionally, that something shows through, he's the person I love. Can he bring it out on command - when he senses it's crunch time? Yes. No - he's not devious enough. Sometimes I think he never thinks beyond his next meal or his next pint or his next session of what passes for lovemaking these days. So what do I do? I could play along until my plans are complete; I guess that would be less stressful. Would that be fair to him? Building him up, and then knocking him down. If I'm going to make the break, I should just do it, not string him along. Damn it, I wish I knew if I'd got the job - then I'd feel I was getting somewhere.*

It was only three weeks since she'd seen the ad in the local paper, and she remembered her nervous excitement, when, after the usual breakfast rituals mixed with a variety of grunts - the children's version of conversation - she finally had the house to herself.

*****

It was a Friday. She made a cup of strong tea, picked up the morning paper, and turned straight to the jobs section. She had completed her computer courses a few months earlier. Now she quickly scanned the columns looking for anything suited to her newly acquired skills. One particular ad caught her attention.

Part-time Administrator wanted. Basic computer skills and excellent organisational skills required, along with a mature attitude. Hours can be flexible.

It sounded ideal. Kathy quickly wrote down the contact details, and then jumped as she heard the front door slam.

'KATHY!' Tony was bellowing from the front hall.

Almost spilling hot tea all over herself, she quickly stuffed the job information into her dressing gown pocket. She closed the paper just as he walked into the kitchen.

'Did you forget something?' she asked nervously.

'My mobile. Have you seen it?' Tony looked around distractedly. 'You're still not dressed,' he said, looking Kathy up and down. 'What if that was a stranger at the door? Or that guy Pete from next door who fancies you? You give off the wrong signals, Kathy. Put some clothes on.'

Obediently, Kathy headed up the stairs, leaving Tony to search for the missing phone. She felt the crumpled paper in her pocket and squashed it tightly inside her clenched fist. In the shower, with the steam swirling around her, she indulged in her usual fantasy. It was the same every day. Always the same. Whether she was in the shower, or on the bus, cooking the dinner, or in bed, lying beneath his sweating, fleshy body, Kathy dreamt of a new life. One without Tony. Without his constant put downs, his barrage of demands, and his sweaty, pawing hands. A chance to find the real Kathy Forrester.

Once she heard the front door slam, she turned off the shower and dressed quickly.

She smoothed out the crumpled ball of paper. Wrestling with her conscience she re-read the advert. She really should discuss it with Tony first. He wouldn't like the thought of her meeting people that he didn't know, making a life for herself; she knew he'd never agree.

But this was all part of her plan, to get a job, a house of her own - and finally break free of him.

Without giving herself a second to change her mind, she picked up the phone and dialled. Her heart was racing; she didn't have a clue what she was going to say. *Oh, this is stupid. I can't do it.* She was about to hang up when a lady with a sing-song voice answered.

'Hello, Williams & Son, can I help you?'

'Hi, I'm enquiring about the job ad in this morning's *Echo*,' Kathy replied, amazed at how calm and confident she sounded. *Is this really me?*

'Can you email in your CV, the closing date is next Wednesday.' The receptionist told her.

Kathy struggled for two days with the CV, not knowing what to put. What had she done with her life so far? Left school at sixteen, become pregnant at eighteen, married at nineteen – and never had a job. She felt once again that this whole plan was a waste of time. But the tiny flame of determination within her flickered and grew. She attacked the CV with renewed vigour, hoping that her recent training courses - all passed with flying colours - would show that she worked hard, and could learn new tasks. And that managing a home and three children would show off her organisational skills.

*****

Voices ahead on the footpath brought Kathy out of her reflection on her employment status. Thinking it must be Joy and Daniel she sped up a little. Feeling exhausted by her inner conflict and debates, she was looking forward to some real conversation.

She stopped dead in her tracks. She saw them together, just where the path opened out onto a gravel beach. Joy had her back to Daniel.

'I don't need you to go on. You win. It was my fault. I drove you to it,' Joy said.

Daniel's response was low, resolute. 'I'm not the winner, Joy.'

Kathy barely heard the words. She stepped back, embarrassed, yet compelled to watch and listen.

'DANIEL. I GET IT.' Joy fired the words like bullets. 'It was an office fling. A one-night stand. She flattered you. Seduced you. Stuck her tongue down your throat. You fucked her. End of.'

Kathy backed further away and turned, retracing her steps, distancing herself from the scene as quickly as she could. She had never seen Joy like this, in all the years they'd known each other. *Hopefully she will have calmed down before the others catch up. And Daniel - he deserves whatever's coming to him. Men. They're all bastards, the lot of them.*

*****

Within a minute or two, Kathy met up with the rest of the group on the footpath.

'Hey, you're going the wrong way, Kathy,' Brad called out. 'What's up? Did you think you were lost? Or were you just lonely?' he teased.

'You're such a joker, Brad,' Kathy replied with sarcasm.

'Did you see that goat?' Ruth asked.

Kathy shook her head.

'Back there.' Ruth threw her arm back distractedly. 'He looked as though he were about to charge any second, I didn't fancy those huge horns anywhere near my nether regions, thank you very much.' She put her hands on her bum, protectively. 'He was a bit whiffy too.'

'Oh, stop exaggerating, Ruth,' Rob said.

'You OK?' Trish asked, squeezing Kathy's shoulder. She leaned closer. 'We haven't fallen out or anything, have we?' she whispered. 'I wasn't gossiping. Joy's our friend. I really feel for her - I just want to help.'

'I know – and it's fine,' Kathy said. She pulled Trish along the path a little way, out of earshot of the others. 'I came back because I caught up with Joy and Daniel,' she said. 'It was awful; they were having a terrible row. I felt like I'd crept up on them - I was mortified.'

'Did they see you?'

'No, thank God. They were too busy hurting each other to notice me. That's why I came back, to slow you lot down. Give them time to pull themselves together, and for Joy to get a grip on herself. Trish, I've never ever seen her like that.'

'Right, we'll tell the others we need to rest for a few minutes,' Trish said, taking charge.

VIII

'Wow, look at this place.' Brad pointed to the Drover's Inn, their accommodation for the night. It stood proud and tall. Imposing, yet welcoming. On the green outside, the benches and picnic tables were bustling with walkers, their rucksacks and poles heaped at their feet.

Ruth winked at Brad. 'It's haunted, you know, or so rumour has it,' she said, eyes wide. 'I might be scared in that room on my own. Can I share with you?' She gripped his arm. 'I might need protecting from the ghost.'

'Ruth, stop accosting the poor guy,' Trish said. 'We'll make sure your room is close to ours. Just yell and Rob will come to save you.' She nudged her husband 'Won't you?'

'Yup. I've seen *Most Haunted*; I know the ropes.' Rob gave a mock salute.

'Ghosts or no ghosts, what a magnificent building,' Brad said. He'd whipped out his camera and was taking shots from all angles.

'Let's get checked in then. Tony's here already.' Rob pointed to the bus across the car park. 'I don't know about anyone else, but I'm gasping for a pint,' he said.

Kathy had spotted the bus already. She was anxious about how Tony's mood would be this afternoon, and she couldn't see him anywhere. Did that mean he'd hit the bottle again as he had the previous evening? She followed the others into the hotel reception area. The décor was dark with lots of wood panelling and dim lighting.

They knew The Drovers Inn was extremely popular, they'd been lucky to get the last available rooms for that night.

'I'm not into old and musty,' Ruth muttered as she looked around. 'Personally, I think I would have preferred a light and airy modern hotel.'

'Well, like it or lump it you're stuck with it.' Trish threw her a key. 'Here, catch,' she said.

Ruth looked at the key fob. 'Room thirteen... Great.'

Kathy looked around for Tony and spotted him standing by the bar with a pint in front of him. She waved and he waved back, drained his glass, and began to make his way towards them. He seemed steady enough as he moved through the tables. She stepped back from the others slightly as he approached – just in case. The last thing she wanted was a scene.

'How are the walkers?' he called, as he approached.

'Gasping for a pint, mate,' Brad replied. 'How's the beer?'

'Wet and cold.'

'That'll do me. I'll be down in five.' Brad nodded, heading up the stairs.

Kathy let out a sigh of relief. Tony was obviously still in a good mood.

'Are we checked in already?' she asked him.

'Yes, your stuff's upstairs. Come and have a drink,' he said, catching her hand in his.

'Let me get a wash and change my shoes.' She wriggled her hand free. 'I'll be five minutes,' she said, moving towards the stairs.

Her heart sank as he joined her. *Damn, I know what he'll be looking for.*

At the top of the stairs, they turned left, and halfway along the corridor, Tony stopped outside room nine, and opened the door for Kathy.

*****

The room was quite small, again with dark panelled walls, and a tiny window draped with heavy dark, reddish brown curtains, which had obviously once been rich red brocade. There was a picture of an ugly hunting scene on the wall by the bathroom door. Kathy shuddered at the forlorn look in the eyes of the deer as it was dragged along the ground by a pack of savage-looking dogs. The oak bedstead was old and creaked loudly as Tony sprawled across it.

He winked at her.

'The whole floor will know what we're up to,' he said wickedly, bouncing on the bed, making it creak and whine even louder.

Kathy made a bolt for the bathroom. *Great, that's all we need, a fucking creaky bed. Well, he can forget that idea.* She splashed cold water on her face, washing off the heat of the day.

'Come on; let's get back down to the bar.' Tony called out to her through the open bathroom door. 'I bet you could murder a drink,' he added.

Amazed that he wanted to go back downstairs, rather than indulge in his usual habit of pawing her like a piece of meat , Kathy quickly brushed her hair, coated her dry lips with Vaseline, and left the bathroom. She was surprised to see Tony standing at the open door, ready to go, and as she passed him, he stood aside courteously to let her go first.

Walking down the broad carpeted staircase, Kathy couldn't decide if she liked the place or not. She couldn't abide hunting and there were stuffed animals everywhere. She looked at them with distaste, feeling desperately sorry for the poor creatures.

IX

Daniel was already in the bar. He sat at a large round table, beneath an enormous stuffed stag's head, with antlers that must have been four feet long. He had an empty glass beside him and was half way through his second pint. Kathy sat down opposite, despite being angry with him; he looked so dejected that she couldn't help feeling sorry for him.

'Do you want another?' Tony asked.

'Please,' Daniel replied.

'Did you tell her?' Kathy said, once Tony was out of earshot.

'Yes.'

'Are you OK?' She knew he wasn't, but didn't know what else to say.

'Fucking great, Kath. What do you think?' Daniel drank the remaining beer in his glass. 'Anyway, why are you asking? You couldn't give a fuck about me. You think I'm the worst bastard on the planet.' He slammed down his empty glass and stood up. 'But do you want to know something?' he growled. 'You don't know the half of it. You know nothing.' He pushed past her, and stormed out of the bar.

Kathy watched him leave the room, shocked at his outburst. She remembered the tense scene she'd witnessed earlier that day, and wondered what it was that she wasn't supposed to know.

'Where did he go?' Tony asked, returning from the bar with the drinks. 'I thought he wanted another pint.'

'Oh, something about a phone call.' Kathy played it down.

Tony shrugged and pulled up a chair next to her, putting the drinks down on the table. His arm came around her shoulders and instinctively she tensed.

'I really enjoyed this morning, Kath... my little sex siren,' he whispered, kissing her ear.

She pulled away slightly. 'Don't spoil it, Tony.'

'No, no, I won't. And I meant it all – everything I said this morning – I love you, Kath, I couldn't bear being without you. I'll change, I promise I will,' he said, his voice rising with every promise. People nearby turned their heads and Kathy felt hot with embarrassment.

'OK, OK, just keep the volume down, will you? We don't want everyone knowing our business,' Kathy hissed. 'One rocky marriage among us is enough to cope with.'

Shit, I shouldn't have said that.

Tony pulled away from her. 'What do you mean? Who?' he asked.

The expression on Kathy's face showed clearly that she wished she could take back her words.

'Come on, you can tell me. I'm not going to say anything,' said Tony, searching her face for clues.

Kathy said nothing. She picked up her glass of ice-cold cider and took a long slow drink. She looked around hoping to see Ruth or Brad enter the bar.

'Daniel?' Tony sat back in his seat, folding his arms across his chest. 'I thought he was looking miserable earlier. Has she been playing around? I always knew she was a sly one. The stuck-up bitch.'

He looked so smug, sitting with his arms resting on his beer belly. Kathy wanted to slap him.

'Tony, shut up,' she snapped. 'Joy's my friend. And no, she hasn't been playing around, as you put it. He has.'

'She must have driven him to it.' Tony shuffled in his seat, turning to face Kathy. His expression changed. 'Probably kept her legs crossed in that prissy cold house of theirs,' he sneered.

Kathy was incensed. *You have to bring it down to your level, don't you? It's always about sex, crude, vile, gutter sex. You really do disgust me. I can't see you'll ever change. I'm deluding myself if I think you will.*

'What? What's that look about? What have I done now?'

'You really don't know?' she asked, shaking her head. 'Well, it doesn't matter now.' She drank the last of her cider. 'Can I have another drink please?'

X

Joy was in the bath when she heard Daniel come in, slamming the room door behind him. She heard the bed groan gently under his weight.

She immersed herself completely under the bathwater. She felt deflated. Not even angry - just exhausted and relieved. She held her breath, listening to her own heartbeat until finally, when she felt her lungs would explode, she surfaced, breathing in the steamy air and sloshing water all over the floor. She took a deep breath, feeling the pressure that had been building finally released. The first hurdle was over, even though Daniel's words had been hard to take.

He's right. I did want everything perfect, in perfect order. Who doesn't? Engagement, marriage, house, kids. But I wanted you more than anything else, Daniel. I wanted it all to be perfect for you. You should have talked to me, told me it was going wrong. Instead of letting me railroad you down a path you didn't want to take. I'd have listened, wouldn't I?

Joy stood up and wrapped a towel around her. She pulled out the bath plug, watching the water swirling down the plughole faster and faster. And as the water level receded, she was gripped by the feeling that her life was going the same way.

Daniel sat on the end of the bed, flicking aimlessly through the three TV channels, each with a snowier picture than the one before. He and Joy hadn't spoken for hours, not since her outburst had ended their talk on the rocky footpath earlier that afternoon.

Joy dropped the towel and walked around the room naked, trying to cool down after the heat of the day and then the warm bath. She moisturised her whole body slowly and methodically. Daniel used to help her once, now she didn't want his help, and he hadn't even looked at her since she came out of the bathroom. Fully moisturised, she put on a pair of white pants, then pulled a simple pale blue, cotton shift dress over her head. It felt soothing and cool as it slithered over her skin. She dried her hair quickly and applied her makeup carefully, finishing with a deep red lipstick. Pouting at her reflection, she caught sight of Daniel through the mirror, still aimlessly flicking through the TV channels.

'We should go down to eat.' She hadn't spoken for so long that her throat felt rusty. 'We must try to keep things normal.'

He continued playing with the TV remote, and didn't respond. For a second, Joy wondered if she'd actually spoken the words aloud.

'Did you hear me?' she said.

'Yes, I heard you.' His voice was raspy. He cleared his throat. 'Normal. This isn't normal. Why pretend it is?'

'Because it's a holiday; our friends' holiday.' Joy felt like a petulant child, fighting for her own way.

'What's the point? They all know anyway.' Daniel continued pressing buttons on the remote control.

'No, they don't.' Joy felt panic rising. She wanted to snatch the TV remote out of his hand. 'Only Trish knows. I told her and she won't say anything. She promised.'

'She'll have told Rob by now.' Daniel finally looked at Joy. 'You know what she's like. And she's bound to have told Kathy, they're sisters.'

'She won't, she promised.' Joy defended her friend, feeling her confidence lessen.

'Well, Kathy knows.' Daniel spoke almost carelessly.

'How?' Joy demanded. She could feel her chest tightening.

'I told her.'

'Oh, that's fantastic, Daniel. You talked to Kathy but you couldn't talk to your own wife.' Joy paced up and down the room, fighting to keep control. 'That's just great. What's she going to be thinking now?'

'You wouldn't let me talk to you. What the fuck was I supposed to do?' Daniel flung the remote onto the bed. 'You'll be happy to know that she called me a bastard,' he said, and marched into the bathroom.

Joy was shaking, cold now despite the stifling heat in the room. *Stay calm. Remember to breathe.* The band tightened around her chest until she thought she was going to pass out. She sat down heavily, putting her head between her knees, trying not to think, just breathe.

She didn't hear Daniel come out of the bathroom. He handed her a crumpled paper bag he'd pulled from his rucksack.

'Breathe into this,' he said, handing her the paper bag. 'Come on, take deep breaths.'

He stood beside her, rubbing her back in gentle rotating movements, until she sat up again.

'OK?' he asked.

She nodded, not trusting herself to speak.

'Look, I'll go down with you.' He spoke quietly. 'But I'm not pretending everything's normal. What's the point? They're our friends, and they're not stupid. They know something's wrong. Tell them what you want. I don't care. I won't talk about you to other people, Joy, I promise you that.'

'You nearly did... to Trish, earlier outside the toilets. I heard you.' Joy whispered.

'I know, and I'm sorry. I was angry. I needed you to hear me out. And then along comes Trish, having a go at me without knowing the facts.' He walked over to the window. 'I just snapped. I'm sorry.'

XII

Everyone else was already seated, studying menus when Joy and Daniel entered the bar. They sat in the two remaining chairs, between Brad and Kathy.

'You two took your time, didn't you?' boomed Tony.

His eyes looked a little glazed and Kathy gave him a swift dig in the ribs.

Joy hid behind the enormous menu, convinced that all eyes were on her. *Of course, they all know. Trish was bound to tell Rob - after all, that's what married couples do – tell each other stuff. And Kathy - I wouldn't have thought she'd tell Tony, even though they seemed very cosy earlier, as though they've sorted out some major issue, so maybe she has. Shit, that's all I need. Once he gets pissed, there's no telling what he might do or say.*

'What are you having?' Brad waved his glass at Joy as he stood up to go to the bar.

'Just water for me thanks. I had enough last night to keep me going for the rest of the week.'

'Well, I'm not on the water,' Ruth said. 'I'll have a vodka and cranberry juice, please.'

'I'll give you a hand, Brad.' Tony pushed back his chair.

Relieved to see Tony leave the table, Joy put down her menu. She'd decided on chicken salad with honey and mustard dressing, and rustic potatoes, and hoped it would be gentle on her churning stomach. Picking at a drop of hardened candle wax on the edge of the stained and chipped wooden table, she smiled politely as Ruth held court with woeful tales of life on the farm.

Trish sat across from her. She looked strangely disjointed through the large candlestick holder, its iron limbs bleeding thick rivers of hardened wax, the dim glow from the lit candles casting shadows over her face.

Joy could see Trish was trying to attract her attention; she was looking at her quite intensely, nodding at her discreetly and tipping her glass ever so slightly in her direction, but she studiously ignored her. Instead, she gave Ruth the occasional glance, smile, or quiet chuckle, even though she wasn't listening to a word of what she was saying. She began analysing each of the people sitting at the table around her, a game she often played when she didn't want any attention to turn her away.

Through the shadows dancing around the candlestick, she studied Rob. *He absolutely adores Trish. Look at him. Even while he's talking to Kathy he's got an arm around Trish's shoulders, stroking her neck. He's always so open - there never seems to be any hidden agenda with Rob. Smiling, relaxed, nothing's ever a problem to him. Is it all really so perfect? Trish makes you believe it is. So much so that we mere mortals feel complete failures. She always wants to listen, to help. It's just so hard to open up to her, to expose your wounds in the face of such perfection.* She watched Trish put her hand over Rob's, and then turn and kiss him.

Joy quickly picked up her glass of water, not wanting to be caught staring.

Her eyes moved around the table. Tony was back from the bar. His hand covered Kathy's delicate one, resting on the table between them. *No mystery there, anyway. He's a prize prick, a bully and a lazy sod. He's had her locked tight in his clutches for years.* Joy pondered for a moment, trying to catch a look at Kathy, hidden slightly by Daniel, sitting beside her. *Kathy seems different today, less jumpy. I can't put my finger on why, exactly. I mean, look at her now – in a simple T-shirt with no cleavage in sight, and a pair of jeans. Usually when they're out together she wears hideously short skirts and some of her tops leave nothing to the imagination. Daniel would hate me wearing anything like that, and, anyway, I just wouldn't. It's asking for trouble from any leering dirty-minded blokes - ugh! Tony makes her wear that stuff, I'm sure. She says it's her choice; she knows he likes her to dress that way and she likes to please him. But I don't believe it. She hates it, you can tell. She sits still all night, only getting up to go to the loo, then she scuttles off with her head down - obviously completely embarrassed that she looks like a hooker.*

Joy took another sip of water as her food arrived, catching Brad watching her from the corner of her eye. She smiled politely at him.

'You're very quiet tonight,' he said.

'Just tired.'

'Mmm, it's hard work walking fourteen miles with a hangover from hell,' he teased.

'Exactly. I won't be doing that again.' Joy began eating in the hope that he'd turn his attention elsewhere. She went back to her thoughts on Kathy, who was looking very relaxed, sipping her vodka, and matching Ruth drink for drink.

Everyone seemed so happy. Even Daniel was laughing at one of Rob's work stories.

Joy felt as if there was a dead weight inside her. She just wanted to curl up and cry. She couldn't allow herself that luxury; she had to keep it together - at least until the end of the week. She drank some more water and turned to Rob, focusing on his story and trying to laugh as enthusiastically as the rest of them.

As the evening wore on, the volume around the table rose and Ruth, as always, started a singsong. Carrying on the theme from the night before, she belted out another track from *Grease* – 'Summer Nights' - and was quickly joined by Trish's rousing, if slightly off-key voice.

'Before you girls get into full swing, let's get some pictures. The lads in the pub won't believe this place,' Rob said. He aimed his camera at the stag's head above them.

'All of you gather underneath this beast,' he added.

Obediently, the group shuffled into place, while Rob lined up the shot. He asked a burly walker at the next table, with a thick welsh accent, if he'd take the picture, and took his place in the centre of the group, beside Trish. Joy rested her hands lightly on Daniel's shoulders, not wanting any sign of their rift showing up on the pub notice board at home. She saw Kathy, who by now was tipsy, draping her arms around Brad's neck and leaning heavily into him. *I bet that'll mean trouble when Tony sees it pinned up in the local.*

'Everyone smile,' the Welshman said.

The photo shoot over, Trish and Rob said their goodnights, and Tony headed off to the loo. Joy sat on an empty chair beneath the stag's head.

'I'm off to bed as well,' Daniel said from across the table. 'Night, all.'

Joy nodded. She didn't need to reply. Brad and Ruth were still singing, although now more quietly, and nobody was looking their way.

*****

She watched him as he wove his way through the still busy bar area. She was exhausted, but she couldn't face going up too. Not yet, anyway. Then she frowned. Kathy had followed Daniel through the crowds, and was talking to him, one hand on his arm. *What's she doing? He must have asked her to follow him. I bet he's telling her what happened today. The bastard. After everything we said earlier, and what he said about not talking about me. And now... what the fuck is she doing with her arms round him? And kissing him as well! Is she making a play for him, or what?* Joy watched as they disappeared into the hallway. She had to use every ounce of her self-control to stay put. She held her glass so tightly there was a very real risk of it shattering in her hand. *Just the once, my foot. No fucking way. If he can kiss my best friend... ex best friend, while in the same room as me, it's obvious. They're probably in bed together already. II bet they planned the whole thing. Well, she's welcome to him.* She drank her water, feeling the vicelike grip around her chest again. Fighting for control, she looked around wildly, hoping desperately that nobody would notice her distress.

XIII

Kathy's feet felt alien to her and the people around her looked all warm and fuzzy. She knew she'd probably had far too much to drink and would have a stinking headache in the morning. So what? She was on holiday, and for the first time in God knew how long she was happy, even with Tony around. She knew she was staggering and starting to slur her words. It was definitely time she went to bed; she just needed to find Tony first.

Daniel had stopped to let an elderly lady, inappropriately dripping with diamonds and adorned with a peacock-blue feathery headpiece, through the narrow doorway to the bar area, when Kathy barged into him from behind. The diamond-studded one swept past with a look of disgust, as Kathy fell against Daniel's chest.

'Careful.' He put his arms out to steady her. 'Are you OK?'

'No, I'm pished,' Kathy slurred, making no effort to extract herself from him.

'I'll second that. Maybe you should go to bed.'

'I'm looking for Tony.' She concentrated on her words, and gazed up at him, doe- eyed.

'Come on, he's through here, I think.' Daniel tried to move forward.

'You look so sad. I want to kiss you better.' She spoke to him as if he was a child, and quickly pulled his head down to meet hers, kissing him full on the lips. 'Mmm, nice.' She smiled.

'Behave yourself, Kath,' Daniel hissed as he straightened up. Taking her by the hand, he guided her out of the bar.

In the relative quiet of the hallway, Kathy squinted, trying to focus on the man walking towards them. 'Tony?' she enquired. Daniel gently handed her over to Tony, like a parcel.

'She was looking for you,' he told him. 'I think she wants to go to bed.'

Tony nodded his thanks at Daniel, and picked his wife up, carrying her up the stairs in his arms. She laid her head on his shoulder, trying not to close her eyes, and focusing her gaze on Daniel, walking two steps behind them He looked weary and sad. Battling the fog enveloping her brain, Kathy tried to remember something she'd heard earlier... something Joy had said about it being her fault. What did she mean?

As soon as Tony put her down in their room, she felt sick and stumbled into the bathroom. Nothing happened, so she drank a glass of water and went back into the bedroom. Tony was watching a foreign football match on the TV.

He looked her up and down. 'You'd best get into bed,' he observed.

His tone and expression didn't give anything away, and foggily she tried to weigh up his mood. Was he still her gentle giant Tony of this morning, or his usual surly self, looking for his marital rights. *Oh God, if he's all over me, sweaty and pawing at me, I'll throw up. Or I'll say something I'll regret – like I do when I'm pissed.*

He continued watching the match while she undressed, not commenting. Even when she pulled out a pair of childish pyjamas, half expecting him to say, 'What do you want those for?' he remained silent.

Once Kathy had climbed unsteadily into bed, he placed a glass of water beside her, switched off the lights, and got into bed. He pulled her to him and instantly she tensed.

'Don't, Tony, I feel sick. I can't - I'll throw up,' she said.

'I only want a cuddle.' His voice sounded strained, as if he was trying to stay calm.

She felt the weight of his heavy body, as he pressed against her tightly.

'I told you, I'll change,' he murmured. I'll be what you want me to be. I need you, Kath.'

She lay still, trying not to close her eyes, desperate to avoid the feeling of the room spinning. She wanted to turn to him; she knew he wanted her and he was tempting her with his gentleness.

XIV

'C'mon, have ye nae homes t'go tae?' the barman called out as he gathered the empty glasses.

'Guess that's our cue to leave.' Ruth stood up; remarkably steady on her feet, despite the copious amount of vodka she'd drunk. She giggled.

'Come on, Brad, would you care to escort two gorgeous ladies to their rooms?'

'With pleasure.' He offered Ruth his arm and held out a hand to Joy.

She ignored the gesture, picking up her bag and moving towards the door, leaving the others to follow. She still felt so angry. *I can't go back up there yet. I can't face another confrontation.*

Two girls came in through the open front doors, smelling faintly of cigarette smoke and cool night air. Joy stepped out into the darkness.

'Hey, where are you going?' Ruth asked coming up behind her, Brad still in tow.

'Go on to bed, Ruth, I just need some fresh air for five minutes. I'll be fine.'

'I'll keep her company,' Brad said.

'OK then,' Ruth said, clearly disappointed at losing her escort.

'Night, Ruth.' Brad kissed her cheek.

'Night. Night, Joy.' She sighed as she turned and headed for the stairs.

'I don't need company,' Joy snapped, as Brad followed her.

'I need some fresh air anyway,' he replied.

Joy sat down on a bench under a window, and Brad plonked himself down beside her.

For a few minutes neither of them said anything, both lost in thought as they watched the last departing revellers leave the bar, their voices quickly swallowed up into the darkness.

'Tough night, eh?' Brad finally said, without looking at her.

When she didn't answer, he carried on.

'Daniel looked rough too.'

'What are you, a counsellor?' Joy said.

'No, I just noticed that things looked strained between the two of you, that's all.'

'Are you married, Brad?' she asked, her tone almost pleasant.

'No.'

'Girlfriend?'

'No.'

'Gay?'

'Definitely not.'

'So you're hardly an expert on relationships, are you?' Her tone was biting.

'I guess not.' Brad shrugged.

The dark silence surrounded them again. Joy had hoped to be sitting out in the sultry heat, counting the stars, with Daniel's arm around her. The reality, she reflected grimly, had turned out rather differently.

Who are you trying to kid, girl? You know perfectly well that this was just waiting to happen. All the holidays, the new cars, the house - everything; they were all just pieces of sticky tape that you hoped would hold the two of you together.

Brad fidgeted beside her, his thigh touching hers and reminding her that he was still there. He cleared his throat uncertainly.

'I've had a few girlfriends, but things just never felt right, you know?'

'I always thought Daniel felt right.'

'And he doesn't now?'

'Forget it, Brad, I shouldn't have said anything. I really don't want to discuss it.' She stood up to leave.

'Come on, Joy, I'm sorry. I won't ask any more questions.'

Joy sat down stiffly, putting a bit more distance between them. Neither of them spoke and gradually she felt herself begin to relax a little.

XV

'There was one girl, a long time ago,' Brad began. 'Her name was Jennifer, I always called her Jen. Gorgeous she was, giddy and completely mad - not a girly girl at all. She was one of the lads, really - screaming at football matches, or diving about in the sea, when all the other girls were tanning themselves and worrying about getting sand in their hair.'

Joy opened her mouth to speak, then thought better of it. Brad seemed to be in another time and place.

'We were just mates for ages,' he continued. 'She said over and over again that she wasn't interested in boyfriends. Her mum and dad were divorced and she'd seen too many men come and go in her mum's life. She used to say the relationship game was very overrated.'

'She wasn't wrong, there,' Joy muttered under her breath.

Brad continued his story.

'I was at this beach party, in the sand dunes. There was a group of us, all seventeen, or eighteen, and we had a portable barbeque for sausages and burgers. The girls brought music and vodka and the lads brought cans of lager and cigarettes. It was a hot night and everyone got pretty pissed. Then most of the group went skinny dipping which of course always ends in sex.'

'Not always,' Joy interrupted. 'I went to beach parties like that when I was at college. Maybe I was at that one! And I went skinny dipping, too, but I didn't end up having sex. We weren't all like that.'

'No, you're right, I'm sorry,' Brad said.

He looked at her as if he'd just realised she was there.

'Jen wasn't like that either,' he said. She wouldn't go in the sea that night. She said she was going home, so I walked with her. It was a fair walk; she lived right at the other end of town. The tide was out so we walked the whole way along the beach. I guess I fell in love with her that night, although it was weeks before I plucked up the courage to kiss her. I was convinced she'd thump me.' He laughed.

'And did she?' By now Joy was listening intently, almost relieved not to be thinking of her own problems for a while.

'No, she kissed me back.' He smiled. 'And beneath that boyish bravado, I found a real girl. We started doing all the usual stuff. Going to pubs and clubs, staying out until all hours, and then sneaking her back to my room after my dad had gone to bed. Or going back to hers and letting myself out at five in the morning, before her mum got up.

We'd only been going out six months when we got engaged. Her mother had a fit. She said Jen was far too young, and that I wasn't good enough for her. She ranted at Jen saying that I had no prospects, because I worked in McDonald's, and I didn't even have a car! They had a huge row in front of me, and I felt a pathetic failure. Jen screamed at her mother, grabbed a few clothes and stuffed them into her college bag. Then, dragging me with her, she flounced out of the house and told her mother she was never going back.'

'You were working in McDonald's?' Joy asked. 'I thought you studied accountancy.'

'Yes to both. My dad couldn't afford to pay for me to go to college, so I had to help pay my way. I was determined to make something of myself, and if I didn't see any shame in working McDonald's in order to do it.'

'So didn't Jen's mother know you were studying to be an accountant?'

'She wasn't interested in me. She wasn't really interested in Jen either. She just wanted her to find some rich bloke they could latch on to. Jen hated her for it.' Brad fell silent for a moment.

Joy shivered involuntarily.

'You're cold,' said Brad, concerned. And I must be boring you.'

'No, I'm fine.' Joy rubbed at her bare arms. 'Just a shiver. Go on – what happened next?'

'I took Jen home with me and Dad said she could stay. He didn't want us sharing a room though, said it wasn't proper. So she put her stuff in the spare room but always crept into mine. I think he knew - in fact, I know he did. It was just easier for him to deal with if she had a room of her own.'

'So how did it all go wrong?' Joy whispered, guessing that this story wasn't going to have a happy ending, and subconsciously asking the same question of her own situation.

'I was working a shift at McDonald's one evening, when Jen came in with her mate Sammy. She wanted to borrow the car. Sammy had missed the last bus home, and Jen said she'd drop her off. I asked them to wait – I said my shift finished in less than two hours and I'd drive. Jen said that Sammy and she wanted a girly chat and that she'd be back before my shift finished. So I threw her the keys and she blew me a kiss.'

Joy's hands flew to her mouth. 'Jennifer Alderton and Samantha Blackburn,' she mumbled through her fingers.

'It was a head-on collision with a truck on Loftus Bank. She didn't have a chance. She didn't suffer. At least that's what they told me. It was instant, they said.'

Instinctively, Joy hugged him, but he didn't move a muscle. It was as if she wasn't there.

She remembered how shocked everyone in college had been when they heard the news. Both the girls had been in her business studies class. She hadn't known them well, but the sudden death of two eighteen- year- old girls had affected everyone deeply.

'She took me with her, really,' Brad said as Joy kept one arm loosely around him. 'I never felt like that about anyone again. I had a few relationships after that, but I was just going through the motions really. Nobody else ever came close.'

He turned to Joy, the moonlight catching his unshed tears.

'I never wanted to hurt anybody,' he said earnestly. 'So each time, I'd end it, before things got too serious.'

Standing up suddenly, he pulled Joy to her feet. 'So now you know all about me, I'm not gay, not a love rat, just a single bloke trying to get through life as best he can.'

Joy allowed herself to be steered inside, and together they walked up the stairs. At the door of her room, he gave her a small smile.

'We all have our demons, Joy. Things in our past we wish we could change. But as you know, there's no going back. Night.'

TUESDAY
I

It was early when Kathy entered the dining room for breakfast. Only the girls and Rob were at the table. Joy said that Daniel was having coffee in his room, and Brad hadn't shown yet.

Tony had decided he'd have a lie-in and eat later. He'd wanted her to stay in bed with him, but she couldn't do that again today. She felt she could hardly say she'd walked the full distance if she kept taking mornings off, and besides which, she was hungry. Too much drink always made her hungry the next morning.

Everyone was pretty quiet, which suited Kathy just fine. She was beginning to realise that it was no easy task spending seven days, morning noon, and night with a group of friends; but then perhaps that depended on your friends.

She glanced around at the others while she ate her cereal. Rob was reading the *Times*, with Trish peering over his shoulder at some article that had attracted her attention. She was dropping toast crumbs everywhere, and Rob didn't say a word. *Tony would eat me alive if I did that to him. Not that he'd be reading the* Times. *More likely to be eyeing up the page three girls in the* Sun.

Ruth was munching her way through her second bowl of cereal. After a failed attempt at conversation with Joy, she shrugged her shoulders and began flicking through some tourist leaflets.

'Imagine that, there's a shop called The Green Wellie. It's in Tyndrum, ' she said, looking around the table. 'Looks really interesting. Might be worth a mooch around, this afternoon,' she continued, smiling hopefully at Kathy.

Kathy smiled back and nodded.

Joy was peeling an orange, and looking like she had no intention of ever eating it. Slowly and methodically, she removed every last bit of skin and pith, before splitting the segments and placing them on her cereal. Kathy hardly dared to look in her direction. *That smouldering anger in her eyes and the way she directed it at me, I was convinced she was about to launch herself across the table that very second. It doesn't make sense to Kathy, but I'm dammed if I'm going to ask questions this morning.*

'Brad's probably overslept,' Ruth said. 'Should I go up and give him a knock? You were both up pretty late last night, weren't you?' She spoke directly to Joy.

'Not that late,' Joy snapped. 'I'm here on time, aren't I?' She dropped her spoon into the uneaten cereal. 'Ready to leave at nine, is it?' she asked Rob, leaving the table without waiting for an answer.

Ruth watched her stride out of the dining room.

'What is it with her?' she asked. 'She's definitely off with me today.'

'It's not you,' Trish reassured her, before throwing a warning look at Kathy.

Kathy hated Ruth being out of the loop. It wasn't fair, especially when she was always so open about everything.

'It's probably her hormones or something, making her a moody cow. She'll snap out of it, I guess,' Ruth decided.

'Women. More bloody trouble than they're worth,' Rob grumbled, lifting his paper quickly to shield himself from a bombardment of sugar sachets.

II

Joy packed the last of her things into the suitcase. She was exhausted. It must have been after one when Brad had left her at her door. She'd lain awake for hours, careful not to let one inch of her touch Daniel. She didn't think he'd slept much either.

'I'm going down. Can you manage that, or shall I take it?' He pointed to her suitcase.

'I'll manage.' She glared at him, her eyes steely cold. 'Tony's having a lie-in, so the coast is clear.'

'What?'

'Oh, don't look so innocent. We're fucked anyway. Why pretend?'

'Joy, you really need to get a grip,' he said shaking his head in bewilderment as he left the room.

Once he'd gone Joy threw herself on the bed. *I just want to go home, lock myself away, and hide. Where is home anyway? Maybe I should just go away completely, where nobody knows me. Somewhere I can just be me. I'd need a job. What could I do? I haven't worked since I left school. How useless am I?* She allowed herself one or two tears, then stood up quickly and brushed herself down. *This is not the time to let my guard down, I can't let the cracks in this brittle facade I call my life widen any further.*

She remembered Brad's story the night before. Such a tragedy – two young lives wiped out in the blink of an eye. She'd been with Daniel the night it happened...

A group of them were in someone's house - she couldn't even remember his name now. Sammy's brother, Alan, was there too. Music was blasting out and everyone was eating pizza and drinking beer, when a policeman had knocked at the door, looking for Alan; a nervous hush spread around the room.

Daniel went with Alan out to the police car. He was crying when he came back. She'd never seen Daniel cry before and didn't know what to do.

'Alan's sister Sammy and her friend Jennifer are dead,' he blurted out. 'Killed in a car crash. The cop has taken Alan to the hospital,' he told everyone, then ran off up the stairs.

All the girls in the room started crying, too.

Joy followed him, and wrapped her arms around him while he sobbed, burying his face in her hair.

'Come on, let's go,' he said. 'The party's over.'

Back at Daniel's house they just sat in front of the blank TV screen for a while. Then Joy led him upstairs, into his bedroom. Stunned and shell-shocked at the news, she just wanted them to feel close. She took off all her clothes. It was the first time she'd ever been completely naked with him. She wanted more than ever to make love to him, to take away all the hurt.

'No, stop. Not like this. You wanted to wait,' Daniel said, pulling away.

'Why wait?' Joy cried. 'We could be dead tomorrow too!'

'We won't be, I promise.' He stroked her hair, her face, and then her whole body, with incredible tenderness. 'I love you, Joy. Marry me. I'll look after you forever. We'll die together when we're ninety-five.'

Well, that all went pear-shaped, didn't it?

III

It was another hot, sticky morning as the group set off to rejoin the footpath, beneath the flawless blue sky. Joy looked back at the Drovers Inn, recalling the sadness in Brad's eyes the night before.

'Am I pleased to be leaving that place,' Ruth whispered as she linked her arm through Joy's. 'I honestly thought I'd get a visit from the ghost of room thirteen in the dead of night.'

'I'm sure it's all talk to get the punters in Ruth.' Joy turned back to the footpath. *The only ghosts around here are those from our own past.*

They crossed the bridge over the rushing tumbling waters of the River Falloch.

'Oh, isn't this fantastic?' Ruth had her camera out, snapping away, taking pictures of the rapids bouncing over rocks and boulders, as the river made its way towards Loch Lomond. 'Take my picture over here, please.' She thrust the camera at Daniel, before stepping backwards, closer to the roaring water. 'The boys would love this.'

Despite her grim mood, Joy found herself smiling at Ruth's excitement. But she didn't linger, instead, she walked ahead, hoping to catch up with Brad. As they descended into the valley, it was deliciously cool and shady, in contrast to the intense morning sun. He was a fair way ahead but she didn't want to call out to him. She didn't even know what she'd say to him, but felt the need to say something; to let him know that she'd shared some of his pain all those years ago, even though she hadn't known him.

The landscape unfolded around them as the dense woodland gave way to open moorland, and the trees began to thin out, allowing the sun to touch her skin once more. Thirsty, Joy pulled out her water bottle. She stopped to put on a thin cotton shirt over her vest top, protecting her shoulders.

Brad was now even further ahead. Joy gave up her chase, slowing to a stroll as the footpath began a steady incline out of the Loch Lomond Basin.

Her thoughts returned to Daniel and Kathy. *What shall I do about Kathy? Daniel didn't admit to anything this morning, but I saw them with my own eyes last night. Shall I confront her, or give her the cold shoulder? I don't know what would be worse. I can't believe she'd do that. Not just because she and I are friends, but to run the risk of Tony finding out - knowing how possessive he is. I wouldn't like to be in her shoes. If I say anything at all, then the whole flaming lot of them are going to know everything. That's a big can of worms I'd be responsible for opening. Do I really want that?*

Joy turned at the sound of footsteps. It was Trish. *Maybe she knows something.*

'What are you doing, racing ahead? You should be taking it steady. It's supposed to be twenty-five degrees today, you know.' Trish fell into step, looking super cool as always.

Does that woman ever sweat? Joy asked herself. 'I wanted to catch up with Brad; he seems a bit out of sorts this morning,' she told Trish.

'I heard the two of you were thick as thieves, and up until all hours last night.' Trish gave a slightly wicked grin. 'Are you OK?'

Joy knew she was testing the water. Gauging how much she should say. 'I'm fine, I guess.' She gave a weak smile. 'I have to be.'

'Did you talk to Daniel, listen to what he had to say for himself?'

'Mmm. And what do you know; it's my fault... of course.'

'It's not your fault.' Trish grabbed her arm, giving it a shake. 'I've told you that already.'

'It is. I know it is.' Joy pulled free of Trish's grip. 'End of discussion. Can we please change the subject?' she said.

Trish gave an exasperated sigh, but said nothing. They were still walking beside the river, surging its way over low boulders, cutting through the open moorland, as they continued their ascent, leaving Loch Lomond behind and moving into new and wilder territory.

It was very peaceful, and Joy felt a comfortable silence develop between herself and Trish. Yet still she was itching to know how long Kathy had been at it with Daniel. She weighed it up in her head. *Daniel's had plenty of opportunities. He gets out and about visiting clients. We hardly ever talk about his job and what it involves – we haven't in ages. It pays the bills. What else matters? There's nothing to stop him going to her place during the day. How would I know? I wouldn't have a clue. And of course, Tony's at work all day. Right little den of sin they'd have for themselves, very cosy.*

'Do you think she's having a fling?' Joy blurted, without stopping to think.

'Who?' Trish asked.

'Kathy.'

'No.' Trish shook her head. 'What makes you say that?'

'I don't know. She seems happier, more confident,' Joy said. 'Did you see her last night? She was pissed; singing her heart out, not hiding behind Tony's shoulder, or in a corner somewhere.' Joy tried to pad out her reasons, hoping to lighten things. Kathy was Trish's sister after all.

'No. She wouldn't have the bottle.' Trish shook her head, dismissing the very idea. 'Anyway, Tony's got her completely under his thumb - she'd never get away with it.'

'So what's with all the new found frivolity then?' Joy persisted. She didn't really think Trish knew anything, but wanted to plant a seed of doubt.

'Tony probably cut her a little slack. He's definitely been mellower the past couple of days.'

'Don't you think she's been showing more spark, confidence - whatever you call it - for months now, on and off?' Joy pushed.

She watched Trish wrinkle up her forehead, always a sure sign the cogs were turning.

'Like she's hugging some exciting secret.' Joy left it there, hanging between them.

When Trish didn't answer, Joy mulled over something Kathy had said to her a few days ago. They'd been talking about the way life pans out, when Kathy had become agitated, saying her life was a nightmare.

'... I hate him. I'm planning my escape route,' Kathy had spat.

So she has an escape route... Daniel. It has to be. Why else would he have chosen now, the night before this holiday, to tell me about the despicable Stephanie? An affair that happened ten years ago. What was the point? Kathy of course. He probably couldn't bear her to see me whisking him off to bed, right in front of her eyes. So he brought all this up, just to cover his tracks with her. They're probably trailing behind right this minute, stealing a quick snog or more behind a bush. Fuck it. And I laid everything on the line.

'You think it's Daniel, don't you?' Trish interrupted her thoughts.

She'd hit the jackpot; just as Joy has known she would.

'You're being ridiculous. You do know that,' Trish said.

'It seems pretty obvious to me.'

'Why, for God's sake?' Trish asked. 'OK, I agree she could be tempted into an affair. Wouldn't we all, with a husband like Tony? But, Joy...'

Joy winced, knowing she'd gone too far with this.

'...You're her best friend, she loves you to bits. She'd never do that to you. I can't believe you could even think it.'

'I saw them together last night,' Joy defended herself. 'She was draped all over him. Kissing him right there in front of everyone.'

'I can't believe it.' Trish shook her head.

'Are you saying I'm lying?' Joy fumed. 'Why would I? What's the point?' My life is shitty enough as it is, without making things up.'

'No, I'm saying I can't believe it,' Trish said.

Joy could see Brad in the distance. He seemed to be waiting for them.

'Sorry,' she said sullenly. 'I shouldn't have dumped all this on you. I don't know what it is with me at the moment; I usually sort out my own mess.' Joy let out a frustrated sigh. 'She was kissing him though. I guess I just saw red. It must be all this fresh air.'

'And all the walking, it gives you too much time to think,' agreed Trish. 'I'll talk to Kath.'

'No, don't. It's over with me and Daniel anyway.'

'Don't say that, Joy. You need to wait until you get home, sort things out properly. I'm sure you can.'

'Well, I'm certainly not going to say anything out here – it would just cause pandemonium, and Tony would go off on one. It would be awful. This is a holiday – at least for some. The rest of us have to be adult about things and get through until Saturday.'

'OK.' Trish put an arm around Joy's shoulders.

Joy shrugged her off. They didn't do the touchy feely stuff and she felt uncomfortable with it. Plus it didn't feel right to be accusing Kathy of anything, when they'd known each for such a long time and been such good friends.

IV

The two women lapsed into silence, Joy thought back to when she first met the sisters.

She was fifteen when her grandma died. Joy's mum didn't get on with her father, Joy's granddad, and without her mum there to keep the peace, they all – Joy, her mum and dad, and her sister Caroline - had to up sticks and move out of Joy's grandparents' house. They had lived in the lovely old semi since Joy was seven. It had a long back garden with a sprawling apple tree and a dilapidated old air-raid shelter, with a tin sheet roof that leaked in one corner when it rained.

Joy and her sister Caroline loved the air-raid shelter. It was their den. Somewhere to hide away when their mother was ranting - usually at their father because he'd forgotten to put out the rubbish on bin day, or hadn't brought in the washing when it started to rain, while she was out on her regular Saturday morning shopping trip. Sometimes the tirade would be at the girls; they might have put a book back in the wrong place, making the shelf look disorderly, or perhaps they hadn't opened the curtains when they'd got up. Joy's mum was a control freak; at least she seemed to be through Joy's fifteen-year-old eyes. Everything always had to be perfectly prim and proper. And nothing was ever up for discussion. It was always mum's way or no way.

When they moved into the tiny two-bedroom terrace in South Bank, things got a hundred times worse. It was only ten minutes' walk from Joy's grandparents' house; it could have been a hundred miles away, it was so different. Rows and rows of tiny terraced houses lined the narrow streets, which teemed with noisy children racing up and down on bikes or skateboards. Their mothers stood constantly gossiping besides their open front doors, and Joy's mother felt very uncomfortable there.

The house had no garden, only a tiny yard, which was all mossy and slimy, until her mum scoured it with bleach. She scoured the whole house with bleach, too, scrubbing every inch and moaning that nobody helped, then belittling their efforts when they did. She was convinced that it wouldn't be clean until she'd cleaned it herself.

Joy and Caroline tucked themselves away in their room. It was much smaller than the one they'd left, and they had bunk beds, to save on space. Joy got the top bunk because Caroline always needed the loo in the night. The two girls weren't particularly close, but they were united in their gripes about their mother, and her controlling ways. For weeks after the move, she wouldn't let the girls out in the evenings, telling them it wasn't safe, but Joy and Caroline knew it wasn't that bad. Eventually she allowed them a little freedom, as far as Trish and Kathy's house at the end of the street. Joy and Kathy were in the same year and both played on the school netball team. Their tentative friendship soon developed into inseparable best friends.

Kathy and Trish's house always seemed happy and relaxed. Their mum loved nothing better than having a full house and cooking huge meals for everyone while the stereo was blaring away. She was friendly and caring, and talked to her children's friends as if they were adults – without demanding answers - unlike Joy's mum.

Sometimes Joy would stay over. Wedged in tight between the wall and Kathy, in Kathy's small single bed, the two girls would whisper late into the night, sharing their secret hopes and dreams, while Trish slept in the bed opposite, inches away from them, dreaming of her new boyfriend, the gorgeous Rob.

They used to talk about sex and what it would be like. Joy hadn't even kissed a boy. Kathy had, and she said it wasn't up to much. She said the boy smelled of stale cigarettes and he'd tried to push his tongue into her mouth. She said it was the most disgusting thing ever. With the superior experience of someone five years older, Trish told them loftily that sex was great. Listening to her, Joy could never imagine having a boyfriend - let alone having sex with him. She wouldn't have risked the wrath of her mother, who appeared to be still living in the dark ages, and believed that you should be married first.

V

Both lost in their separate thoughts, the women were surprised to find that they had caught up with Brad – who stood staring intently up into a tall pine tree. They stopped and followed his gaze.

'What are you doing?' Trish asked him.

He pointed. 'I spotted a red squirrel just a few seconds ago. It scooted up the tree trunk,' he said, his voice soft and animated. 'Have you got your camera, Trish? Take it out quietly; we don't want to scare him off.'

Joy stared hard into the dense foliage, looking for signs of a red bushy tail, while Trish stood poised, camera at the ready. They'd been waiting there about five minutes, when Ruth, followed by Rob, caught up with them.

'What are you doing?' Ruth asked.

'Watching for a red squirrel,' Joy whispered.

'I should think you're wasting your time.' Rob burst the bubble. 'Those little fellows jump through the treetops at high speed – he's probably half a mile away by now.'

'Oh, you little ray of sunshine.' Trish kissed her husband.

Joy turned away. 'Show's over then.'

Kathy was just drawing level with them, trailed by Daniel, thirty yards behind, and without glancing at her, or saying anything else, Joy moved off, heading north, with heavy heart.

'Joy, hang on!' Ruth called.

Joy slowed a little.

'I need some help to keep going this morning - I'm struggling a bit,' Ruth puffed. 'I think I might need the afternoon off.' She pulled out a hanky and paused to mop at her sweating face. 'Will Tony meet us for lunch, do you think?'

'Probably,' Joy said.

'This holiday's been harder than I thought it'd be. I guess I'm just not fit enough, really.'

'I don't think any of us are, except Trish and Rob,' Joy agreed. 'And Brad perhaps.'

'Yes, Brad. Talking of whom, what do you think my chances are?' Ruth asked.

Joy glanced at Ruth, wondering if she was joking. She sounded a bit dreamy.

'You're steaming ahead, girls. Are you buying the first round?' Brad called out from just behind them.

'If it suits the gentleman,' Ruth drawled in an atrocious American accent.

Joy nudged her friend playfully, spotting her rosier than normal cheeks.

Brad caught up with Joy and Ruth and the three of them marched along in companionable silence. He carried the guidebook in his hand, referring to it from time to time.

Joy glanced at him surreptitiously from behind her sunglasses. It was as though they'd never spoken at all the night before.

Look at him now - bright and chirpy, with a spring in his step, you'd think he hadn't a care in the world. It was plain to see last night that he will never get over Jen's death; her memory will stand in the way of any relationship. He hides it well, just like me. Here I am with more shit than a pig farm in my life - and does anyone suspect? Nope, they don't know the half of it. They think my life is perfect. Thanks for that, Mother. If I learned nothing else from you during those miserable teenage years, I learnt how to be distant, how to put on a face that others expect to see, to be agreeable, prim and proper, and keep my feelings under wraps.

Ruth and Brad struck up a conversation about nothing in particular, which quickly rose to a passionate debate about the Labour Party. She slowed down, choosing to opt out of the small group. Maybe Ruth did have a chance with him. Joy didn't really think so. Still there was no harm in Ruth having a little fun trying.

VI

Kathy was confused and mystified by Joy's frostiness at breakfast. She still hadn't spoken two words to her, and had moved away very obviously, whenever Kathy got close.

She'd tried talking to Daniel, when the two of them were lagging behind earlier.

'You look exhausted,' she said. 'Maybe you should have taken the morning off.'

He just grunted. Not to be deterred, she took a braver approach.

'I take it you finally got Joy to listen to your side of the story. The atmosphere seemed quite charged around the two of you last night.'

Daniel glared at her.

'Why are you asking?' he snapped. 'You told me I was a bastard the other day. *She's* your friend, and you couldn't give two fucks about me, so just keep your nose out.'

'That's not fair,' Kathy said, taken aback by the venom in his words. 'I've known the two of you forever. Both of you are my friends. But you messed up, Daniel.'

'So did she,' he muttered under his breath.

Kathy heard, and responded in a flash.

'She had an affair?'

'Huh. If only it were that easy.'

Kathy frowned.

'Look, forget I said anything. I promised her I wouldn't talk about her.'

Impulsively, Kathy put her arms around him. Her normally strong dependable friend looked as though the mountains of Scotland rested on his shoulders.

Shaking off her attempt at a hug, Daniel stopped and sat down on a grassy mound and rested his elbows on his knees. His long lean fingers cupped his face, still covered in two days' worth of dark stubble.

Kathy knew he was crying. She felt like an intruder and wanted to slink away. Instead, she took a step forward, stopping as he reached out to grab her. She sat down beside him, holding his hand.

After a few minutes, he rubbed his eyes with the backs of his hands, tore a length off the toilet roll stuffed in the side pocket of his rucksack, and blew his nose. He drank some water, stood up, and pulled Kathy to her feet.

'I know you want to help and I really appreciate it,' Daniel said, turning to look straight at her. 'But I can't talk about this with you. I'm sorry.'

Kathy nodded. 'I understand. But please talk to someone else about it, Dan,' she said quietly, as they reached the others.

Joy turned around as they approached. She glared at Kathy, who flinched, wondering yet again, what she had done to upset her so much.

The group walked in a long straggling line. All a little subdued, wrapped up in their own thoughts.

Kathy checked her phone again for missed calls or texts. Nothing. It clearly wasn't a good sign and she resigned herself to not having got the job. On the scale of things, it was a minor setback, she told herself. At least Tony was proving easier to live with at the moment.

'Have you got that phone out again?' Trish shouted from ten paces behind her. 'Are you and Tony on a second honeymoon or something?'

'Ha ha!' Kathy retorted, without turning around, and relieved that her sister couldn't see her flaming face.

Seconds later Trish caught her up, and Kathy sighed inwardly.

'I was only joking,' Trish said.
'It's fine.'
'You were walking with Daniel earlier,' Trish said.
'And Ruth. And Rob.' Kathy knew Trish was fishing.

'Yes, but you and Daniel ended up way behind.' Trish raised a questioning eyebrow. 'We waited ages for you to catch up.'

Kathy said nothing; she concentrated on her footsteps, trying not to make eye contact with Trish.

'Did he tell you how it went with Joy yesterday?' Trish asked. 'I know he told her everything, but she hasn't said much.'

'No. He said he can't talk to me about her,' Kathy said. 'But Joy's really off with me today. Did she tell you why?'

Trish hesitated for a second.

'Joy's just off, full stop,' she said lightly.

Trish had taken too long to answer, and Kathy was convinced her sister was keeping something back. She resolved to catch up with Joy in the pub at lunchtime and try to sort things out with her.

The group were gathered near the railway. Kathy and Trish were the last to join them.

Brad led the way, as one by one, they entered the gloomy, low roofed passageway that passed under the railway line.

'It's known as cattle creep,' Rob called out, his voice echoing through the tunnel.

Ruth cringed. 'That's a good name for it. It's creepy as hell.' She shuddered. Then she gave small shriek. 'Ugh,' she said in disgust. 'Is that cow muck I'm walking through?'

Emerging from the tunnel, the group made their way onto a grassy footpath that had once been an old military road. It ran parallel with the road below, and went all the way to Crainlarich. There was no shade at all, and the constant heat was sapping all of their energy. People were definitely getting a little fractious.

Kathy watched the road below, imagining how wonderful it must be to live and work surrounded by such magnificent scenery. *Do the people living in those little cottages down there realise how lucky they are, living in a place like this?* For most of her life, Kathy would have given anything to live in the countryside. The farm Ruth had shared with Paul was just amazing, and Kathy knew she would have been in her element living somewhere like that.

'Oh look, is that our bus down there?' Ruth cried.

The lights flashed as it whizzed past them.

'Can't be. It's going in the wrong direction,' Daniel told her.

'Well, it looked like it,' Ruth grumbled. 'And I'm definitely hitching a ride this afternoon. My feet are killing me.'

'Come on, Ruth. It won't be long until lunchtime.' Kathy linked her arm through Ruth's, hoping to encourage her.

'I think I've got countryside-itus.'

'What's that when it's at home?' Kathy asked.

'I'm allergic to its smells,' Ruth said solemnly. 'It was the tunnel that set me off - that terrible cow smell.'

'Don't tell fibs,' Kathy chuckled.

'I'm not, honest. I get suffocated by all these country smells and wide open spaces. Give me three days in the countryside and I start to go doolally,' grinned Ruth. 'I need shops and nice clothes. And I need to see people; not just farmers in wellies and grubby wax jackets, but men in suits and women in high heels with designer handbags – it doesn't even matter if they're fake.'

They all laughed at Ruth's little speech.

Kathy felt sad for her too, she knew how much it had hurt Ruth to leave Paul and the kids, and that beneath all the wisecracks she was feeling desperately lonely.

Ruth pouted like a sulky child.

'Are we nearly there yet?' she asked.

VII

The pub was pleasantly cool and gloomy after the brightness outside, and the group were all longing to get out of the heat for an hour and have a cold drink. Tony was already inside, sitting at a long table with benches either side. He beckoned Kathy over, patting the seat beside him. An orange juice with ice was waiting for her and she drank it thirstily.

He kissed her, his lips cool on her burning face. 'How did it go?'

'Tough. It's hot out there today. Nobody can believe it. They never get weather like this.'

'Do you want another drink?' Tony asked.

She nodded.

'Get us another orange juice here, Brad.' His voice boomed around the small room. 'Cheers,' he added, when Brad raised his thumb in acknowledgement.

Kathy cringed. He was always so loud. It was embarrassing. Still, she was surprised by his continuing efforts to be nice, although she couldn't help wondering how long it would last.

'Why don't you have the afternoon off?' Tony asked. 'I've checked out Tyndrum, and it's a cosy little town. We could explore, have a few beers, check in early...' He winked. 'What do you think?'

'I can't, Tony.' Kathy shook her head. 'I missed yesterday morning, and if I miss any more days, I won't be able to say I walked The West Highland Way. Not really, anyway - and I want to.' She was trying to be firm, knowing it sounded slightly as if she was pleading with him.

'This is something I really want to do. OK?' she finished, with more conviction than she felt.

He wiped the condensation off his pint glass, and said nothing. Kathy was convinced she'd blown it and that he was about to go off on one any second, just when everyone had sat down around the table.

'The days get a bit long sometimes, you know,' he said quietly.

'I know,' she whispered. She was determined not to back down. 'But you knew what it would be like before you came, didn't you?' she added.

Right on cue, Ruth's voice broke into their conversation.

'Tony!' she yelled up the table. 'I need an afternoon off. Any chance of a lift into Tyndrum after lunch?'

'There you go.' Kathy smiled. A bit of company for the afternoon.'

'Great,' Tony replied. He didn't return the smile; he didn't go off on one either. 'No problem,' he called back to Ruth.

Kathy felt her phone vibrate in her pocket. It wasn't stopping, which meant a phone call, not a text. She didn't dare pull it out in front of Tony, so she let it go to voicemail. She was glad now that she had set a proper voice message before she'd come away. She'd agonised over it for days, hating the sound of her own voice; trying to sound professional and confident, yet not too assertive. She wondered if they would leave a message, and if the call was about the job. It could be Alison or one of the boys. The vibration stopped. She waited. A few seconds later, it went off again, shorter this time. That was a message. She had butterflies in her stomach. Desperate to check it out she made her excuses and dashed to the ladies; locking the cubicle door, before she dared pull her phone from her pocket.

You have one new voicemail, the message told her.

Her fingers shook as she pressed the numbers and hit call. She placed the phone to her ear and waited.

'This message was left today at 12.55pm.'

'Hello Kathy, this is George Williams, Williams & Son... regarding your recent job interview... unsuccessful on this occasion...'

Kathy's heart sank. Unsuccessful was all she'd heard. His voice continued, droning in her ear but she wasn't listening. She felt gutted and wiped away an angry tear.

What was I thinking of anyway; pinning all my hopes on a part time job on a poxy industrial estate. It would never have paid the bills.

She held her breath as she heard someone come in. It was probably one of the girls- there weren't too many other people in the pub. She wiped her face and took a deep breath. A minute or two later, feeling in control once more, Kathy left the cubicle.

Joy was at the washbasin, splashing water on her face and then patting it dry with the hand towel she'd pulled from her rucksack. She massaged sun cream into her shoulders and around her neck, ran lip-gloss around her lips, and then brushed her hair, all the while looking at her reflection, and not once acknowledging Kathy's presence.

Kathy looked into the mirror at Joy's reflection.

'Joy, will you talk to me? It's obvious I've done something to upset you. I'm damned if I know what it is.'

Without a word, Joy turned to Kathy and glared at her, before flouncing out, letting the door slam behind her.

*****

An hour later, everyone had finished their lunch and they began gathering up their belongings ready for the next stretch.

Ruth was still keen to go in the bus with Tony.

'You will come for a walk-around with me, won't you?' she asked Tony, who was standing beside the open bus.

'Oh, I don't know,' he grunted. 'I like to have a kip in the afternoons.'

'Come on,' Ruth said nudging him playfully in the ribs. 'You'll sleep like a baby after a brisk walk.'

'We'll see,' Tony muttered, kicking one of the back tyres.

Trish rummaged in her bag for sun cream, and then began rubbing it into the back of Rob's neck as he and Brad stood discussing the football match that they hoped to watch later that evening.

Seeing Joy standing alone, rhythmically tapping her walking pole as she waited for the others, Kathy tried again to talk to her.

She looked her square in the eyes 'We've been friends long enough to be straight with each other. Now will you just tell me what I've done to upset you?' she pleaded.

Joy's eyes glistened, changing from blue, to grey, to silver ice, as she stared at Kathy.

'We all know your husband's a bullying bastard,' she began. 'But what gives you the right to steal somebody else's husband?' Her voice rose with every syllable. 'Keep your hands off Daniel. All right?' She jabbed Kathy in the chest before striding away.

Kathy was shaking. She hadn't a clue where Joy's outburst had come from. She only hoped the others hadn't heard. She glanced around. Everyone still seemed pre-occupied –where was Tony? She couldn't see him.

She sighed with relief as Tony emerged from behind the bus, with Ruth following behind him.

What am I to do about Joy? Maybe Trish can talk to her and find out what I'm supposed to have done.

*****

'Let's get moving, guys.' Rob pointed to the path with his walking pole 'This way.'

'Have a lovely time; don't walk too hard,' Ruth said, smiling and waving through the open bus window.

'Go on, be off with you, you dosser,' Trish replied, giving her an exaggerated wink.

The group quickly got into their stride again, quiet in their tranquil surroundings, as they left Crainlarich behind them.

Knowing her own T-shirt was damp with sweat Kathy idly studied the varying degrees of moisture on the backs of those walking a few strides ahead of her.

Trish fell into step beside her.

'I never thought I'd be asking for rain on my holiday, but today I'd give anything for it,' she said. 'Nothing too dramatic though. A ten-minute shower would do the trick, don't you think?'

'Mmm.'

'Don't sound too enthusiastic, Kathy, will you?'

Kathy turned to her sister.

'Sorry, I was miles away,' she said. Then pointing to Joy, a good thirty metres ahead added, 'She's going to make herself ill, you know. Look at her, head down, back ramrod straight. The angry vibes she's emitting are enough to shrivel up the leaves on every tree she passes.'

'I agree completely. Getting her to talk is like trying to get the last dregs of toothpaste from an almost empty tube.' Trish nodded.

'Huh. She had no problem giving me what for back there. I thought she was going to punch me.' Kathy's voice wavered slightly as she recalled the encounter.

'Come off it, Kath. Joy would never hit anyone, least of all you. You're one of her best friends,' Trish said.

'Well, I tell you, she's losing it big time. You should have heard the venom in her voice and seen the hatred in her eyes as she poked me in the chest and accused me of stealing...' Kathy's voice shook, as she tried not to cry, '... her husband.' She sniffed as she searched for a tissue in her pocket.

'Oh, for fuck's sake,' Trish snapped. She put an arm around Kathy's shoulders. 'That woman needs to get this mess with Daniel sorted before she destroys more than her marriage. Until she does she's like a walking time bomb.'

'Why, Trish? How could she think I would do a thing like that?'

'She's just trying to make sense of everything.'

'He had an affair. With some girl called Stephanie - years ago. Not with me. I wouldn't do that. Not to her; or to any other woman for that matter.'

'I know that, and she does too - when she's thinking straight. The trouble is that she's not. She's weaving things together; and seeing incriminating evidence in perfectly innocent activity. She's putting two and two together and coming up with a dozen.'

Kathy knew Trish cared for Joy as much as she did, and was defending her actions, but as much as she cared, right now, Kathy just needed answers.

'You do realise that if she says any of this to Tony, there'll be murder... probably mine,' Kathy said. 'He's not going to listen to my side of the story.'

'She saw you kissing Daniel,' Trish whispered.

'What?'

'Shhh, keep your voice down.' Trish pulled her to a halt. 'The fewer people know what's going on, the better,' she said, looking directly into Kathy's eyes.

'When?' Kathy was totally shocked.

She racked her brain, trying to figure out what possible scenario Joy could have witnessed that would make her think she had seen her and Daniel kissing.

'It was in the bar last night,' Trish said with a sigh. 'She said you were all over each other.'

Kathy shook her head.

'No way,' she said. 'She's totally lost the plot.'

'She saw you kissing. He had his arm around you and you were hanging off his neck, and then you left together.' Trish looked at her sister. 'She's convinced you went off to bed with him right there and then.'

Kathy saw the look of doubt on Trish's face, and realised that she didn't trust her.

'That's ridiculous,' she raged. 'I've a good mind to go up to her right now and shake her out of this crazy hole she's digging herself into.'

Trish gripped Kathy's arm tightly.

'Calm down,' she told her. 'She'll only take your anger as guilt.'

'I might be guilty of a lot of things, but not of cheating with my best friend's husband,' Kathy hissed.

Rob turned around at their raised voices and gave them a quizzical look.

Trish waved a hand at him, giving him a clear gesture to keep out of it.

Kathy took a deep breath. 'I was very drunk last night and happy for once. Tony was being really nice to me. It was as if we were young again. I went looking for him, to say I was going to bed, when I bumped into Daniel... literally. He put his arm around me to stop me falling. I kissed him to say thank you. Because I was happy... and pissed, perhaps the kiss looked like it was more than it was.'

She looked at Trish for reassurance that she believed her story. 'He took me out into reception to find Tony, which we did. And Tony carried me up the stairs to our room. End of story,' she added.

'I believe you.'
'But will she?'

'Maybe. I'll try and talk to her first. It might be better for both of you, if you have a mediator,' she said. 'You need to remember that she's in a dark place at the moment, where there are no rational thoughts.' Trish hugged her sister briefly.

'You have to make her see sense Trish. This is such a bloody mess.' Kathy saw Rob turn and walk back along the path to join them, and she ended the conversation abruptly.

*****

'What is it with you girls today?' he asked as he reached them. 'You two are trailing behind, and Joy is half a mile in front. Am I missing something?' He gave them a good-natured smile.

'No, darling, just girl talk,' Trish said sweetly. She stroked his face gently with both hands, before cupping his chin and kissing him on the lips.

'And now I'm off to do a little more girl talk. See you later,' she said and jogged off ahead to catch up with Joy.

Rob shrugged his shoulders. 'Women,' he said, to nobody in particular.

IX

Kathy gave the men a brief smile as she passed them. She was still seething over Joy's accusations. She was also annoyed with herself for getting so drunk the night before. She took a few deep breaths and thought how difficult her escape plan was going to be now that she hadn't got the job – even without the added complication of Tony getting wind of some imaginary affair between her and Daniel.

The Way meandered pleasantly through the forest plantation, where the grass verges, protected from the scorching heat by the canopy of conifers, were still a lush green. Kathy was lost in thought as she trekked along the footpath. So much so that, when Brad fell into step beside her, she barely acknowledged his presence. After a few minutes, impressed with his restraint in not interrupting her thinking time, Kathy finally broke the silence.

'You didn't fancy an afternoon off then?' she asked, deliberately lifting her voice, in an effort to hide her frustration and disappointment at recent events.

'Not at all. I'm actually really enjoying the walking. Anyway, what would I do all afternoon?' he said. 'I'd probably end up ringing the office,' he added with a grin.

Kathy rose to the bait.

'I hope not. We had an agreement,' she said. 'You haven't rung in already, have you? I bet you have. You just can't help yourself, can you?'

'Calm down.' Brad was laughing at her. 'I haven't rung the office, ok? I never renege on a deal and we had a deal, didn't we?'

'We did.' Kathy nodded.

'Talking of which, have you given any thought to a theme?'

'A theme?'

'Yes, for my apartment. I was thinking football. Maybe red and white, the Boro colours...'

Kathy pushed up her sunglasses and stared at him.

'What do you think?' he asked, frowning.

'You've got to be joking, right?'

'Gottcha!'

Kathy punched him in the arm, while trying unsuccessfully to keep a straight face.

'That's better. You were looking way too serious earlier. You should laugh more often. In fact, we all should. Apparently it's good for our health.'

As Kathy relaxed, she found herself warming to Brad more and more. They walked in silence for a while, and the quietness between them felt comfortable.

A low murmur of voices floated towards them, from Rob and Daniel walking behind. She could see Trish and Joy ahead and wondered once again, what was going on in Joy's head.

Where is all this shit about me making a play for Daniel coming from?

'You're frowning again,' Brad said, interrupting her daydreaming.

'Can I trust you?' Kathy shocked herself with the question.

'One hundred percent.'

Kathy didn't miss his serious tone, and it gave her confidence to go on.

'This is so top secret I can't believe I'm speaking the words out loud, let alone telling a virtual stranger,' Kathy whispered.

'I'd like to think I'm more than a stranger, Kathy.'

'Sorry. I didn't mean it like that. It's just that this is about people here, and there are enough rumours flying about.'

'Whatever you say will go no further than me and this mountainside,' Brad said. 'Cross my heart and hope to die.'

Kathy nodded.

'And most definitely nowhere near Tony,' he added.

Kathy's heart hammered in her chest.

'Why Tony especially?'

'Come on, Kathy, I'm not blind; or stupid for that matter. I've seen the way he treats you and how withdrawn - scared almost - you are around him.'

The silence stretched between them as Kathy psyched herself up to speak. She was surprised at his perceptiveness.

'I don't know where to begin really.'

'Is the beginning too obvious?' he asked gently.

'Too difficult.'

'OK, try lunchtime,' Brad suggested. 'You looked distracted, upset, angry even...'

'Disappointed.' She sighed. 'And angry... and upset as well, I guess.'

'Why?'

She felt the smoothness of her phone as she pushed her hand into her pocket. 'I applied for a job a few weeks ago. Only a part time position, office admin stuff. But I really wanted it, you know?'

She looked up.

Trish and Joy were just ahead of them.

I should be talking to the two of you about this, not a stranger.

Kathy sighed.

'Anyway, I didn't get the job. My phone rang at lunchtime but I couldn't answer it. Tony has no idea about the job. He'd go ape. So I had to dash off to the loo to listen to the voicemail.'

Brad nodded with understanding. 'There were probably loads of applicants...'

'I know, younger, more experienced, and all that. It's just a kick in the teeth, that's all. I'll have to keep looking, and something else will come along eventually, I suppose. It's just that I'm so desperate to get out...'

'What, out of the house? You can do that by helping me with the apartment. I'll pay you, you know.'

Kathy shook her head.

'It's more than that. Out of the house, out of the marriage, out of my life,' she whispered.

'That's a lot of "out ofs", Kathy.' Brad looked concerned.

'I've thought of nothing else for the past twelve months. I've had enough of thinking. It's time to act. I feel suffocated, Brad. I can't stand it.' Kathy forced the words past the lump in her throat, willing herself not to cry.

Brad said nothing.

'Sorry, I shouldn't be putting this on you,' she said. 'I have to do something. I'm thirty-five going on sixty. My life feels like it's over already, I may as well be six foot under.'

Brad looked shocked.

'That's a terrible thing to say,' he said. 'What about your daughter? Alison, isn't it? How old is she?'

'She's ten - and I know it's terrible to think this way, which is why I have to do something.' Kathy was angry now. 'And why I've taken computer courses and why I'm looking for a job,' she snapped.

It hurt her that Brad could think she didn't care about Alison. The lump in her throat wasn't receding.

'This is all coming out wrong.' She sniffed, loudly.

'I didn't mean to make you cry, I'm sorry.' Brad fished in his pocket and produced a packet of tissues. 'Here.' He handed one to her. 'Please stop crying, otherwise I'll have to give you a hug, and that might set tongues wagging.'

'Things can't get any worse, I've already been accused of messing around today. The sight of me with another man's arms around me wouldn't make any difference,' she said. And indeed at this point, she wanted nothing more than to lay her head against his chest and cry her heart out.

'In that case, come here.' He pulled her to him, wrapped his strong arms around her, and kissed the top of her head, before releasing her again just as quickly.

As brief an encounter as it was, Kathy languished in the sensations: the smell of sun cream and spicy aftershave, the rhythmic beat of his heart beneath her ear pressed against his chest, the featherlike touch of his kiss on the top of her head. She committed them all to memory, to be replayed later, when she was alone. In that fleeting moment she felt protected against the world. She wondered what it would be like to kiss him. Would his lips be warm or cool?

'Now,' he said. 'Dry your eyes, and let's work out the next step.'

Kathy snapped out of her daydream.

'What was the name of the company you applied to?' Brad asked her.

'Williams & Son, on the Skippers Lane estate,' Kathy told him, still a little distracted by his closeness.

'The window company?' Brad asked.

Kathy nodded.

'Then it's probably just as well you didn't get the job. They're a client of ours - an absolute nightmare to deal with. You're worth more than that, Kathy. We'll find you something.'

'We?' she asked.

'Yes. I'll help you,' Brad said. His tone became businesslike. 'I have a lot of contacts, as well as a large client base; there's always some company or other looking for staff.'

Kathy smiled. He was obviously in his comfort zone.

'That's better,' Brad said.

'What's slowing you two down?' Rob called out.

Kathy jumped, and turned to see Rob and Daniel just feet behind.

'Debating life and the universe - as you do when you're miles from the nearest pub,' Brad replied smoothly, not giving so much as an inkling of what they'd been discussing.

'Well, if I were you, I'd speed up while you carry on your debate. Otherwise it'll be closing time when you do reach the pub,' Rob said over his shoulder as he passed them.

Kathy noticed that the girls were now well out of sight.

'We'd best keep up,' she said.

'Wait a second.' Brad touched her arm.

He crouched down, fiddling with his boot. After a minute or two, he looked up.

'I wanted them to get far enough ahead to be out of earshot,' he said.

Kathy suddenly felt the urge to kiss him again.

Does he really care about me? This is madness; I can't believe I'm even thinking this.

They set off again, confident now that the others couldn't hear their conversation.

'Now,' he said. 'What kind of job are you looking for? Would it be purely a means to an end, or would you like to build some kind of career from it?'

'A career?' Kathy laughed. 'I don't think so. I'm a bit old to be starting a career.'

'You're thirty-five, not fifty-five, Kathy,' he said. 'You've got a good twenty-five working years ahead of you; plenty of time to build a career.'

'Brad, get real, will you?' Kathy shook her head, dismissing his words. 'I've never had a job in my whole life; I didn't even finish college, and I've got three kids. I don't think an employer would find me a very attractive candidate,' she said.

'I didn't know you were in college. So did you have a career in mind at that point?'

'I wanted to be an accountant,' she said. Her voice fell flat as she remembered all her broken dreams. 'Then I got pregnant, got married, and got pregnant again.' She sighed. 'And the rest, as they say, is history. So, Mr Jameson...' She tried to sound positive. 'An opportunity to use the new skills I've learned, plus earn a few quid, will do me fine for the moment.'

'Being an accountant is a stressful job,' said Brad. 'Just look at me.'

'That's because you haven't got the work/life balance right,' she said, bossily, speaking to him as if he was one of her kids. 'I've told you that already.'

'I'll give you a job.'

Kathy stopped dead in her tracks.

'Say that again,' she said, sure that she had misheard.

He pushed his sunglasses up into his sun-bleached hair and looked her in the eye.

'I said I'll give you a job,' he repeated. 'If you really want a career, and you want to be an accountant – though God only knows why, it's pretty boring, you know, looking at numbers all day – then I'll give you a job. I'll put you through college, pay you a trainee salary, and then, when you qualify, you'll get the going rate.'

Kathy was stunned. She didn't know what to say.

They began walking again.

'Look, have a think about it. You don't have to decide right now.,'

Eventually, Kathy found her voice.

'Why?' she asked.

'I like you, Kathy.' His answer was simple. 'And I like it when you smile. I've come to care about you a lot in the last few days, I want to see you happy – and I want to help. The offer of a job is my way of doing that. I do have one condition though.'

'What's that?'

'We have to renovate the apartment first... and we both agree to be honest. If the job isn't working out for either of us, we call it quits and don't let it ruin our friendship.' He held out a hand to her. 'Deal?'

She took his hand, and then impulsively she hugged him instead. The temptation to kiss him was so strong she had to pull away.

'That's two conditions,' she said shakily.

'Then we're even.' He laughed.

'Can I think about it?'

'Take all the time you need. The offer will still be there in six weeks or six months.'

'Thanks, Brad.'

He looked at his watch and frowned slightly. 'Now, perhaps Rob had a point about closing time at the pub – let's step it up a gear.' He placed his hand beneath her elbow and propelled her forward until they were jogging along the footpath giggling like teenagers.

X

Joy yanked up her T-shirt and used it to wipe away the sweat that was running down her forehead, before it dripped into her eyes. She let her tears flow, however, tasting their salty wetness on her hot, dry lips, and knowing that the others were too far behind to see her distress.

She was walking at a relentless pace - too much in the heat of the afternoon sun. She could feel her heart pounding against her rib cage, and her breath came in short gasps, but she didn't care. She wanted to hurt. She wanted to feel so much physical pain that it made her cry.

God, I need to release this pressure before I do something I'll regret. Look what happened with Kathy back there. I wanted to hit her and keep on hitting her. How did I get into this state? I'm disgusted with myself. How could I think that of Kathy? Because all the signs are obvious, and I saw with my own eyes, that's how.

'Joy!' Trish's voice hurtled through the space between them.

Joy turned, instinctively.

'Wait up, will you?' gasped Trish, continuing to jog towards her.

Joy slowed down, but didn't stop. She needed the time it would take Trish to catch up, in order to compose herself. She took several deep breaths, and pulled out her water bottle, gulping thirstily, before splashing the tepid water on her face. She ran her hands through her hair, smoothing away the damp tendrils that clung to her forehead, and hid her telltale, red eyes behind her sunglasses.

'What are you playing at?' Trish panted. She grabbed Joy's wrist, pulling her to a halt. 'The last thing we need is a visit from Mountain Rescue!'

'What are you on about?' Joy forced normality into her voice.

'You, storming ahead like that. Look at the state of you. Your face is like a beetroot, all blotchy from the heat and the sweat is pouring...'

'Do I smell?' Joy interrupted, attempting a joke.

'No,' Trish said. 'I'm not joking, you'll end up dehydrated. You could get really ill or collapse out here, in the middle of nowhere - and that's when we'll be looking for Mountain Rescue,' she finished in a rush.

'Oh, stop being so melodramatic. I'm fine.' Joy said flippantly, trying to keep her anger at bay.

'I'm just worried about you,' Trish persisted.

'Trish, you'll be the one who gets ill, with all this fretting about everyone else. It's not good for you, we're grownups now, you know, well able to fuck up our own lives... and sort them out again – and fuck them up some more....'

'Don't put me in the frame here,' Trish retaliated. 'You're the one who's at boiling point. You're totally stressed out, and you're creating an atmosphere among everyone.'

'I am not.' Joy said. 'I'm perfectly polite when the others are around.' Her voice trailed off.

Nevertheless, she knew that Trish was right, and there was an atmosphere.

I should have just bailed out, said I was ill, gastroenteritis or something, that I couldn't move away from the loo. That would have been convincing enough; then I'd have had time to sort my head out and put a story together. It would have been better than going through all this embarrassing shit, making a complete fool of myself...

'Are you listening?' Trish sounded exasperated.

Joy looked up in confusion.

'Sorry, what did you say?'

'I asked what was all that with Kathy earlier? You scared the life out of her - she thought you were going to hit her,' Trish said.

'I thought I might too,' Joy whispered. 'I just saw red. But if she is messing around with Daniel, and flaunting it in my face, what does she expect me to do?'

'Nothing is going on between her and Daniel,' Trish said. 'She told me what happened. How she was pissed and Daniel caught her when she fell. He helped her find Tony; that was all. No fling, no secret affair; just friends.'

'And you believe her?' Joy gave a brittle laugh. 'Of course you do. She's your sister. Blood's thicker than water and all that crap.'

Trish gave an exasperated sigh. 'Look, Joy, will you just get a grip? Yes, she's my sister, and she's your friend too. We both know she would never do anything to hurt you.'

Joy said nothing, and they walked faster along the footpath, matching each other stride for stride, a wall of ice between them that no amount of heat from the burning sun could begin to thaw.

Joy knew it wouldn't be long before Trish spoke. She hated strained silences and would witter on about anything to avoid them. It's better than having an atmosphere, she'd say. When everyone knew it was just her way of trying to get you talking again, hoping you'd open up and discuss your problems. Then she could find a solution, and all would be well with the world again.

Trish spoke quietly, seemingly undeterred by Joy's lack of response.

'Mum hated it, you know - when Kathy got pregnant. Not so much that she was unlucky enough to get pregnant when she was still a kid, but that she wanted to get married. Mum tried everything to talk her out of it. "I'm at my wits end, Trish," she'd say. "There's something about that lad; he has her wrapped around his little finger, he does." I'd tell her they were in love, and not to be so cynical, but there were endless rows. And Mum pleaded with Kathy not to give up college. "I'll take the bairn. I'll bring it up as my own," she'd say. "Have a bit of a life for yourself first, Kathy, before you settle down." You know Kathy as well as I do, Joy. She had to do things properly. The way Kathy saw it, this was her mess, and she would deal with it. That meant getting married before she was showing and becoming a dutiful wife and mother. "What's the point in finishing college?" she'd said to Mum. "I'm going to be a proper mother." You've no idea how much that hurt Mum. I don't think Kathy meant it, but Mum took it personally. I found her crying in the kitchen. "I just want you girls to have an easier life than I have," she'd tell me. Then she'd blow her nose and get on with cooking the tea. "Mark my words," she'd say. "It'll end in disaster, and that poor little mite will be in the middle of it." Then she'd shake her head sorrowfully.'

Trish paused, although Joy knew the routine, she wasn't ready to contribute to the conversation yet. Anyway, this was nothing new to her. Joy had witnessed the rows between Kathy and her mother, and she'd listened to Kathy's arguments in favour of the marriage. About how great Tony was, and that he loved her to pieces and would make a brilliant dad.

As her best friend, maybe I should have tried to talk some sense into her, but we were seventeen. A wedding was just another excuse to buy a new pair of shoes. We couldn't imagine being thirty, let alone spending the next thirty years living with someone. Waking up beside them every morning, waiting for them to come home every night, consulting them on every decision. And now... now I can't imagine being without Daniel; no matter how awful it is to be with him. Is that why Kathy is still with Tony? Is she scared of being on her own too?

Trish continued her reflection of the past.

'In the end, when she could see that there was no changing Kathy's mind, Mum told Kathy she'd always be there for her whatever she decided. And she has been. She worships the kids, and never says a bad word about Tony – at least not to Kathy anyway.'

'That must be hard for your mum.' The words were out before Joy could stop them.

'Aha.' Trish smiled.

'What?'

'She speaks.'

'Oh, shut up, you.' Joy laughed, feeling some of the tension spilling from her body.

'That's why I'm a walking wreck whenever I've been round to visit,' Trish said. 'Never a month goes by when she doesn't quiz me about Kathy and what's going on. It does my head in, I tell you.'

'It's only because she cares.' Joy used the same words that Trish had spoken not long before.

'I know that, but sometimes...' Trish's voice hardened, 'I wish she'd remember that I'm her daughter too, and that my life isn't always a bed of roses.' She sighed. 'When I had Seb, life was just a nightmare...'

Joy waited a few seconds for Trish to continue.

'Why?' she finally asked. 'What are you talking about?'

'Nothing, I'm just waffling. Anyway, the point of all this is that I care. About you, about Kathy, about Daniel, even. And I truly believe nothing is going on between them.'

Joy shrugged, still not convinced, and distracted from her own problems by Trish's expression.

'What happened when Seb was born?' she asked.

For a second Trish looked like a wounded animal.

'It's not important. Just forget it,' Trish said, walking half a stride ahead of Joy; just enough to avoid eye contact.

XI

During the final couple of miles to Tyndrum, their stop-off for the night, the bristling tension between Joy and Trish abated. And while their silence was no longer hostile and their shoulders were relaxed, their legs were weary as they passed through the gateway and turned right, along the narrow footpath leading into the town.

'Civilisation at last!' Trish said, breaking the silence. 'There has to be a very cold pint of cider with my name on it, waiting in Paddy's Bar.' She licked her lips and smiled at the thought.

'I'll fight you for it,' Joy said. She could almost taste the sweet amber liquid, and feel the fizzy bubbles sliding down her parched throat. 'Anyway, how do you know there's a pub called Paddy's?'

'Don't you remember?' Trish asked, surprised. 'It's a part of the hotel we're booked into.'

'Oh yes,' Joy said, distracted. Then she pointed and frowned. 'Is that Ruth?'

Trish shielded her eyes, peering into the distance. 'I think so. What is she wearing on her feet?'

A loud whistle came from one of the men a few yards behind, and Ruth waved frantically.

'It looks like she's wearing wellies.' Joy sounded perplexed. 'Why on earth would she be wearing wellies? Its twenty-five degrees out here, and as dry as a five-hundred-year-old bone.'

'And with a skirt? She is a serious worry at times.' Trish laughed.

Joy shook her head. 'And you thought I was the one to be worrying over. You were obviously focusing your attention in the wrong direction,' she said with a playful smile.

'It's good to see you smiling anyway,' returned Trish.

Joy gave her a nudge, before calling out to Ruth.

'You'll be locked up, walking the streets dressed like that!'

'What?' Ruth yelled back. 'Don't you like them?'

As she drew closer, Ruth held out a foot, showing off a lime green welly covered in daisies, their white petals surrounding bright yellow centres.

'They're lovely,' Joy told her friend, 'for the appropriate location and occasion.'

'That would be St Luke's, in the company of men in white coats,' Trish joined in.

'Oi! Less of your cheek,' Ruth quipped, before turning her attention to the others behind. 'What do you think, guys?'

She did a little jig along the footpath, her indigo cotton skirt swirling around her flamboyant wellies. 'You lot look wrecked,' she sang out, still dancing. 'Was it a hard stretch?'

'No, not really, just hot,' Brad said. 'Although I do think we're all in need of some liquid refreshment,' he added, looking at Kathy walking beside him.

'Absolutely,' Kathy said, nodding in agreement.

Ruth linked arms with Kathy and whispered, 'Tony's having a snooze I walked the legs off him.'

'Really?'

'No, course not! He came into The Green Welly with me for two minutes, and then he said he needed to get something from the bus. Next time I saw him was in Paddy's Bar, three sheets to the wind.'

'That sounds more like him. He doesn't do shopping,' Kathy said trying to suppress a sigh.

The after-effects from the night before were taking their toll now, and she was tired. The last thing she needed was Tony's aggressive behaviour after an afternoon's binge drinking.

'He wanted me to have a drink with him but I thought he'd had enough,' Ruth told her. 'He was all gaga about how much he loves you and how beautiful you are! I sent him off to bed before I threw up.'

'Give over,' Kathy said, a little embarrassed. 'Let's hope he's sobered up before we meet later. I can do without my virtues being bandied about the dinner table.' Conscious of Brad beside her and wary of a difficult evening ahead, she was trying to keep the conversation light.

They passed by the railway crossing and walked the short distance through Tyndrum to Paddy's Bar.

Ruth rounded everyone up outside the entrance to the hotel.

'Now, before we go inside, you need to know about a little hiccup in the arrangements that I encountered when I checked in earlier,' she told them.

'Please don't tell us we're double booked. I'm desperate for a shower,' said Joy.

'No, it's not that bad.'

'So what is it then?' Rob asked.

'They booked us four doubles, instead of three doubles and two singles. We tried to change it but they're fully booked, the best they can offer is to change a double bed to two singles in one of the rooms.'

'OK, so how do we work this then?' Trish asked, looking around for suggestions.

'Well, I don't mind sharing with Brad - if he's game.' Ruth winked.

'Don't worry, I'll spare your blushes, Brad,' Joy piped up quickly. 'I'll share with Ruth, you go with Daniel. That's ok with you, isn't it, Dan?'

Brad looked at Daniel. 'Do you mind?'

'Do you snore?'

'Not that I've heard,' Brad replied, getting a smile from Daniel and a ripple of laughter from the others.

'Right, now that's sorted, let's get to the bar, pronto.' Rob pushed open the door.

'I think it would be a good idea to freshen up and get changed first,' Trish called after him.

'Don't be daft!' Rob tossed the words over his shoulder. 'Look, I'm sure plenty of other weary travellers in here smell as sweet as we do.'

'What about that glass of cold cider we've been salivating over for the last mile and a half?' Joy reminded Trish.

'Mmm... Oh what the hell! Come on, let's have that drink.' Trish put her hands on Rob's shoulders, and steered him towards the bar.

'Spoilsport.' Ruth grinned. 'I quite fancied a cosy night with Brad,' she said.

Joy gave a chuckle as they followed the others into the bar.

The bar was quite busy, for five in the afternoon. They managed to find a couple of tables by the window. Rob and Brad pushed them together and Trish cleared away the empty glasses.

She took them up to the bar.

'Do I get a discount for clearing tables?' she asked the young barman, giving him a wink.

He gave her a sheepish smile.

She helped Daniel to carry the round of drinks back to the table.

Brad tapped the side of his glass.

'I think we should congratulate ourselves,' he announced. 'We've passed the halfway point now. Only forty-something miles to go.' He raised his glass. 'Cheers, everyone.'

'Cheers!' they said in unison, clinking glasses.

'So what did you get up to all afternoon, apart from buying eccentric footwear?' Joy asked Ruth.

'Oh, I just moseyed around. Checked in, took a shower, and went for a stroll. This is a lovely little village, buzzing with activity - it has a really nice feel to it.'

'You certainly look smitten.'

'Why don't you get changed and come for a wander with me?' Ruth said. 'I can show you the sights and where to buy this wonderful footwear.' She wriggled her feet.

Joy drained her glass and stood up.

'OK, give me ten minutes to get changed. Do I need to check in?'

'Just sign in at reception and I'll show you where our room is,' Ruth said. She sat down between Trish and Kathy. 'How about you two? Will you join us on a sightseeing tour of Tyndrum?'

'We might catch up with you later.' Trish sloshed the small amount of cider left in her glass. 'I think I'll have another first.'

Ruth linked Joy's arm in hers as they left the bar. 'They look a bit serious back there do you think?' she said.

'Probably talking about me,' Joy muttered.

'Why would they be talking about you?' Ruth tossed her head and looked surprised. 'It's more likely they're saying look at that mad cow in her flower power wellies.'

'You could be right.' Joy smiled, relieved by Ruth's light-hearted reply. 'Give me a sec,' she said, as they reached the reception desk.

XII

Kathy watched Joy and Ruth leave the bar. 'So did you speak to her?' she turned to ask Trish.

Trish nodded. 'We can't talk here,' she whispered, looking over at Daniel.

Kathy followed her gaze. Daniel appeared to be in a world of his own, sitting beside Brad and Rob, who were discussing a tennis match showing on the TV screen in the corner above the bar.

'Do you girls want another?' Rob asked, winking at Trish from across the table.

'No, thanks. I think I'll go and grab that shower after all,' Trish said. 'Are you coming up?' She stretched out her hand to him invitingly.

'I'll have another with the lads first, if that's all right with you.' Rob took her hand and raised it to his lips, kissing her fingers.

'Of course, my darling,' Trish answered theatrically, making Kathy smile.

'What about you, Kathy?' Rob asked.

'I'm ready for a shower too,' Kathy said. 'See you guys later.'

'So what happened?' Kathy asked as soon as they were out of earshot.

'Come up to my room and I'll tell you.'

As Trish made small talk while they wandered the corridors, Kathy's stomach churned with dread.

Trish is stalling for time, I know she is. Things can't have gone well. Joy doesn't believe me, but does Trish? Or is she on Joy's side?

Trish let them into the room.

'Did you tell her? What did she say?' Kathy tripped over her words. She perched on the edge of the bed, wringing her hands together.

'The honest truth?'

Kathy nodded. 'Of course.'

'I really don't know what to tell you.' Trish sighed. 'She's angry, understandably. Her husband has just told her he had an affair. She saw the two of you and put two and two together, making six. I don't even know if she was listening to me half the time. I think you'll just have to give her a little while to get her head around things.'

'I suppose so.' Kathy began pacing the floor. 'I'm just worried about Tony getting wind of her wild accusations. If he does, God knows what will happen.'

'Calm down, it won't come to that.' Trish tried to reassure her sister with a hug. Kathy shook her off distractedly.

Trish sighed. 'I'm going for that shower, stay here a while if you want.'

'Its fine, I need to check on Tony.' Kathy opened the door, hating herself, knowing she'd hurt Trish by dodging her hug. 'I'll meet you downstairs in an hour.'

XIV

Kathy could hear the shower going and Tony humming something unrecognisable when she went into their room. She sighed inwardly, closing the door as quietly as possible. She'd hoped he'd be sleeping off the effects of his afternoon session; allowing her to soak her aching limbs, while reflecting on the day's events.

Now he'll be expecting me to join him in the shower and everything that goes with it.

Kathy was seriously considering skipping the shower and making a swift exit when Tony walked out of the bathroom, naked bar the towel around his neck. He was rubbing at his hair. She turned away and began rummaging in her suitcase.

'Hello, gorgeous,' he said, wrapping his arms around her from behind. His breath smelt of toothpaste with a lingering tinge of lager, as he nuzzled her neck.

Feeling vulnerable, she tried to pull away.

'Hi, yourself,' she said lightly, still trying to free herself. 'I'm all sweaty, Tony, I need a bath.'

'You should have joined me in the shower,' he whispered, moving his hands upwards inside her T-shirt.

She felt his interest growing. 'Give me ten minutes,' she said as she wriggled free and bolted for the bathroom.

'How about you give me ten minutes? I've been lonely without you,' he said, following her.

Without answering, Kathy ran the bath, pouring in a liberal amount of the complimentary bath oil from the glass shelf above the basin. She stiffened as Tony pulled her into his arms again.

'This bath looks big enough for two,' he said, kissing her. 'And I don't mind getting wet again.'

At first, she responded, enjoying the gentle pressure of his lips and his hand ruffling her hair at the back of her head. Then her back was up against the open bathroom door, his heavy weight pressed against her, and his fingers gripping her hair so tightly her scalp began to ache.

'Tony!' She pulled her mouth away and tried to push him off her.

'Ah, come on, Kath,' he groaned, not releasing his hold.

'Will you just let me go?' she pleaded.

He dropped his hands, leaving them hanging limply by his side, but didn't step away.

'I asked for ten minutes, that's all,' Kathy whispered. 'A relaxing soak in the bath. Is that too much to ask for?' She looked him in the eye and took a deep breath. 'What happened to all those promises you made yesterday; of changing, doing whatever I wanted because you didn't want to lose me?' She was shaking inside but she kept her voice strong.

Saying nothing, Tony walked away.

Kathy watched him pull on T-shirt and shorts then flop onto the bed and switch on the TV.

'I won't be long,' she said, closing the bathroom door with a quiet click.

XV

'This will be like old times,' Ruth said, bouncing on the double bed like an excited teenager. 'Are you sure you don't mind sharing? I'd have been more than happy to share with Brad,' she added, with a twinkle in her eye.

Joy laughed. 'I really don't mind, but we won't have a bed to sleep in if you don't sit still.' She rummaged in her suitcase, pulling out clean underwear. 'I'm having a shower,' she said.

Joy went into the bathroom. A second later, she stuck her head around the bathroom door.

'You terrified the life out of him,' she called out to Ruth. 'He was ready to run all the way to Fort William, rather than share with a temptress like you.'

'You cheeky mare.' Ruth laughed and threw a pillow at Joy's disappearing head.

Inside the shower cubicle, as the water cascaded over her sunburned shoulders, Joy gave herself a stern talking to.

I'll have to speak to Kathy tonight, give her a chance to explain. Trish was right, I know Kathy isn't capable of doing anything to hurt a friend. It did look like something was going on. Surely, no one could blame me for being suspicious.

I have to start thinking logically about things. If I alienate my friends now, what chance do I have of their support once they know what I've done?

I know one thing for sure anyway: Daniel will be relieved I offered to share with Ruth tonight. The little bit of breathing space might help us talk more rationally about all this shit... just so long as he doesn't go spilling his guts to Brad in the middle of the night. That's all I need in the morning, a lecture from Mr Perfect.

Emerging from the bathroom in a short cotton robe, Joy proceeded to set up the travel iron. She placed a towel on the dressing table and began smoothing out the creases in the simple white, cotton sundress. She was conscious of Ruth watching her, but thought it would appear churlish if she took the dress into the bathroom. She dropped her robe, revealing her evenly tanned and toned petite frame, in white lace matching underwear, before slipping the dress over her head.

'God, you are soooo unfair,' Ruth groaned, raising her eyes to the ceiling. 'Why does she get a body like that and I end up looking like a dollop of lard?'

Joy wished she had gone into the bathroom now.

'You look nothing of the sort,' she said, hoping to comfort her friend.

Ruth was curled in the foetus position in the middle of the bed.

'You have a wonderful, womanly figure,' Joy told her.

'Fat.'

'Curvy.' Joy pulled her to her feet. 'Now come on, let's get out of here.'

XVI

Joy and Ruth left the hotel through the main entrance and stepped outside into the balmy evening sunshine. They quickly merged with the swarming mix of walkers, tourists, and locals on the street outside.

'Come this way, I want to show you something.' Ruth turned to follow the road sign posted Lower Tyndrum Station.

'I thought we were going to the Green Welly?' Joy frowned.

'Mmm, we are. I just wanted to take another look down here first.'

Joy had to admit it was lovely, strolling around this pretty village with its white houses nestled amongst pine trees, and surrounded by mountains. All set against the backdrop of a cloudless blue sky. Despite having walked twelve miles already that day, her feet didn't ache at all. Free from the restraints of cumbersome boots, with the soft breeze tickling her bare arms and legs, and lifting her hair, she felt light and free, like she was walking on air, as she sauntered alongside her friend. And she'd forgotten what good company Ruth could be.

'What are we looking for?' she asked.

'It's just along here. Come on, we're nearly there.' Ruth pushed up her sunglasses. Her blue eyes were bright and dancing with fun.

A few moments later, they stopped outside a beautiful old lodge. Shiny black iron gates were invitingly open, and a pristine 'Vacancies' sign creaked gently, despite the lack of a breath of wind.

'It's lovely.' Joy gave what she assumed was the expected comment. 'Really lovely,' she added, at the sight of Ruth's wide grin. 'Pity we didn't see it on the internet, we could have stayed here.'

'I want to buy it,' Ruth gushed.

'You what?'

'I want to buy it and run the B&B.'

Her enthusiasm was infectious and Joy found herself jumping in on the dream.

'I'll go shares with you,' she cried. 'You can do the breakfasts and I'll look after the beds.'

'Oh yes, and what about Daniel?' Ruth laughed.

'I'm sure it wouldn't take him long to find a replacement bed warmer. There's probably one lurking in the hall cupboard as we speak.' Joy said, with more than a hint of sarcasm.

Ruth laughed.

'I think this gravel might have to go. Lovely as it looks and despite the fact that I do like the crunching sound, it's murder when it gets between your toes,' Ruth said as she steered Joy up the driveway.

'What are we doing?' Joy whispered.

They stopped a few yards from the open front door.

'It's OK. I cleared it with Jane. It's her house. I want to show you around properly. Get a second opinion.'

'A second opinion?' Joy was puzzled. 'On what exactly? I thought we were just larking about.'

'No.' Ruth gazed at the grey stone building. 'I mean it.'

Taken aback at Ruth's serious tone, Joy looked up at the large house. Three freshly scrubbed stone steps led up to the front entrance. The forest green paintwork on the double doors was gleaming. The doors were flanked both sides by massive bay windows that continued up to the first floor. Higher still, three attic windows with shiny white lattice fascia rose out of the neat slated roof. Tall grey chimneystacks stood like sentinels on the gable ends.

'It's lovely,' Joy agreed. 'But Ruth, this is the West of Scotland; we're hundreds of miles away from home.'

'Look, do me a favour. Just come and have a look around. Forget about the location for a few minutes... please.'

'OK, but we can't just go waltzing inside like this.' Joy paused to admire the mosaic tiled floor in the entrance.

The inner glass door opened and a tall, painfully thin woman in her late fifties, with tightly cropped salt and pepper hair, smiled at them.

'Hello again,' she said, reaching out for Ruth's hand.

'Hi, Jane, this is my friend Joy, I've brought her to have a look around if that's still ok.'

'Of course, come in, come in.' Jane ushered them into a long wide hallway. 'It's nice to meet you, Joy.'

Smiling politely, Joy took Jane's hand, which was cold despite the heat of the day, and the skin felt paper-thin. She noticed too how her eyes, pale watery blue in colour, looked too large for her sunken face. Her lilac, short-sleeved cardigan was buttoned up to her sallow neck and her navy linen trousers hung loosely from a waist so tiny Joy was sure she could span it with her hand.

'It's nice to meet you too,' she said. 'Thank you for allowing us to look around.'

'Not a problem. As I told you earlier, Ruth, I have no guests at the moment so feel free to wander wherever you like. I'll be in my study if you need me, just off the kitchen.' Jane smiled at them both and left them standing alone in the entrance hall.

Joy and Ruth wandered around the large house. Every room they went into was more impressive than the last. The parquet flooring in the long hallway was exquisite. There were seven double bedrooms, all decorated in soft neutral colours, and each room had a different tartan on the cushions and throws. Even the towels in the en-suite bathrooms had matching tartan trims.

The vast reception room was filled with comfy sofas. The shelves that lined the back wall were jammed with books of all sizes. The fireplace was magnificent, its thick oak mantelpiece was adorned with photographs and postcards, propped up against each other. A pristine, shiny black hearth surrounded the ready laid fire, just waiting for the strike of a match to set it ablaze.

Ruth perched on one of two small brick pillars built into the hearth on either side of the fire.

'Can you just imagine this room in the winter?' she said dreamily. 'Warming your toes and making toast in front of a roaring fire?'

Joy left her to dream. She strolled down the hall and ventured though a doorway, which led into a large octagonal conservatory. Mahogany-stained wicker furniture and brightly coloured cushions littered the room. She sat at a small round table and looked out of the window. Her gaze travelled across the lawn garden, dotted with vibrant flowerbeds and meandering pathways, to the panoramic mountain views beyond.

Ruth found her there. The wicker chair creaked as she sat down.

'So, what do you think?' she asked.

'Dream location, mad idea,' Joy said.

'No, make that dream location, complete and utterly crazy idea, but I love it, I want it.' Ruth hugged herself. 'I'm going to make her an offer,' she squealed. She leapt to her feet, obviously intent on doing so there and then.

'Whoa.' Joy grabbed her arm as she swept past. 'Let's talk about it a bit more first. Do you even know the asking price?'

'She wants a quick sale, so I could haggle.' She pulled free just as Jane came into the room.

Joy jumped to her feet and stretched out her hand.

'We should be getting back to the others,' she said briskly, shaking Jane's hand warmly. 'They're probably starving by now. So nice to meet you and thank you again for letting us look around your lovely home.'

'Not at all, my dear. My pleasure,' said their hostess.

'Thanks, Jane, I'll give you a ring tomorrow,' Ruth said as Joy ushered her firmly towards the front door.

As quickly as their flip-flops would allow, Joy marched Ruth back to the hotel, anxious to quell her excitement and talk some sense into her.

'You can't just jump into this with both feet, Ruth,' she said as they retraced their steps.

'But it's like someone flicked a light switch in my head. I feel alive. I'm excited about something for the first time in an age.' Ruth grinned.

'Don't tell the others,' Joy said. 'They'll make fun; think you're being a scatterbrain.'

'Is that what you think?'

'No, I think it could work, honestly,' Joy said, 'it just needs careful planning.'

*****

By the time they entered Paddy's Bar the sweat was running between Joy's shoulder blades, beneath her thin cotton dress.

'Didn't you do enough walking already today, Joy? Your face is like a beetroot.' Rob said, as she plonked down beside him. 'Need a drink?'

'You're a lifesaver. Cider, please.' Joy pushed her fingers through her damp hair.

'Did you go somewhere interesting?' Trish said quizzically. 'You don't look as though you were shopping in the Green Welly.'

'Just exploring the village,' Joy said, giving Ruth a warning dig in the ribs. 'It's still roasting out there,' she added.

At that moment, Kathy came into the bar, followed by Tony and Brad.

When Trish looked over and waved to them, Joy turned to Ruth. 'Let's talk about this in our room, Ruth, before you say anything to anyone else,' she pleaded.

'I'm rubbish at keeping secrets.'

'Just try, Ruth, you know what they are like, especially Trish, they'll all have to give their opinion and it'll get confusing.'

'Mmm, OK.' Ruth didn't sound too sure. 'Promise you'll hear me out later? Help me plan the best way to get what I want.'

'I will, I promise.' Joy nodded, turning a little too eagerly to smile at Brad as he sat down opposite her.

'What are you two plotting?' he asked.

'Nothing,' they said together, then immediately raised their glasses to drink, preventing further conversation.

Brad shrugged his shoulders and asked of no one in particular, 'Are we ready to eat? I'm famished.'

Just as he spoke, Rob returned from the bar with a handful of menus, and passed them around the table.

*****

Behind the veil of her menu, Joy allowed a slow silent sigh to escape. She was tired now; tired of all the false joviality and fake smiles she'd pinned on for the last few hours. She wanted nothing more than to disappear off to bed, to be alone with her own thoughts. Having quickly decided on the pasta carbonara, she surreptitiously studied her fellow diners. Kathy was wearing a low-cut top again, and looking a little anxious. Joy saw her look over at Daniel, and then quickly back down at her open menu.

That's a guilty expression if ever I saw one. Why is she looking over at Daniel like that? I know Trish fought her corner earlier and I kind of believe her, but there's no smoke without fire. And look at Daniel; he's deliberately not making eye contact with her. Is he still trying to keep his dirty little secret under wraps? Has he told her it's over?

Feeling the heat of her anger rising again, Joy shifted her gaze to Trish. A secret conversation appeared to be going on between her and Rob, and Trish, usually calm, seemed jittery tonight.

Rob was looking down at his menu, his shoulders pushed back, and his jaw tense as he listened to his wife.

What's that about, I wonder? What was that weird thing she said earlier today... she nearly blurted something out... shit what was it again? Life was a nightmare, that's it. She said that when Seb was born, her life was a nightmare. What did she mean by that?

Suddenly, at the other end of the table, there was a minor commotion as Kathy knocked over her drink and Daniel rushed to help mop up the spillage, dabbing at it with his napkin. Joy watched, catching a glimpse of Tony from the corner of her eye. She shivered involuntarily.

My God, he thinks something's going on too. He looks ready to punch someone. And Kathy's like a cat on hot bricks again. Her face is crimson. Well, I'm damned if I'm sitting here watching.

She stood up and grabbed her bag.

'You'll have to excuse me, guys. I don't feel well,' she said, before fleeing the room and racing up the stairs two at a time.

XVII

Kathy grabbed her napkin, frantically dabbing at the amber river that threatened to cascade off the edge of the table. Her face was burning and her hands were shaking. She felt all eyes on her.

'Here, let me help.' Daniel jumped up, throwing his napkin over hers.

Their fingers touched briefly, and Kathy cursed herself for the guilty way she recoiled.

With order restored once more, Kathy checked her phone as a distraction, hoping her flustered face soon returned to its normal colouring. She hadn't missed Tony's exaggerated sigh, as he ordered another drink, or Joy's swift departure.

As if things aren't bad enough already without a stupid accident adding fuel to the fire.

She looked up to see Brad watching her. He gave a half smile and a wink so brief she might have imagined it. Her heart skipped a beat and she looked away quickly. She couldn't wait to get dinner over with and escape to her room. And judging by Tony's behaviour earlier, his turning over of a new leaf was heading towards disaster already. There was anger in his eyes, earlier, up in their room. Admittedly, he backed off when she asked him to, but Kathy knew he'd used every ounce of willpower to walk away. After what he'd already drunk that afternoon, it wouldn't be long before he'd be the worse for wear, and she couldn't face another public humiliation. Besides, she wanted to think about Brad's job offer. She caught him watching her again. *Is it only a job offer though? Or does he have ulterior motives?* She threw him a brief smile, just as Tony placed a fresh glass of lager in front of her.

'Try not to spill it this time. The beer's not cheap in here, you know,' he grumbled.

'Same in all the tourist spots, Tony.' Brad gave a wry smile. He pointed to the TV behind the bar. 'What's Mr Cameron spouting on about now?'

Kathy zoned out as they discussed the state of the economy.

His hands are lovely. Strong, tanned, with clean clipped nails. Not like Tony's, all rough skin and dirt and grime, from years of working under car bonnets; embedded into the skin surrounding his chewed fingernails…

She imagined Brad holding her, touching her. His lips kissing hers...

'Kath!'

Kathy looked up. The colour raced up her neck, flooding her face.

'Earth to Kathy,' Ruth was calling out.

'Sorry,' Kathy mumbled. 'Miles away.'

'You don't say,' Ruth drawled. 'Come sit over here with Trish and me. There's some boring political debate going on with that lot.' She nodded towards the men and patted the seat beside her.

'OK, but I'm not staying up late.' Kathy shuffled round the table to join them.

'Me neither. In fact, I think I should check on Joy. She disappeared fairly sharpish,' Trish said.

'I'll check on her. She's sharing with me anyway. Besides...' Ruth lowered her voice. 'We have something to discuss.'

'Oh yes, what's the big secret?' Trish asked.

'Can't say; sworn to secrecy for the moment.' Ruth tapped the side of her nose.

'Sounds intriguing.' Trish pushed.

'And daring... risky even... For now, my lips are sealed.' Ruth drew a finger across her pursed lips, shaking her empty glass at them with an enquiring look.

'Another?'

'Please,' Trish said.

Kathy shook her head, covering the top of her glass. She turned to Trish once Ruth was out of earshot.

'What do you reckon that's all about?'

'Don't know.' Trish frowned. 'Maybe Joy's pissed off with the pair of us now, and has decided to take Ruth into her confidence instead.'

Kathy looked at her sister.

'I thought you said she believed you,' she said anxiously. 'I thought we had things sorted. Between her and me, I mean. I know it'll take a bit more to sort things with Daniel.'

'I thought so too.' Trish nodded. 'Look, this could be totally unrelated. It might just be one of Ruth's jokes or harebrained schemes.'

XVIII

Joy feigned sleep when she heard the door to their room open. She listened to Ruth feeling her way across the room in the dark, switching on the bathroom light and then closing the door until only a thin ray of light stretched across the bed and up the wall, fading out as it reached the ceiling. She watched Ruth's shadow blocking the light's path, as she moved around preparing for bed.

'Are you awake?' Ruth whispered into the darkness.

Joy remained silent as Ruth climbed into the king size bed. She felt the pillows being placed along her back.

'Don't want you turning over in the middle of the night and thinking I'm Daniel. What a fright we'd both get.' Ruth giggled.

Joy smiled, despite her tear-stained face.

Ruth continued her whispered ramblings. 'There was me thinking we were going to discuss my big adventure - the B&B – and what do you go and do? Fall asleep. Huh. Well, don't think you can get out of it that easily. Wait until tomorrow, up on Rannoch Moor. You'll have nowhere to hide, and then you'll have to listen to me, won't you? Night then.'

After a couple of minutes tossing and shuffling, Ruth finally seemed to be comfortable, and Joy let out a sigh when she heard gentle snoring coming from the other side of the bed. Her head ached, she was thirsty, and hungry too, after missing dinner. All she'd eaten were the two shortbread biscuits left on the tea tray. She didn't dare get out of bed to get a drink, in case she woke Ruth.

Her problems filled every pore of her body. Her eyelids were like lead, but still she couldn't sleep. She checked the time on her phone: 1.30 a.m. She heard footsteps and deep voices passing the door. Sounds like Tony and Brad.

*****

She must have fallen asleep at some point, because she was woken violently by her own crying. Great heaving sobs that threatened to burst her ribcage. Her pillow was soaked through.

Ruth was crouched beside her, stroking her hair and rubbing her back. 'Come on, Joy, wake up. It's just a dream. Everything's ok, I'm here.'

'It's not, it's not OK. It'll never be OK again.' Joy gulped. She was crying uncontrollably, mortified that Ruth was seeing her like this, yet unable to stop.

'You were dreaming…it was a bad dream - or a nightmare.' Ruth's tone was soothing, as if she was talking to one of her boys when they'd woken, distressed, in the night.

Joy thought her heart would break as she fought to regain control.

'I'll get Daniel.' Ruth leaned over her, trying to see her face. 'I'll be back in a sec.'

'No!' Joy howled, holding Ruth's arm in a vicelike grip.

'OK, it's OK. But tell me what you want me to do. You're scaring me.'

With a huge effort, Joy regained control and her sobs died down. She let out a shuddering sigh.

'I'll be fine,' she gulped. Sorry for frightening you. Just bad dreams, that's all. Like you said.' She released her grip.

Rubbing her wrist, Ruth got out of bed. 'I need a cuppa now to calm the nerves. Want one?'

'No, thanks.'

Ruth flicked on the bedside light and quickly made tea. She carried her cup around to Joy's side of the bed and sat down beside her.

'You scared the shit out of me. What were you dreaming about anyway?' she asked. 'Demons and banshees, by the sound of it.' She gently pushed Joy's hair back off her face, revealing red raw eyes and a blotchy face.

Joy closed her eyes quickly; embarrassed that Ruth had witnessed her in such a state. 'Yes,' she said, 'in the shape of Daniel and Kathy chasing me down the driveway, pelting me with shoes and handbags and suitcases.'

Ruth snorted with laughter. 'How weird is that?' she said.

'They're having an affair.'

'What, in your dream?' Ruth asked. She wrinkled her nose, like a child who didn't understand what she was being told.

'No. For real.'

Ruth gasped. 'No way! What are you talking about? She's your best friend.'

'Well, you read about it all the time, don't you - best friends and husbands being found in bed together.'

'How long?'

'Years, apparently.'

'I'm sorry, I don't believe it.' Ruth was pacing the room. 'And you had no idea? It doesn't fit. How did you find out?'

Strangely enough, Joy found she wanted to talk. It was easier here, in the dark, with Ruth's blunt questioning.

'He told me, on Friday night,' she said quietly.

'What, as in this Friday, before Saturday, before we came up here?' Ruth shook her head. 'Talk about timing.'

They said nothing for a short while. Ruth paced some more, and then went into the bathroom.

Joy felt her body relaxing. The tears had stopped now; her crying storm had released the pressure that had been building up. She blew her nose, pushed the pillows up behind her, and sat up in the bed, hugging her knees.

Ruth emerged from the bathroom.

'So he just came straight out with it? Me and Kathy are having an affair. We love each other and have done for years.' She mimicked Daniel's deep voice.

'Not exactly.'

'So how, exactly?'

'He said he'd had a fling.'

'A fling!' Ruth pounced on the words. 'A fling, not an affair?'

'Same thing. It's still betrayal,' Joy retorted.

'And he told you it was Kathy he had this fling with?'

'No.'

'Not even a hint?'' Ruth persisted.

'No, but I've seen them together, this week. Something's going on still.' Joy defended her theory fiercely.

'For fuck's sake, Joy, get a grip will you?' Ruth sat crossed legged on the bed in front of her.

'The signs are all there, Ruth.'

'Look, think logically. Get that totally in control head of yours back in place again.'

'But the evidence is staring me in the face. The looks, the trailing behind, the whispered conversations. They both say nothing is going on...'

'Daniel told you he had an affair, right?' Ruth interrupted.

'Yes.'

'So, what has he got to gain by not admitting it's Kathy?'

'Not being flattened by Tony, for a start.'

Ruth let out an exasperated sigh. 'Joy, he's in bits. By telling you what he'd done, he risked blowing your marriage apart. Why would he lie about Kathy? He's got nothing more to lose... besides which, Kathy would never do the dirty on you, and well you know it.'

Joy shuffled back under the duvet. 'I know I want to believe she wouldn't, I just hurt so much, Ruth.' Her words were barely audible.

Ruth lay down beside her. 'I know you do. And you will for a long while yet. It takes time.' She put an arm around her friend's shaking shoulders.

WEDNESDAY
I

Joy opened her eyes, rubbing at the dried-on saltiness of last night's tears. Carefully, she lifted the dead weight of Ruth's arm, still wrapped protectively around her, and slid from the bed. She checked the time on her phone: still two hours before breakfast. Her head felt muggy, as if her brain needed fresh oxygen.

Ruth turned over and, groaned, but slept on.

Joy decided to go for a walk. She pulled on cotton trousers and a white T-shirt and slipped her bare feet into sandals, rubbing a wet wipe over her face before creeping out into the deserted hotel corridor. She passed the cleaner, polishing tables in the reception area, and stepped outside the main door.

It was only 6.30 a.m., so Joy was surprised at the number of people out on the streets. Even some holidaymakers were up and about, studying maps as they strolled along in the early morning sunshine. All spurred out of bed at this early hour by the good weather - almost unheard of in the Scottish Highlands.

Joy sauntered along the main street, relieved to be on her own for a while, away from questions and pitying glances from her friends. She tried not to dwell too much on her embarrassing display of emotion the night before. Instead, she admired the neat white cottages dwarfed beneath the towering mountains. Like Ruth, she felt lured by the magic of the place.

She found herself on a road that looked familiar, and soon she came across the B&B Ruth had brought her to the day before. Stopping at the shiny black gates and gazing at the imposing yet welcoming house, she saw once again why Ruth was hooked. Even so, it was a massive plan, logistically and emotionally, and she really didn't think Ruth was strong enough to hack it. Just as she turned to go back the way she had come, Joy heard the crunching of gravel.

'My, what an early bird you are.' Jane's soft lilt floated down the driveway.

'Hello again.' Joy stopped and smiled at her, amazed to see her so perfectly groomed at this hour of the morning.

Jane dropped the black bag she was carrying into the wheelie bin at the side of the house and dusted herself down, patting at the lilac floral apron she wore over a crisp white blouse and the navy linen trousers she'd had on the evening before.

'Would you like a cup of tea?' she asked smoothing down her short hair, tucking it behind her ear. 'I have the kettle on.'

Joy hesitated, checking the time. 'A quick one would be lovely, and then I must get back. We have a long stretch ahead of us today,' she said, following Jane into the bright kitchen.

'Please sit down,' Jane said. 'Will you have some toast?'

'No, thanks, I'm fine. I'll be having breakfast at the hotel shortly.'

'I made the bread fresh this morning.'

'Really?' Joy was impressed. 'OK then, thank you. Just one slice though,' she said with a smile.

Jane cut thick slices from the batch loaf and placed them under the hot grill.

'It never tastes quite the same from a toaster,' she said.

Joy saw a flash of pain in her eyes and noticed again, as she had the day before, Jane's grey pallor beneath her make-up.

'Do you have help running this place?' she asked. 'It must be a massive task for one person.'

'Jack, my husband, was here, once upon a time. Now Helen helps out with the breakfasts and Dot comes in to clean the rooms,' Jane said. 'So it isn't too bad,' she added, turning the toast under the grill.

'Is Helen your daughter?' Joy asked, wondering if Jack had died.

'No.' Jane smiled. 'Helen is a very good friend... I was never blessed with children.'

'I'm sorry. It was very rude of me to ask. I just assumed...' Joy was flustered. 'I should go, you look tired,' she said, getting up from the kitchen table.

'It's OK. Please sit down,' Jane said, putting a plate of hot toast on the table. She smiled in a resigned fashion. 'The pain is tiring, but I've learned to live with it as the months have gone by.'

She moved back and forth between the table and worktop, bringing butter, jam and marmalade. Then she filled the teapot with boiling water, carried it to the table, and sat down across from Joy, who was waiting for her to speak again, and not wanting to ask about the cause of the pain.

'The medication makes me tired too – and I'm a bag of bones – just look at me.' Jane laughed gently. Then her smile faded. 'I'm not long for this world now,' she said softly.

'Don't say that, Jane.' Joy suddenly felt she'd made a friend she didn't want to lose.

'It's true. The dreaded big C will take me soon,' said Jane calmly, and began buttering a slice of toast.

Joy felt a huge sadness. Her eyes filled with tears and a lump in her throat the size of an apple prevented her from speaking.

'Don't cry.' Jane handed her a tissue from a box on the table. 'I've known it was coming for a long time. And I'm ready... well, almost. Once I find the right person to take over here, then I'm ready to go.'

Joy dabbed at her eyes. 'Won't Jack want to take over?' She felt intrusive asking the question.

'Oh, he's not interested now, financial or otherwise. We divorced over fifteen years ago. He has a new family now and a new life in Canada. It's over ten years since I've heard from him...' she said.

Joy waited quietly, feeling Jane might say more.

'The happiest years of my life have been in this house, running the B&B, I'd like to think it could make someone else happy; perhaps turn their life around, as it did mine.'

'Ruth's hooked you know,' Joy said.

Jane nodded.

'I know she and this place would be good for each other.'

'It's a long way from her home, and her kids.'

'If it's meant to be, she'll find a way,' Jane said.

'I suppose so.' Joy nodded. She'd nibbled half heartedly on her toast, and now gave up any pretence of eating it.

Jane rose briskly and began clearing the table.

'Now, you'd best get moving,' she said with a smile. 'You have a tough few days ahead. Keep your chin up.'

They walked down the driveway together. At the gate, Jane reached out and gave Joy a hug. Her embrace felt so delicate, and her body so fragile, like that of a small child. Joy was almost afraid to hug her back in case she broke.

'I hope things go well for you with the sale of the house,' she said reluctantly releasing her hold. 'You're a brave woman, Jane. I hope the pain doesn't get too much worse.' She squeezed her hand gently. 'It really was lovely to meet you.'

'You too, my dear. Bye,' Jane said, waving to Joy as she set off back to the hotel.

II

It was almost half past eight when Joy let herself back into the hotel room. As soon as she closed the door, Ruth pounced.

'God, I was so worried,' she berated her friend. 'Where did you get to?'

'Just for a walk. I'll tell you later. Right now I need a shower,' Joy said, walking into the bathroom.

'Did you have more bad dreams?'

'No, Ruth, I'm fine, honestly.'

'OK, well you'd best get a wriggle on,' Ruth said, as she threw her hairbrush into her suitcase and closed the lid. 'We're leaving in half an hour.'

Joy closed the bathroom door, turned on the shower and pulled off her T-shirt.

'I'm going down for breakfast,' Ruth called through the bathroom door.

'Won't be long, I promise,' Joy replied, then closing her eyes she tilted her head back and let the lukewarm water pour over her face.

I could quite imagine Ruth playing hostess in the B&B. I think Jane could too. Although imagining her living five hundred miles away from her kids is not quite as easy. Jane is so lovely and so unbelievably calm and accepting of her situation. I felt a real connection with her this morning, as if I could have told her everything – Daniel, his affair and the whole sorry mess I've made of my life. I just know she would understand completely.

III

By 9.30 a.m., the group had left the hotel, with Tony waving them off, to take the path out of Tyndrum and join the 'way-marked footpath' once more.

'Today we'll be doing twenty-two miles - quite a challenge,' Rob announced. 'Can everyone be sure to drink plenty of water?' he added, looking around at his flock.

'Oh, I'll never make it.' Ruth wiped her forehead with a tissue. 'I'm sweating buckets already.'

'Of course you will,' Joy said taking her arm. 'Come on, walk with me.'

'What if we're in the middle of Rannoch Moor and someone breaks a leg... then what will we do?' Ruth dramatised.

'Trust you to wish disaster on us,' said Joy, making a face.

'She's got a point,' Brad said.

'We do have mobile phones,' said Trish.

'But what if there's no signal up there,' Ruth continued worriedly.

'Well, Rob would do the heroic thing and run up mountains and across streams to get help.' Trish put her arm around her husband. 'Wouldn't you, darling?'

'Yup, no problem. Superman in disguise, that's me.' He laughed and the others joined in.

'Ruth, you can decide what you want to do when we reach the pub at lunchtime,' Trish said.

'Yes, you can always duck out of another afternoon's walking and hitch a lift with Tony again,' Joy said, giving Ruth a playful nudge in the ribs.

They all laughed at the absurdity of the conversation, and as the footpath took them further away from the village, they spread out, each finding their own pace.

Kathy found herself walking beside Brad at the back of the group.

'I was thinking,' he said, 'maybe we should perform a rain dance. It's going to be pretty damned hot up on Rannoch Moor.'

Kathy looked at his serious expression.

'You're totally mad. You do know that?' she said with a shake of her head.

'So I'm told.' He grinned. 'Still, it got you smiling.'

'Ha ha,' she said half sarcastically.

What do I have to smile about? I should have known Tony couldn't change. He's all talk as usual. Well, that's it, no more talk. DD Day is back on. No more stalling, it's full steam ahead from now on.

'You're not listening to a word I'm saying, are you?' Brad interrupted her thoughts.

'Sorry, miles away,' Kathy apologised.

'I asked if you'd given my job offer any thought.'

'You do realise it will finish your friendship with Tony if I take it?' she told him.

'I think I can cope with that.' He grinned. 'Anyway, the rewards will be far greater.' He gave her a flirty wink.

A pink flush crept up Kathy's neck. 'I'd really love the job but...'

'There's a lot involved – a lot of hard work, study, exams,' Brad said.

'I understand that.'

'So is that a yes?'

'I think so.'

Kathy felt butterfly wings banging against her stomach walls, as Brad put his arms around her in a bear-like hug.

'Great,' he said and kissed her cheek.

Kathy blushed, thankful that the others had rounded a bend on the footpath and were out of sight. Impulsively she threw her arms around his neck and pulled his head down towards hers. His lips, soft and smooth, rested against hers for a fleeting second, before he pulled away.

What are you doing, Kathy?' he said, visibly shocked.

'I thought...' Kathy was mortified; she wished the ground would open up beneath her.

'Listen,' Brad said, stopping and pulling her down to sit beside him on the grassy bank of the footpath. 'Tony is proving to be the biggest asshole on the planet. I hate to see the way he treats you, and I'll do anything I can to help you get out of that situation. I'll give you a job; help you find a new home; whatever you need, but Kathy...' He paused looking at her crimson face and the threatening tears of humiliation welling in the corners of her eyes.

He took her hands in his. 'I want us to be great friends, the kind who look out for each other. I don't want to end up in bed with you, and ruin our friendship. And I don't think that's really what you want either,' he said gently.

Kathy pulled her hands away. 'Point taken,' she said in a shaky voice.

They set off once more, the silence between awkward. Kathy didn't know what to say. She felt such a fool.

After a few minutes Brad spoke. 'I'm sorry,' he said.

'No need,' she told him. 'It's me who should be apologising, and anyway you're right. I need a friend who can help me turn my life around, not another complicated relationship.'

She smiled suddenly, liking the feeling of having a strong reliable chap like Brad as her friend. She began to chuckle.

'What's so funny?' he asked with a smile.

Kathy shook her head, but her chuckles were infectious, and he couldn't help laughing with her. Before long, the two of them were howling with laughter, with tears streaming down their faces.

Kathy struggled to get the words out. 'I feel such an idiot,' she gasped.

'Don't. Anyway I'm flattered.' Brad's eyes twinkled.

'Bullshit. You've probably got tons of women beating a path to your door.'

'Not the one I'd like to see.'

'Aha.' Kathy dried her watery eyes with a tissue 'So you've got your sights set on someone?'

'Mmm. She's a non-runner though,' he said vaguely. 'Destined to be a bachelor, that's me.'

Kathy didn't miss the note of resigned sadness in his tone. 'Oh I don't know. Life can change when you least expect it,' she said, linking her arm through his. 'We'd better catch up with the others, before they call out search and rescue.'

IV

Joy was only half listening to Ruth's voice as she walked beside her. They were heading up the group, and Ruth's excited babble about her afternoon off, along with her plans for the B&B, was fuelling the pace - despite her apparent worries over the desolate Rannoch Moor. Joy was also very much aware that Daniel, only a few paces behind them, was able to hear every word. She kept her fingers crossed that Ruth wouldn't want to talk about her distressed state during the night.

'Are you listening at all?' Ruth broke into her thoughts.

'Yes, of course I am,' Joy said.

She searched for the right words to say to her friend, to get her to consider the implications of moving lock, stock and barrel over five hundred miles away.

'I've worked it out roughly,' Ruth pressed on excitedly. 'With the money from the sale of Mum's house, plus what I'll get from selling mine, I can raise around two hundred and fifty thousand.'

'You'd never get the B&B for that though.'

'I know that – I'm not stupid,' said Ruth, indignant at Joy's negative response. 'But it would be a good deposit to approach the bank with.'

'What about the boys?' Joy still thought that, as idyllic as the place was, Ruth would find it very hard to be so far away from them.

'Maybe they'll find coming to Scotland to visit me more exciting,' Ruth said. 'They hate coming to stay with me at the moment. They say it's boring, and that there's nothing to do.' She gave a small sigh. 'They've been asking me to go up to the farm instead, but I can't do that. It feels too awkward now.'

'Why is it awkward?' Joy asked. 'They're your kids and it was your home.'

'Paul's seeing someone else.' Ruth dropped her voice to a whisper. 'She stays over sometimes – the boys told me - she's quite the farmer's wife by all accounts.'

'Oh, right.' Joy didn't know what else to say.

Why didn't I know that? Have I been so wrapped up in myself? Did she tell me and I forgot? No, I wouldn't forget something like this.

'Don't be feeling sorry for me, Joy,' Ruth said, interrupting her thoughts.

'No?'

'No. I left them, remember?' She smiled. 'I'm glad he's found someone he can be happy with. The boys like her, and actually, she's quite nice,' she added.

'You've met her?'

'Yes, a few weeks ago, when I was dropping the boys back at the farm.'

As Joy listened to her friend and watched her excitement at the impending adventure, she thought of all that Ruth had been through.

I have to find a way through this mess called my life. Look at Ruth... She's finding her way and I should be able to find mine. That's it. I'm going to talk to Daniel. Now. This morning.

'It's OK, you know, Paul moving on with his life.' Ruth was talking again. 'It doesn't hurt any more, not really. Well, not very often.' She grabbed Joy's arm. 'I'm so excited about this B&B - more than I've been about anything in ages,' she said, her eyes sparkling.

'I can see that.' Joy smiled. Then her expression grew serious. 'I met Jane this morning,' she said. 'My wanderings took me past the house, she was outside, and she invited me in for tea and toast. She's very ill, Ruth. Did you know?'

'No. I thought she looked a little frail, but then some people are like that.'

'She told me about the house and how important it is to her, how important it is that she finds the right person to take it over,' Joy said, remembering Jane's passion as she spoke about the B&B. 'She liked you, Ruth,' she added.

'How ill is she?' Ruth asked.

'She has cancer,' Joy whispered. 'It's terminal and she seems to think the end isn't too far off,' she added.

'Oh, that poor woman,' Ruth cried.

'I know, suddenly our problems seem trivial, when someone like Jane is faced with tying up all the loose ends in her life.' Joy gave Ruth a sad smile.

'It felt special, right for me, you know.' Ruth said, looking into the distance. 'Like, suddenly I knew the right path to take.' She turned to look at Joy. 'I can do it, run the B&B: I know I can.'

Joy could see the determination in Ruth's face. *She'll do this with or without support from her friends.*

'Look, why don't you offer to run it with her for a while? See how you cope with living so far away from the kids. Be sure you can settle in Scotland, at least until you sell the house?' Joy suggested. 'That way you can get a real feel for the place and Jane can get to know you too.'

'Joy! You're a genius! I'll ring Jane tonight.' Ruth threw her arms around her. 'Now I'm going to skip back down the path to tell Trish all about my new adventure!' Suddenly she lowered her tone dramatically and whispered in Joy's ear. 'And you're going to talk to Daniel, right?'

'I'd decided to anyway,' Joy whispered back.

'Good girl.' Ruth turned and skipped away like a ten-year- old.

V

Joy watched, happy for her, before falling into step beside Daniel.

'Can we create a little distance?' she asked him. 'I think it's time we talked.'

Neither of them spoke until they'd widened the gap considerably between themselves and the rest of the group. When they were safely out of earshot, Joy spoke first.

'The only way out of this mess is to be completely honest.' She looked at Daniel intensely as though she was trying to read his mind. 'We have to tell each other everything. All the facts, however ugly they might be. And how we really feel, however painful it is.' As she spoke, fear twisted inside her stomach at what she was about to hear.

'It'll hurt, Joy.' Daniel's voice was hoarse, as if he hadn't spoken in weeks.

'It already hurts.'

Daniel cleared his throat and took a long drink of water. 'I guess it started... what, over ten years ago. More, even, before Stephanie...'

Joy balked at the mention of her name and opened her mouth to deliver a scathing retort.

Daniel glared at her. 'Please, Joy, let me finish before you say anything, it's the only way to get through this.'

Joy bit her lip. 'I know. I promise,' she said.

She looked straight ahead, hands by her sides, and fists clenched, feeling her nails biting into her palms.

Daniel cleared his throat for a second time.

'It was so hard. We were trying for a baby and as the months went by you became so obsessed that sex was just a mechanical procedure. And then there was the fallout - the tears, the silences - every month when you weren't pregnant... anyway we've been through that.'

He gave a sigh before continuing. 'It was a drunken fumble, after the office Christmas party you wouldn't come to. That's all it was.'

Daniel looked across at Joy. She didn't alter her expression.

'I promise you, Joy, I've never looked at another woman, before or since. I only ever wanted you,' he pleaded. 'And after it happened, I was mortified - so ashamed. I couldn't look at you without being consumed with guilt. I'd work late, or just walk the streets to avoid you –'

'To avoid me!' Joy spat, clenching her fists even tighter.

'Joy, listen, please. I was terrified you'd find out and leave me. If I came home when you were in bed, it was easier. Easier to lie beside you and hold you, lie to you... in the dark.'

He drank more water.

'Then, overnight, you changed - just like that. Suddenly getting pregnant didn't matter. It would happen when it happened; babies weren't top of the agenda. You were full of life and energy, wanting to move house, buy fancy furniture and nice cars, go on exotic holidays. And at first it was great. I was so relieved to have the old Joy back again, I agreed to it all. I'd have given you anything - and I did - to see you happy. Anything to make it up to you, to ease my conscience, always hoping you'd never find out what a bastard I'd been.'

Daniel paused to catch his breath.

Joy couldn't work out if he'd finished. She let out a shaky sigh and released the tension in her hands, feeling the blood flow through her fingers.

'Wait!' Daniel put his hand up before she could speak. 'The thing is, Joy; it's always all or nothing with you. When your attention moved from babies to material things and "raising our social status" as you put it, you went at it full throttle.'

'I get focused,' she interrupted. 'That's all.'

'To the point of obsession; the exclusion of all rational thought. I work for an accountancy firm. I don't own it. There was never enough money, Joy. I started taking on private work after hours, so that we could manage, so that I didn't have to say no to you.'

'I would have understood about the money,' Joy said, hurt afresh that Daniel had felt he couldn't talk to her. 'You should have told me.'

'I tried; I suggested you get a job a while back,' he said, his voice less aggressive.

'But you didn't say we needed the money.' Joy tried to make sense of it all.

He earned decent money. Not megabucks, I know - but then I wasn't mega extravagant either.

'I couldn't,' he said, shaking his head. 'All of this would have had to come out, and I would have lost you.'

He stopped to drink more water, never taking his eyes from hers.

Joy felt the searing heat burning into her, searching, probing, for what... forgiveness, honesty?

'I spent hours, days, poring over our finances. Nothing would add up.' His eyes pleaded with her to understand. 'I was desperate, Joy.'

The questions struggled to break through her pursed lips.

'I borrowed money through the company, to keep us afloat,' Daniel said.

'Borrowed? They let you do that?' Joy asked in surprise.

'They don't know.' He lowered his voice. 'It was only meant to be a temporary thing, until I'd spoken to you, but the time was never right. The debt just got bigger. The stress became more than I could handle...' He flicked at a bee that was buzzing around his face. 'I quit the job – I walked out,' he finished, letting out a deep sigh.

Joy swung around staring at him in horror.

'Well that's just great,' she snapped. 'Well done, Daniel. That's really sorted things out.' The jibe was out before she could stop it.

'Thanks for understanding, Joy!' he snapped. Turning his back on her, he stormed ahead.

'Dan, wait!' Joy ran after him. 'I'm sorry. I didn't mean it to come out that way. It's just so much to take in.'

She saw that he was crying and she wanted to cry too.

'I want to tell you it'll be OK. But I don't know if I can,' she said sadly.

'At least you're being honest with me now.' His words were barely a whisper. 'If you hadn't been such a closed book all these years...'

Joy decided to stick to the facts, before they both drowned in the emotion of the whole mess.

'When did you quit?' she asked. 'Was it last Friday?'

'No.' He shook his head. 'Over a month ago. I've been walking the streets, visiting the job centre, trying to figure out how I was going to tell you everything.'

'Four weeks ago!' Joy's anger flared up again.

'You didn't even notice anything was wrong.' Daniel sighed. 'That's our real problem, Joy. We're so far apart now, each of us harbouring secrets and lies, insecurities and fears of what the future has in store.' He looked at her. 'We're just going through the motions, and that's not living.'

'I can't do this.' Joy sat down on the edge of the footpath.

'What are you doing?' Daniel towered over her, his shadow blocking the heat of the sun. 'I thought you wanted to talk. We've only just got started,' he said.

'It's too much. It's too hard.' Joy rubbed at her face with the small towel she pulled from her rucksack, trying not to cry. 'I need a breather. I have to get my head around this.'

'But there's more to be said, I need to know stuff too.'

'I realise that,' she said. She didn't want to beg but suddenly she felt exhausted. 'Later, Daniel, please.'

She watched as he widened the distance between them and disappeared around a bend in the path. Whilst catching her breath, her mind went into overdrive. She didn't know what to say or what to think, other than this had to be all her fault.

Ten minutes had passed when Joy stood up quickly; realising that they hadn't been that far ahead and the others would soon be upon her. She wasn't ready to talk to anyone else just yet. She pulled her iPod from her pocket, dragging at the wires and stuffing the earphones into her ears. Selecting a Guns n' Roses track, she turned the volume as loud as she could stand, until she could no longer hear herself think, and set off in pursuit of Daniel. She kept up a relentless pace, hearing her own heart pounding as loudly as the drumbeat of the music.

VI

It was some twenty minutes later when Joy eventually caught up with Daniel. He came out of the tiny village shop in Bridge of Orchy, carrying two bottles of water. He passed one to her.

'Thanks,' Joy panted. She took a long drink and leant against an old stonewall.

'What are you doing to yourself, Joy?' Daniel shook his head. 'It's twenty-five degrees out here; and we still have miles to go.'

'I don't know.' She rested her hands on her knees, taking deep breaths. 'I want to be with you. And then, when I am, I want to punch you. I want to talk to you but I don't know what to say. I don't know who you are any more. I don't even know who I am any more – and I feel as if our whole life together has been a lie.'

Daniel drank his water in stony-faced silence.

They set off again, walking more slowly, side by side.

'I didn't want to hurt you,' Daniel said. 'I didn't want it to be this way, blurting it out the night before our holiday. I'd been walking the streets all day, I got soaked to the skin in that freak thunderstorm, thinking, weighing up my options...'

She watched his furrowed brow, saying nothing.

'Maybe I chose the wrong option, telling you like that.' He sighed. 'It's turned out all wrong, that's for sure.'

'There was never going to be a happy ending.'

'Option two might have been less painful.' Daniel glanced across at her. 'They do say ignorance is bliss.'

'What was option two?'

His face took on a distant expression. His voice was so low Joy had to lean forward to hear the words.

'Option two. I could jump off this bridge and sink through the dark cold water. If I opened my mouth, letting the water in, the end would be quick. My problems would be over. Would you be sad? Would you be relieved that you didn't have to live a pretend marriage anymore? Or would you be angry that I had disgraced you, and you'd have to make up some story to tell everyone why I had done it?'

Joy grabbed his arm, pulling him to a standstill. She took both his hands in hers. 'Listen to me, Daniel Crathorne,' she snapped. 'Our marriage might be over. We might never want to speak to each other ever again. But I would never, ever, wish you were dead.' Her voice shook with the fear of what he might have done.

Daniel's shoulders slumped as if defeated, and he pulled his hands free.

'I know, and I couldn't do that to you.' He sighed heavily. 'But I can't live with it all any longer either. So here we are. Instead of trying to sort this out in the privacy of our own home, we've become gossip fodder for all and sundry.'

'Perhaps being here has helped us talk more rationally to each other,' Joy said, still distracted by what Daniel had just told her.

'What, dropping your bombshell on me and then leaving me to stew for five days? You call that rational?' He stared at her in amazement.

Joy could hear Ruth's laughter, and began to panic. 'The others are just behind us, Daniel,' she told him through gritted teeth.

'Like I give a fuck,' he snarled. He dropped his voice anyway. 'I need to know when you found out, and how long you've kept it from me. Was it when things changed - before we moved...?'

'Daniel, please,' she hissed as Ruth trotted up behind them.

VII

'Hi, guys. Phew, it's hot. Did you get an ice cream at the shop? I did, it was heavenly,' Ruth gushed.

'No, just water,' Joy said, letting out a sigh as Daniel gave her an exasperated glance, and walked on ahead.

'How did it go?' Ruth linked her arm through Joy's. 'I'm guessing not that well, but it's still early days.'

'Yes, early days is right. There's a lot of talking still to be done,' Joy said, firmly closing the subject.

Ruth seemed to take the hint, and continued to witter on about the heat as they followed the path towards the Inveroran Hotel.

'Oh, wow. She gasped pointing towards Loch Tulla in the distance. 'Look at the trees - and that perfect reflection! Where's the camera?'

Joy was impressed too and waited patiently, enjoying the view, while Ruth clicked away; capturing the moment. Kathy walked past and gave Joy a half smile.

'Did Daniel tell you?' Ruth whispered, once Kathy was out of earshot. 'Has something been going on between them?'

'He said nothing is going on.'

'And you believe him?'

Joy nodded.

'So...'

'I know. I'll talk to Kathy, apologise,' Joy said.

'Good.' Ruth gave her a wide smile. 'Friends are important.'

'Come on, girls, lunch is just around the corner,' Brad said, muscling his way between them. He linked their arms and started to jog along the path, dragging them both with him.

IX

Kathy spotted Tony waiting by the bus, his hand shading his eyes as he sought her out in the group.

She took a deep breath and painted on her best smile.

'Hi, love.'

'How'd it go?' He hugged her possessively.

Kathy wrinkled her nose and held her breath, as she wriggled free.

'Tony, let me go, you're all hot and sweaty.'

'Give us a kiss then,' he said, planting his lips on hers.

Suddenly all Kathy's misgivings were back with a vengeance and she felt nervous about what the future held. Having Brad as an ally, and knowing he believed in her, felt good. All her confidence and resolve in the plans she'd discussed with him that morning had deserted her the moment she spotted the bus outside the pub. She almost wished the holiday was over; she was willing to forego the breathtaking scenery that surrounded them, just to get back and set the ball rolling.

As she squirmed in Tony's embrace, she made a silent promise to herself. Once the holiday was over and they'd left Scotland, she would never let him touch her again. She caught Brad's eye as he passed. He raised an eyebrow and her face burned with shame.

Tony was a stride ahead, with a tight grip on Kathy's hand, pulling her along. Inside the bar, it was cool and gloomy, with only the bartender and a farmer, who appeared to be engrossed in his newspaper, to witness her embarrassment.

'Don't let him do that to you, Kathy,' Brad whispered, from behind.

'What am I supposed to do?' she hissed back. 'If I say or do anything to upset him now, he'll lose the plot - and ruin everything for everybody. In a few more days, we'll be home, and then that's it.'

'I'll clock him one myself in a minute, if he doesn't let you go.'

'Brad, please,' she whispered, wriggling to free her hand. 'Tony, stop pulling me, you're hurting my hand,' she said, trying to sound assertive, but failing miserably.

'Tony!' Brad called out, waiting until he had Tony's full attention before continuing. 'She asked you to stop pulling.'

Kathy cringed, wishing the floor would swallow her up. It suddenly felt as though all eyes were on the three of them.

'What business is it of yours? She's my wife?' Tony spat.

'Yes, she's your wife. Not your dog,' said Brad calmly.

Kathy squeezed her eyes shut, waiting for the onslaught. The grip on her hand tightened until she thought her fingers would break.

Suddenly the pressure was gone. Tony barged past, knocking Trish against the table and stormed out of the pub. Kathy raced after him, rubbing the circulation back into her hand, her heart racing.

'Tony! Wait!' she called out.

He threw open the driver's door, almost tearing it off its hinges. Stony faced, he jumped into the driver's seat, and slammed the door shut. He started the engine and revved it hard.

She hammered on the window. 'Don't go like this! Come back - I'm ok,' she said, trying to calm him down. He was clearly enraged, and she was worried he'd have an accident.

He drove away without acknowledging she was there, and Kathy stared after him, praying he'd get to the hotel safely. At the crossroads he stopped, then reversed with a screech to where she stood.

He leaned out of the window; his face inches from hers. 'Get in!' he barked.

Kathy took two steps back.

'Tony, you're scaring me.'

'Nobody tells me how to treat my wife. Come on, you're coming with me.'

'No, Tony, I'm not.' Kathy spoke with a calmness she didn't feel. 'I'll see you at the hotel,' she said and turned away.

'Kathy!' Tony yelled. 'Fuck it, Kathy, get back here NOW!'

She kept on walking, not sure her shaking legs would carry her, without looking back. She heard the squeal of tyres spinning in the gravel, as the bus pulled away.

X

Brad found her sitting on the bank of the stream that ran through the beer garden, hugging her knees, her whole body shaking with fear and anger.

He plonked himself next to her. 'I've asked you if you're OK too many times already this week. I can't face saying it again.'

'I will be,' she told him. 'No thanks to you.'

'I know, I'm sorry,' he said meekly. 'I just can't stand the way he treats you.'

'And you think I can?' She turned on him, finally able to release her pent-up anger. 'It's easier to do as he says – it always has been. And I could have gone on doing that for just three more days, because I knew it was going to be over then. But now... God only knows what he'll do.' She rested her head on her knees and let out a shuddering sigh.

Brad didn't speak. Kathy heard him stand up and move away, but didn't look up. She suddenly felt exhausted; the prospect of walking a further twelve miles seemed insurmountable. Lying back on the grass, she closed her eyes trying to conjure up pleasant soothing images of mountains and flowing rivers, sunsets, anything to blot out Tony's raging expression before he'd pulled away.

She felt Brad return and sit down beside her again.

'Peace offering,' he said quietly.

Kathy opened her eyes to see a plate of sandwiches and a pint glass of water on the grass between them.

'I told the others everything is fine,' he said, offering her the plate. 'So hopefully they won't bombard you with questions.'

She took the water and drank thirstily, ignoring the food.

'Please eat something, Kathy. We've a long way to go still.' He pushed the plate towards her again.

She picked up a sandwich and bit into it, and they shared the food in silence.

When they'd finished, Brad stood up, extending his hand to Kathy. Unsmiling, she accepted it and he pulled her to her feet.

'I'm sorry.' He held his arms open and she leaned against his chest.

As Kathy gave in to the hug, a feeling of safety enveloped her for a few seconds.

Following Brad as they joined the others, she frowned.

Was that our bus that just passed the crossroads, or am I imagining things?

'Gather round, everyone,' Rob called out, in his official voice. 'Now you all know how tricky this stretch can be; we could be subject to all kinds of weather. So, have we all got plenty of water?'

'Yes, sir,' they chorused.

'Sun block?'

'Yes, sir.'

'Waterproofs?'

'What, like it's going to rain?' Ruth laughed.

'We have to be prepared,' he told her. 'Now, waterproofs?'

'Yes, sir.' They were all laughing now.

Even Kathy raised a smile, saying a silent thank you to Rob for keeping things normal.

XI

As the group began the climb to the summit of Rannoch Moor, they gradually spread out once again. Joy deliberately held back, wanting to keep a distance from Daniel. She was still trying to digest everything he'd told her, and although she knew he was looking for explanations too, she wasn't ready to give them. Not yet.

Bending to tighten a bootlace, she let the others pass.

Kathy and Brad were in the lead. Joy hadn't missed Kathy's shaken appearance, or Brad's arm draped casually across her shoulders as they'd passed, reminding Joy that she wasn't the only one with problems. Daniel and Ruth were twenty paces behind them, walking side by side, each engrossed in their own thoughts. Joy was well aware of the issues dominating those thoughts. *What a sad bunch we are. Daytime TV would have a field day with us lot.*

Trish and Rob strolled past.

And what about you two?

'Why are you raking all that up again?' Trish grumbled. 'What's done is done.'

Rob dropped Trish's hand and stuffed his own hands deep into his pockets.

'And what about Seb?'

Joy's ears pricked up.

What about Seb? And why is Rob angry? That's not like him. Is the heat getting to those two? God, I hope not, they're the only hope of credibility – and sanity and honesty - us lot have. Even though one or two green-eyed monsters in the Ship pub used to say the two of them were too good to be true. Maybe they're right. No. Don't be so stupid, Joy. Stop wishing something on them, just because you feel like shit.

Daniel had stopped, and Joy knew he was waiting for her, and as she caught up to him, she threw the first shot, hoping to take control of the situation.

'So it was a one-night stand, a grope in the dead of night.'

Daniel sighed.

'Yes, I told you.'

'And you never saw her again?'

'No.'

'Don't lie to me, Daniel. You worked in the same office.'

Joy lowered her voice.

'Please, no more lies, Dan. I don't want us coming out of this hating each other.'

'OK then; I never slept with her again.'

'But you did have some communication with her.'

'Not really. She left about four months later. She got a job in Leeds.'

'So that was the end of it?' Joy felt a glimmer of relief. Maybe they could get through this, if she could only find a way to make Daniel understand her side of things.

He nodded, and for a few minutes they didn't speak.

Joy stole a glance at Daniel as they walked. His brow was creased, his lips set in a firm line. Despite the intense heat on the exposed footpath, a shiver ran down her spine. She was certain he was about to ask her to explain her own deceit.

Daniel cleared his throat and took off his sunglasses.

'Actually, Stephanie did contact me again, indirectly.'

He hesitated, fixing his eyes on her for a moment before looking at the ground.

Joy held her breath, as icy fingers gripped her heart. *He's going to leave me for her. That's what he's going to say, I know it.*

He mumbled into his chest. 'A year later I received a letter from the Child Support Agency.' He looked up at her. 'I have a child,' he whispered.

Joy released the breath she had been holding, like a deflating balloon, and suddenly lightheaded, she stumbled. The footpath rose up to meet her and before she knew it, she was in a heap on the ground, the ever-present band of steel tightening around her chest as she fought to get air into her lungs.

Daniel was beside her in an instant.

'Joy, come on now, sit up,' he said calmly. 'Put your head between your knees. That's it. Now count, Joy, nice and slowly, and breathe. One, two, three ...'

Joy lost all concept of time as they sat at the edge of the path. Distantly, as if through a fog, she'd heard one or two concerned voices asking if everything was OK. She allowed Daniel's rhythmic counting to calm her, and the band loosened, her shoulders relaxing under the gentle pressure of his hands.

'We'd best get going,' she said shakily.

Daniel pulled her to her feet. 'Are you sure you're OK?'

'No, of course I'm not OK.' She glared at him, shrugging off his hold on her arm.

'Joy, I'm sorry...'

Save it, Daniel.' She cut him short. 'I can't deal with any of this now. I need to concentrate on getting off this fucking mountain.'

She set off again, focusing on the task of putting one foot in front of the other.

Daniel said nothing. He took her arm again as he walked beside her, his hand gently cupping her elbow, ready to catch her if she stumbled.

Joy mentally added up the years. *Eight? Ten? Ten years of lies. Ten years of hiding the maintenance payments he must have been making. Ten years of knowing he had a child, yet never getting to know him or her.*

Hang on a second, how do I know that? He never said he hasn't had contact. There was never any evidence, any signs, but that only means he's a damn good liar.

She pulled away, swinging round to face him.

'What is it?' she asked.

'What's what?'

'The child, stupid.' Her voice was croaky. 'A boy or a girl?' She pushed the words out.

'Oh, a boy,' Daniel whispered. 'He's called Jason.'

Joy could see how uncomfortable it was for him to talk about it, but she didn't care. She wanted him to hurt like she was hurting.

'Are they still living in Leeds?'

Daniel shook his head and Joy's heart began to pump faster once more.

'Where, then?' she asked.

When he didn't speak, she answered for him.

'They're in Redcar, aren't they?'

'Stockton, actually.' His words were barely audible.

'Fan-fucking-tastic.' Joy stopped him in his tracks, squaring up to face him. 'So while I'm being the dutiful wife, waiting to have dinner with her husband, in that mausoleum of a house we call home, you...' she poked a blood red, polished fingernail into his chest 'You're off playing happy families in Stockton.'

'It's not like that.'

'Then what exactly is it like, Daniel?' she exploded. 'You have a child who's what, ten years old, and you never thought to tell me... your wife.'

'I've never met him.' He sighed. 'I didn't even know they lived nearby, until two months ago. I just paid the CSA.'

'I don't believe you,' Joy interrupted. 'You must have seen him – at least once.'

'No, I wasn't interested. She was a mistake I wanted to forget.'

'So you just blindly handed money over to that tart who, for all you knew, could have just been screwing you for money to support some other bloke's kid.'

'I'm not totally stupid,' he said glowering at her. 'I asked for a DNA test. Jason is my son. I had a responsibility for his welfare; that was as far as it went.'

'This makes no fucking sense, Daniel,' Joy screamed at him. 'You're not interested in the tart. You're not interested in the child. It all happened ten years ago, yet you choose now to spill your guts. What the fuck is it all about, Daniel?'

Daniel grabbed her by the shoulders. 'If you just stopped for five minutes to listen, instead of jumping to your own conclusions or storming off refusing to hear me out, I might get a chance to explain,' he snapped. 'Stephanie rang the office a few weeks ago, totally out of the blue. She said we should meet; that Jason was asking questions, that he wanted to know about his dad.'

Joy's shoulders slumped. She shrugged him off and marched ahead, rhythmically stabbing the ground with her walking pole, allowing her mind to go into overdrive. So many unanswered questions crowded into her head that she didn't know where to start. So she asked the question that scared her most.

'Are you going to meet him?'

'Yes, next week,' Daniel mumbled. 'We're meeting at the Riverside Football Stadium; going on a tour round the stadium and stuff.'

'What, her as well?'

'She's hardly going to let him go on his own, is she?'

'Right.'

Her head pounded and she thought she might throw up any minute. If she could wave a magic wand and be anywhere but here, with anyone but him, she would gladly do it. The reality was she was trapped in the prison of this footpath and the enormity of the news she'd been given, and a man who, at this moment in time, she hated more than anyone or anything, as her cellmate.

'Daniel just go,' she said. 'I can't bear to look at you for another minute.'

'I'm not leaving you on your own.'

'We're on one of the most walked footpaths in the country,' she spat. 'And anyway, I'm a big girl. I can look after myself – which is just as well, because it looks like I'm going to have to from now on.'

Daniel flinched, and then frowned.

'Stop it, Joy. You're not the only injured party here, you know.'

'Don't even go there, Daniel. Not now. Look, forget it. Stay back here, I'll go on ahead. Just give me some space, OK?'

Daniel gave a frustrated sigh. Shaking his head, he dropped his rucksack and sat down on the rough grass beside the footpath.

Joy threw him a look of contempt before jogging off, quickly widening the distance between them.

XII

The River Ba, with its torrent of water flowing beneath the stone bridge, was an oasis of delight along the arid path across Rannoch Moor. Its roar echoed around the mountains, meaning that the walkers could hear it long before they reached it. And when they finally saw it, they reacted like children in a sweet shop.

Ruth leaned over the bridge. 'Come on, let's go in; it'll be heavenly,' she yelled excitedly, pulling Brad along with her, she ran down onto the riverbank, throwing her backpack onto the parched grass.

'Fully dressed?' Brad questioned.

'Well if you want to strip off, be my guest,' she said with a wink. 'We won't object, will we, Kathy?'

Kathy felt a blush flood up her neck, into her cheeks. 'She's only teasing,' she told Brad. 'Go on, you'll dry in no time in this heat.'

Ruth stepped into the cool water, treading carefully across the uneven surface to sit on a flat stone where rushing water washed over her.

'Ooh, aah, Oooh...' She swooned with delight. 'Better than sex any day!'

'Ruth!' Kathy admonished. 'Do you have to be so...'

'Honest?' Brad volunteered, giving Kathy a wink that heightened her blushes.

'Crude.' Kathy's voice disappeared amid Ruth's yells and the thunderous water.

She watched Brad, hearing him gasp as he sank into the icy flow.

'Here Brad, sit here.' Ruth wobbled, fighting to keep her balance as she struggled up from the flat stone she'd plonked herself on. 'It's like a Jacuzzi, only a hundred times better.'

Trish and Rob peered over the bridge.

'Ooh, looks like fun,' Trish yelled as they ran to join Kathy and the bathers.

She dropped her bag beside Kathy.

'Come on Kath, let's cool down.' She pulled Kathy to her feet.

'Oh, I don't know,' Kathy faltered. 'I'm not great with water.'

'You'll be fine, just sit on that stone, and soak your legs; it's really refreshing,' Brad called out to her.

Gingerly she stepped into the fast flowing water, glad of Trish's support.

'Brad, come here, you have to try this,' Ruth called from a few feet downstream, where she stood under a mini waterfall.

Kathy had to admit it felt good, the rushing water washing over her, cooling the blood, relaxing the mind. She could see Ruth and Brad under the curtain of water up ahead. Ruth shrieked like a schoolgirl, losing her footing, almost falling as Brad caught her.

'Come on in, Joy, this is fantastic!' Trish called out.

Kathy looked up to see Joy pass by in a streak of dust, her cap pulled down low, earphone wires dangling either side of her grim face.

Her heart went out to her, and Daniel too. She couldn't believe that this apparently perfect couple were being blasted apart before her very eyes. And there didn't seem to be a damn thing she or anyone else could do about it.

Stepping out of the water, she caught a glimpse of Ruth pulling Brad towards her, fixing her lips on his. She felt a pang of envy at seeing them kiss, quickly replaced by satisfaction, when Brad pulled away, shaking his head.

'Can't blame a girl for trying,' Ruth called after him, as he moved towards the bank.

XIII

They were already making their way back to the footpath, when Daniel reached them.

'You should have taken a dip, Dan,' Rob said, drying his face. 'It was brilliant –really refreshing.'

'I'd rather push on,' Daniel replied. He reached into the flowing waters anyway, scooping handfuls over his face and arms, before taking to the footpath again.

Kathy left the riverbank with him, struggling to keep up with his lengthy strides. Throughout the next long, arduous stretch, Joy remained in their sights, a mere blip on the canvas of the impressive landscape of the towering mountains that surrounded them.

'Look at that.' Kathy pointed to the mountains on her left. 'Can you believe there's still snow on those peaks? Even in this heat?'

Daniel didn't react.

'Do you want to talk?' she asked, when the silence became embarrassingly uncomfortable.

'Not really.'

'It might help.'

'It hasn't so far. The whole thing is just one big fucking mess.'

She felt the anger emanating from him.

They continued in silence along the winding footpath, Kathy keeping pace with him.

'I can't stand this heat a minute longer,' she finally blurted out. 'Surely we must be near the finish.'

Daniel checked his watch. 'About another half hour or so.'

Kathy thought his shoulders were more relaxed his jawline less rigid.

'Will you two work it out?' she asked, nodding at Joy, not so far in the distance.

'No, it's over,' he said. 'There's no coming back from this.'

'I'm sorry.'

'Don't be, it was inevitable. I've told her everything now.' He gave a half smile. 'And I have to say the relief is indescribable, Kathy. For years, our whole life has been a lie. And the pressure and the stress... it's enough to make you top yourself.'

Kathy shuddered. 'Don't even think that, Daniel, it's too awful to imagine.'

He shrugged and pointed to a white speck in the distance.

'Look,' he said. 'Kingshouse Hotel. We're on the home run.'

'I thought I'd never make it,' Kathy said, feeling suddenly revitalised at the sight of the finish line.

Soon the speck of white became a hotel; coloured dots became cars and pinpricks became people milling around or sitting at picnic tables, soaking up the sun.

Kathy spotted the bus, and her heart sank. She slowed down and began dragging her feet, remembering Tony's performance at lunchtime.

'Kathy.' Daniel stopped on the path. 'I've just shattered my marriage into a million pieces, but I had to tell her. I don't know if it was the right thing to do or not – I couldn't continue living this way.' He looked towards the hotel and the bus parked outside it. 'You have to do the right thing for you too.' He hugged her tight. 'You deserve better than him.'

Kathy pulled away, looking around wildly.

Here we go again. Who saw that? Did Joy see us? Will she kick off again? What about Tony... could he have seen from that distance?

She pulled free and moved ahead of Daniel, along the downhill path, drawing ever closer to the Kingshouse Hotel. She could hardly wait to take off her boots and her sticky, sweaty clothes, and sink into a fragrant bathtub.

The picnic tables set out in front of the hotel were now clearly visible and Kathy easily picked out Tony, sitting with a pint in front of him, staring up at the footpath. She felt his eyes burning into her. Then she saw Joy pass by the table and Tony's arm stretch out to stop her. Joy pushed him away and turned to look back up the mountain.

What poison is he spreading now?

Kathy allowed her anger to build. She needed to be angry, very angry, to have the courage to do this. DD Day was only days away.

XIV

Compared to the tranquillity of the moor, the hustle and bustle surrounding the hotel felt like a London tube station during rush hour. Kathy took a deep breath as she drew level with her husband.

His appearance disgusted her. His eyes were glazed and bloodshot and his face bloated, glowing red. His shorts were stained with lager, and an encrusted dribble of curry sauce trailed down his white T-shirt. He stared right through her as if he hadn't seen her at all and she released the breath she'd been holding. Suddenly she yelped, as his hand shot out, grabbing her trouser leg, and pinching the skin on her thigh.

'Get off!' She pulled away, hearing the thin cotton rip, and rushed into the hotel. Her heart was racing as she stumbled into the ladies, praying he hadn't followed her. In the cubicle, she examined her trousers, finding a two-inch tear along the seam joining the pocket.

'Bastard,' she hissed. Her whole body trembled. She'd never been so afraid of him. She'd never seen him look at her like that. Not ever.

God knows what's going on inside his head.

She sat on the closed lid of the loo, waiting for her breathing to return to normal. She heard the door open: Ruth and Trish walk in, chattering and laughing.

'I'm wrecked,' Trish announced, entering the cubicle beside Kathy.

'I couldn't walk another inch,' Ruth called out to her from the other side. 'I say we just grab a drink and something to eat – and to hell with getting cleaned up first. We're all in the same boat anyway.'

'You're right,' Trish agreed. 'If I have to go up those stairs, I'll never make it back down again this side of morning.'

Kathy held her breath, not moving a muscle. Her heart was still racing. *I couldn't bear for the two of them to see me now, in tears over that bastard.*

'Besides,' Ruth lowered her voice, 'there's too much shit going on here, between a few, who shall remain nameless... 'A storm is brewing, and I'd rather have our meal before it breaks.'

Feeling her lungs about to burst, Kathy released her breath, as slowly and quietly as she could, wishing the two of them would just go.

'I know. Tony is in an awful state.' Trish had left the cubicle and her voice could just be heard above the hand drier blowing. 'I've asked Rob to try and get him up to bed, before he causes a scene. Poor Kathy.'

Angry tears pricked Kathy's eyes. She didn't want their pity.

I should march out there right this second and tell them. I'm not poor Kathy.

But she didn't move. Not until she heard the noise from the bar, filtering through the open door as they left. She counted a full two minutes, then left the cubicle and splashed cold water on her face. She took a deep breath and pushed her shoulders back, before striding into the bar with head held high and fingers crossed.

XV

Everyone was there, except Tony. Kathy hovered on the edge of the group, listening to them deciding on when to eat. Trish and Ruth got their wish for an immediate dinner, and the decision was finalised just as a long table became free, on the far side of the room.

'Shall I go and fetch Tony?' Rob asked.

'Judging by the spills on his clothes, it looked like he'd eaten already,' Trish said, making a face.

'Even so...' Rob began.

'I'll go.' Kathy squeezed past Ruth. 'Won't be a minute,' she said, hating the artificial brightness of her tone.

Her hands trembled as she stepped outside into the evening sunshine. The mountains surrounding the whitewashed stone building of the hotel were stunning. She paused for a few moments to soak up the view and steel herself for a yet another scene. The bench where Tony had been sitting was empty; and he was nowhere in sight. She walked around the hotel to the car park and saw the locked bus, but still no sign of Tony.

Back in reception, she got their room number and a second key. She climbed the stairs, her heart hammering loudly, blocking out everything else around her.

She placed an ear against the door before unlocking it, preparing herself for the inevitable confrontation. Hearing nothing, she opened the door a crack and peered inside, scanning the room. The bed was untouched, her suitcase standing neatly beside it. The bathroom door was slightly ajar, with whispers of steam filtering out.

'Tony, we're going to eat now,' she called out from the doorway. 'Are you coming down, or have you eaten enough?'

'Can't hear you,' he yelled. 'Come in here.'

Gingerly, Kathy walked across the room, and pushed the bathroom door further open, with her foot.

'Ruth's with me,' she lied. 'Are you coming down to eat or not?'

'Order me steak and chips and a pint. I'll be down in a minute,' he slurred.

Kathy left without replying, her heart sinking at the prospect of a drunken Tony at the dinner table once again.

*****

Five minutes later, she watched her husband approach the table. He'd made an effort - she'd give him that. A fresh white shirt, skin glowing from the hot shower. His stagger was so slight, you'd only notice if you were watching for it.

'You all made it then?' he boomed, slapping Rob on the back as he took the empty seat between him and Joy to his right.

Kathy cringed and buried her head in the menu.

Just listen to him, they might not have noticed his stagger, but there's no hiding his drunken slur. Poor Joy having to put up with his waffle. I'm so relieved to be at this end of the table – although in hindsight perhaps sitting across from Daniel wasn't the brightest move.

'Yes. It was a tough one all right. Still, tomorrow will be a cushy number - only nine miles.' Rob laughed.

'What's so funny?' Ruth piped up. 'It might only be nine miles, but we have to climb the Devil's Staircase. And that's meant to be a killer.'

'Don't panic, Ruth,' Brad said. 'Take your time and it'll be fine.'

'Will you hold my hand if the going gets tough?' Ruth put on her little girl lost voice.

'Sir Lancelot, that's me.' Brad grinned widely. He caught Kathy's eye, giving her that almost invisible wink.

Kathy blushed.

Damn it, why do I keep doing that? We're just friends - it's a friendly gesture, nothing more and I go acting like a love struck teenager, like I fancy the pants off him, and I don't... well, OK, maybe I do, but as he's told me, it's not going to happen.

She felt an elbow in her ribs.

'Is he OK?' Trish threw a glance towards Tony.

Kathy picked up her drink. She peered over the top of the glass, careful not to make eye contact with Tony. He was glaring intently at Brad. She recoiled at the raw aggression she saw in his eyes. Suddenly he switched his gaze to Kathy and their eyes locked. She spluttered on her drink, coughing uncontrollably, and Trish jumped up, whacking her on the back.

'I'm OK,' Kathy said breathlessly. 'Just went down the wrong way.'

'Wow, there's enough to feed a small army on just one plate here,' Trish said, looking at the chicken fillets covered with a creamy white wine sauce, placed before her by a rosy-faced cheery waitress.

Kathy nodded, still breathless from her coughing fit.

'Och, we're well used to feeding hungry walkers here,' said the young waitress. 'You'll manage it all, I'm sure,' she added.

XVI

Joy knew without doubt that she wouldn't finish hers. She pushed the fillet of wild Scottish salmon around her plate.

What goes around comes around, isn't that what they say? Living a lie to hold on to him all these years could only ever have one ending... heartache. It's over, I know, so what do we do next? How do we get through the next three days for a start? Maybe I should just cry off now; get myself back to Glasgow and catch a train home. I can't stand all this false joviality. I mean, look at them all, it's not just me- are any of them being honest?

Brad's a workaholic, preferring to go through life all alone rather than take the risk of getting close to someone again, after what happened to Jen all those years ago. With his easy come, easy go attitude, people only ever see the joker or the womaniser. I wonder how many of his so-called friends have seen even a glimpse of his sadness.

And Daniel. I know to my cost what lies beneath there. The question is how will he handle what's happened? And how will the others react? Will they say, 'great news, Dan, nothing can beat being a parent, there's no other love like it.' Or will they be disgusted that he not only cheated on his wife, but also left such a tangible reminder of that infidelity.

Rob. I thought he was such an open book, now I'm not convinced. Watching him and Trish this week, there's definitely something underlying. The happy normal couple scenario seems to be wilting under the spotlight of the sun and the twenty-four seven company of strangers. Hang on a minute... strangers? We're supposed to all be friends here.

Abandoning her meandering thoughts, along with any attempt at eating, Joy pushed her plate away. Exhausted, she wondered how quickly she could make her excuses and escape to the sanctuary of her room. She longed for the safety and comfort of her own bed; they'd only been away five days, but it felt like a lifetime. Unable to maintain any sort of pretence at being sociable, Joy decided enough was enough.

'I'm off,' she announced, pushing back her chair. 'See you all in the morning.' Before anyone had a chance to object, she had bolted, disappearing through the door marked 'residents only'.

XVII

Kathy watched Tony move on from pints to whiskeys, and wished she were anywhere but here. As soon as he'd demolished his food, he'd left the table, and was now slumped on a high stool at the end of the bar, bending the ear of an old man with a mop of white hair and a long straggly beard, who was trying to read a newspaper. She was ashamed to even be associated with him, let alone married to him and wished fervently that he'd stayed at home.

She had no idea how she was going to get through these next few days.

If the truth be known, I'm scared, scared of my own husband. How sad is that? What can I do? I can't share that with anyone here, not even Brad. You don't talk about things like that. What happens behind closed doors usually stays there, and Tony makes out we're the perfect couple, like everything's hunky dory between us. It's such a farce.

Folding her napkin neatly, she slid out of her chair and stood up.

'See you in the morning, everyone,' she said quietly, hoping not to draw too much attention to herself.

XVIII

Kathy woke with a start. The room door almost came off its hinges as Tony fell through it, staggering and cursing and tripping over her suitcase.

'Where's the fucking lights?' he muttered, eventually hitting the switch, flooding the room with brightness.

She didn't move a muscle.

He stumbled over to the bed. 'Kathy? You awake?' he slurred.

Kathy said nothing.

He thumped the bed at her feet. 'Wake up!'

She curled up instinctively.

'You're avoiding me. What the fuck's going on?'

Her heart hammered against her ribcage, as he lumbered around the bed towards her.

Do I stand my ground, or try to calm the situation?

Calming the situation seemed the best approach. Kathy shuffled herself across the wide bed, and stood up on the far side with the bed a barrier between them, relieved that she was wearing pyjamas.

'Stop yelling, Tony. It's the middle of the night.' The words came out more smoothly than she expected.

'You're at it with Crathorne, aren't you?'

'Don't be ridiculous.'

'Don't you dare lie to me, Kathy.' He slammed his fist into the pillow she'd just vacated.

Kathy flinched.

'I've seen you - the way you've been looking at him. You were all over each other today, up on that track where you thought no one could see you,' he sneered, climbing onto the bed and advancing towards her.

'What are you on about?' Kathy moved backwards towards the far wall, as she tried desperately to keep her voice, and the situation, calm.

'That bastard Crathorne, he's Alison's father. Just admit it, woman. And you two have been at it ever since.'

He looked so pathetic, clawing his way across the bed in an effort to reach her.

Kathy pressed herself against the wall, edging towards the bathroom. She would have laughed at the sight of him, if she hadn't been so scared.

'Not all this again, Tony. You know nothing's going on; there never has been and never will be.'

He continued ranting, as if she hadn't spoken at all.

'Well I've had it with your excuses. "I'm tired, I want more romance..."' he mimicked. 'When the truth is, you're getting it elsewhere. And now, tonight, not satisfied with one bit on the side, I see you throwing yourself at Brad! Some fucking friend he is, sleeping with my wife!'

'For crying out loud, Tony, I'm not sleeping with Brad.' Kathy was furious.

If he wants a fight then he can have one.

He clambered off the bed and stood up, swaying slightly, just feet away from her.

She saw his eyes try to focus, and she turned away feeling utterly repulsed.

'Where do you think you're going?' He lunged forward, grabbing the back of her T-shirt, catching her hair in his grip, dragging her backwards.

'Tony, stop it!' she yelled, wrenching free and running to the bathroom.

Despite his drunkenness, he was quick to catch her. He grabbed her arm and spun her around, slamming her back against the wall. His fingers bit into her shoulders as he pinned her there.

'It's time you behaved like a proper wife should. Or maybe you like playing the tart,' he sneered, his spittle spraying her face.

Tony forced his mouth onto Kathy's. She could hardly breathe. She squeezed her eyes tightly shut, twisting her head from side to side, terrified of what he would do next.

'Stop it. You're hurting me.' Her words were lost against his bristly cheek, as she squirmed, freeing her mouth from his.

'Come on; put a bit of effort into it. Get those stupid things off.' He tried to pull her pyjama top over her head.

'No!' She grappled with him, desperate to keep her body covered.

'Take them off now!' he barked, stepping back.

'No. No more, Tony.' She was amazed at how controlled the words sounded. 'I won't keep taking this shit.'

She watched his eyes widen, before narrowing to tiny slits, as her words registered.

He wiped the back of his hand across his mouth.

'I asked you nicely. Now I'm telling you,' he ordered.

She lashed out as he came towards her again, drawing angry red lines down his neck, digging her nails into his flesh.

'You bitch.' His hand came up in a reflex action, striking her across the face.

For a split second, shock took over and neither of them moved.

'Fuck it.' He turned away.

She jumped at the sound of splintering wood, as he punched the bathroom door.

'Fuck it, Kath; I'm sorry, I'm so sorry.' He swayed towards her again. 'Why did you make me do that?'

Kathy thought she'd pass out. Her face felt like an explosion had taken place. The pain was so intense she was sure her cheekbone was broken.

Tony reached out to touch the angry mark. She reacted instinctively, bringing her knee up hard.

'Aghh,' he roared, falling to the floor.

Kathy ran to the door, pulling it open and fleeing out into the corridor.

XIX

Panicking, she tried to remember which room was Trish's. She looked anxiously behind her, before hammering on a door, too frightened to care if she had the right room or not.

'Trish, Trish!'

After what seemed like an eternity, Rob opened the door, wearing only his boxers, pulling a T-shirt over his head.

Kathy pushed past him running to the farthest corner of the room. She sank to the floor, hugging her knees. Her whole body shook uncontrollably. Her brown eyes were huge and terrified.

Trish was beside her in seconds, wrapping a white towelling robe around her shoulders.

'My God, Kath, what happened?' She stroked Kathy's flaming cheek with her thumb.

Kathy couldn't speak. Silent tears spilled from her eyes, and her teeth chattered.

'Rob, fetch some whisky from the minibar,' Trish called out as she hugged her sister.

Kathy stared ahead unseeing, vaguely aware of Trish's movements and a cool glass being put into her hand.

She held it tightly, willing the amber liquid to remain steady, as it sloshed against the sides of the glass. Trish's hand gently covered hers, guiding the glass to her mouth, tilting it, until the bitter taste of whisky hit her lips. She swallowed, concentrating on the burning sensation, as the whisky travelled down her throat.

They could hear Tony's raging voice in the corridor.

'Stay here,' Trish told her.

She nodded, never once letting her eyes stray from the open doorway.

'Kathy! Kathy!' Tony bellowed. 'Where is she?'

Kathy shrank back further into the corner when he appeared at the doorway. Rob valiantly blocked his way.

'Come on, Tony, keep it down, mate or you'll have us all thrown out.'

Then Trish was in the doorway, next to her husband.

'What have you done to her, you bastard?' she screamed at him.

'Kathy, get out here now, before I drag your fancy men out of their beds and give them what's coming to them,' he ranted.

'Leave her alone.' Trish blocked his way. 'Or I'll call the police.'

Tony turned away in disgust, and stormed off down the corridor hammering and kicking on more doors.

'Crathorne! You in there?' he shouted.

Kathy couldn't think straight, her face was throbbing, her head pounding. She needed to get out there, calm him down, before he hurt someone. She heaved herself to her feet and took a wobbly step towards the door. The glass fell from her hand and the floor came up to meet her.

XX

Joy woke at the sound of ructions in the corridor. Recognising Tony's roars and Trish's screams, she quickly pulled on her jeans. She threw a cushion at Daniel, sleeping in the armchair.

'Dan, wake up, something's kicking off in the corridor. Can't you hear them?'

They both jumped as the door rattled.

'Crathorne, I'm warning you!' Tony kicked the door repeatedly.

'What's going on?' Joy asked, wide-eyed and anxious as she looked from Daniel to the door.

'How the hell do I know? I was sound asleep until two seconds ago.'

'Well, it sounds like he's after your blood. No surprises there then,' she snapped. 'You and Kathy - I knew it! I'll let him in, shall I?'

'For fuck's sake, Joy, he's as deluded as you are.' Daniel pushed her away from the door.

They both jumped and Joy screamed when the door splintered and flew open.

Daniel didn't stand a chance. Tony's fist slammed into his nose, causing a spray of blood as he fell backwards. He immediately launched himself at Daniel again, punching him repeatedly in the ribs.

Joy threw herself at Tony, jumping onto his back. She dug her long nails into his scalp, grabbing handfuls of hair, pulling with all her weight.

'Get off him, you bastard,' she screamed, scratching Tony's face.

All the pent-up anger and emotion of the past few days broke free, and like a lioness she continued her assault. Just seconds later, Joy felt herself being lifted away from him. She had clumps of black and silver hair in her hands and Tony's blood and skin under her fingernails. Rob put her down in the corridor. She watched breathlessly as he and Brad grappled with Tony. Then instinct took over and she raced towards Daniel.

'Oh my God.' Her hand flew to her mouth.

Daniel struggled to sit up. Blood poured from his nose and one eye was swollen and closed completely.

'We need a doctor,' shouted Joy.

'I'll be OK,' Daniel whispered, wincing in pain as he touched his ribs.

'Get the fuck off me!' Tony roared. His rage intensified. He struggled free from the two men and then lunged at Brad, grabbing him around the throat, pushing him back against the wall.

Feeling like an extra in an episode of *Taggart*, Joy watched in horror, expecting to hear some director shout 'Cut!' any second.

'I knew you fucked about with women,' Tony shouted. 'Well, not with my wife you don't!' With every word, he shook Brad's head violently. 'Keep your fucking hands off her! Do you hear me?'

Suddenly, and without warning, he released his grip.

'She's my wife, do you hear me... my wife,' he muttered and pushing past Rob, he staggered back out into the corridor.

Rob and Brad were right behind him. Brad coughing and spluttering as he rubbed at his throat.

Joy kissed the top of Daniel's head before following them.

Doors were opening right and left, and people in all states of undress crowded into the corridor, horrified at the spectacle unfolding before them, in this usually tranquil place.

'Kathy, get out here!' Tony marched back towards Trish's room.

The spectators rushed to clear a pathway for him.

'We're getting out of this fucking hell hole right now,' he yelled.

Ruth stepped forward into the corridor and as Tony drew level, she threw her walking pole out in front of him.

'Stop right there matey,' she hissed.

Tony fell head first, flat on his face, and lay spread-eagled on the worn red carpet. Brad leapt on top of him, twisting his arm up his back.

Joy winced, convinced she'd heard the bone crack, and Brad pushed Tony's face into the carpet.

'You lay a hand on her again... or so much as touch a hair on her head,' he whispered, 'and I'll kill you myself.'

The intensity of the controlled anger in Brad's voice shocked Joy.

Heavy steps pounded along the corridor as hotel staff, accompanied by uniformed police officers, ran towards them.

'Right, sir, I'll take over from here.' A burly police officer helped Brad to his feet. Another officer with tightly cropped red hair, bushy eyebrows, and a thick moustache to match fixed the handcuffs onto Tony's wrists and pulled him to his feet.

'Get the fuck off me,' Tony roared, thrashing against the officer's firm hold.

'Sir, I'm arresting you for breach of the peace.' The red-haired officer read Tony his rights.

Tony slumped forward, all the fight gone out of him as the officer walked him through the gawping crowd, towards the staircase, and the squad car waiting outside the hotel.

With the show over, the other residents gradually disappeared behind their doors, leaving only Joy, Brad, Rob and Ruth in the corridor.

Brad rubbed his throat. His neck was red and angry looking, where Tony's hands had been.

'I think I need a drink,' he croaked.

'I think you need a doctor,' Joy told him. 'Daniel should go too,' she said taking control of the situation. 'Rob, will you take them, please? Ask at reception, you might have to go to Fort William, to A & E.

'I need to check on Trish and Kathy first,' he said.

'We'll take care of them, won't we, Ruth?' Joy said. 'Please, Rob, look after Dan.'

Rob nodded his agreement. 'I will, but I do need to talk to Trish first. I'll be two minutes.'

'Ruth, go find the bus keys, and lock up Kathy's room,' Joy instructed, before going back to Daniel.

Daniel was pushing his feet into his shoes. He held a wad of tissue under his bleeding nose.

Joy saw the pain in his eyes and knew it wasn't just physical.

'Rob's taking you to a doctor,' she said calmly, without a trace of the turmoil of emotions she was feeling.

'He's obsessive and controlling, as well as being insanely insecure,' Daniel said. 'You do know that, don't you?' He took her outstretched hand and she pulled him to his feet. When she tried to pull away, he kept hold of her hand.

'Joy, look at me,' he persisted.

She looked directly into his eyes.

'If we never speak another word to each other, or spend another night together, please believe me when I tell you, nothing ever happened between me and Kathy.'

She tore her gaze away, looking at his hand clasping hers. He fingered the chipped nails, the gold, and diamonds of her rings.

Should I give them back?

They almost reached the knuckle of her finger. How strange it would feel without them.

'You ready to go, mate?' Rob asked, from the doorway.

'Coming,' Daniel said, and bending slightly, holding his ribs, he let go of Joy's hand and followed Rob.

Joy's hand fell to her side. She looked around the room, seeing Daniel's blood, crimson on the white duvet. The dented door and the overturned chair. She felt violated.

Ruth stepped aside to let the men pass.

'Come on, you,' she said, putting an arm loosely around Joy's shoulders. 'I think we need a drink, girl.'

Suddenly all the fight went out of Joy, and she began to shake as she let Ruth lead her out into the corridor.

'Let's raid the minibar in my room,' Ruth whispered, closing the door softly behind them.

XXI

Kathy opened her eyes to see Trish kneeling beside her.

'Come on, Kath, take another sip. It'll help with the shock,' Trish said, holding the glass of whisky to her sister's lips.

Kathy couldn't. She knew that if she opened her mouth, the most inhuman sound ever heard would erupt from her. She sat up, hugging her knees tightly, rigid with fear. She could hear the chaos in the corridor. It was surreal, like a TV playing in a distant room. Recognising the voices, yet unable to move, she tried to focus. She could make out the doorway. It was slightly ajar allowing a shaft of light to enter the darkened room.

The official voice of a police officer reading someone their rights stirred her into speech.

'Someone called the police?' Kathy looked at Trish, forcing the words past the hysteria that threatened to engulf her.

'The management, I'd imagine,' Trish said. 'There's one holy ruckus going on out there.'

'Has he hurt anyone?'

'Well, you, for a start.' Carefully, Trish helped Kathy to her feet. She peered cautiously around the open door to see the police officers leading a subdued Tony away.

'What'll happen to him?' she whispered.

Trish gulped down the whisky she'd been offering her sister.

'They should lock him up and throw away the key, if you ask me. Sorry, Kathy - but after that performance, surely to God you won't take him back?'

'I don't know. I don't know anything anymore.' Kathy sighed heavily. She was exhausted, physically and mentally. 'I should go to the police station.'

'Like hell you should!'

'But...'

'Never mind the buts,' Trish said. 'Get into bed. You need some rest.' She gave Kathy a gentle push.

Too tired to object, Kathy fell into the bed, shuffled down under the duvet, and closed her eyes. She couldn't sleep. The image of Tony's contorted rage-filled face swam behind her eyelids, while her silent tears soaked the pillow.

'He went berserk out there...' Rob whispered. 'I'm taking Brad and Dan to the hospital in Fort William,' he told Trish. 'Do you think Kathy needs to go too?'

'No, I think she's better here with me,' Trish said looking over to Kathy.

Kathy listened to Trish and Rob's urgent whispering, unable to make out many of the words and lacking the energy to ask any questions.

'Are you awake, Kath?' Trish called quietly across the room.

Kathy didn't answer.

'I'll be back in a minute.' She closed the door with a soft click.

XXII

Joy and Ruth sat side by side, propped up against pillows on Ruth's bed, nursing glasses of whisky. Exhausted and shell-shocked they watched the TV's silent flickering as it played an old episode of *One Foot in the Grave*. Any other time they would have laughed aloud at Victor Meldrew's antics, but not tonight.

There was a firm knock at the door and the two women jumped, slopping whisky over the rim of their glasses.

'Can I come in?' Trish called out.

Ruth heaved herself off the bed, let her in without a word, and resumed her position.

Trish helped herself to a drink, grabbed a spare pillow, and sat cross-legged on the bed, facing them.

'How are you doing?' she asked Joy.

Joy shrugged, giving a weak smile.

'Kathy's asleep, thank God.' Trish threw back her drink. 'That bastard's made a right mess of her face.'

Ruth switched off the TV and stared at Trish.

'He hit her?' she asked. Her eyes widened in horror. 'What the fuck is he playing at?'

'Uncontrollable jealously,' Trish spat. 'He got some notion in his head that she was seeing someone else, and he just snapped.'

'Daniel,' Joy croaked. 'She was seeing Daniel.'

'Oh, Joy, we're not going down that road again,' Trish said, shaking her head.

'I think we should all try and get some sleep,' Ruth interrupted. 'It's too late, or too early, whichever way you want to look at it, to make any sense of this.' She pointed at the window and the streak of light spreading slowly through the blackened sky.

'You're right,' agreed Trish. 'We'll talk in the morning. I guess we'll have to decide then what we're going to do.'

Once Trish had left, Joy turned to Ruth.

'Can I stay with you?' she asked.

'Of course.' Ruth smiled and gave her a reassuring hug. 'Everything'll look better in the morning. You'll see.'

XXIII

With a feather-light touch Kathy traced her little finger around the angry red handprint, shocked at her reflection. The imprint of his fingers decorated her cheek, scarlet and purple, against a grey complexion. Her eyes were dull, lifeless, and half hidden beneath puffy lids. She gripped the edge of the basin for a second, before turning away.

It was three in the morning, and there was no sign of either Trish or Rob. Kathy desperately wanted a shower. She needed to wash away the touch of Tony's hands, the feel of his violence and rage. She needed her own things and her own space.

Straightening up the bed covers, Kathy began looking for the key to her room. Engrossed in the task, her feet almost left the floor when the door swung open and Rob appeared.

'Lost something, Kath?' he asked.

'The key. I'm looking for the key to my room.' She felt like a child, caught hunting for Santa's stash of presents at Christmas. Her voice shook as much as her hands. 'I need a shower - and I need to get my stuff.'

'I have it.' He pulled the key card from his pocket. 'Are you sure? Shall I get Trish to go with you? She's in with Ruth and Joy.'

'No, really, I'll be OK.' Kathy took the card.

She scurried across the hall, let herself in, and closed the door quickly. Without looking too closely at the crime scene, she locked herself in the bathroom. She turned on the shower and watched the steam fog up the mirror, until her reflection was reduced to nothing, symbolising the disappearance of her other self. The one she'd wrestled with for so long – the one with the eyes that so often scared her into holding back from saying or doing what she really wanted.

Kathy stepped under the shower. The hot water stung as it splashed her tender face. She bit her lip, holding in the tears, waiting for the intensity of the sting to dull. Something inside her had escaped tonight, like an airbag bursting out from its compartment in a car, never to fit back inside again. She recalled the emotions of the past few hours. Her repulsion at the pathetic drunken state Tony had got himself into – and her fear when he had her pinned against the wall. That's when the airbag burst. When she acted on the anger she'd felt so many times, but had held onto, on the advice of the 'other Kathy' who lurked beyond the foggy depths of the bathroom mirror. Then, terrified at what she'd done and the recriminations that might follow, she'd fled to Trish.

Now despite this ache in my face and my pounding head, I feel different, surprisingly calm. I finally did it. I actually fought back – and I guess there's no going back now. There's only one road to take, and that's straight ahead.

Ten minutes later, scrubbed and glowing, Kathy left the steamy bathroom wrapped in a towel. She slid the chain across the bedroom door - just in case, and hit the light switch. In the soft glow of the breaking dawn, she flopped onto the cool bed, before falling into an exhausted sleep.

THURSDAY
I

Kathy woke with a shiver just before seven. Despite the sun flooding the room, she was chilly, and quickly pulled on jeans and a daffodil yellow T-shirt. In the bathroom, the steam had cleared and her reflection studied her intently.

Don't look at me that way. I'm strong. I can do this.

The deep brown eyes appeared doubtful. Worry lines creased her tanned forehead.

I'll show you; you'll see.

She turned away, angry at the visible uncertainty and closed the bathroom door behind her.

'I can do this. Today is D-T-Day,' she told the empty room loudly. She threw her suitcase onto the bed and began packing her things.

Fifteen minutes later Kathy left the room and went downstairs. The reception area was deserted. Feeling in need of some air, she ventured outside.

The view really was spectacular. The mountains surrounding the valley of Glencoe were bathed in soft morning sunlight to the east, while still shrouded in darkness to the west. Their magnitude and vastness took her breath away.

The picnic tables scattered around the green were deserted, their umbrellas not yet unfolded. She sat down at one of the tables, thinking how nice it would be to be artistic.

Picture the scene, men and women in bohemian dress, standing behind easels, holding paint palettes and using lavish brush strokes to create stunning paintings of this beautiful mountain scenery.

She jumped at the hand that touched her shoulder.

It was Daniel.

'Couldn't you sleep either?' he asked.

She shrugged in half-hearted agreement.

'Isn't this the most amazing place? Look at these mountains,' she said hoping to divert the conversation she knew would come. 'They are huge. So majestic, oozing confidence and power.' She pointed to the arc around her. 'They make me feel tiny and insignificant.'

'Can I sit down?' he asked, showing little interest in the mountains.

'Of course.' She looked back at the sleeping hotel. 'But windows have eyes. We could be fuelling the gossip flames.'

Daniel shrugged and sat down opposite her.

'Could things be any worse?' he asked with wry smile.

Kathy saw him wince as he moved.

'How badly did he hurt you?' she asked.

'I'll live. How about you?'

Her expression hardened.

'Enough to break the mould. He won't hurt me again.'

A delivery truck passed by the hotel and they sat in silence for a moment listening to the dull drone of the engine echoing around the mountains, until it faded away into the distance.

Kathy turned back to Daniel. 'He's ruined the holiday, that's for sure,' she said, shaking her head. 'And the hotel... all the damage he's done, broken doors, chairs... It's a wonder they didn't throw us all out last night.'

The purr of a car engine and the sound of tyres crunching over gravel made them both look up. Moments later two police officers appeared from the side of the hotel and crossed the grass towards them.

'Excuse me, sir.' The red-haired policeman from the night before stopped in front of Daniel. 'We'll need to take a statement from you.'

'What'll happen to Tony?' Kathy asked.

'This is his wife.' Daniel introduced Kathy.

'Madam.' The officer gave a brief nod.

'Will you charge him?' Kathy persisted.

'He could face charges of drunk and disorderly, damage to private property, assault...' The officer looked at Daniel. 'If you decide to press charges.'

'Oh, I don't know,' Daniel said.

The officer stared at Kathy's blackening eye and bruised cheekbone. ''Did he assault you too madam?' he asked. 'Will you be pressing charges?'

'Will you let him go?' Kathy avoided giving an answer.

'That'll depend on the charges. Either way, I'll need an account of what happened. And the hotel *is* pressing charges.' The officer nodded at Kathy and touched Daniel's arm. 'Now if you could come with me, sir.'

As he stood up, Daniel's eyes pleaded silently with Kathy.

'It's your call,' she said. 'I have my own decisions to make.'

'We'll be in touch, madam,' the officer said.

Kathy nodded and walked back indoors.

II

In dribs and drabs, the others came into the dining room. Besides a few murmured enquiries to Kathy on how she was doing, they kept a low profile as they collected their fruit and cereal from the breakfast bar. They were all well aware of the sideways glances from some of the other guests, understandably cranky from their disturbed night.

'Shall we take our coffee outside?' Ruth asked when the full Scottish had been demolished, or toyed with, depending on whose plate it was. 'At least we can talk out there,' she added in a whisper.

Everyone nodded in agreement and left the dining room to trek across the grass and gather around a picnic table.

'That's better. What a load of nosy old beggars. Craning their necks and straining their ears to get a sniff at the gossip.' Ruth blew off steam before grabbing Kathy in a warm hug. 'Come here, you. How are you doing?'

'I'll be OK, Ruth,' Kathy said, glad of the moral support.

As usual, Rob took charge. He stood with one foot resting on the bench and addressed the group.

'Right, everyone. Last night was pretty horrible.' He looked around the table. 'There's only one person to blame and he's not here. The question now is how we all feel about carrying on. Do we continue? Do we go home? So shall we vote and go with the majority, or each do our own thing?'

Brad was first to speak.

'What do you want to do, Kathy?' he asked.

As Kathy looked at Brad, she saw the other Kathy reflected in his sunglasses, - ready to give in and bend to the will of the other people. Her face grew hot under the group's scrutiny, as they waited for an answer. She closed her eyes and took a deep breath.

I have to be strong. Today is DD Day. From now on, I do what I want, and I'll do it my way.

'I came here to walk The West Highland Way, and I'd like to finish it,' she said, her voice as strong as she could make it. 'But I'll understand if, after what Tony did, you'd rather I wasn't around.' She looked down at her hands clasped together tightly on the table.

'Tony's behaviour was disgusting last night,' Trish said, reaching across the table to place a hand on Kathy's. 'Kathy, you're married to him. That's all. You're not answerable for his actions.' She looked across at Rob. 'We'll finish the walk with Kathy, won't we?'

He smiled and nodded. 'Of course.'

'I'm with you on that.' Brad nodded too, and then winked at Kathy.

Ruth nudged Joy in the ribs. 'You can count us in - we're in it to win, aren't we, Joy?' she said firmly. 'That's if I can get past the Devil's Staircase,' she added with a grin.

'What about you, Daniel?' Rob asked. 'Are the ribs too painful?'

'I'm fine, count me in too,' Daniel said.

'What about the bus?' Kathy asked. 'Even if they let Tony out, I don't want him anywhere near me - or any of us.'

'I'll talk to the hotel staff. We'll work something out, don't worry,' Rob told her.

He went back inside and came a few minutes later, with a plan.

'For a fee, the hotel will drop the bus down to the B&B in Kinlochleven,' he told them. 'I also rang ahead to the B&B and Mrs Galbraith, the landlady, said there was no problem getting the bus over to Fort William tomorrow,' he added. 'So, now that's sorted, let's be ready to roll in ten minutes. OK?'

By 9.30, they were walking single file along the side of the road, in a westerly direction, towards the head of Glencoe.

III

Joy felt dwarfed by the towering mountains.

It's as if they are closing in around me, reaching inside me and, pulling out the person that's locked in there. The one hidden behind the armour I've been building around myself for as long as I can remember. I know I have to talk to Kathy. Back there, outside the hotel we skirted around each other avoiding eye contact - that's no good. I have to face her; I have to face them all. I have to explain my actions to Daniel – he has a right to know. But now that the armour is cracking, it's just so hard - and I'm scared. Scared the real me will be left exposed and vulnerable, like fodder in a lion's den.

'Those damn mountains. They're suffocating me,' she said aloud, stabbing the ground with her walking pole.

'Are you OK?' Daniel asked, stepping forward to walk beside her.

'As OK as I can be, considering my life is total shit.' She stabbed at the ground once more.

'Did you get any sleep?' he asked.

'Not much, you?' Despite their situation, she was concerned about him. 'You look as if you're in pain. What did the doctor say?'

'The ribs are bruised, that's all. Nothing's broken.'

'Don't you think you should rest today? You could have driven the bus to Kinlochleven, taken things easy.'

'I'll be fine. I'm doped up on strong painkillers. Can't feel a thing.' He tapped his chest. 'Never mind me, you look really tired, Joy. Yesterday was a tough day in more ways than one. Are you sure you're up to this?' His eyes bore into hers.

Something inside Joy snapped. 'Of course I'm fucking tired,' she exclaimed furiously. She stopped dead, and so did Daniel. Ruth and Trish collided into the back of them.

'Hey, watch it, you two,' Ruth said.

Joy waited a second or two, until Ruth and Trish were out of earshot.

'We've failed at practically everything in our lives,' she hissed. 'Friendships; marriage; parenting; business; we've even failed to be decent members of society...'

'Stop it!' Daniel shook her shoulders. 'Stop it now!'

'That's exactly what I'm doing,' she said tightly. 'I'm stopping it now. No more failure. No more lies. I'll finish this walk if it kills me, and I'll tell you everything. Then I'll tell them everything.' She pointed to the others gathered at the foot of the Devil's Staircase. 'Because I can't be Joy Crathorne anymore.'

'You want a divorce?'

'You just don't get it, Daniel. You just don't get me.' She gave a sad little laugh and marched off to join Trish and Ruth.

'You're not talking sense! How the fuck am I meant to understand?' Daniel shouted after her.

*****

Joy walked one step ahead of Ruth as they began to climb the Devil's Staircase. She kept her head down, concentrating on the arduous climb.

'I knew this would be torture,' Ruth puffed. 'Didn't I tell you it would be the death of me?'

'Shut up, Ruth, conserve your energy, and just keep walking.' Trish had a hand on her back, pushing her forward.

Joy could see Kathy ahead, moving with the energy of a teenager, disappearing and then reappearing, as they zigzagged their way upwards.

Why am I treating her like this? I know, deep down, there's nothing between them. Maybe it's just easier to be angry and accusing than to be open and honest about who I really am.

IV

Kathy reached the top of the staircase and slumped to the ground, resting her back against a huge craggy bolder. Her lungs were craving air so badly she felt they might burst. At the same time, she felt exhilarated and free, despite all that had happened - not just the night before, but during all those times she'd bowed down to Tony and his bullying ways.

'What are you smiling about?' Brad sat down beside her.

'I feel free, Brad. Like an enormous weight has been lifted from me - and if I don't hold on to something, I'll float away.'

'I'll hold you down,' he said, smiling and gripping her hand tightly. 'Have you thought about what you're going to do back home?'

'I won't be spending another night in that house with him, that's for sure.'

'Where will you go?'

'I don't know. To eat humble pie at my mother's, I suppose. She always said he was a wrong 'un. I'll take Alison with me, but I can't decide for the boys. They'll have to make up their own minds.'

'Do you think they'll stay with their dad?'

'I doubt it. Ever since they were old enough to notice things, they always hated the way Tony was with me. No, they'll probably crash with friends for a few days, until we sort something out.'

'Wouldn't it be easier to kick Tony out?' Brad asked.

'I suppose...' Kathy hesitated. 'The thing is that I want to be me, without the emotional baggage stuffed in every corner of that house. Do you see what I mean?'

'Kind of.'

'You know that ad on TV, about moisturiser or something, where she says "Love the skin you're in"? Well, I don't.' She plucked at her bare arms. 'I want to shed this skin, and reveal what's underneath - a new me. The real me.'

Her words hung in the air between them.

They took in the panoramic view of the rugged peaks around the head of Glen Coe and Glen Etive.

Brad broke the silence. 'Did you know this is the highest point on the way? Five hundred and fifty metres, and it's all downhill from here.' He stood up, offering her a hand. 'Well, for today at least.' He laughed and Kathy did, too.

'Did anyone ever tell you what a pain in the backside you are?'

'Frequently.'

The footpath followed the flat ridge for a while, the bulk of Ben Nevis looming in the distance ahead.

Brad pointed it out to Kathy.

'The final milestone.'

'Still looks a long way off to me. Anyway, it's better that I take one day at a time at the moment.'

'You could move into my flat, you know,' Brad said.

'What?'

'I said...'

'I heard what you said. But what do you mean?'

'I can move out, stay with a friend,' he said with a shrug of his shoulders. 'You and the kids could stay there, until we sort somewhere more permanent.'

'We?'

'I want to help,' he said. 'No strings.'

'I don't know.' Kathy was speechless. It was the last thing she'd expected.

'Look, no pressure. It's an option. That's all.'

Why is he doing this? Tony almost killed him last night. If he had any sense, he'd keep as far away from me as possible. I know Tony won't give up without a fight, and Brad doesn't need to be in the middle of all of that. There's no way I can stay at his place.

'Does it hurt?' Kathy pointed to the angry bruising on his neck, where Tony had attacked him.

'Not really. Throat's a little sore, that's all.'

'Did the police talk to you?'

'Not yet. I said I'd call into the station in Kinlochleven.' Brad touched her cheek gently. 'What about you? Are you pressing charges?'

'Do you want him charged with assault on you?' she asked, without answering his question.

'I want him to stay the hell away from you. And if having him charged and locked up can achieve that, then I think I do.'

Kathy flinched.

'I don't think I could bear for the kids to see him locked up. I couldn't do that to them. He'd had too much to drink, that's all. I'll talk to him. He'll be sorry, I know he will.'

'I can't believe it.' Brad turned to her in amazement. 'You're defending him. He almost raped you - he could have killed you.'

'I'm not defending him,' said Kathy hotly. 'It's over between us and I'll tell him that now - today if I have to. But my kids come first, and he's still their dad. If he were to be locked up they'd be so ashamed, and I won't put them through that if I don't have to.'

She marched ahead, her jaw set determinedly.

Brad caught up with her. 'Kathy, wait,' he said. 'I'm on your side, believe me. I want to be your friend – and you need your friends. We all do.'

V

Joy was ready to stride ahead of Ruth and Trish, once they'd reached the ridge at the top of the Devil's Staircase. She wasn't in the mood for chitchat, and when Trish spoke, she sighed inwardly.

'How's Daniel?' she asked. 'Back there he looked as if he was struggling a little.'

'Battered ribs and a bruised ego. He'll survive.' Joy was flippant, hoping to end the conversation.

'Did you see Kath's face? It's a mess,' Trish continued. 'I feel so sorry for her. He's such a bastard.'

'Who, Daniel?' Joy knew she was being catty, but she couldn't help herself.

'Oh stop it, Joy.'

'Well, maybe Tony was onto something,' Joy sniped back.

'Can the pair of you cut this out? This is serious.' Ruth's stern tone silenced them instantly. 'We're supposed to be friends. We should be able to sort this like adults.'

With a sinking heart, Joy knew she was behaving badly.

How will I ever explain the lie my life has been, with any sense of conviction, when I can't exchange a few civil words up here, without it turning into a cat fight.

She turned and saw Daniel come around the bend behind them. She deliberately slowed down, letting Trish and Ruth move further ahead and allowing Daniel to draw closer.

'That's the hard bit over with,' Daniel said tentatively, clearly unsure of her mood.

'You reckon?'

'From a walking perspective at least.'

They walked side by side along the wide footpath, neither of them speaking for a few minutes.

'Does he look like you, Dan?' Joy asked finally.

Daniel sighed. 'Not now, Joy. I need all my energy to walk. I can't face another row.'

'I'm not going to row, I promise,' Joy said quickly. She took a deep breath, exhaling slowly before continuing. 'You know, I always thought that when we had kids, if it was a boy he would look like you. Be like you. Loads of dark curls, tall, good at sports, intelligent, all the things I loved about you. And if we had a girl, she'd be blond with big blue eyes. Pretty and cute. She'd learn to dance and sing and play piano and be full of confidence. She'd be warm and caring and loved by everyone.' Joy stared off into the distance.

'Neither of us are blond, Joy,' Daniel cut in. 'You're letting your imagination run away with you.'

'Sorry. It always did, I guess. And as time passed, I just kept adding to the wish list...'

'I have a photograph,' Daniel said. 'I didn't think you'd want to see it.'

He fiddled about in his wallet and handed her a picture.

She studied the snapshot of a boy aged eight or nine. He was dressed in a football kit, the pale blue shirt streaked with mud. His blue eyes shone as he held a trophy high above his head.

'I thought he'd have curly hair,' she whispered.

'It probably would be, if he let it grow.'

'There's no denying he's your son anyway.' She handed the photo back.

'No.'

Joy saw his eyes light up as he looked at the photo. She knew that despite everything, he was looking forward to meeting his son. She took a deep breath.

'I should have let you go when I found out,' she said.

'What, you knew about Stephanie? Is that what you're saying?'

'No, no.' Joy shook her head. 'I was selfish, Dan. I loved you. I knew I couldn't keep you forever, but I kept on hoping...' Her voice trailed off.

'You're not talking sense, Joy.'

'For a baby...' she whispered. 'I never stopped hoping that one day I'd be pregnant, despite what I was told. After all, even doctors can get it wrong sometimes.'

'I never stopped hoping either, Joy,' Daniel said putting the photo back in his wallet. 'I guess it just wasn't meant to be. '

'Do you remember the estate agent who sold us our house? He pointed out the pastel colours and Beatrix Potter characters painted on the walls of the back bedroom. It was obviously designed as a nursery and he smiled - and asked us if we had a little one who could make good use of it.'

Daniel nodded.

'I couldn't stop the tears welling, so I pretended to have something in my eye. And you smiled at him politely and moved swiftly on to the bathroom. It was six months before we decorated that nursery, painting over Peter Rabbit, and his friends in a harvest gold emulsion. You said we should leave it for a while. Then you put your arms around me, telling me one day we'd have a baby of our own. I knew it wasn't going to happen. Still I kept on hoping.'

'Being married to you made me the happiest man alive, Joy. Kids would have been a bonus. I never felt they were a necessity.' He took her hand, and stroked her thumb. 'We had each other. And to me, having you was all that was important. Nothing else mattered.'

'Not having children mattered to me, Daniel.' She pulled her hand free. 'It really mattered to me. You can't see that, can you? You don't understand how it made me feel. I'd failed you. Failed myself. The plan went wrong.'

'What plan?' Daniel asked.

Joy walked a stride ahead so that he couldn't see her face.

'My whole life,' she said, spreading her arms wide. 'It's been one big plan. And when it goes wrong, I paint on a face and make another plan.' She glanced back over her shoulder at her husband. 'That's what I do. I plan and plan and plan - and then, when something goes wrong, I don't know what to do.'

'I don't understand why you couldn't talk to me. Besides the fact that I had a right to know how you felt, I thought you loved me.'

'That was the problem, Dan. I loved you too much.'

'Not enough to trust me.'

'No. Just not enough to let you go.'

The hurt enfolded them like a mist rolling down from the mountains and neither of them spoke for a moment.

'And that day, at the hospital, when that doctor called my name, I was still hoping...' Joy said.

Daniel's shoulders slumped. 'You should have let me in, Joy. I should have been there with you.'

'I'm sorry.' Joy kissed his cheek and lengthened her stride to walk ahead of him.

She was exhausted, both physically and mentally.

This is all too hard. Why didn't I just stick to my shallow artificial life? Accept Daniel's confession, scream and shout at him – and then forgive him. Instead, I thought that heart to hearts, and deep and meaningful conversations, like in a tearjerker film, or a good book, would put the Crathorne world to rights.

VI

Joy continued her solitary trek as the path began its descent. She was thankful it was only a nine-mile walk today. It hadn't gone well with Daniel, and there was so much more to be said. She just couldn't seem to find the right words.

I might not be able to fix things with Dan, but I'm determined to get things back on track with Kathy before this walk is over.

Hoping to distract herself from the turmoil in her head, she turned her attention to the others in the distance. Ruth and Kathy were nearest, and there didn't appear to be much talking going on there.

But look at Trish and Rob. Trish's head's bobbing, like the nodding dog Dad used to have in the back of the car. Rob doesn't appear to be responding much and I'm still convinced something isn't quite right there. I wonder where Brad's got to. I almost feel sorry for him, caught up in the crossfire of all this. It's obviously not what he thought he was signing up for when he agreed to come on this trip.

Joy trailed her fingers across the tips of the long cool grasses with their different shades of green; the darkness of the strong mature blades contrasting with the vibrant bright young shoots. Even out here, in this vast open space surrounded by mountains, with the heat of the sun on her face, she could feel the stark coldness of that hospital waiting room. She could smell the antiseptic and the disinfectant. She could almost taste them as she remembered with a shudder how they seemed to permeate every pore, no matter how many times you showered. Just the mention of the word hospital sends Joy hurtling back there, watching herself in the horribly familiar scene playing out in her head.

*****

Sitting tall and straight on the grey plastic chair, her stomach in knots as she crossed and uncrossed her legs, Joy smoothed her already smooth dark hair, straightened her skirt and scraped at the skin around her fingernails until she drew blood. She stared at the bleak white walls of the hospital waiting room. A poster, its edges torn and curled, showed the stages of pregnancy, from tiny cell to full term baby. Another showed a picture of a smiling woman, proudly displaying her bump. A large speech bubble ballooned from her mouth extolling the advantages of folic acid. She read the message at least fifty times before her name was called.

'Joy Crathorne.' A matronly, West Indian nurse with a mass of afro hair scanned the waiting room with her black-brown eyes.

It took Joy a second to register that it was her turn before she stood up. She straightened her skirt, smoothing it across her stomach, as if to still the trembling butterflies inside. Her heels tip-tapped across the tiled floor as she crossed the corridor and entered the consulting room.

'Sorry to keep you waiting,' Dr Melrose said without looking up. 'Please sit down,' he added, his tone brisk and business like.

She sat opposite him, absently picking at the skin on her thumb, watching him shuffle files.

Come on. Get it over with. Just tell me, will you?

Finally satisfied his desk was in order, he looked up.

Joy wanted to scream. 'Tell me now! Tell me now!' Instead she took a deep breath and spoke calmly. 'Don't be gentle with me, Doctor. I just need to know one way or the other.'

He cleared his throat. 'I'm very sorry Mrs Crathorne...

Joy could see his mouth still forming words, but the screaming in her brain drowned them out.

She jumped up, knocking her chair over.

'I know it's a lot to take in; but other options are open to you... Mrs Crathorne.'

Joy wasn't listening. She fled the room and raced along the corridor. Her legs felt alien, the furious tapping of her heels on the tiled floor vibrated up through her body. She pushed past the matronly nurse, ignoring her concerned questions. Dodging trolleys that cluttered the corridor, she broke into a run, her chest heaving, panicking, fighting for breath. She burst through the main doors out into the hospital car park and ran to her car. She struggled with the key before wrenching open the door and falling into driving seat and allowing the tears to erupt, in a torrent to rival Niagara Falls.

She didn't know how long she sat there, sobbing, the doctor's words still repeating, like a scratched old vinyl record, in her brain as she stared unseeingly through the windscreen.

She gripped the steering wheel as she focused on getting home in one piece. Every light along the way was red. Every zebra crossing had a lollipop lady. The pavements seemed to be filled with schoolchildren, skipping along in their uniforms of red and grey, clutching lunchboxes and paintings; women pushing buggies with babies well wrapped up against the brisk winter air. Joy watched them as the traffic crawled along and her heart hurt.

Finally home, she let herself in to the empty house. It was almost dark but she didn't bother with the light. She dropped her bag and slid to the ground. Leaning back against the front door, the huge gasping sobs wracked her body. She covered her ears trying to block the words *not able to conceive... not able to conceive.*

Much later, stiff and cold, shuddering with leftover tears, Joy dragged herself up and into the kitchen. She took the vodka from the kitchen cupboard and drank straight from the bottle. Spluttering at the bitter taste, she welcomed the heat burning her throat, calming her body as it travelled. She took another mouthful, this time hungry for its taste and heat, before climbing the stairs, with the bottle in her hand.

'Daniel will be home soon,' she whispered into the emptiness.

Daniel. What use am I to him now? About as much as a blow-up doll... empty.

Upstairs, Joy undressed and stepped into the steaming shower, desperate to wash away the day, the tears, the smells, the reality. The water ran in rivers, down her face and neck; over her breasts, never to feel heavy with milk; down across her flat stomach, never to expand to carry a baby.

How can I tell Dan? He'll be devastated. He'll leave me. I just know it. And who could blame him? He's always wanted children. And now I've failed him. It's only right that he should know... I can't tell him. I just can't. I'm not ready to lose him, not yet.

She turned off the shower and wrapped a thick white bath sheet around her slim frame. She poured a large measure of vodka into the glass beside the washbasin, and sipping it slowly she went into the bedroom, faltering for a moment at the sight of the king-size bed that dominated the room, remembering the endless baby-making attempts. Turning her back to the bed she dropped the towel and began moisturising, covering every inch, slowly and methodically, willing the cool lotion to block up her pores and prevent the misery seeping out. She searched through her underwear drawer until she found her favourite black silk matching set. Her hands shook as she reached behind her back to fasten the bra.

Joy took another gulp of vodka.

Come on, start working. I need to feel calm. I have to look relaxed and happy when Dan gets home.

She wrinkled her nose as the alcohol burned down her throat and tentatively lifted her eyes to meet her reflection.

Why can't I be one of those women who cry attractively? I'll need foundation an inch thick to hide this mess.

She applied her make-up with extreme care, anxious to hide her puffy eyes and blotchy skin. And once the thick lash mascara and dark eyeliner were in place, it was time to lock the tears away for good.

Joy opened the wardrobe, knowing exactly what she was looking for. She pulled out a red dress, with a deep v back and front, and dropped it over her head. It slid down her body, clinging to her curves. She coated her lips with the seductive ruby lipstick that Daniel had bought her two weeks before, hoping to cheer her up, and pouted at her reflection.

I think I could pull this off but I'll need a little more of you first. She drained the last of the vodka from the glass and went back to the bathroom in search of the bottle.

Swaying slightly she knew that finally the alcohol was dulling the ache inside. She drank from the bottle, leaving lipstick smudges around the rim.

Drinking myself into oblivion would be the easy way out.

'No,' Joy said aloud. 'I need to be in control.' With a sudden burst of determination, she poured the vodka down the sink and took the empty bottle downstairs, dropping it into the kitchen bin.

For the next hour, she kept herself busy. She ordered an Indian takeaway – Daniel's favourite – and dressed the table in the dining room as she would for a dinner party, with their best dinner service and the crystal wine glasses she had bought on a trip to Prague. She tidied up the magazines in the sitting room, wiping away imaginary specks of dust on the coffee table, before switching on the oven to keep the takeaway warm.

Her heart skipped a beat when she heard a car pull into the drive, and then Daniel's key in the front door. She waited in the kitchen gripping the edge of the sink. She felt her skin tighten, as if forming a protective shell, locking her secret hurt inside.

'Hello. What's the occasion?' Daniel asked as he passed the dining room and saw the table set with candles and wine glasses. 'It's only Thursday.'

'No occasion. Just because I love you,' Joy called out from the kitchen, in a bright cheery voice she didn't recognise as her own.

He gave a wolf whistle when he reached the kitchen. 'You look amazing.'

'I wanted to make the effort,' she said, walking towards him. 'I've been too preoccupied with getting pregnant, for far too long. I think we should have a little fun in our lives again.' Joy wrapped her arms around his neck.

'Have you been drinking?' he asked, pulling back a little.

'Mmm, just a small one,' she whispered before kissing him deeply, pressing her body close to his.

The red dress was soon a puddle on the kitchen floor, and they tore the rest of their clothes off as they stumbled towards the stairs. Tumbling onto their big bed in a haze of passion, for the first time in a long while they made love just for each other. Not for a baby. During their lovemaking, Joy kept her eyes tightly closed, locking the pain away along with her tears in a secret place that she told herself Daniel must never find.

*****

Back in the mountains, Joy placed one foot mechanically in front of the other. It was a long downward path into Kinlochleven and her feet felt swollen, as if her toes might break through her boots. The town was in sight and had been for some time, but she never seemed to get any closer.

'Hello there,' Brad said, unfolding his crossed legs and standing upright.

'You scared the shit out of me,' Joy snapped. 'What are you doing? I didn't even see you there.'

Brad moved away from the rock he'd been leaning against, half hidden behind overgrown shrubbery.

'Evidently, I've been watching your trancelike state as you've walked down this hill for the past five minutes,' he said pointing to the incline behind her.

'Why are you watching me?'

'Hey, chill out. It's nothing untoward – I'm just taking a break.'

'Sorry,' she mumbled.

'Apology accepted.' Brad smiled with a half wink, and fell into step beside her.

'I imagine this didn't turn out to be quite the holiday you expected,' Joy said, after a minute or two of silence.

'A little livelier than I thought a hill walk with a bunch of married thirty-something's would be, I must admit.'

'I'm sorry you had to witness all that crap,' Joy said. 'When I booked this holiday I thought we were a bunch of half-decent thirty-something's too... well, most of us, anyway.'

'Meaning Tony?'

'Not just Tony.'

'Daniel?' Brad raised an eyebrow.

'Daniel, me, Kathy, even Trish perhaps. I mean who are we, Brad? Who are you? Who are any of us?'

Brad didn't answer at first. She watched him, noticing the tiny wrinkles at the corner of his eyes and his nose twitching as he pursed his lips and rubbed his chin.

'You should just say it. Whatever it is you're thinking, say it,' she said. 'That's half the problem. We never say what we really think, instead we try not to offend and then what happens... we end up in the shit that we're all in now.'

Brad nodded. 'You're right. But it's not always easy to change things.'

'Well, I can't change you or Kathy or Daniel. But I can change me.' Joy stabbed the ground with her walking pole.

'I'm so angry, Brad. I'm angry and hurt and scared...' she blurted, 'and I don't know how to deal with it.' *Oh, I can shout and cry in the privacy of my own bathroom, then paint on another layer of armour. Now the shell is so hard, no air can get through. I'm shrivelling up into nothingness inside. This can't be living. Why can't I tell him what I'm feeling? Why is it so difficult to tell Dan how I feel?*

Joy let out a quivering sigh.

Brad put an arm around her shoulders, giving her a brotherly hug.

'You'll find a way through this, Joy,' he said, kissing her forehead.

'Are you seeing Kathy?' Embarrassed by her outburst, Joy threw the unexpected question at him.

'No.'

'I've seen you together. You look very cosy to me. And Tony obviously thought you were.' She pushed Brad for an answer, annoyed at his calm expression.

'Tony is a bully and a control freak,' Brad said. 'Kathy isn't seeing anyone. Not me and not Daniel.' He shook his head.

Now Joy could see the frustration in his face.

'Can't you have some compassion for her?' He turned to look Joy in the eye. 'She's totally demoralised and humiliated by the way he's treated her in front of her friends,' he said. 'We can keep feelings and emotions under wraps but not physical damage. Kathy's chosen to finish this walk, knowing she might well get pitying glances or curious stares. She should be commended for that.'

Joy felt shame wash over her. She knew she was piling pressure on Kathy with her unfounded accusations.

'For a second or two, last night, I wanted Tony to kill Daniel. I was so angry with him for all the lies he'd told me.' She spoke slowly, only just admitting this fact to herself. 'Then I saw Dan's bloodied face and suddenly I was like a banshee, tearing into Tony. Not just to pull him off Daniel - I wanted to really hurt him. To make up for all the times I'd stood on the sidelines, doing nothing – just watching my happy confident friend turning into...' She stumbled and almost fell on the gravelly footpath.

Brad caught her hand, pulling her upright again.

'Are you OK?' He kept hold of her hand.

'I'm just so tired, and that flaming town's getting no closer.' She wiped her clammy forehead with the back of her hand. 'Can you pass my water from the side pocket of my rucksack, please?'

'Hold on to me for a while,' he said, handing her the bottle.

She let Brad's arm take her weight as she took long gulps of the warm water. The town ahead looked fuzzy around the edges and her legs felt as though they didn't belong to her. Her head was pounding and her eyes were dry and itchy.

Oh God, please don't let me faint. I have to make it to the B&B at least. Trish will kill me if she has to call out mountain rescue!

'Are you ok?' Brad asked again. 'You're as white as a ghost.'

'I will be when I get to the end of this flaming path,' she said. 'I have to keep talking. It's the only way I'll make it.'

He tightened his hold on her arm.

'Do you know why it's over with Daniel?' she asked him.

'He had an affair?'

'Which resulted in a child,' she said bluntly.

Joy went on to tell Brad the entire story, rattling it off without emotion, as though it were a film review or an article in the Sunday tabloids.

'You know...' Brad interrupted. 'What Daniel did was wrong. Sleeping with someone else when you're in a relationship is always wrong - and there's no excuse good enough.' He paused, choosing his words carefully before continuing. 'But he's a decent guy. He made a mistake. Ok, as it turned out, a massive one. One that's probably lost him the woman he loves.'

'So you're defending him?' she asked.

'I didn't say that,' Brad said, looking her in the eye. 'Finding out that one mistake created a child must have scared the shit out of him. Yet he did the right thing,' he added.

'The right thing would have been to tell me,' she snapped.

'OK, he did the right thing by the child. Paying maintenance, giving financial support and now... well, doesn't every child have the right to know who their parents are - good or bad?'

'Of course they do. But didn't I, as his wife, have the right to know where our money was going – the whole story?'

Brad shrugged his shoulders. 'That's why I was never any good at relationships.'

VII

Kathy felt weary as she trudged along the dry footpath. It ran parallel to some huge water pipes lining the hillside, which then plummeted towards the aluminium works dominating the town below. Ruth, who'd walked with her for a while, complaining about how tired and achy she was, had now fallen behind, leaving Kathy to walk alone, which suited her just fine.

Her earlier bravado had deserted her on the Devil's Staircase, now she was shattered and worried about Tony. *Will the police have released him by now? Will he be at the B&B waiting for me? What shall I do if he is?*

Her thoughts drifted to her kids.

Alison will be on her way home from school, the lads on their way home from college; probably picking up pizzas or some other fast food.

She knew she'd have to ring them later.

They need to know what's happened... well, maybe not the full story – an edited version. I'll have to tell them I'm moving out. I'll have to tell my mother too. I don't know if I can do this. It's all too much. It would be so easy to just accept Tony's apology - no doubt there'll be one - and stay.

Rob and Trish were waiting at the end of the footpath, where it joined the road.

'I thought it would be a good idea to round everyone up here,' Rob told Kathy. 'Then we can decide if we're going to the pub first or the B&B.'

'Anywhere we can sit down, I say.' Kathy wiped her clammy face with the bottom of her T-shirt. 'Is it just me, or was that downhill path never-ending?'

Rob nodded in agreement. 'No, you're right, it was definitely tough today.'

Kathy noticed Trish's painted-on smile and lack of comment, but said nothing. She listened to Rob as he chatted casually about the history of the aluminium works they had passed, knowing that he was covering up for Trish's silence.

Ruth arrived, hobbling like a lame duck along the last few feet of the footpath.

'Traitor - abandoning me up there,' she accused Kathy playfully, as she sat down beside her on the narrow grass verge by the dusty footpath.

'I had to keep the momentum going, Ruth. Otherwise you'd have been carrying me down,' Kathy said.

'Were the others far behind you, Ruth?' Rob asked.

'Not far, no. Brad's with Joy - they seem to be holding each other up, and Daniel's just behind them. Five minutes, I suppose.'

Shaded from the sun, the four of them sat in weary silence for a moment.

'Will Tony be at the B&B?' Ruth looked directly at Kathy.

'I don't know,' Kathy said. 'I've had no phone reception for most of the day.'

'You don't have to see him, you know. If you don't want to, it's OK. One of us will talk to him.'

'Thanks, Ruth, but I need to do this myself.'

'What if he goes for you again?' Ruth asked, with a trace of panic in her voice.

'He won't. Not if he's sober,' Kathy said, with a confidence she didn't feel. 'And if he's not, then I'll make sure I speak to him in a public place. Don't worry about me - really.'

Kathy looked up as Brad and Joy reached them. She was shocked at Joy's appearance. Her hair was plastered to her head, her face fiery red and beaded with sweat, and she was leaning on Brad so heavily that Kathy was doubtful she'd stay standing if he released her.

'What happened?' she asked, getting to her feet.

'She's tired and a bit dehydrated, I think.' Brad gave a weary smile. 'Once she gets some fluids into her, and has a good rest, she should be fine,' he added.

'I've been trying to catch you up,' Daniel gasped, as he reached the group moments later. 'Is she OK? Joy, look at me. What's happened, are you ill?'

'Tired, just tired,' Joy whispered, slumping against Daniel's chest.

He winced at the pressure on his bruised ribs, and allowed Brad to take her weight again.

'I think we'd best get her to the B&B.' As usual, Rob took charge. 'Do you think she needs a doctor?'

'I'm sure the landlady will phone one for us if need be,' Trish said.

Concern for Joy was etched on all their faces as they made their way through the streets of Kinlochleven. The town was busy for the time of day with walkers strolling around, town folk going about their business, and children racing home from school, a reminder that normal life continued as usual, something easy to forget for those trekking through the wilderness of the mountains.

'I'll walk ahead to that grocery store and pick up a bottle of fresh water,' Kathy said.

'I'll come with you,' Trish said.

Kathy came out of the shop just as the others approached. Daniel and Brad were either side of Joy. Brad had his arm around her waist while Daniel carried her rucksack and kept a steadying hand on her elbow.

'Here, drink some water, Joy.' Kathy took the top off the bottle and held it to Joy's dry lips.

'You should have one of these too,' Trish added, handing her a glucose tablet.

Joy rested for a minute, eating two glucose tablets and taking small sips of water.

'I could carry you the rest of the way if you'd like,' Brad said with a twinkle in his eye.

'I don't think so,' Joy said with as much energy as she could muster. 'I'm sure I can manage a few hundred yards more.'

VIII

Ten minutes later, they reached the B&B on Douglas Street, at the far end of town. Despite their concern for Joy, the picture postcard beauty of the house wowed them all.

The whitewashed walls were stamped with eight gleaming windows framed by glossy black paintwork and draped with white lace curtains. Four attic windows rose out of the eaves of the black slate roof. A narrow gravel footpath led from the wrought iron gate to the open front door. It cut sharply through the manicured lawn, the firm lines of which were softened by lilac campanula spilling from its borders.

Kathy was last to walk through the gate, and the only one to notice Tony sitting on the bench in the shadow of the hedge, just to the left of the gate. He wore a clean white cotton shirt and blue jeans and his holdall was parked neatly beside the bench. She stopped beside him, as the others went inside.

'What's up with her? What's going on?' he asked, as though the previous night hadn't happened. 'Everyone looks very serious. I thought you'd be in the pub - I didn't think you'd be here for ages yet.'

'Joy's ill. They think it's dehydration. She might need the doctor,' Kathy said bluntly. 'I should go and see if she's OK.' She stepped towards the open door. He reached out a hand towards her.

'The bastards charged me,' he complained.

'What did you expect? A commendation?' Kathy stopped and turned to confront him. 'You assaulted people. You trashed the hotel. You're lucky they didn't keep you locked up,' she said, and moved away.

'Wait.' He grabbed her arm.

'Get off me,' she snarled.

'I'm sorry, Kath, I just want to talk,' he said, dropping his hand and patting the seat. 'Please sit down. I won't touch you, I promise.' He sounded like a contrite child.

She sat, but only because she thought she'd fall down if she didn't sit down, and at the farthest end of the bench, well away from Tony. She pulled a leaf off the privet hedge, and examined it studiously as she waited for him to speak.

'Where do I start?' He paused.

She didn't look up.

'Kath, you have no idea how much I love you -'

'Bullshit,' Kathy snapped. 'Not this broken record again. Just get to the point, Tony.'

'I didn't mean to hit you.' He reached to touch her face.

Kathy jumped up again, suddenly feeling less vulnerable. She was only a few feet from the open doorway. She'd seen Brad look back before he went inside and was certain he'd be watching out for her.

'Don't be scared of me, Kathy.' His voice cracked.

'You were disgusting; drunk – vile – and disgusting.'

'I should never have got drunk, I know. I just got so worked up, seeing you and him together...'

'There is no me and anyone, Tony. It's in your head.'

'And then you rejected me, Kath. Every day we've been here, you've pushed me away. Like you're someone else - not my Kathy. It's as if I don't matter to you any more. I just saw red.'

'You would have raped me.' She looked directly at him.

'You're my wife. You can't rape your wife.' His look was so incredulous, she almost laughed.

'The police asked if I wanted to press charges.'

'What, for giving you a slap?'

'Assault - attempted rape - domestic abuse - mental abuse, I could take my pick,' Kathy spat, glad to see fear and uncertainty in his eyes.

'Come on, Kathy, we can sort it out ourselves. We don't need the police,' he pleaded. 'It's this place. I don't know what it's done to you. We'll be fine when we get back home.'

But Kathy was resolute now, and more than anything, she wanted to make him suffer.

'Daniel's pressing charges for assault,' she told him. 'Brad too.'

Tony stood up, his bulk blocking out the evening sun. Instinctively Kathy stepped back, closer to the open door - and the protection of Brad who was now standing in the doorway.

'Sit down, Tony,' Brad said loudly.

Tony sank back onto the bench.

'I should have finished off the pair of them when I had the chance,' he hissed. But he remained seated.

Trembling uncontrollably inside, Kathy took an enormous breath. This was it. The moment she had been building towards for the past two years. That had consumed every waking thought of every step of the last eighty-odd miles. Ditch-Tony-Day had arrived!

'It's over, Tony,' she told him, the words rushing out. 'I'm moving out. I want a divorce.' She clasped her hands together tightly, trying to control the shaking.

'What are you on about? Don't be stupid, woman.'

'Don't call me stupid,' she snapped. 'I'm telling you it's over. I'll never set foot in that house again. Never, do you understand? I've had it with your controlling mind games. Your possessive pawing of me in public. Your slovenly ways. Your groping hands. The way you treat me like a slave.' She raised her voice until she was screaming at him.

'Kathy, stop it. Stop it now.' Trish was racing across the garden towards them.

'Trish, I'm fine.' Kathy took a deep breath.

'Please, Kathy.' Tony's shoulders slumped.

'I want you to go home, Tony. Tonight. Right now,' Kathy said, lowering her voice with an effort.

Tony stood up again and glared at her.

'If you do this, then that's it, we're finished,' he shouted, as she turned away. 'Don't think you can come back, crying to me...'

'You're right, Tony. We *are* finished.' Kathy didn't look back as she went inside.

'Well done.' Brad squeezed her shoulder as she passed, not taking his eyes off Tony for a second as he sank back onto the bench.

Hearing the sound of crunching gravel, Kathy peered through a tiny porch window. She saw Brad strolling towards Tony, who was sitting with his shoulders hunched and his head in his hands.

If he's crying I know it will just be a ploy to get me out there. I'm not falling for that.

Brad was talking. She could see his hands moving, making gestures, pointing to the gate. Tony responded. She couldn't make out what he was saying either. She was about to go over to them, worried that Tony might have another go at Brad.

Then Tony was on his feet, inches from Brad, and Kathy's heart was pounding against her ribcage. Brad grabbed the neck of Tony's shirt, and yanked him forward, so that their faces were almost touching.

Kathy raced through the door.

'Don't!' she yelled. 'No more fighting, please!'

'He's just leaving, Kathy,' Brad called, without releasing his grip. 'Aren't you, Tony?' He passed Tony his bag

Kathy watched Tony silently walk away, through the wrought iron gate and past the neatly trimmed hedge. His head was down, and he never once looked her way. She watched until she could see him no more, and then, letting out a shaky sigh, she sat down heavily on the now empty garden bench.

'I can't believe I just did that,' she whispered, turning to Brad who had sat down beside her. 'What did you say to him to make him go?'

Brad gave a wicked grin. 'I told him there's a bus to Fort William at six o'clock.' Then his expression became more serious. 'It doesn't matter what I said. The main thing is that he's gone, and he knows you mean business. So now you can just relax,' he added.

'I need to check on Joy now, but thank you,' said Kathy, and gave him a kiss on the cheek.

'Behave yourself, that's how rumours start, you know.' Brad gave her that irresistible wink.

IX

Propped up on pillows with her legs stretched out on the old-fashioned chintzy sofa, Joy felt suffocated by the concerned faces crowded around her. Ruth sat on the floor looking up at her anxiously. Daniel was perched by her feet, absently rubbing a hand up and down her shin and trying to get her to drink more of the foul tasting rehydrating drink. She already felt a little better, just being out of the heat and off her feet. Everything looked sharp again, instead of fuzzy around the edges.

'Come on,' she said, struggling to stand up in the crowded space. 'Drama's over, I'm fine, really. And I don't know about you lot, but I really need a shower and some food,' she added, trying to make her voice bright and cheery, and hoping desperately that she wouldn't faint.

'We can eat here. I've spoken to the landlady and the menu looks fantastic,' Trish said, looking around for approval. 'And we can always stroll down to the pub afterwards.'

'Sounds like a plan, Stan.' Ruth hauled herself up from the floor. She gave Joy a brief hug. 'What are the sleeping arrangements?' she whispered in her ear.

'You look after Kathy. I'll be fine with Daniel,' Joy whispered back, touched at Ruth's thoughtfulness.

Putting all her energy into looking normal, knowing that all eyes were upon her, Joy walked unsteadily out of the sitting room into the hall, with Daniel hovering anxiously beside her.

Her legs felt like jelly as she climbed the stairs, gripping the banister tightly with one hand and hanging on to Daniel's arm with the other. The vibrant jumble of pictures lining the stairwell filled every available space and made her feel quite claustrophobic. The frames were all colours and sizes. The pictures themselves ranged from Scottish snow-covered mountains, to African tribesmen dancing against the backdrop of an orange sunset. Along the upstairs landing, colourful ornaments crowded into the pristine white shelving that lined every nook and cranny. A set of Spanish castanets sat beside a commemorative plate of Charles and Diana's wedding, along with a pink teddy bear wearing an 'I love Scotland' badge, and a tall Lladro figurine of an angel. The shelves were so busy that they made her head spin afresh, and she gripped Daniel's arm tighter.

When they reached their room, Daniel unlocked the door and ushered Joy in. An unspoken truce had developed between them and she was relieved he was there with her now.

She immediately dropped the bravery act, and curled up into a ball on the bed.

'Oh God, Dan, I feel like crap,' she groaned.

'I'll run you a bath. Take off your clothes and cool down for a few minutes,' he said and went into the bathroom. 'And keep sipping that drink,' he called out to her.

Joy sat up and removed her trousers and tee shirt, and then flopped back down onto the pillow. Wearing only her bra and pants, she was glad of the coolness of the room. She closed her eyes and drifted in and out of sleep for a few minutes. The running water from the bathroom became the rushing river on Rannoch Moor. She opened her eyes again to see a shaft of evening sun from the window casting a golden glow over her glass.

Is it water or whisky? Whisky would be good. It would numb the senses. Dull the ache. Calm my racing mind. Let me sink into oblivion. She moved her hand, casting a shadow. The glass held only water.

Daniel came back into the bedroom and helped her to stand up. Like a child, she let him guide her to the bathroom. He held her steady as she removed her underwear and, stepped into the tepid water. It rippled around her calves, making her feel woozy.

'I think I need to be sick,' she slurred, putting a hand over her mouth.

'Sit down, you'll be OK,' he reassured her, supporting her while she lowered herself gingerly into the water and rested her head back. 'I'll find you a bowl or something,' he said, rushing out of the room.

He returned moments later, with her glass of water and the waste paper bin.

'This was all I could find,' he said placing it bedside the bath.

'I'm ok now my eyes are closed.'

'I'll just sit down here a while.' Daniel sat on the floor, resting an arm on the side of the bath. 'I don't want you nodding off and sliding under.'

Joy opened one eye a chink, to see Daniel with his head resting on his arm, inches away from her face. She said nothing and remembered that it had been only the night before they came away that she was doing the exact same thing to him. It seemed a lifetime ago now. Her eye closed again. She let her mind drift, remembering that night.

*****

She should have been packing; instead, she stood at the bedroom window, watching for Daniel to come home. Her arms were folded tightly across her chest, and she was tormenting herself.

I can't work it out, yet I can't ask either. He normally approaches the house from the opposite end of the road. Where has he been? What has he been doing? Who was he with?

Just after nine, she saw him cross the road and walk towards the gate. She turned away, relieved that he was home. Her head was banging with the stress she put herself under; she took a painkiller from the foil packet beside the bed, and swallowed it down with a glass of vodka and a shudder. Curling into the foetal position, she closed her eyes, disgusted with herself that she wasn't strong enough to ask the questions that haunted her.

She could hear Daniel moving around downstairs, walking into the kitchen. Then the sound of cupboard doors opening and closing, the clatter of dishes, and silence. She waited for the sound of the TV. Nothing.

He'll call my name any minute, come upstairs looking for me. Then I'll have to talk. What do I say? Should I confront him? Ask what he's been up to? Then who am I to talk, with my own secret eating away at me?

Her mind was drifting; she was sinking into the blackness of sleep. She fought to keep her eyes wide open, suddenly frightened. The dark, heavy furniture created even darker shadows. It felt as if it was closing in on her, reaching out, touching the edge of the bed.

Why doesn't he come looking for me? Why don't we talk anymore? We say good morning, pass the salt, or discuss the weather, that's not really talking.

Her eyelids refused to stay open.

Think, Joy. When did things start to go wrong? I have to talk to him, find out the truth. Tell him the truth.

*****

Joy spluttered as bathwater washed over her lips. She opened her eyes.

Daniel's hand was under her chin. 'Do you feel any better?' he asked. 'You were nodding off there.'

He stood up and reached for a towel. 'Let's get you into bed now. I can bring you up a sandwich or some soup.'

He held out a huge lemon bath sheet. She stood up and let him wrap it around her.

She felt safe in the thick towel that smelt of jasmine with Daniel's arm around her waist.

How can he be so lovely - looking after me, being so nice to me - after everything that has happened and the way I've spoken to him?

Not that being Mr Nice Guy will make up for ten years of lies and deceit. It'll take more than a few kind words and a sweet-smelling towel to sort our mess out. I just don't have the energy for more sniping and bitter accusations now.

Almost without realising it, Joy spoke her thoughts aloud.

'How can you do this – be nice to me and look after me like this, after everything that's happened... after all the things I've said?'

'Because I love you.' He had tears in his eyes.

He led her through to the bedroom and held back the candy-striped duvet. She dropped the towel and lay down on the crisp white sheet, allowing him to cover her with the duvet, tucking it under her chin, revealing only her face, pasty white except for the two rosy spots on her cheekbones.

She looked up at him. 'But who do you love? The girl you first met. Or the woman she became?' she asked, her eyes wide as she waited for his answer.

He didn't speak, and Joy eventually closed her eyes. She heard him go into the bathroom and turn on the shower. She tried hard to stay awake.

Sometimes I just want to fall asleep and never wake up. Surely, life doesn't always have to be this difficult.

He came out of the bathroom with a towel around his waist. Joy watched him through her lashes as he pulled out a clean shirt from his bag. Only after he'd finished getting dressed, did he answer her question.

'I love the woman I watch sleeping, her eyes flickering as she dreams, her face relaxed and real,' he said quietly. 'But you've hidden her away, Joy. Underneath layers of perfection and artificial claptrap. I want her back, but I don't know if she can free herself. Do you?'

Joy couldn't speak. His sadness completely overwhelmed her. Tears squeezed out from behind her closed eyelids, running into her hair and her ears, soaking the pillow. She felt as though the weight of the ceiling was bearing down on her chest.

Daniel crouched down beside the bed and leaned forward to kiss her forehead. He ran his thumb across her wet cheek before standing up.

'I'll bring you some soup in a few minutes,' he told her, and left the room, closing the door quietly behind him.

Joy pulled the duvet up over her face.

X

Kathy met Daniel at the bottom of the stairs.

'How is she?' she asked.

'Asleep.'

'You look exhausted. I'm so sorry for what Tony did to you,' she apologised.

'Don't be, you're not his keeper.' There was a flash of anger in his voice. 'How are you, anyway? We could end up with matching black eyes.'

'Oh, I'll get over having a black eye,' Kathy said. 'It's just the rest of my life I'm stressing about,' she added, with a lightness she didn't feel.

'Have you ended it with Tony?'

'I had to,' she said, faltering slightly. 'We only have one life and we have to live it the best way we can – if we're lucky, with someone we love and who loves us back. Above all, we need to be happy... at least some of the time, and I wasn't... ever.'

'Do you want me to press charges?' he asked.

'I can't answer that, Daniel. He assaulted you. It's your decision.'

'Will you?'

'I don't know. I need to talk to the boys first. I'm just about to ring them now.'

'Good luck.' Daniel gave her a hug.

Kathy went outside. She walked across to the bench by the hedge, deciding that as Anthony was the eldest, she should ring him first. He'd always been more sensitive than Joe, her middle child, and she knew he hated the way his father treated her.

Joe spent most of his time playing football or running on the athletics track, and was always too busy to notice what was going on. Home was just a place where muddy, dirty clothes miraculously appeared in the wardrobe, clean and ready to wear again. Where there was always a meal on the table and grazing food in the fridge. Kathy often worried he might turn out like his father.

'I wouldn't sit out now, my dear. You'll be eaten alive.' Mrs Galbraith, the well-built, jolly landlady appeared at the door. A frill-trimmed, pristine white apron covered her purple and pink floral summer dress.

Kathy smiled politely.

'I just need to make a phone call. It won't take long. I'll be fine.'

'Really, dear, it wouldn't be wise. It's almost dark; the midges will be out soon.' She beckoned Kathy towards the house. 'Come, you can use my office. It'll give you some privacy.'

'Thank you,' Kathy said following her to the back of the house, where she opened a door marked 'private'.

The office was as cluttered as the rest of the house, filled with papers, brochures, leaflets and photographs, rather than ornaments, paintings and soft furnishings.

Anthony answered on the first ring.

'Hiya, Mam.'

'Is that phone permanently stuck to you?' Kathy asked.

'Ha ha. How's it going?'

They exchanged chitchat for a minute or two, while Kathy psyched herself up for the real business of the call.

'Anthony, something has happened -' she paused a second. '- I've left your dad,' she said quietly.

'What?'

Kathy rushed on, filling him in on the situation, being as fair as she could be. She didn't want to make any of the kids think they had to take sides.

'The bastard.'

'Anthony!'

'Well, he is. Is he coming back here now, tonight?'

'I don't know. It could be tomorrow before he gets back.'

'He's not coming back here.' Anthony was raging.

Kathy felt a surge of sadness at Anthony's low opinion of his dad. *He's always been a sensitive kid. Always trying to protect me when Tony was having a go. It's so unfair that he should have to deal with this shit.*

'Listen, love, of course he'll come back,' Kathy tried to calm her son. 'It's his home. He won't know what else to do. I've left him, so I'll be the one moving out. I'll take Alison with me, but I can't tell you and Joe what to do.' She took a deep breath before continuing. 'I want you to come with me - of course I do. But it's your decision and it will be Joe's decision too.'

'No way am I staying here with him,' Anthony spat. 'Where are you going to live? Are you going back to grandma's?'

Kathy explained about Brad's offer to loan them his flat.

'So, why don't you stay at a mate's place until I get back on Saturday, and then we can talk it over properly? It'll be OK, trust me,' she said. 'Now, is Joe home?' she asked briskly. 'It'll be better if I tell him myself.'

Typically, Joe's reaction was much more laid back than his brother's.

'I'll be fine, Mam. Dad will have calmed down by the time he gets back,' he told her. 'I'll see you on Saturday.'

Next, there was Alison. As perceptive as she was, Tony was still her dad and Kathy knew she would have to tread carefully.

After twenty years, I know Tony only too well. He'll go straight to the pub, drink himself senseless, have a greasy fry-up supper, and then sleep it off until lunchtime. He won't give Alison a second thought.

As she debated her next move, there was a gentle tap on the door and Trish's head appeared.

'Mrs Galbraith told me you were here. Did you talk to Anthony?'

'Yes, and Joe. I'm just thinking what to say to Alison now.' Kathy sighed.

'Can't you wait until we get back?' Trish asked. 'She's staying with Mam isn't she?'

Kathy nodded.

'So, it'll be easier to talk to her face to face,' Trish reasoned.

I know, but what if he calls round to Mam's? What if he rings and talks to her? He'll poison her with his lies. He's convinced she's not his as it is and now that I've ended it, God knows what he'll tell her,' Kathy panicked. 'I need to figure out a way of protecting her from that. She's only ten, Trish.'

'I know,' Trish soothed. 'Look, we'll make sure he doesn't see her before you do. Now ring Mam.'

'I haven't got the energy for her "I-told-you-so's".' Kathy felt like crying.

'She won't be like that, Kath. She'll want to protect Alison as much as you do. You don't have to tell her everything now. Just get her to make sure that if Tony turns up, she doesn't let him in.'

'You're probably right - as usual,' Kathy said, giving her sister a weak smile. 'I'll ring Alison first, and then I'll have a quick word with Mam.'

'Right, I'll leave you to it,' Trish said, squeezing her shoulder affectionately. 'Food's in half an hour, and it smells divine,' she added, before closing the door behind her.

*****

Ten minutes later Kathy felt more relaxed. Her mother had taken the news calmly, and as yet, there'd been no recriminations. She'd promised to take Alison out straight after school for some shopping and then to McDonald's for tea.

Soothed at the feeling of having got another job done, Kathy went upstairs, looking for room number seven. She'd agreed to share with Ruth now that Tony had gone. It helped with the costs, and the landlady was grateful of the additional room for a weary walker who'd just arrived at the door.

Kathy smiled at Ruth's brightly coloured clothes spread out on the bed, adding to the general cheer of the room. The door to the bathroom was ajar, and she chuckled to herself when she heard Ruth singing the hit 'Don't you wish your girlfriend was hot like me?' at the top of her voice.

Her hands flew to her eyes as Ruth appeared in the nude, her ample hips gyrating to the song.

'Ruth!'

'Oops, didn't hear you come in.' Ruth had the grace to blush as she hurriedly wrapped the towel she'd been dancing with, around her. 'You can come out now. Hopefully there's no lasting damage.'

Kathy laughed at Ruth's apologetic smile –and suddenly found she couldn't stop. It was as if a tap had been turned on, and it was infectious. Within seconds, Ruth had joined in and the two of them were laughing so hard they could hardly breathe, as tears ran down their faces. Ruth clutched the top of her towel, which kept slipping dangerously low as she wobbled beneath it, which only served to fuel the laughter.

Finally spent, they flopped onto the empty bed. Legs dangling over the edge, they lay side by side, staring up at the ceiling.

'Thanks, Ruth, I haven't laughed like that in years. I feel two stone lighter.'

'I wish I did.' Ruth hitched up the towel. 'Glad to be of service, all the same,' she said grinning.

XI

Downstairs in the dining room, Kathy admired the large, oval-shaped mahogany table, adorned with crystal wine glasses and elaborate candlesticks. It looked amazing, although everyone seated around it looked tired.

Ruth voiced what everyone was thinking.

'We seem a small group tonight. Could Joy not face dinner?' she asked Daniel.

'Mrs Galbraith gave me soup on a tray, to take up to her,' Daniel said.

The courses were enormous, and so delicious that everyone just kept on eating, and dessert was a juicy apple and blackberry pie. The light flaky pastry was stained dark purple by the berries and covered in thick cream. By the end of the meal, Kathy had to release the button on her jeans before it popped off itself.

'Shall we stroll down to the pub?' Rob asked. 'Apparently they have live music on a Thursday night,' he added, waving a leaflet advertising the Leven Arms Bar & Restaurant.

Trish and Brad nodded in agreement.

'Can we get a taxi?' Ruth asked. 'I don't think I could face walking again tonight.'

'I could murder a pint all right,' Daniel said. He stood up. 'I'll need to check on Joy first, but I don't think she'll be up to it.'

'I can stay and keep her company,' Kathy volunteered. 'I don't think I can face the pub. I couldn't eat or drink another thing.' She tapped her empty plate.

'Oh come on, Kath.' Trish nudged her in the ribs, making her groan. 'We need to walk some of this off, or we'll never sleep tonight.'

'Anyway, it's not the best time for you to be spending time with Joy.' Daniel looked down at her. 'You two have stuff to sort out, but not a good idea for you to do it when you're both as wrecked as you are now.'

'Point taken,' Kathy nodded. 'I'll have to get out of these before I go anywhere.' She looked down at her jeans, straining across her usually flat stomach.

*****

Ten minutes later the group gathered at the front gate and set off towards the other end of town and the Leven Arms.

The pub was heaving, filled with a mixture of people. Old and young, visitors and locals. The music wasn't quite what they were expecting. As they walked in, Kathy cringed at the sound of droning bagpipes and fiddles, whining and screeching as they churned out traditional Scottish tunes to the clapping and whooping audience.

Trish spotted a free table near the bar and the girls quickly gathered stools around it. The music was so loud it was difficult to talk and be heard. This suited Kathy, she didn't really want to talk about Tony, or what the future held. She tapped her feet to the music, smiling at Daniel when he took the stool beside her.

He looks different tonight, less troubled somehow, although he must be worried about Joy, despite their problems. She really didn't look well this afternoon.

'You seem happier,' she said.

'What?' he mouthed, with a frown.

'No, that was the wrong thing to say,' she corrected herself, raising her voice to be heard above the music. 'Calmer, less angry perhaps?' she said.

Daniel leaned over to speak into her ear.

'We've said all we can say now,' he said, and then turned to clap along to the music.

Kathy took that as a sign he didn't want to talk, and sipped her drink.

'Are you OK?' Trish shouted into her other ear.

'Just wondering about Tony – where he is, if he's OK,' Kathy said.

'Don't. He's not worth it,' Trish said dismissively.

Kathy wanted to shout back at her sister, '*Do you think I don't know that? But it doesn't stop me worrying about him.*'

Instead, she shrugged and turned to watch the musicians.

At eleven o'clock, the musicians took their final bow and an air of calm settled on the bar as people finished their drinks and began to leave.

'Are we all finished?' Rob asked, draining the last of his pint. They all agreed, and began moving towards the pub door.

'Let's hit the road,' Brad said, opening it.

As he did so, an eerie black mass confronted them, and shocked they all took a backward step. Brad closed the door quickly.

'What the hell was that?' Trish asked. 'Did you see that black, quivering mass? It looked like a swarm of bees or locusts or something.'

An old man with a withered face was sitting at the bar, chewing on his unlit pipe.

Midges,' he told them. He looked at their thin cotton clothes, exposing bare legs and arms, and nodded knowingly. 'You'll have to make a run for it,' he said taking his pipe out of his mouth, and giving them a toothless grin.

During the evening, Kathy had seen people coming into the pub, ruffling their hair and wiping their faces, but she'd thought nothing of it. Now she realised why.

'We'll be eaten alive,' Ruth moaned.

'Oh don't be such a drama queen, Ruth,' Trish said. 'Come on! Let's do like the man said.'

She opened the door again and ran across to the other side of the road. They all followed, one by one, arms flaying as they beat a pathway through the black biting cloud.

'Ugh, they're in my hair!' Trish said, rubbing vigorously at her scalp. 'It's disgusting!'

'It's worse than that.' Ruth squirmed. 'I'm sure they've found their way down my bra.'

'Well, I won't say where I think I can feel the little buggers,' Rob grinned. 'Imagine living here and dealing with that every night.'

The group laughed, itched, and scratched their way back to the B&B.

XII

'It's our last day of walking tomorrow, Kath,' Ruth said, climbing into the bed across from her. 'I never thought I'd manage it, you know.'

'You did really well.'

'Did you get bitten?' Ruth rubbed at her forehead. 'I'm sure I did.'

'Yes, I have at least two or three under my arm, and I'm sure more will appear by morning.'

Kathy stared at the ceiling, listening to the odd creak and squeak that old houses make, interspersed with Ruth's gentle breathing. She felt a sadness creeping over her.

'Ruth,' she whispered.

'Mmm.'

'Nothing's going on between me and Daniel,' Kathy said. 'You do believe me, don't you?'

'Of course I do, you dozy mare,' Ruth answered.

'I need to put things right with Joy, make her see the truth,' Kathy said, suddenly feeling a little panicky that she might not be able to sort things between her and Joy.

'You will, tomorrow.' Ruth's voice was sleepy. 'Night, night, Kath.'

'Night, Ruth.'

Kathy kept her eyes open. In her head, she recited the words she would use. She went over them again and again, deciding where they could talk, and when. Until her eyes would stay open no longer.

FRIDAY
I

Joy's eyes twitched behind her lids. She rubbed at the sleep clogging her lashes, and opened her eyes.

I'm not dead, then.

She looked around the room, confirming her hazy recollections of the night before. She sensed she was alone in the big double bed and looking to her left, she saw Daniel, on the floor beside the bed, sleeping soundly, his mouth slightly open, producing reassuring snores.

The roof of her mouth felt like the Artex ceiling above her head. She reached over for the remains of the fruity Dioralyte drink on the bedside table and took a few sips, pulling a face at the now warm liquid.

Her phone told her it was 6.25 a.m. – far too early for Daniel. Joy tried not to wake him, as, becoming increasingly aware that she was desperate for the loo, she attempted to get out of bed. Her legs felt like bendy pipe-cleaners and buckled as she stood. Quickly she sat down again.

Damn it, I really need to pee.

She prepared for a second attempt and shuffled herself to the foot of the bed. One step and a lunge for the bathroom door got her onto the toilet seat. She left the door slightly ajar, allowing a thin streak of light in from the bedroom.

She left the bathroom on legs less bendy but still slightly wooden, and took a few tentative steps around the bedroom, pausing by the window to peer out at the sleeping street below.

A few more laps of the room and I hopefully I should make it to the finish line in Fort William.

Passing the mirror, she gasped at the sight of her bloodshot eyes, puffy sockets, scarecrow hair, ashen face and cracked lips.

What the hell happened to me? I look as if I've been crying for a month.

She struggled to remember what had happened; what made her cry. She tried to smooth her scarecrow hair.

I feel calmer. As if that hard protective shell has weakened – a little scared, I'll admit, but definitely calmer.

She leaned forward, her nose touching the mirror and looked deep into the eyes of her reflection.

I can almost see MYSELF inside there now.

Spying Daniel's wallet, on the corner of the small table beneath the mirror, she picked it up. The photo of Jason was sticking out a little. Daniel was still snoring softly. She carefully pulled out the photo.

He does look like Daniel, although his eyes aren't quite as bright. Does he laugh like Daniel? Does he have the same sense of humour?

Noticing again the aura of calm she seemed to have developed overnight, and surprised by it, Joy put the picture back inside the wallet.

Feeling ready to tackle the shower, she went into the bathroom and closed the door, hoping not to disturb Daniel. She brushed her teeth vigorously, before stepping under the warm water.

Maybe I could meet Jason. What was it Daniel said last night, about loving me?

She couldn't remember but knew that it had sounded good. It gave her hope that maybe they could work things out.

He's an honourable man, that's why he supported Jason, not Stephanie. I could see the look on his face was different, almost disbelieving, when he took out the photo. I don't think he can quite believe that Jason's real and that he actually has a son. I think he's really looking forward to meeting him, he just hasn't realised it yet.

The quiet tapping on the door gave her a start.

'It's open,' she called out.

'I just need to pee,' Daniel said.

'Go ahead,' Joy said from behind the curtain. She listened to the trickle against the toilet bowl.

How surreal this is? The two of us sharing the bathroom after being at war with each other all week.

Daniel flushed the toilet and left the bathroom. Joy finished her shower and emerged five minutes later, feeling almost human again.

Daniel was making tea at the small table by the window. He'd opened the curtains and sunlight flooded the room.

'How do you feel this morning?' he asked, offering her a cup.

'Surprisingly good actually.' Joy was surprised to find that it was true. She was feeling stronger and more capable by the minute. She took the tea and padded over to the bed, propping up the pillows and making herself comfortable while she drank.

'Are you up to doing the distance today?' Daniel asked. 'We don't get a lunch stop, apart from a picnic in a field somewhere. You might find it a bit much.'

'To get this far and not finish would be a disaster,' Joy said. 'I have to finish it.' She couldn't contemplate the thought of not doing so. 'I feel good, honestly. I don't know what she put in that soup last night, but whatever it was, it worked.' She gave him a wide smile, hoping to convince him of her fitness.

Daniel nodded. 'I'll have a shower, and then we'll take a short stroll before breakfast,' he said, disappearing into the bathroom. 'Just to be sure,' he added.

In less than ten minutes, Joy was walking, albeit rather stiffly, down the stairs, with Daniel following closely behind her. The house was quiet, apart from a distant humming from Mrs Galbraith, as she busied herself in the kitchen. They let themselves out of the front door, and closing the garden gate behind them, they set off slowly, Joy with her arm linked through Daniel's for support.

*****

The early morning sun was warm on their backs as they walked through the quiet streets, and after a while, Joy's wooden gait began to loosen. Daniel told her all about the traditional music entertainment in the pub, and 'the attack of the killer midges', the night before.

Joy found herself laughing along with him, and she felt curiously light and free.

'Am I dreaming this?' she asked, stopping to look at Daniel. 'Is this the calm before the storm or something? It can't be right. We've gone from almost ripping each other's throats out, to walking along arm in arm, laughing and joking like we haven't a care in the world.' She frowned, shaking her head. 'I don't get it.'

Daniel shrugged.

'I don't know,' he said. 'Maybe we've exhausted all the anger. And all the secrets are out, so perhaps now we can talk our way through everything. Make it work, or end it as friends.' He shrugged again. 'I'm really not sure.'

Joy nodded and held Daniel's arm a fraction tighter, chilled by the casual reference to ending it.

Does he really think we could split up, and just be friends? I think there's more hurt and decision-making to come. But for the moment, I'm going to allow myself this brief interlude of normality.

They walked back to the B&B in companionable silence.

'Are you excited about meeting Jason?' Joy eventually asked.

'Kind of - nervous too.'

'Does Stephanie have a partner?' She kept her tone light, surprising herself at how easily the words came out.

'No idea,' he said. 'It worries me though, that she might think we can get together.' He looked at Joy. 'Because that will never happen.'

They were almost at the gate. Joy could see Kathy's bent head beyond the hedge.

'I could come with you.' Joy couldn't believe she'd said that. 'If you like?'

Daniel looked at her in surprise.

'I'm not sure that would be a good idea,' he said.

*****

Kathy stood up as they entered the garden.

'Well that's a relief,' she said to Joy. 'You look better than I expected.'

'Thanks. I definitely feel better than I did yesterday afternoon.' Joy looked embarrassed. 'Kath, can we talk?'

Before Kathy could answer, Ruth and Brad appeared in the doorway.

'Come on you lot. Breakfast,' called Ruth.

'Later, OK?' Kathy whispered to Joy as they walked down the footpath and into the house.

Joy felt the hunger pangs stirring, at the tantalising aroma of freshly baked bread and fried bacon wafting from the dining room.

Everyone was relieved and delighted to see her up and about. Trish hugged her tight and Rob kissed her cheek.

Ruth pushed the plate of hot toast across to her.

'Come on, eat up,' she said bossily. 'You need to build up your strength again.

Joy felt uncomfortable at all the attention, and was relieved when Mrs Galbraith breezed into the dining room carrying plates of bacon, eggs and fried tomatoes.

'Give over, you lot,' she said, her voice a little shaky.

She broke a corner off her slice of toast and dipped it into her fried egg, smiling as she caught Brad's eye and received one of his flirty little winks.

There was very little talk around the table as everyone tucked into the delicious breakfast.

After a second cup of coffee, Joy pushed back her chair and stood up.

'I need to brush my teeth and finish packing,' she said. 'What time are we leaving?' she asked looking at Rob.

'We'll meet out in the front garden in half an hour,' he said checking his watch. 'If that's OK with everyone,' he added.

They all nodded and murmured their agreement.

'Fine,' Joy said before she left the dining room.

II

Half an hour later, their bags were piled outside the minibus and they were ready to set off on the final leg of the walk.

'I'll have the bus outside your hotel in Fort William before you arrive this afternoon,' Mr Galbraith said as he helped Rob load the luggage.

'We need photographs, please,' Ruth hollered from the front doorway.

They gathered at the bench, the four girls sitting with their arms around each other, and the guys lined up behind. They were all laughing and smiling as Mr Galbraith took several pictures with Ruth's camera.

Mrs Galbraith was busy fussing like a mother hen; she had prepared sumptuous packed lunches, and was handing them out to everyone. She wagged a finger at Joy.

'You drink plenty of water now. And wear a hat.'

'I will. Thank you so much for your kindness,' Joy said.

Mrs Galbraith clucked and fussed until, finally satisfied, she waved from the gate as they set off back down to the village, to pick up the footpath again.

III

Daniel and Brad showed equal concern for Joy on the steep uphill climb out of Kinlochleven, walking either side of her, each taking an arm and propelling her upwards.

'Stop!' she called out, panting hard.

'What's wrong?' Daniel asked.

'Look, I know you're worried about me, but I'm fine. Our strides don't match, I feel like I'm being dragged along.' She rested her hands on her knees. 'I'll be better at my own pace,' she told them. 'Go on; wait for me at the top.'

'Well, if you're sure,' Daniel said, clearly uneasy about the decision.

She waved them off, smiling at their anxious backward glances, pausing for a few seconds to look back at the town, nestled in the valley below. After a minute or two, although daunted by the height the zigzag path rose to, she set off again. She could see Brad and Daniel up ahead. They had passed the hairpin bend in the path and were now walking parallel, thirty or forty feet above her. She waved, giving them an encouraging thumbs-up. By the time she reached the spot where they had been, she had developed an irritating stitch in her side.

I must have eaten too much at breakfast. I need a distraction. Maybe I should count. You're supposed to count sheep when you can't sleep. And we used to count cars when we were kids, on a long car journey. I won't find many cars up here, but I could try trees, or bushes.

She heard Ruth's voice chanting rhythmically behind her.

'Ninety-two, ninety-three...' Ruth pointed to her feet as she passed.

Joy decided that counting could work. After all, Ruth was probably the least fit of the group, and yet here she was, making steady progress.

'One hundred and thirty-three...' Joy puffed as the path levelled off to a gentle incline. 'Thanks for the counting idea, Ruth,' she said to her friend.

Ruth nodded and wiped the sweat from her glowing face.

'I'll tell you what, the Devil's Staircase was a walk in the park compared to this,' she gasped.

They paused a moment to look back down at the zigzag path chalked out on the mountainside, giving a wave to Trish, Kathy and Rob who were behind on the final section of the steep zigzag.

'When are you going to sort things out with Kathy?' Ruth asked.

'Today,' Joy replied, watching her friends draw closer.

'Well, now's as good a time as any,' Ruth said squeezing her arm.

The trio paused beside Joy and Ruth.

'Come on, girls,' Rob said briskly. 'We can't be dawdling too much this early in the day.'

'Just a sec, Rob,' Trish interrupted. She turned to Joy. 'How are you feeling?' she asked with concern. 'That was tough going.'

'You're not kidding,' Joy said. 'I'm OK now I've had a few minutes' rest. And Rob's right. We should get moving,' she added.

The group set off once more. Rob was sandwiched between Trish and Ruth, and, behind them, Kathy fell into step beside Joy. Their similar height and build meant that their steps matched evenly.

Neither of them spoke for a long while and Joy slowed down slightly to allow the gap to widen, not wanting the three in front to overhear what might be said.

Joy silently rehearsed her speech. Nothing sounded right.

'I'm sorry' seems too easy. Meaningless, almost. Anyone can say I'm sorry. But she's probably waiting for an apology.

'I'm sorry, Kath,' Joy said, without turning her head. 'I know it's not enough. I don't know where to begin to apologise properly.'

'I'm sorry too,' Kathy said quietly.

'What for?' Joy looked across at her. 'There was nothing going on with you and Daniel. I know that now.'

'I'm sorry that I gave you any reason to think it in the first place.'

Joy waved her hand dismissively. 'Don't be,' she said quickly. 'You didn't – and you can't be responsible for my paranoia.' She took a deep breath. 'Can we put this right?'

'Of course we can.' Kathy put her arms around her in a reassuring hug.

Joy pulled away, embarrassed at the tears that threatened to fall. 'So, what about you?' she asked quickly, eager to take the attention away from herself. 'That was a massive step you took with Tony last night. Daniel filled me in briefly. What will you do? Do you think you can work it out?' She paused for breath. 'Sorry, that's a million questions. Don't feel you have to answer if you think I'm being nosey,' she added, remembering her own anger at being questioned, just a few days before.

'Friends aren't nosy, they're caring,' Kathy said. 'Anyway, in a nutshell, we're well and truly over. I'm moving out.'

'Where will you go?' Joy was shocked at how strong and resolute the usually mouse-like Kathy was.

'I have it sorted, I'll be fine. Don't worry about me,' Kathy said with breezy confidence.

Joy was impressed.

'I wish I could be so sure, about my own mess.'

'You need to let people in, Joy. That's what I did eventually,' Kathy said gently. 'It wasn't easy, but I couldn't get any further on my own. Problem and solution scenarios became a spinning top in my head. The solution became a problem and the problem a solution - until I thought I'd crack up completely. Then I let someone in. Suddenly there was a fresh perspective - a clear set of eyes and bingo. The endless head debates stopped, and steps for a plan of action appeared.'

Joy listened and sighed.

'It's different for me, I'm in the wrong. I failed,' she said, stopping to tighten her bootlace. She imagined she could feel tiny fragments of the hard protective shell she wore, breaking away, falling to the ground.

'You were wronged, Kath,' she added.

'But I failed too,' said Kathy sadly. 'He was a bully. I should have stood up to him years ago.'

'Who helped you see things differently? Was it Daniel?' Joy asked. She wondered if that would explain their apparent closeness.

'No. Actually it was Brad.'

Joy raised an eyebrow.

'He talks a lot of sense, once you get past his flirty charm,' Kathy said.

They realised they had fallen quite a way behind, when they heard Daniel calling them.

'What's the holdup?' he shouted back down the footpath.

He walked back to meet them.

'Are you OK? Are you tired?' he asked. He put a hand on Joy's shoulder, his eyes wide with concern. 'Do you feel ill?'

'Stop panicking. I'm fine. We were just talking,' Joy said.

'Well, I'm glad to see you're getting on again,' Daniel said with relief. 'But try to keep up. We still have miles to go.'

They nodded and as he turned back, conscious of his watchful eye, they increased their pace, not speaking until he was well ahead.

'He loves the bones of you, despite what's gone on,' Kathy whispered. 'Everyone makes one mistake in their life. Sometimes more than one,' she added softly.

Joy nodded and the two of them continued to trek along the pathway, each lost in their own thoughts. She could see the others up ahead, all walking in single file with some distance between them.

Is everyone deep in thought, trying to sort out their own issues, like me? Or are they just trekking mindlessly, now that the end is in sight?

She could hear Kathy breathing as she walked beside her.

I really want to tell her everything, but I'm scared. Scared she'll hate me - that they'll all hate me.

IV

It was just after twelve when Joy and Kathy joined the rest of the group by a low stone wall just off the footpath.

'This could be a good place to stop for lunch,' Rob announced. 'There are great views over the valley and a grassy bank to sit on.'

The others nodded in agreement, and, pulling off their rucksacks, they sat on the bank below the footpath, resting their backs against the low stone wall.

Despite thinking they wouldn't eat another thing after the mammoth breakfast that morning, the group delved eagerly into their rucksacks, keen to start on the excellent packed lunches provided by Mrs Galbraith.

'Wow, look at the size of this!' Brad held out a sandwich made up of two doorstep-thick slices of granary bread, stuffed to overflowing with ham and salad. 'That woman's an angel. I could marry her,' he drooled.

'I can make sandwiches like that too,' Ruth said, fluttering her eyelashes and giving an exaggerated wink.

'What, an available angel?' Brad gasped. 'Is there a priest hiding in these mountains?' he called out giving Ruth a playful wink.

Ruth blew him a kiss as the rest of the group laughed at the joke.

Like children on a school outing, they sat with legs outstretched and lunches on laps. Nobody spoke as they munched their way through the doorstep sandwiches followed by crisp juicy apples.

Joy gazed across the rolling hills as she bit into her apple.

It's almost over, less than six miles to go. In just twenty-four hours, we'll be back in the real world and whatever it may have in store for us.

'Oh my God, oh my God' Ruth's sudden squeals shattered their harmonious lunch. 'Look up there... clouds!'

'Would you credit it, four hours to go, and finally the shade we've been praying for since Sunday,' Rob said.

'I might get to use those new waterproofs after all,' Trish said.

'Steady on, Trish, I gave up packing mine two days ago.' Kathy pointed upwards. 'They're only little clouds.'

*****

Half an hour later, the group packed up their lunch things. Rejoicing at the pockets of shadow falling across their face and arms, they were now anxious to see the finishing post.

Ruth struck a pose, flinging her arms wide to get their attention. 'Before we go, everyone,' she shouted, 'I have an announcement to make.' She paused for effect.

'Get on with it then,' Brad groaned.

'I'm moving to Scotland,' she gushed. 'Tyndrum actually. In two weeks' time,' she added, hugging herself with excitement.

'What's all this about?' Trish and Kathy asked in unison.

Ruth rattled off the details of her afternoon in Tyndrum. The perfect B&B. The idyllic house with its large rooms, conservatory, and beautiful gardens.

'And,' she said, glancing coyly at Brad. 'I can cook like Mrs Galbraith.'

'When did you decide?' Joy asked, wondering if she'd missed something. 'Did you speak to Paul, or the boys?'

'No, but I did speak to Jane at the B&B. I told her I was really interested, and that I should be able to get a mortgage and stuff. I just needed to sell the house first.' Ruth's eyes shone. 'She suggested that I work for her for a few months; the rest of the summer if I want to. You know, to get a feel for the place.' She paused, lowering her voice. 'She's very frail, you know.'

'I know she is and she really cares about that house,' Joy said. 'She's probably vetting you, before she commits to selling,' she joked. 'Seriously though, I'm really happy for you.'

Joy hugged Ruth tight. She felt more fragments of her protective shell breaking away imagining them sticking to Ruth's damp hair and T-shirt.

'It's a big decision moving so far away from home, you should think it through carefully,' Daniel said taking Ruth's hand and giving her a quick hug. 'The best of luck whatever you decide,' he added.

'Yes, good luck with it, Ruth, I hope it all goes well for you,' Brad said as he picked up his rucksack from the ground.

'It sounds like a great adventure, Ruth,' Rob said smiling. 'Now we really should get moving again.' He set off along the footpath with Brad and Daniel. 'Don't be long, girls,' he called over his shoulder.

The girls were still shrugging on their rucksacks as they prepared to follow.

'This has been the best experience ever,' Ruth said. 'Last Saturday when I first put on my boots, I didn't think I'd make it to the end of the High Street in Milngavie. Now look at me - almost ninety-five miles later!' She held her arms wide. 'And do you know, I'm sure I've lost weight.'

'We probably all have.' Trish patted her flat, tanned midriff. 'It was definitely an experience. Different for everyone, I think.'

'I've had a great time,' Kathy said.

'Yes, me too. Fantastic.' Joy's sarcasm was obvious.

Trish shook her head and turned away.

Joy felt a sharp pang of annoyance with herself.

Why did I do that? That was the ideal opportunity to tell them the truth, and I pushed them away. I'm running out of time. If I don't tell them now,- before we go back home, I'll never do it. I'll just go back to hiding behind my false lifestyle again. I need to stop being such a bloody coward and tell them now, here in this wide-open space where there's nowhere to hide. If they're my friends, they'll understand... and if not well fuck the lot of them!

She felt her fury rise, like the valve on a pressure cooker. Releasing, pushing up from the pit of her stomach, through the half-digested sandwich, squeezing the air from her lungs, until the words escaped through her mouth.

'My life is one big lie,' she blurted. 'One massive fucking lie.' There was a moment's stunned silence and they all stared at her.

Trish spoke first.

'Isn't everyone's?' she snapped. 'Why does that mean you have to behave in such an obnoxious way?' With an exasperated glance, she turned on her heel and set off at a brisk pace.

Joy leant against a tree, shocked at what she'd said.

'Go after Trish.' Ruth nudged Kathy.

'No, you go. She won't talk to me.' Kathy pushed Ruth forward.

Joy sank to the ground, to sit with her back against the knobbly bark of the tree. She took several deep, invigorating breaths, filling her lungs with mountain air.

I've made a start. Not a great one, but it's helped. It's as if something's shifted. For the first time in years, I feel as if I can breathe properly.

She watched Ruth jogging awkwardly after Trish, who was marching so fast she was almost running, and thought not for the first time this week, that something was troubling Trish.

V

Joy and Kathy sat quietly, each immersed in their own thoughts. The rest of the group were out of sight when Kathy reached out a hand to Joy, who grasped it tightly.

'That was quite a statement,' Kathy said, pulling her up. 'I'm sure you feel better getting it off your chest,' she added with a wry smile.

Joy was shaking from the adrenalin rush.

'Like you wouldn't believe,' she said. 'Something inside just cracked. It came from right down there, Kath.' She rubbed her T-shirt below her ribcage. 'Once it started, I couldn't stop. The words just spilled out.' She looked intently at her friend. 'You've known me forever, Kath. Have I changed that much since we were younger?'

'We all change Joy,' Kathy said. 'You're still pretty much the same. Maybe a little sharper, a little stronger minded - and you can appear quite aloof at times. But then, even when we were fifteen, you could be like that sometimes.'

Joy nodded, taking in what Kathy was saying and adding it to her collection of thoughts.

They put on their rucksacks and set off after the others.

'It's all been an act,' Joy said suddenly. 'For as long as I can remember my life has been an act.'

Kathy looked at her, but didn't speak.

'Ever since I was a child everything came easily to me: schoolwork; riding a bike; ice skating; playing piano. I never failed at anything. I got good exam results and passed my driving test first time. Little Miss Perfect, that was me.'

'That's what my mam used to say whenever she saw you pass the window. "Here comes Little Miss Perfect.".' Kathy smiled at the memory. Then she laughed. 'You've no idea how much I wanted to be like you.'

'That wasn't me, Kath. I wanted to play in the mud, have dirty fingernails, fall on the ice, fluff an exam, crash the car - anything to break the mould. But I couldn't. Failure was a forbidden word in our house. And I became obsessed with it - and terrified. Terrified of failing, and of what might happen to me if I did. So I buried myself inside this protective force, which got thicker and stronger, every time failure loomed in any shape or form.'

'Joy, everyone does that at some point in their life,' Kathy said.

Joy didn't look at her. She couldn't. Not if she was going to finish what she'd started.

'And then there it was. Failure with a capital F - no amount of practice or re-sits could fix this one. I was thirty years old and I'd never failed at anything. I had no choice, Kath. I had to bury it. So I piled on the layers and hardened the shell.'

Kathy took hold of Joy's hand.

She snatched it away.

'I need to be me,' she panted. 'It's who I am.' She thumped her chest. 'You need to know who I am. They need to know who I am. I want to be accepted for being me. With all the failures that I have no control over - the mistakes I can only try to put right.'

VI

Kathy felt exhausted for Joy and the effort it must be taking to get out all these long-buried feelings.

What do I say? Is it better to let her keep going? Does she need to talk about this 'big failure'? I'm out of my depth - we don't do this kind of thing. Where's Trish when you need her? She'd know what to do. Or even Ruth to throw in a stupid joke or two. Help!

'Do you remember years ago, when we were fourteen?' Joy asked. 'I had that deep plum, taffeta bridesmaid dress. You tried it on and I did your hair all curly. You looked lovely. Then I put on your faded jeans. The ones with holes at the knees and ragged frayed bottoms, and that goth style black T-shirt you practically lived in. You put the make-up on for me, purple eye shadow and thick eyeliner...'

'Of course I remember. My mam took a photo. I still have it, somewhere,' Kathy said. 'I felt so posh in that dress. I thought it would change my destiny. And that some rich boy would come and whisk me away from our shabby terraced house and my second-hand clothes and market tat.'

'I would have been happy in market tat.' Joy sighed. 'I never wanted to be something I'm not. Both of my parents were fixated on exactly that. When it didn't happen for them, and then Caroline rebelled and left home, they turned their attention to me. Well, I can't do it anymore, pretend to be something or somebody that isn't me. And if I end up with no husband, and no friends, then so be it.'

'We're not going to desert you, Joy.' Kathy tried to sound reassuring.

'I haven't told you what I've done yet. It was wicked and selfish of me to treat Dan that way. I can never fix it.'

The words played around on Kathy's tongue, but she was almost afraid to speak them.

It must be to do with kids. They never had any. Did Daniel want them? Was Joy too caught up in her social life to make time? Did she know about his affair? Has she punished him ever since, keeping him out of the bedroom?

This time it was Joy that reached for Kathy's hand with a grip so tight that it hurt. Kathy knew it was crunch time.

'We tried. Really tried,' Joy said. 'Like everything else I'd ever done, I expected immediate success. And when it didn't happen after the first couple of months, I felt I had to make it happen. Like a military operation, I plotted temperatures, and kept thermometers and ovulation charts to hand. I even called Daniel out of work when I was most fertile. I was so desperate for this to happen. But nothing was working. Every month was a nightmare. And in the bathroom mirror, where there should have been a pregnant belly, all I could see was failure, with a capital F.'

Joy sniffed loudly and took a deep breath, before continuing.

'Daniel couldn't handle it. He didn't know what to say to me. He tried, but I couldn't listen to him saying 'It will be all right, it's you I love'. All I could think was: How can he keep loving me when the one thing I'd failed at in my life was what woman was put on this earth for...?'

Kathy's fingers were white and she had lost feeling in her hand. She found it hard to take in what Joy was telling her. For as long as she could remember, she'd thought of Joy and Daniel as having the perfect relationship. *How could we have known what she was going through? Their attitude was always 'Kids - yes, lovely when they come along, but we're not going to sit around waiting.' I remember Joy saying, 'Do all the fun things first, that's what I say.' Now that I know the reality, what can I say to her?*

'Everyone's here for a reason, Joy. It's not always about reproducing,' Kathy said, thinking how lame that sounded.

She wasn't surprised when Joy didn't react.

'Eventually when I could stand it no longer, I made an appointment to see a doctor.' Joy was immersed in her confession. 'Maybe I wasn't a failure, I thought. Maybe the problem was with Daniel. I saw this doctor, a specialist, on my own. I pretended it was happening to someone else. It was the only way I could keep up appearances in the outside world... the inside world too. And he told me what I already knew, deep down. It was me. I'd failed the test.'

'Surely he didn't say that?' Kathy blurted out.

'He worded it politely, of course, told me all about my blocked fallopian tubes, but it all amounted to the same thing. I didn't stay to listen. Inside I was breaking into a million pieces – something Joy Crathorne didn't do outwardly. She was cool, calm, and collected. And when I was safely out of sight of the world, and I'd finished coming apart inside, I put myself together again. But the pieces were brittle and hard with sharp edges, so that with every breath they stabbed at my heart, my lungs. And over time, the outside layers got thicker, hiding the pain... and the lies.' Joy took a deep breath, shuddering slightly.

'Oh, Joy.'

'Don't, Kath, I need to finish.' Joy dropped Kathy's hand and put both of hers up to her face, rubbing at her dry eyes before continuing.

'I couldn't let myself admit I'd failed. Not even to Daniel. Every man wants kids; it's a natural progression in marriage. I was convinced he was only saying they weren't important for my benefit. That would be another failure. I was terrified I'd lose him - and without him, what would I have left?'

'You didn't tell him?'

'It was only supposed to be for a little while. I always promised myself I'd tell him, and then let him go. Time slipped by and while living without a baby was a well hidden, dull ache, I couldn't contemplate being without Dan. It niggled away constantly, deep inside that jagged shell, that I was living a lie. But we were liked and respected and the person I'd become needed that security. If I told the truth, Dan might leave me – and then it would all be gone.'

'Is that when he had the affair? When you told him?' Kathy asked.

'No. It was a one-night stand. He never meant to hurt me. I know that now. He never expected the repercussions it would bring either.' Joy spoke robotically, as if she was reading a police statement. 'That's what ate away at him, his secret, in exactly the same way that my secret was eating away at me. And so for years we lived this pretence, this artificial life. When in fact the people we had become weren't really us at all. So when cracks started to appear in our relationship we were both so wrapped up in our own guilty secrets that neither of us could see them.'

'Did she blackmail him?' Kathy asked.

'He has a son.'

'Oh My God, I didn't see that one coming'.

Joy continued her story, oblivious to Kathy's reaction.

'He's been paying maintenance for years, apparently. Now I know why he went on at me about booking yet another holiday, or buying another pair of boots. Money was tighter than I ever realised. His guilt made him want to give me everything I wanted – but we couldn't afford it.'

'Does he see him?' Kathy asked. She wanted to cry. All this had been going on in her friend's life and she hadn't been able to offer support.

'Next week will be the first time. His name is Jason and he's ten years old. A miniature Daniel.' Joy gave a sad smile.

'So his secret's out,' Kathy ventured. 'Is yours? Have you told him about when you found out you couldn't have children?'

Joy nodded. 'Is that Ben Nevis?' she asked suddenly, stopping and pointing northwards.

'I think so. Not far to go now.' Kathy paused beside her.

Joy looked at her friend. 'I couldn't hold onto it any more, Kath. I thought he was having an affair. Oh, not back then, just in recent months. It was eating away at me and I suppose I knew the time had come. Make or break, the truth had to come out. All of it.' She rested her arm on one of the fence posts that bordered the forestry path.

'Are you OK?' Kathy asked.

'I just need a minute, you go on,' Joy said.

'No, I'll wait with you. I could do with a breather myself.'

'I'll be fine, really. Look, the campsite is just ahead in the distance,' Joy insisted.

'I'll wait with you all the same,' Kathy repeated.

*****

Joy took several deep breaths and thought of how far they had come that week.

Friday night seems like a lifetime ago. Waiting for Daniel to come home, drinking too much, waking up after midnight with a pounding head and scratchy throat, seeing Daniel's side of the bed empty.

The bedroom was in darkness. Joy held her breath, listening, straining to hear a sound from downstairs. There was only silence. She switched on the bedside lamp.

'Damn it. Why did I drink that vodka?' she muttered struggling to make sense through the fuzz in her head. 'Where the hell is he? Gingerly she got out of bed, her legs alien to her as she crossed the room.

Her head bounced painfully with each step as she went downstairs. She found Daniel in the sitting room, lying on the sofa, her heavy winter coat thrown over him. His eyes wide open, staring at the ceiling.

'Daniel,' she whispered.

He was lying so still, he could have been dead.

Her heart pounded as painfully as her head. Kneeling on the floor beside the sofa, she touched his face. He was icy cold.

'Oh my God. Daniel! What's happened? What's wrong?' Joy was scared. She'd never seen him like this before.

His eyes slid to the right, the pain she saw shocked her to the core. She felt as if she could see into his soul.

Her throbbing head forgotten, briskly she pulled off the heavy coat covering him. His clothes were soaked through. He'd obviously been caught in the torrential downpour earlier.

'You're freezing. Come on, you need a hot bath.' Joy rubbed at his icy hands, helping him to his feet.

Like a child, Daniel followed her up the stairs and into the bathroom.

The steam from the hot bath water distorted their reflection in the mirror tiles, misting over their faces. Joy sat on the bathroom floor, watching Daniel's body turn from grey to pink, as he began to thaw beneath the steaming water.

'I can't do this anymore,' Daniel whispered, his eyes locking on to hers.

'Can't do what, Dan?' Joy asked, her heart hammering at what he might be about to say.

'Come here.' Daniel gestured towards the bath water. 'I really need to hold you.' He stroked her hair.

One last time. He wants to hold me one last time before he tells me it's over.

Joy undressed, her eyes never leaving his, and stepped into the water to sit between his legs, leaning back against his warm chest. He held her, his arms wrapped tight around her waist, his chin resting on her head.

I'll hold onto that moment forever, no matter what happens. We never said a word. We just sat there until the water turned cool, my hands resting on his.

*****

'Joy?' Kathy handed her a tissue.

Joy wiped her damp cheeks.

'We said we'd never have secrets. ' She looked at Kathy. 'And then, at two in the morning, there we were, sitting across from each other at the kitchen table. Dan said he had something to tell me. I felt calm; I thought I was ready to hear it, whatever he had to say. Since we were sharing secrets, I'd written him a letter, afraid I'd bottle it when my turn came. I could feel it, digging into my leg through my dressing gown pocket. Pushing me, goading me.'

'But you were going on holiday the next day,' Kathy said shaking her head, confused.

'I know. You'd think you could choose the time to blow your marriage out of the water, but you can't, no matter how much you plan.'

'True.' Kathy nodded.

Joy began walking again and Kathy fell into step beside her.

'So he told me, and even though it was what I expected to hear, it wasn't, if you know what I mean? I thought the affair was in the here and now, not ancient history.' Joy looked at Kathy. 'I was raging. I ended up spitting out the truth, about our childless marriage, and then locking myself in the bathroom, refusing to talk. It was awful, and we spent the few hours before you and Tony arrived saying horrible hurtful things to each other. There were no explanations, no saying I'm sorry. Just anger.'

'Are you still angry?'

'No. I've had ninety miles to walk it off.' Joy looked intently at Kathy. 'But I am sad, sad that I may have already lost Daniel - the most important person in my life.'

'You don't know that you've lost him,' Kathy protested.

'I feel it in here.' Joy banged her chest. 'And I'm scared. Scared I'm going to lose my friends too.'

'That won't happen,' Kathy said forcefully.

'It might. The person I want to be, the real me, isn't the person you all know.' Joy stopped once again, to look Kathy in the eye. 'You'll all hate me, for deceiving Daniel the way I did.'

'No one's going to hate you. Come here and give me a hug.' Kathy opened her arms. 'I think I'm going to love the new Joy. The others will too. You're a brave lady.'

Joy began to cry. Huge fat tears of exhaustion. She felt completely drained from the effort of telling her story, of finally letting someone else into her secret world.

'You know, you can't share everything with everyone.' Kathy held her at arm's length. 'But you need to be able to talk to someone, sometimes. A problem shared and all that.'

'Thanks, Kath.' Joy dropped her gaze.

'What about Daniel? Can you work it out?'

'I don't think he wants to.' Joy looked at the ground as she spoke.

'Maybe now's the time to find out.' Kathy pointed up ahead to where Daniel sat with his back against a tree. Joy followed her gaze and panicked.

'No, don't leave me, Kath. I haven't got the energy for another row.'

'Come on, this is the real Joy now; open and honest.' Kathy encouraged her. 'If you don't want to lose him, then you need to tell him.'

Daniel stood up as they approached.

'Are the others far ahead?' Kathy asked him.

'Five minutes or so,' he told her. 'It's a straight path to the bottom now. You can't get lost.'

VIII

Kathy walked ahead and Daniel fell into step beside Joy.

Neither of them spoke.

How will he react? There's been nothing but anger and hurt between us for days, and before that, years of pretence. How do you get past that? It's not like wiping a blackboard clean of chalk, erasing everything bad that ever happened - everything wrong that has been said.

'I'm surprised you're still standing.' Daniel broke the silence. 'I really didn't want you to walk today – I had visions of calling out air rescue and everything,' he said lightly.

'You know me. I never did like to fail.' The words sounded harsher than she'd intended.

He ignored her comment.

'Did you and Kath sort things out?'

Joy nodded.

'I was wrong, accusing her like that.'

'What did you tell her?'

'Everything, pretty much; about your affair, Jason, my lies. How much I've hurt you.' She looked up at him, meeting his gaze directly. 'How much I still love you.' Her voice trailed off.

Daniel took off his cap and scratched his head. Without speaking, he put it back on, pulling it low, shielding his eyes.

Shit, shit, shit, I've blown it. I've said it too soon. You stupid cow, is this the new you? Blurting stuff out without thinking it through, not caring for the consequences. If he tells me no, he can never forgive me, then what? Or if he wants to kiss and make up just like that. Then what will I do? I'm not ready for that either. Help!

Daniel cleared his throat and looked at Joy from beneath the peak of his cap.

'I've got a lot to get my head around. There's Jason for a start. I don't know how that meeting will go. I don't even know how I want it to go.' He shook his head and kicked at a loose stone on the footpath. 'For so long I've been consumed by the guilt and the lies that I've never really thought of him as my son. He was just a mistake I had a duty to pay for. Seeing his picture suddenly made him real. But he's something I created without you... and somehow that doesn't seem right, especially not now.'

'You don't have to choose,' Joy told him.

Daniel took her hands in his and turned her to face him. 'There's still so much we need to talk about,' he said, stroking her fingers with his thumb. 'I still love you, Joy.'

The air around them was charged with emotion and Joy was momentarily speechless.

He said he still loves me. So he doesn't hate me! Maybe we can work this out after all. But what if he doesn't like the real me? What if he can't forgive me for what I didn't tell him? Joy felt the remains of her energy leaking out through every pore in her skin.

She could see the rest of the group just a hundred yards or so ahead at the end of the path. There were cars passing behind them.

'Come on, you two,' Ruth yelled.

'The home run,' Joy said, pushing her exhausted face into a smile.

Daniel released her hands and waved in acknowledgement to the others, as they walked the short distance to join them.

'We were waiting for you,' Rob said when Joy and Daniel reached the roadside. 'We thought it would be good to walk to the finish line together.'

'Sounds like a plan,' Daniel said, taking hold of Joy's hand.

Joy had no energy left. She felt woozy as she struggled to see the way ahead. Just a couple of feet in front of her, Trish and Rob looked blurry. One minute there were two of them and the next they merged into one. She stumbled as she lifted legs of lead, to put one foot in front of the other, cringing at every car that passed as the roar vibrated through her head.

Kathy took hold of her other arm, offering support.

'Do you think she'll make it?' she asked Daniel over Joy's head.

'She's a stubborn one,' he whispered. 'She'll keep pushing on to the end.' He turned to Joy. 'Do you want to rest a minute?' he asked her. 'You don't look so good.'

'No. Come on, we're almost there,' she said, with forced brightness. 'I'll be fine. I'm not giving up now, not with the finish line just around the next bend.' She gripped Daniel's hand even tighter.

The voices of Daniel and Kathy flitted in and out of her consciousness, like a badly tuned radio station, as Joy willed the end of the road to draw closer. *One hundred strides, that's all. Ninety-nine, ninety-eight...* She counted down, putting one foot in front of the other with dogged determination. *Fifteen, fourteen...*

IX

'There it is! Oh my God, I can't believe I made it!' Ruth yelled with excitement, breaking into a jog.

Joy broke free of her trancelike state to focus on the present. She watched Ruth fling her arms around the monument with exuberance, hugging it like a long lost friend.

'Congratulations from the Ben Nevis Highland Centre,' Ruth read aloud, caressing the words on the stone. 'We bloody well deserve it, too!'

Amidst hugs and laughter, they all gathered around the monument and congratulated each other on their achievement.

Joy leaned heavily against the plaque, obscuring the word 'congratulations', for a few moments. She drank thirstily from her water bottle, before splashing the rest of her water over her face, hoping to re-energise her look before Rob started taking photographs.

'It's almost an anticlimax, don't you think?' she asked Kathy who stood beside her. 'We walk ninety-five miles and the finish line is this simple sign plonked on a bit of lawn.'

'I totally agree,' Brad joined in. 'The least there should be is a fanfare of trumpets and a bunch of scantily clad girls handing out champagne.' He grinned.

Joy and Kathy stepped away as other walkers approached the monument, to allow them their moment of glory.

'It's supposed to be a personal achievement in the natural beauty of the Scottish Highlands, not some celebrity award ceremony,' Kathy laughed.

As other walkers were still hovering around the finish line, Rob quickly asked one of them to take some victory shots for him. The group gathered again around the finish sign, grinning widely, looking as energetic as if they'd just finished a walk in the park. Not content with smiling victory shots, Brad encouraged everyone to take off their boots and socks.

'Come on, I bet no one has feet as bad as mine,' he challenged.

'You'd be surprised,' Trish laughed. 'I've got bites up my calves almost to my knees,' she said sitting down beside him and removing her boots.

'God, this feels good.' Joy sat next to Trish and wriggled her toes in the cool soft grass of the carefully manicured lawn.

'How is that fair?' Ruth plonked herself beside them. 'Look at your legs, bronzed and smooth, with not a blemish in sight...' She placed her pale, bitten leg alongside Joy's. 'And I've got more spots than a Dalmatian.'

'You're obviously much tastier than me, Ruth.' Joy gave her a hug.

Ruth grinned. 'I wish Brad thought so,' she said ruefully.

The others joined in and soon they'd formed a circle on the grass, sitting with their legs outstretched and their toes touching, as they compared their bites and blisters.

'This is definitely one for the photo album.' Brad clicked the camera. 'Did you ever see such a motley crew?'

'OK, so who's up for another walk?' Rob stood up, pulling Trish to her feet.

'No way.' They all protested in unison.

'What? Not even to the pub?' He grinned and pointed to the Walkers Inn, just yards away.

XI

The bar was busy with a mixture of customers. There were walkers in long shorts and boots with thick socks turned over the tops, drinking pints of beer or orange juice. Businessmen lingered over the remains of a late lunch, their ties loosened and top buttons of their shirts undone. A group of young women wearing sundresses herded schoolchildren dressed in matching maroon polo shirts to a large round table, where they dished out plates of chicken nuggets and chips.

Suddenly Joy felt claustrophobic. 'Can we sit outside?' she asked Kathy, holding her rucksack up high as they squeezed past a woman with a buggy and two toddlers. Kathy turned to answer her, but Joy was feeling panicky and light-headed.

'I need to get out right now,' she told her.

I'll either faint or throw up if I don't get out of here.

Turning around, she fought her way back, almost falling through the doorway. Never had she been so thankful to feel the glare and the heat of the sun.

She leaned against the wall, battling the nauseous feeling rising in her stomach, taking deep breaths as she waited for the panic to subside.

All the outside tables were occupied. Some people had taken their drinks beyond the walled patio, to sprawl on the grassy area beyond. Knowing she couldn't bear it inside, Joy contemplated moving onto the grass. She noticed a couple of businessmen packing papers into leather briefcases, and she stepped away from the supporting wall.

'Are you leaving? Do you mind if I sit here?' she asked.

The larger of the two men nodded his balding head at the empty end of the bench.

'You look like you need to take the weight off your feet for a while,' he said, giving her a paternal smile.

'Thanks,' she said, smiling back, before fiddling with her rucksack to avoid being drawn into conversation.

The businessmen finished their drinks and said goodbye to her as they left. Joy moved to the other side of the bench where she could see the entrance to the bar. A minute later, she saw Kathy at the doorway, scanning the patio looking for her. She raised a hand in a discreet wave and watched as Kathy weaved her way through the crowds towards her. She frowned at the two pint glasses of clear liquid that Kathy placed on the table. They were topped with slices of lemon.

'What, no beer?' she asked.

'I think we need rehydrating first.'

'We should be celebrating our great achievement.'

'Celebrating will have you in hospital if you don't get some fluids back into you,' Kathy said sternly. 'Do you realise how awful you look?'

'Gee, thanks.' Joy sighed and took the glass. The ice cubes clinked, and condensation rivulets formed on the outside. She ran her finger up and down, wiping the glass clean. 'OK, I admit I don't feel the best,' she said, raising the glass to her parched lips.

'Lemon and lime,' Kathy told her. 'It's very refreshing.' She took a long drink. 'Trish and Ruth are following me out. Is that OK?' she added.

Before she could answer, Joy looked up to see the pair of them crossing the patio.

'You look a bit rough, Joy,' Ruth said with concern. She touched Joy's clammy forehead with the back of her hand.

'I'll be fine after a shower and a power nap,' Joy reassured her.

'I hope so,' Ruth said, unconvinced. She put her drink on the table and sat beside Joy.

Trish sat next to Kathy, and for a second, or two, nobody spoke.

Joy went back to wiping the condensation from her glass.

Trish looks uncomfortable. Either she's still stewing on some personal issue, or she's distinctly off with me. Yet another relationship I need to sort out. She dried her fingers on her shorts.

'Are the lads joining us?' she asked.

'No, would you believe they bumped into some guy from Redcar, who Brad knows,' Ruth answered 'He's climbing Ben Nevis tomorrow. And get this. Brad's thinking about doing it with him.' Ruth shook her head. 'He must be mad.'

'It'd be a fitting end, I guess. For anyone who thinks they can manage it,' Kathy said.

'Not for me,' said Ruth firmly. 'As far as I'm concerned, the end is right here, right now.' She set her glass down a little too hard, making the ice cubes jangle and the liquid slosh over the top.

'I don't think I'd quite manage it anyway,' Joy smiled.

Trish looked up. 'I don't think any of us would,' she agreed.

They lapsed into silence again.

Joy knew that Trish and Ruth were unsure of what to say.

This feels so uncomfortable. Ruth and Trish can't tell if Kathy and I have sorted things out between us or not. And poor Kath, after everything I've just dumped on her shoulders - along with her own problems - she's probably exhausted. It's up to me to sort this out. It's time to tell them what's been going on - what I've done... and find out how strong our friendship really is. Not here though. Not all sweaty and tired, looking like death. I need to prepare myself.

Joy drained her glass and stood up.

'I think the four of us need to talk,' she announced. She felt, rather than heard, the intake of breath around the table. 'Let's check in and meet down in the bar in an hour.' She looked at them all in turn.

'I'll ask the lads to go off and watch football or something,' Kathy volunteered.

Trish nodded her agreement.

Ruth linked her arm with Joy's, as they walked to the small hotel just alongside the pub.

'Shall we put on our glad rags?' she asked.

'If it makes you feel good, then absolutely,' Joy said with a tired smile.

Just a couple of minutes later, the group gathered around the minibus, collected their bags and headed into the hotel.

Joy spotted the door to the bar on the left of the reception.

'I'll see you in there in an hour,' she said to the other women, before heading up the stairs.

XII

Joy surveyed the room. It was dominated by a king-size bed piled high with plump pillows in shades of chocolate and vanilla, with splashes of vibrant lime green. She could see no armchair large enough for Daniel to be comfortable in.

I suppose it wouldn't be so bad sharing the bed; after all, it's big enough.

The window looked out over the car park, beyond which she could see the towering height of Ben Nevis, its summit barely visible amongst the wispy white clouds that had been gathering since lunchtime. She pulled back the natural voile curtains and stood, arms folded, watching. Just for a moment, instead of seeing the Scottish mountain scenery beyond the glass, she saw her own street, as she had so many evenings, while waiting for Daniel to come home.

She shuddered, turning away from the window.

This time tomorrow, we'll be home. I don't even know where home will be... or where I want it to be.

She lay down on the bed and closed her eyes.

The only thing I know right now is that I have to talk to Trish, Ruth, and Kathy, tell them about the lie my life has been, and test the friendship theory. Perhaps then, I can work out what to do next.

Joy woke with a start as the door clicked closed. Daniel walked across to the bed.

'How are you feeling?' he asked.

'Tired. I must have nodded off.' She yawned as she sat up. 'What time is it?'

'Twenty to six,' Daniel told her, looking at his watch.

'Shit, I'm supposed to be meeting the girls at six,' Joy said, swinging her legs off the bed and crossing the room to the bathroom. 'Do you mind if I take the first shower?' she added.

'No, go ahead,' Daniel said dropping onto the bed, filling the space that Joy had just vacated. Picking up the remote control, he switched on the TV and flicked through the few channels offered by the area.

Joy stepped into the shower, keeping the water cool, in the hope that she would feel refreshed and able to hold exhaustion at bay, until she'd finished what she'd set out to do. She decided the simple look would be best for the job she had to do, applying a little tinted moisturiser and pale pink lip-gloss. Her reflection looked tired and nervous.

I feel bare and exposed without my usual slap, but then isn't that what I want? To show them the real me without any masks or props to hide behind. At least then, perhaps they will see how sorry I am for the mess I've made of my life.

She dressed quickly in a pair of skinny jeans and a plain white vest, and then pushed her feet into flip-flops.

'See you later,' she said to Daniel as she grabbed a cardigan and her handbag and opened the door to the corridor.

'Joy!' Daniel called out.

She paused in the doorway and looked back at him.

'It'll be OK. They're good friends. They'll be there for you,' he said gently.

'I hope so,' she whispered, before closing the door.

*****

The nervous fluttering in her stomach reached mammoth proportions as she entered the hotel bar. She pushed up the sleeves of her powder blue cardigan, slightly, revealing her tanned wrists and hands.

Her hands shook as she fiddled with her wedding ring, while scanning the room for her friends. She felt like fleeing back to her room, she was so scared at the enormity of what she was about to do – revealing her secrets and lies – and fearful of how her friends would react.

The bar was very traditional in appearance, with dark oak furniture. The chairs and benches covered in burgundy leather, softened from years of use, were cracked and torn in places. The tables were all highly polished and spotlessly clean, despite the dents and scratches, each with a tea light inside a dark green glass, waiting to be brought to life once darkness fell.

There was no sign of the others yet, so Joy crossed to the bar and ordered a bottle of house white.

'Could I take four glasses with that please?' she asked the young barman.

'Aye, have a seat, I'll fetch them over.' He smiled, revealing wire train tracks, pulling his crooked teeth into line.

Joy chose a secluded booth and slid along the seat. She looked up at the old, faded oil painting on the wall. A fierce looking Scotsman in his tartan garb of green and blue stood poised ready to hurl his spear.

'You're not quite Mel Gibson, are you?' she murmured.

The barman placed the glasses on the table and poured wine into one of them for Joy.

'Have a nice evening, madam,' he said politely.

'Thank you,' she replied, and lifted the glass to her lips. It was sharper than she was used to, and made her wrinkle her nose and screw up her eyes.

Ruth arrived just in time to witness her expression.

'Get it down you, girl,' she said, laughing as she slid along the bench opposite. 'Kathy and Trish are right behind me,' she added, and poured wine into the remaining glasses.

Almost immediately, they arrived and greeted Joy, Kathy sitting on the bench beside her and Trish joining Ruth, opposite her.

'You look pretty tonight,' Kathy said smiling at Joy

Joy smiled back and took another sip of the bitter wine. For a minute or two, she zoned in and out, as the usual idle conversation flitted around the table. Her ears pricked up when she heard Trish shrugging off Kathy's question about why Rob had shirked away from Trish's hug outside their room a few minutes earlier.

'Oh he's just tired that's all,' she said dismissing the comment.

Joy felt this was her cue to get down to the real business of the evening, and jumped into the conversation. She looked directly at Trish.

'Is he really just tired? Or is that an evasive answer to keep us all at a distance?'

Their eyes met for a second, and then Trish looked down into her glass.

'He's just tired.' Trish picked up her glass and took a long drink. 'Anyway, who are you to talk?' she spat. 'You've spent the whole week in a strop, refusing to talk or say what's wrong.'

Joy leaned back against the worn leather and looked around at her friends, all silently drinking their wine. She knew Kathy and Ruth felt uneasy at Trish's outburst. She took a deep breath.

XIII

Well, here goes. Once I open up this conversation, I have to see it through to the end, no matter what. She drained her glass.

'Are we friends?' she asked quietly, looking at each of them in turn.

'What kind of a question is that?' Ruth frowned. 'You know we are. We've known each other …forever.'

'But do we know each other?' Joy threw out the question to everyone. She placed her elbows on the table and leaned forward.

'Of course we do. I don't understand where you're coming from, Joy,' Ruth said.

'Ok, so do you know what music makes me cry? What movies make me laugh? What my dreams are? The part of my body I hate the most. Whether I'm happy - or a secret drinker?' She reeled off the questions. 'Or that my life is a lie?' she added, looking down at her glass. She heard Ruth's sharp intake of breath and could feel the three sets of eyes upon her. She counted the seconds.

Will somebody please say something?

'I know you'd be there for me, if I was in trouble.' Ruth spoke first.

'But would you ask? Would any of us?'

Trish looked at Joy.

'I know you're not happy. And I tried to help, but you pushed me away,' she said.

'Did you know I was unhappy two weeks ago - two years ago, even?' Joy asked.

Ruth gave a shocked gasp.

'You and Daniel always seemed so happy and content,' she said.

'Seemed being the key word here,' Joy said with emphasis. 'We *seemed* to be happy. Like you *seemed* to be happy with your decision to let the boys live with their dad. Like Trish and Rob *seem* to be happy, with their idyllic lifestyle and successful son at Uni. Like Kathy *seemed* to be happy, living with a husband who's a possessive bully and a prize prat.' Joy paused, shaking inside as she waited for a reaction.

God, this is so hard, I hope I sound stronger than I feel inside. Stop that. Isn't this what it's all about? It should be OK to show that I'm scared, angry, or vulnerable or whatever.

When nobody spoke, she continued.

'Look, I know we have to protect ourselves. We all build up this tough exterior, putting it on like a winter coat when we leave the house, and that's fine. But with our friends, our real friends, we should be true to ourselves. So...' She paused to top up the wine in everyone's glass, and raised her own to the centre of the table. 'If we're real friends, and I hope we are, let's all be honest about our lives. Then if there is a problem, we can really help each other.'

Kathy clinked her glass.

'I'm in,' she said giving Joy an encouraging smile.

'Me too.' Ruth clinked.

They waited a second or two, before Trish finally raised her glass to theirs.

Joy noticed how Trish's hand shook slightly.

*****

'This could be the shortest new friendship in history, once I've told you my story.' Joy gave a wry smile and took a slow deep breath.

'Daniel's affair was my fault really. I drove him to it...' she began.

She concentrated on her glass as she carried on delving into the past and the hurt, faltering slightly when she told them of her visit to the hospital, what the doctor told her and the way she had hidden it from Daniel.

Reassured by Kathy's arm around her shoulders, she dared to look up. Trish, always so composed, was watching her intently. Ruth – big-hearted Ruth - had tears running down her face.

'Oh, Joy,' she cried.

'Please, Ruth, I need to finish this.' Joy's voice shook as she went on, telling them how paranoid she became when Daniel took to coming home late, and how she'd discovered what he was really doing; working all hours and more to support her spending - and his son.

'Oh, Joy,' Ruth wailed again. 'And to think of all the times over the years that we harped on about our kids, doing this and that...'

'Ruth, stop it. Don't beat yourself up over that,' Joy said. 'I was never desperate for children, not for me anyway. I wasn't really the maternal type. It was just the thing you did after getting married. The hardest part of it all was accepting that I was a failure.' Joy sighed.

'You're not a failure, Joy Crathorne,' Ruth protested. 'Look at your beautiful home, your lovely husband, your gorgeous figure...'

Joy shook her head.

'That's my point. Don't you get it, Ruth? That's not me - not the real me,' she said.

Ruth blew her nose loudly and Trish and Kathy both sipped their wine. Nobody spoke for a second or two.

Joy looked up at the Scotsman on the wall.

Help! I don't think they're on my wavelength at all here. I feel as though I'm in front of a judge and jury.

She took another mouthful of wine.

'I'm not bothered about fancy furniture, posh cars, and dinner with pompous businessmen and their stuck-up wives. Or lunch with the girls from the gym, who only bitch about each other and always have to have something bigger or better, than whatever you've just bought. I don't want to be prim and proper. I want to be carefree, creative maybe. I want to find something I'm good at.' She looked at each of them, trying to work out if she was making sense. 'I want to try things and fail - not caring that I failed, because I enjoyed the experience.' She leaned her head back against the leather seat.

That's it, I've said enough. It's their turn now.

Kathy gave Joy a comforting pat on the arm.

'I'll order more wine,' she said, attracting the attention of the young barman.

'I guess for a long while I knew you weren't yourself,' Trish said when their glasses had been topped up. She looked Joy in the eye. 'It was easier to brush it aside, when you always came out fighting, giving a snappy answer to close any subject you didn't want to talk about.'

'I'm not blaming you, Trish, or any of you. I put up the barriers; and I kept on building them as the years went by. They became so deep and strong that nobody could have broken through. In the end the only way out was to self-destruct...'

She looked around the table. 'So, I suppose the big question now is... Do I still have my friends?'

'You don't get rid of us that easily,' Ruth said with a watery smile. She blew her nose again, with exaggerated loudness, making them all laugh.

'I could become a real pain in the arse. My head's all over the place at the moment,' Joy said.

'Pains in the arse are our speciality.' Trish gave Joy a genuine smile. 'We're not going anywhere,' she told her.

'Well done.' Kathy kissed Joy on the cheek and stood up. 'I'm not running out on you, promise,' she grinned. 'I just need the loo.'

XIV

In the ladies, Kathy checked her reflection, running her fingers through her hair and then smoothing it down again.

Joy was amazing back there, the way she made all of us look deeper at each other and ourselves. She was so brave to tell her story, with no holds barred, and at the risk of losing her friends. But then, if we'd judged her without understanding or compassion, would we really be friends at all?

She dried her hands and returned to the bar.

As she sat down, Kathy noticed her glass was full again. She took a sip and munched on peanuts that Ruth offered round.

'Have you heard from Tony, Kath?' Joy asked.

I guess this is my cue to talk. Can I be as honest and brave as Joy?

'No, but I've no doubt he'll be waiting for me when I get back, all sugary sweet and apologetic,' she said and drank from her glass, washing down the last of the peanuts. 'It's over. I've told him. I'm moving out,' she said.

Ruth gave a little gasp.

'Oh, I know you're all probably thinking: about time too – that I should have done it years ago... and you're right. It's like Joy said. You build up this barrier; show the world you're fine, until you almost believe it yourself. I knew what you were all thinking when we were on a night out and I wore those tarty clothes, while Tony paraded me around like a prize trophy. I'd hide how uncomfortable I felt at the attention - brushing it off, telling you that he did it because he was proud of me; because he loved me. It took me years to finally admit to myself that the way he treated me was wrong. That Tony's love and pride were actually possessiveness and demoralisation. He tapped away at my self-confidence until I became convinced I was nothing without him. And I blamed myself. Everyone around me seemed to have good happy marriages, so how had I got it so wrong?'

'There's that word "seemed" again,' Joy interrupted. 'We're all very presumptuous about other people's lives.'

'Didn't my leaving Paul make you realise we're not all perfect?' Ruth asked.

'It did,' Kathy said. 'But by then I was locked in my own little world, seething and resentful inside, yet a scared rabbit whenever Tony was around.'

She told them of the terror she'd felt on the night he'd said Alison wasn't his, accusing her of having an affair. She spared nothing, talking more graphically than she'd have ever believed possible, of his abusive behaviour, both physically and mentally. Her face burned crimson with humiliation as she admitted how she'd allowed herself to be treated.

Ruth was in tears again and Kathy smiled at her.

'Stop it, Ruth, for goodness' sake. I'm a hundred miles from that point now,' she said, feeling stronger. 'One day something just snapped inside me; it was the way he looked at Alison, as though he was going to grab her by the shoulders and shake her, when she was having a paddy fit over something silly. I couldn't bear the thought of him being as domineering with her as he was with me. Controlling her life, as he did mine. I had to do something. That's when I drew up my DD Day plan.'

'DD Day?' Trish asked.

'Ditch Tony Day,' Kathy said.

Ruth clapped her hands.

'Brilliant, I love it,' she said trying to stifle a giggle.

Kathy smiled as she felt laughter begin to bubble in her throat. Soon they were all laughing, loud and uncontrollably, with tears streaming down their faces.

It must be the wine. Either that or we've all lost the plot completely. She felt lighter and freer than she had in years. It was certainly a much needed relief from the intensity of the evening's revelations.

Joy was first to get her giggles under control.

'What was the DD Day plan then?' she asked.

'It began with lists of what to do,' Kathy said, taking a deep breath to calm her laughter. 'Like where I'd live, could I get a job... stuff like that? I gave myself a two-year time frame.' She went on to tell them about all the training courses she done, in computing and business studies. How she'd applied for jobs, but not got anything yet. She could see the surprise written all over their faces.

'I can't believe you did all that and we didn't suspect a thing,' Trish said.

'That was the whole idea,' Kathy said, looking at her sister. 'The problem was that as I worked my way through the lists, it became harder and harder to keep up the pretence of being the dutiful wife, bowing down to his every command.

'I can imagine,' Joy murmured.

'When he announced he was coming to Scotland with us, my heart sank. I just knew that being with him and being around all of you would be a nightmare. Trying to keep up the pretence. I knew what he'd be like... and how right I was.'

'So, did you plan to end it while you were here?' Ruth asked.

'No way.' Kathy shook her head. 'I haven't even sorted out a job. Without a job how could I support us all or afford somewhere to live?' Kathy sighed.

'Tell him to leave,' Trish said. 'Get him charged with assault for what he did to you the other night, and all those times in the past. Get a court order, whatever. You shouldn't have to leave,' she added, her voice filled with anger.

'I do have to leave. I hate that house and what I became while I lived there. It holds too many bad memories,' Kathy said. 'Anyway, a certain knight in shining armour has come to my rescue.' She grinned at them with a mischievous twinkle in her eye.

'Brad?' Joy asked. 'I thought you two were looking cosy.'

'Humph.' Ruth slumped back in her seat, arms crossed. 'And there was me with my eye on him all week, just waiting for the right moment.' Her face broke into a wide grin.

Kathy rolled her eyes.

'Yes, Brad. But we're certainly not cosy - not like that. He's offered me a job as a trainee accountant, and he said that me and the kids can stay in his apartment for a while, until we sort something else out.'

'And we all know where that will lead,' Ruth said continuing her exaggerated sulk.

'Ruth, if you fancy Brad, then go for it. He's certainly not interested in me and I'm not interested in any man... not for a long while,' Kathy snapped.

'Hey, I was only joking, Kath,' Ruth said. She leant forward, looking concerned.

'Sorry.' Kathy bit her lip, fighting tears. 'It's just been so hard, keeping up the pretence for so long - and now, well, it's hard being just me, too.'

*****

Ruth reached across and squeezed Kathy's hand.

'Can I tell you my plans?' she asked.

Kathy nodded, drinking more wine. They were on their third bottle now. She was convinced that when the time came to leave, she wouldn't be able to stand.

'Is this about moving to Scotland?' she asked.

'Yes, the B&B in Tyndrum. I really want to give it a go. You know, now the boys have settled in at the farm with their dad, and since my mum died, I've just been going through the motions,' Ruth said, her voice tinged with sadness. 'This walk was something to break up the monotony of my life. I'm dead chuffed with myself that I managed to finish. Anyway, as soon as I set foot in that house, I knew it was what I wanted to do, where I wanted to be. It felt so right. I can't explain - you felt it too, didn't you, Joy?' She looked up, seeking encouragement.

'Mmm, it certainly has a lovely feel to it,' Joy agreed.

'It's a long way from home - and the boys,' Kathy said.

'I know that, but like you and Joy, I need to live my life for me. I'll probably see them just as often as I do now, when they're only twenty miles away.' Ruth sighed and then chuckled. 'And we can have great girlie weekends - lots of wine, plenty of deep and meaningful conversations.'

'Have you thought it through? Can you afford to buy it?' Trish asked.

Ruth nodded. 'Once I sell Mum's place. And I could probably get a business loan. Maybe Brad will help me sort out the finances. Or you, Kath, once you start your new job,' she added. 'Jane is quite ill, you know, she has cancer,' she said, her voice tinged with sadness. 'I'll work the rest of the summer season for her. After that, I'll have a good feel for the place, and she'll know if I'm the right person to buy it.'

'Let's have a toast,' Trish said, raising her glass. 'To Ruth and her new adventure,' she announced.

'And to Kathy and her new job,' Ruth added, clinking, and then draining her glass. 'Now, ladies, I think I need a comfort break,' she announced.

'If that's a trip to the loo, I'll join you.' Kathy stood up.

Linking arms and giggling like schoolgirls, they tottered unsteadily across the room.

XV

Joy was feeling relaxed by the wine and the relief of still having her friends around her, despite her revelations.

It's quite shocking to hear what Kathy has been going through, unbeknown to her friends. This proves my point exactly, about really knowing your friends. Trish is a bit of a worry though. She's noticeably less vocal tonight than I would have expected, especially given the enormity of everything that's been said.

Joy was even more convinced now that Trish's perfect life was not as it seemed.

With Kathy and Ruth away from the table, Joy contemplated asking Trish straight out, what the problem was. She still remembered that day, when Trish had almost told her something... what was it?

'You're very quiet tonight,' Joy ventured.

'It's a lot to take in.' Trish looked up. 'I know it wasn't easy for you or Kath, to say everything you did.'

'Much easier than churning it around in my head for as long as I have, believe me.'

'It's not easy listening to it, either,' Trish continued. 'Knowing what you've been through makes me feel so inadequate.'

'Don't be stupid, Trish. How could you do anything to help if neither of us would let you in?'

'Still, if I wasn't so wrapped up in my own life...'

'Rightly so,' Joy said. 'I know it's not always easy, especially with Rob being away so much...'

'It's not just that,' Trish interrupted.

'You're OK though, as a couple, I mean?'

'Yes, well, kind of. It's just difficult at the moment.' Trish paused and took a deep breath.

Joy waited patiently, watching her friend wrestling with what she was about to say.

She'll be arguing with herself now – should I or shouldn't I reveal this problem, secret, or whatever? I know how that feels. After all, haven't I spent half my own lifetime doing exactly same thing?

'It's Seb,' Trish said, taking a gulp of wine, and then leaning forward, towards Joy. 'Rob's not his father,' she whispered.

Joy almost had to pick her chin up off the table. That was the last thing she expected her to say.

'Do you remember Janice Weston from school?' Trish asked, her eyes suddenly misty with tears.

Joy frowned and shook her head.

Trish rushed on.

'Well, we were best friends at the time. It was her wedding day. Rob was ill and had to go home early. Being chief bridesmaid, I couldn't really leave with him, and anyway I was having a laugh. The best man obviously fancied me, and we were just dancing and messing around. He knew I was with Rob. Towards the end of the night I went outside. I'd had way too much to drink and was feeling a bit sick. He followed me out there.'

Joy couldn't believe what she was hearing.

'You cheated on Rob?' she asked.

'No!' Trish cried, and then quickly lowered her voice. 'No. He kissed me. I was drunk. It was nice at first, then I realised what I was doing and pulled away. I went back inside. I still had to decorate the bridal suite. He followed me up to the room. We were throwing confetti onto the bed, messing around. We ended up kissing again, a drunken fumble... I fell back on to the bed, and then he was on top of me... I kept saying no...' Her voice trailed off.

'He raped you?'

'It was a long time ago,' Trish said sadly.

'And you never said a word.' Joy couldn't believe it. 'Oh my God! Trish. Does Rob know? Did you tell him? Why didn't you press charges? Is Seb this bloke's child?'

Trish's nod was so slight that Joy almost missed it. She grasped her friend's hands across the table.

'I'm sorry, I shouldn't be bombarding you with questions like this,' she said.

'It's OK. 'Trish smiled a watery smile. 'After all, it is truth or consequence night, isn't it?'

'Does Kathy know?'

'No one knows, except Rob and now you,' Trish told her. 'Rob's known for a long time. When Seb was born, I didn't know for sure – but I felt it inside that he wasn't Rob's child. It tore me apart, almost destroyed our relationship completely during that first year. In the end I told him everything.'

'How did he take it?' Joy asked.

'At first he was raging, wanted to hunt the man down and knock hell out of him, then he wanted me to go to the police. I couldn't face that.' Trish paused. She picked up her glass, fiddling with the stem before continuing. 'Eventually we agreed to have a paternity test done, which proved what I knew already – that Rob wasn't Seb's father.'

'Rob is amazing, you would never think for an instant that Seb wasn't his,' Joy said.

Trish nodded. 'I know, he loves the bones of him.'

Joy was filled with admiration for her friend.

She did the right thing in telling Rob, and taking the risk that she might lose him. That's what I should have done all those years ago.

She wanted to know more, but already she could see Kathy and Ruth, staggering back to the table. It was Trish's choice to tell them, not hers.

'Does Seb know?' she asked quickly.

SATURDAY

I

[Joy] turned over, wincing as her head hit the pillow with all the [weight] of a medicine ball. Opening one eye with caution, she saw [Daniel]'s head, inches from hers. His eyes were closed, although [she] wasn't convinced he was asleep.

'Whose idea was it to get pissed the night before a six-[hour] bus journey?' she groaned.

'Mine.' She answered her own question.

'Feeling rough?' Daniel asked, without moving or [ope]ning his eyes.

'That's an understatement.' She couldn't remember [gett]ing into bed. She touched her body tentatively beneath the [cov]ers, checking what state of undress she was in.

'Don't worry, you didn't throw yourself at me this time,' [he t]old her.

Joy closed the eye she had opened, and pulled the covers [ove]r her head. She felt Daniel turn over, then the waft of air as he [thre]w back the duvet.

'You want coffee?' he asked. 'Grab a shower, I'll make [you] one.'

Joy frowned.

Is this a dream? Or was the past a dream? We're being [civi]lised. How strange.

'Am I dreaming?' she wondered aloud.

'What?' Daniel snapped.

'OK, so I'm not.' She sighed as she got out of bed and [ma]de her way tentatively towards the bathroom.

The shower water fell like hailstones on her tender head, [but] she stayed put, letting the water beat some life into her. She [sea]rched through the alcohol-induced fog of her brain, trying to [rem]ember the details of the previous night. It proved too difficult, [so s]he gave in to the pummelling water and nothingness.

'No, that's the issue at the moment.' Trish sighed. 'Rob thinks he should know the truth.'

Joy released Trish's hands as Ruth sat down at the table.

'So is it one more for the road?' Kathy asked, slurring slightly, as she slid back into the booth.

'Don't know about anyone else, but I need some food to soak this lot up before we go anywhere,' Joy said, opening the menu.

She gave Trish a brief smile, reassuring her that she would say nothing.

Trish threw back the remainder of her glass of wine, and wiped away a stray tear as she smiled back at Joy.

'Judging by the state you're in, I think some food's definitely a good idea,' she admonished her sister playfully.

XVI

Over chips and burgers, followed by deliciously rich chocolate cake, the four women chattered like teenagers, about the trials and tribulations of everything - men, diets, sex, bad hair days, PMT and politics - laughing until the tears ran into their wine glasses.

Finally, Ruth put down her knife and fork and placed her hands flat on the table.

'Do you want to know what I think?' she asked, struggling to stand up.

'Sit down, Ruth,' Joy said.

'I think, who ever thought up the British Stiff Upper Lip wants shooting,' Ruth said, giving up her attempts to stand, and sitting down with a thud. 'Nobody wants to admit to their failings. Nobody wants to openly celebrate their success - just in case the person sitting next to him isn't so lucky. So we all go around, carrying this huge rucksack of guilt and suppressed emotion. We should have let the Romans rule,' she finished with a flourish.

'Why?' Kathy asked, puzzled.

'Well, just think. All that Italian passion. Mmmm... It could have been quite a different story,' Ruth drooled.

They all erupted into a fit of giggles once again.

Kathy sat up straight, pushing her shoulders back and focusing on Joy until there was just one of her.

'Seriously though, what will you do when we get back? Do you think you and Dan can sort things out?'

'I really don't know,' Joy replied. 'I think I need to learn to be me and like myself. Then – who knows? Anyway, he needs time to get his head around everything, and time to get to know his son.'

'Will you move out?' Trish asked.

'You could come to Tyndrum with me,' Ruth piped up, wiping stray cake crumbs from her mouth.

'You know you can stay at ours, if you wan offered.

'Stay with me and the kids at Brad's place, I won't mind,' Kathy added.

'I wouldn't want to cramp your style.' Joy w Kathy.

Kathy frowned.

'I told you. Nothing is going on between Brad and there isn't about to be anything going on.' Her voic with every syllable.

'Did I hear my name mentioned?' Brad's head up over the back of the seat, smiling, and radiating boyis

Kathy felt her face heat up as the blush crept up from her neck. She cursed her big mouth and the alcohol fuelled it.

'You'll hear nothing good hiding around corners said wagging a finger at him.

Feeling vaguely human after two strong coffees in her room, Joy went down to the dining room.

There she joined the others around the large oval breakfast table. Shuddering at the sight of Brad's full Scottish breakfast, she took a triangle of dry toast and nibbled at it. Kathy and Ruth were equally subdued, both shaking their heads at the offer of a full breakfast.

Joy observed Trish eating a large bowl of cereal and fruit.

'Why don't you look as rough as I feel?' Joy asked.

'Plenty of water and two paracetamol before I went to bed,' Trish said, smugly.

'I can't remember going to bed,' Joy said with a sheepish grin.

She felt her stomach groaning and heaving. *I'm going to throw up, I know it.*

'Excuse me, guys, I need some air,' she said, holding a hand to her mouth. She got up quickly and headed out of the front door.

The air was cool outside, cooler than it had been all week. The wispy white clouds of the day before had grown in size and darkened in colour.

She heard the front door creak and footsteps coming towards her. She sat on the low garden wall, unmoving, head between her knees.

'Reckon I'll need my rain gear today?' Brad asked, sitting down on the bench beside her.

Joy shrugged her shoulders, not confident that she could speak without throwing up over his feet.

'You girls appeared to have sorted out your differences last night,' Brad continued, undeterred by her lack of response. 'I'm glad. Kathy's one of life's good guys. Plus she's a loyal friend who thinks the world of you.'

'I know she is, they all are,' Joy mumbled, speaking to her feet.

'I think you can be good for each other right now,' he said gently.

Joy nodded, getting to her feet, wobbling slightly. The fresh air had helped and she felt slightly better.

'I'd better go and pack,' she said.

'Well, I'm off to climb a mountain,' Brad said, standing up and dusting down the back of his shorts.

'You're nuts,' Joy said with a smile. She took his hand. 'Thanks for our little chats – even if they weren't always what I wanted to hear,' she added.

He pulled her into a hug.

'You take care. I'm sure you'll do what's right,' he said, releasing her. 'Keep in touch,' he added, as he stroked a stray hair back from her cheek and kissed her lips.

'You be careful up there,' Joy called out, as he walked away. She could feel her insides shaking, as she walked back inside, not sure if it was as a result of her hangover or Brad's kiss.

II

An hour later, everyone was ready to go, having all said their goodbyes to Brad and loaded the bags into the back of the bus.

Rob was driving, and as he manoeuvred the minibus out of the hotel driveway, Joy rested her hot head against the cool window, staring unseeingly at the passing houses and shops of Fort William.

Daniel was sitting up at the front with Rob. She was glad they weren't at each other's throats any more. Even though they had a long way to go, she knew it would be all the easier without the pent-up anger and emotion she'd been holding onto for so long.

Kathy sat across the aisle from her.

'You look like I feel,' Joy told her.

'You don't look any better,' Kathy replied with a smile. 'It was a good night though. You did a great job.'

'What did I do?' Joy asked. Her memory of the night before was more than a little fuzzy.

'You were open and honest. You got us all to be honest with each other. Thanks.'

Joy shrugged her shoulders. 'It needed to be said.'

They lapsed into silence for a moment.

'Can you believe Brad?' Joy spoke again. 'Just stopping on like that to climb Ben Nevis today.' She looked at Kathy. 'I could barely climb the steps of this bus, let alone Ben Nevis,' she added, wincing at the pounding in her head as they went over a speed bump.

'I know,' Kathy agreed. 'And it was so good of him to just give me the keys to his apartment. After all, he doesn't know me that well.'

'You'd be surprised how well you can get to know a person in such a short time. Ninety-five miles is a lot of talking.' Joy held her hands up to her head. 'Does he have to hit every bump in the road?'

'Here, have a paracetamol and keep drinking the water.' Kathy threw the box of tablets across to her.

'Thanks.' Joy took two. 'Are you nervous, going back?' she asked.

'A little bit, I suppose. But I feel so much stronger now. The lads are on my side, and once Alison knows that her brothers will still be around, she'll be fine. We'll be OK.' Kathy smiled a genuine open smile, without a trace of the timid nervous Kathy who'd sat in that very seat, just one week before. 'To be honest, I'm more excited than nervous. I've got a new life and new opportunities ahead of me. I'm really looking forward to getting started on the apartment.'

'You've lost me there, Kath,' Joy said, looking puzzled.

Kathy told her of the agreement she had made with Brad, to decorate and refurbish his apartment.

'Of course, it'll be a little more difficult while we're all living there, but hopefully I'll find a place of our own quickly.' Kathy clapped her hands like an excited child.

'You're lucky, you know, Kath, to be excited about what's ahead.' Joy half smiled, happy for her friend. 'I'm terrified of what's ahead for me.'

'Don't be.' Kathy moved across to sit beside Joy. Her warm brown eyes were wide with concern. 'You and Dan still love each other, anyone can see that. It was blatantly obvious all this week - despite the sparks of anger every time you were within ten feet of each other.' She gave Joy a hug. 'I'm sure you'll work through this. It won't be easy, but you're strong, Joy. I bet we'll see the two of you, hobbling down the street, in forty years time, still holding hands.'

'I think you're letting your imagination run away with you, Kath,' said Joy wistfully.

She turned to look out at the towering mountains as the bus took the road through Glencoe. They passed by the Kingshouse Hotel. Walkers were milling around, adjusting rucksacks, and tying bootlaces, preparing for the day ahead.

'I never want to be reminded of that place, that's for sure,' Kathy said. She turned away and went back to her seat.

'Think of it as the catalyst that spurred your DD Day plans into action,' Joy pointed out. 'Otherwise, they could have remained just that – plans - forever. You might never have found the right moment.'

'True,' Kathy murmured sleepily.

Tired as she was, Joy followed the scenery avidly, as the bus journeyed south. She looked out for places she might recognise, spotting walkers as the road ran parallel with the footpath. The clouds gathered in force overhead. The heat wave was coming to an end. The walkers setting out this week wouldn't have the added burden of heat to endure.

'Rob,' she called out impulsively. 'Can you slow down, so that I can get one last view of the loch?' she asked.

'I can't just stop on the main road,' Rob called down to the back of the bus. 'I'll look out for a lay-by,' he added.

Three or four minutes later Rob pulled the bus to a halt beside Loch Lomond. Joy stepped down onto the tarmac, welcoming the cool damp air blowing up from the loch. The crystal clear waters they'd walked beside for two days now looked grey and dull, very uninviting. She stared across to the opposite shoreline, remembering with a shudder the harsh words she had exchanged with Daniel over there.

'Come on, we need to get going,' Rob called from the bus.

Joy went back to her seat and they set off once more.

The threatened rain began to fall. Huge fat dollops bounced off the waters of the loch, splashing against the windows of the bus, spreading tentacles across the glass until the view was completely obscured.

Mesmerised by the movements of the rain on her window, the pain in her head finally dulled by the paracetamol, Joy allowed her eyes to close.

THE END

Printed in Great Britain
by Amazon.co.uk, Ltd.,
Marston Gate.